Love's
Journey
West

D0068524

Love's Journey West

A Collection of Three Complete,
Unabridged Inspirational Romances
in One Volume

Megan's Choice
Rosey Dow

Her Father's Love
Nancy Lavo

Threads of Love
Judith McCoy Miller

BARBOUR
PUBLISHING, INC.
Uhrichsville, Ohio

Published by Barbour Publishing, Inc., P.O. Box 719, Uhrichsville, Ohio 44683
http://www.barbourbooks.com

ecpa Member of the
Evangelical Christian
Publishers Association

Printed in the United States of America.

Megan's Choice

Rosey Dow

ROSEY DOW

Rosey was born in Dover, Delaware, and lived there until college. She minored in English, but despised her creative writing courses. Six months before graduation, she married a preacher boy. Three children later, she impulsively mailed in a coupon for a writer's correspondence course. By the time she finished the course, she had a new hobby. For fourteen years she wrote reams without a single sale. In December 1996, her first book, *Megan's Choice,* appeared in the **Heartsong Presents** line and put her on the 1997 list of ten favorite new authors for **Heartsong**. Since then she's sold several articles, another novel, and a Christmas novella. Serving with her husband as church planting missionaries in Grenada, West Indies, she home-schools their seven children and helps edit a monthly newspaper along with other missionary activities.

Dedicated to

Dave,
my husband and best friend.

one

"Mr. Steven Chamberlin, please," Megan Wescott told the lanky hotel clerk. She had a pleasant, poised voice. It didn't give away the secret that her stomach was full of flying butterflies.

The young clerk gave her a friendly smile as his eyes approved of her large, brown eyes and creamy complexion. "One moment, please," he replied and held up his hand to summon a bellboy. "You can wait inside if you'd like."

Glancing around, Megan entered the hotel lobby to wait. The grandeur of the hotel snatched away her breath for an instant. She hesitated inside the door, feeling out of place and alone. She wished she could slip her hand into the warm shelter of her father's coat pocket, her habit as a child whenever she was troubled or frightened. If only he were here to help her now.

But she was no longer a child. Daddy was gone, and she would have to look after herself. And Jeremy.

"A-hem."

She realized a woman in a stylish black hat was standing close by with an impatient grimace on her painted lips.

"Pardon me," Megan murmured and hastily stepped aside. The woman sailed past without another glance, the swish of silk skirts and the heady scent of French perfume lingering after her. Megan drew a quivering breath. She fought down the desire to turn around and escape to the anonymity of the street. Instead, she crossed the thick carpet to a chair.

Resolutely, she drew the newspaper ad from her handbag and read it for what must have been the hundredth time.

> Industrious young woman needed to cook and clean on a ranch in
> the Colorado Territory. Between 20 and 25 years old. Orphan pre-
> ferred. Top wages. Inquire for Mr. Steven Chamberlin at the Olympus
> Hotel.

The mended edge of her glove slipped from its hiding place beneath the sleeve of her jacket. Carefully, she tucked it back in.

Maybe Mr. Chamberlin has already found someone, she thought, mingling hope and fear. The ad had been published that morning, but she hadn't been able to get away from the shop until quite a while after lunch. Mrs. Peabody had grudgingly given her the last part of the afternoon off.

She noticed a distinguished gentleman who was sitting on a gold sofa reading a newspaper. Discreetly observing his features, she wondered again what Steven Chamberlin was like. Her mind drew a picture of a short man with a middle-aged paunch who smoked smelly, black cigars and had a booming voice. His wife, no doubt, was the kind who would be constantly peering over her shoulder and making clucking noises. She cringed inwardly and again stifled the urge to run away.

It was unthinkable that she, the daughter of a Virginia plantation owner, should be applying for a housekeeper's position. Her family had suffered many forms of humiliation through the last ten years, but nonetheless she was thankful her mother could not see her now.

It's a waste of time worrying about family pride, she reminded herself again. Jeremy, her little brother, was desperately ill, and the sanitarium was far beyond her means. If Jeremy was to get well, she had to have more money than she could earn at the dressmaker's shop.

The years since the War between the States had been a nightmare for Megan. The loss of her father and brother in the war, living in poverty in Baltimore, and her dear mother's death would have been enough to break the spirit of most girls.

How could they have survived without Em? Dear Em, who had been with the family for more than twenty years. Em, who had stayed when the other freed slaves were sent away to find livings elsewhere. Thankfully, Em could watch over Jeremy if Megan had to leave.

Blinking, Megan held back the worried tears that blurred her vision. She drew the scrap of newsprint between two fingers, and the words "Top wages" caught her eye. She had to get this position.

A tall, dark-haired man slowly descending the wide staircase drew her attention. He scanned the lobby, pausing a moment at the foot of the stairs. Megan noticed his tailored black broadcloth suit, white silk shirt with tiny red pinstripes, and black string tie. He had broad shoulders and a square, purposeful chin.

Was that Steven Chamberlin? Her throat tightened when she realized he was striding in her direction.

"You were asking for Steven Chamberlin, ma'am?" he asked, bowing slightly. He spoke pleasantly enough, but his faint, polite smile didn't quite reach his eyes.

"Yes." Megan's tongue felt thick and uncooperative. "I came to apply for this position." She handed him the ad. Her hand was icy and shaking.

"I am Mr. Chamberlin." He sat in the chair facing her. "May I ask your qualifications?"

To her dismay she felt her cheeks growing hot. The speech she had rehearsed all morning flew beyond her reach. Frantically, she groped for it.

"I can cook and clean," she managed at last, then added with spirit, "and I can work as hard as anyone."

The young man took stock of her clothes, which were carefully made but showing signs of wear; the sweet, anxious mouth; the quiet courage in her eyes, and his manner softened slightly.

"What is your name?"

"Megan Wescott. I need employment badly. You see, my little brother is ill, and the sanitarium is expensive."

His wife would be about my own age, she thought, not sure if that was good or bad.

"Your parents?"

"Father was killed in the war, and Mother died five months ago." She met his gaze openly, candidly, and realized for the first time that his thick black eyebrows almost came together. "I've been working in a dressmaker's shop doing fine needlework, but with Jeremy sick I'll have to earn more."

"I'd like to talk to you about some details." He glanced around. The man she had observed shifted position and turned a page of his newspaper. Two men engrossed in conversation walked past. "Would you mind stepping into the hotel restaurant where we can talk more privately? There are some things I need to explain about the position."

"Will your wife join us?" Megan asked, confused.

"That's one of the things I'll need to explain," he said, standing.

Is his wife ill? A vague doubt sprouted in her mind.

An aloof waiter showed them to a small table in a back corner of the dining room. Megan allowed Mr. Chamberlin to seat her. She removed her gloves, clasped them tightly in her lap, and waited. Alive to his every expression, she tried to determine what lay behind the handsome, self-assured face across from her.

"It's quite a long story," he began after ordering coffee for two. "Two years ago, my father bought a four-hundred-acre ranch near Juniper Junction—that's about fifty miles north of Denver in the Colorado Territory—from a man who went back East. It's deeded land. I guess my father was planning to go there sometime, but he never did. He died a month ago, and left a small fortune to my sister and me. My mother died several years ago, you see.

"My half of the inheritance comes with a condition—my father's idea of giving me a test of character." His right eyebrow lifted slightly, giving him a vaguely cynical expression. He paused while the waiter set their coffee before them. "In order to inherit, my wife and I must live on the ranch for a full year and make it profitable."

"And you want a housekeeper for her?" Megan prompted. *Won't he ever come to the point?*

He added a spoonful of sugar to his coffee and stirred it thoughtfully. Megan watched the slow movement of his large, well-groomed hands. She looked up to find his measuring gaze upon her.

"I don't have a wife."

"I don't understand." *Maybe I ought to leave. This doesn't sound right.*

"I mean," he spoke slowly, distinctly, closely observing her reaction, "I'm looking for a housekeeper and cook who would be willing to become my legal wife for that year." He leaned forward, speaking softly. "I'll be frank. I could find a mail order bride if I wanted to. There are plenty of folks who are doing it these days. But I'm not ready to be saddled down with that responsibility. I wouldn't even go this far if it wasn't for losing a fortune in the process.

"After the terms of the will have been met, I'll have the marriage discreetly dissolved. No one in the East need ever know of the arrangement. I'm willing to pay one hundred dollars per month."

"But as your wife. . . ," Megan faltered. She struggled between dismay at his scheme and the knowledge that she desperately needed the amount of money he had quoted.

"A legality only, I assure you," he said. "Call it a make-believe marriage if that eases your conscience. I turned down two women this morning, but I think you and I could be partners. Why not? You need a sizable income, and I need a wife for a year. We can work together to accomplish both."

"But why would your father put your wife in his will if you aren't married?" It didn't sound reasonable.

"He thought I was," Mr. Chamberlin said, ruefully. "The last time I saw him was before the war. I was engaged at the time. What a foolish boy I was." He shook his head. "She was a hostess on the *Mississippi Queen*. I thought she cared for me, but she was only after my winnings at the poker table. She dumped me when a brighter star came along." His lips tightened. "I won't be so foolish again." He shrugged, and his expression softened. "Anyway, I didn't have any contact with my father after that visit. I guess he naturally assumed I had married."

"Couldn't you go to the solicitor and tell him you're not married?" Megan persisted, still puzzled.

"It would break the will." Again that hard look. "And Georgiana, my older sister, would dearly love to chisel me out of my half of the money." He leaned back in his chair and shook his head. "No. There's no other way."

Megan's slim fingers toyed with her china coffee cup. She stared at the painted yellow rose on the inside rim, weighing the possibilities. One hundred dollars a month was almost twice as much as she had hoped for. And what a relief not to have to please the tastes of another woman.

"What kind of work do you do?" She looked keenly at the man across from her. He didn't look unscrupulous, but there must be some reason his father hadn't trusted him.

Chamberlin laughed mirthlessly, gesturing with his hand.

"That's a good question, ma'am," he said, sobering. "It's right prudent of you to ask. I left home at sixteen and found out I could be handy with the pasteboards. That's the cards, ma'am. I rode the Mississippi riverboats for a few years, fought for the Confed'racy under Bragg, and then wandered around New Orleans after the war, trying my hand at this and that, gambling enough to keep me from starving.

"To tell you the truth, I was at a loss until this will came up. I think I'd like to have a go at ranching. Put down some roots, maybe." He shrugged. "At least I'd like to have a chance to prove I can do it even if I decide to come back East later. I don't have a predilection for the idea of marriage, that's all. I've been a loner for too long."

The simple directness of his answer convinced Megan he was being honest with her. There was a lengthy silence while she thought it over.

What would a meaningless marriage matter? Wasn't marriage a commitment of the heart? All he asked was what the ad said: a housekeeper and cook. It would be pleasant on a ranch, too. A ranch and a plantation were practically the same, weren't they? She remembered the corrals, the riding stable, the spreading lawn, and columned plantation house she had known as a child. The ranch would be different, of course, but there were similarities.

What a relief it would be to go back to that life even if she was only a servant.

But I won't be a servant, she suddenly recalled. *I would be the mistress.* Some of the cloud lifted from her mind. *Yes,* she rolled the idea around on her tongue, *I would be the mistress.*

"When would we have to leave?" she asked, slowly.

"Three weeks." He peered at her with half-closed eyes. "Does that mean you accept?"

"I can't see that I have any choice," she said, steadily. "Yes, I accept."

"Good." His expression relaxed. He reached inside his coat. "Here's my card. I'd like you to go to the Hurlick's General Store on Market Street and purchase any household goods you feel will be necessary. I'm afraid I wouldn't know where to begin when it comes to housekeeping, and I think it would be better for you to make your own choices. Give Hurlick this card, and he'll put it on my account. Have everything packed and sent to my address."

"What should I get?" Megan asked, taking the card and glancing at it.

"Whatever you'll need to take care of the house, and fix things up a mite. The house isn't large, I understand, but it has been empty for quite some time. Cooking utensils, curtains, and such like would be in order, I suppose."

Megan slid the card into her purse. Her hands were clammy, and she had the strange feeling she was somehow watching herself from far away.

"We can have the ceremony performed in a quiet corner of the city in about a week," he continued, "but I see no need to change our living quarters until we leave. If you need to contact me in the meantime, you can reach me here. How can I contact you?"

"I live at 148 High Street, Apartment 3B," she said. She pulled her gloves on and stood up. She wanted to have some time alone to adjust herself to the new circumstances.

"Thank you, Miss Wescott," he said, rising with her, the shadow of a smile on his lips.

"Megan," she said seriously. "It's foolish to continue formalities."

"Yes, Megan." He sobered. "I'm sure I don't need to tell you our arrangement shouldn't be known to anyone else. Will you meet me at the park near the big fountain with water spraying out a carp's mouth, say a week from today? At two o'clock?"

"I'll be there." She offered him her hand, and he clasped it briefly. His hand, though uncalloused, was surprisingly firm and strong. "Good day." With a nod, she left the hotel.

Conflicting emotions swept over her as she stepped, blinking, into the bright afternoon sunlight. A flush of exhilaration tingled through her as she mouthed the wage he had offered her. *A hundred dollars a month!* Her brightest hopes had never been audacious enough to rise up that high. The marriage contract was a little disturbing, but livable for a few months. However, now that she knew the problem of the sanitarium fee was solved, she had to face the dark side: leaving behind all she loved to brave the unknown. Many who ventured into the wild new territories were never heard from again.

A whole year. She was heartsick at the thought. *Can I do it? Can I say good-bye to Jeremy and Em?* She pushed back the walls that crowded in on her. She would not succumb to her fears and heartaches. If she caved in, Jeremy would sense it and be afraid, too. She must be strong for him.

She walked blindly along the cobblestone streets, unaware of the chilly May breeze that tickled her burning cheeks. Her feet beat a steady cadence on the sidewalk while she reminisced about the past and wondered about the future.

two

The years since the war were a series of murky shadows in Megan's memory. When the Southern Cause was lost, her family left Virginia and traveled north to Baltimore to stay with Mother's Aunt Alice. Daddy had fallen with a Yankee bullet in his chest. Silverleigh, their home, was a blackened heap of ash and rubble. Friends were scattered, never to be seen again. Gone forever was the world they had loved. They hoped to find rest and build a new life, but those hopes were shattered when Aunt Alice had a stroke and died. Debt swallowed her estate and again the Wescotts were homeless.

Mother was left without friend or advisor. It was up to her to provide a roof to cover their despairing heads and food to ease their gnawing stomachs. She walked the streets of the poorest, dirtiest section of Baltimore until she found an apartment, a dark, wretched cubbyhole, for a dollar a week. Intended for one or at the most two people, it had two closet-sized bedrooms barely big enough for a cot and a chair, a kitchen that was about the size of their dining room table at Silverleigh, and a sitting room that could be crossed in four strides from either direction.

The landlady, Mrs. Niles, looked Mother up and down as though mentally pricing every piece of clothing Mother wore before she grudgingly admitted she had a vacancy. She was a thin-lipped woman who had been middle-aged all her life. Her gown was a cheap imitation of the morning dresses that had filled two of Mother's closets at Silverleigh. However, the cut of the cloth was as far as the resemblance went; because the collar and cuffs were smudged, and there was a small tear under the arm, something Mother would never have permitted even in a servant. Though disgusted, Mother pretended not to notice and handed over the first week's rent, her last dollar but one, and in her mind playfully nicknamed the landlady Nilly-Willy. She made a joke of it to the children later that evening.

What it must have cost Mother's aristocratic pride to knock on door after door asking women if she could do their washing and ironing. The family lived on bread and tea the first few weeks they lived at Mrs. Niles's tenement house. Finally, the news of Mother's and Em's excellent work with soapsuds, starch, and hot iron traveled across the grapevine of Baltimore's housewives, and the amount of work grew until they had money to buy enough food to satisfy a growing boy and, of course, pay their rent.

Mother insisted that Megan, scarcely more than a child, continue her schooling. She found a church with a mission that taught slum children and made Megan attend the classes. Mother filled the gaps in their meager program by teaching Megan by lamplight after a twelve-hour day of bending over a scrub board or iron.

Megan watched her mother's soft, white hands become red and coarse from hours in hot, soapy water. She knew Mother would never allow a word of complaint to pass her lips, and she would not allow anyone else to grumble, either. She never let it be spoken, but she could not hide her suffering, worry-filled eyes.

How could they have made it without Em? Always near with a strong back and willing, loving hands, Em comforted them and offered her earthy wisdom to chase away discouragement.

Years of brutal work and the lack of fresh air broke down Mother's health. She grew weaker and weaker until she had a fainting spell over the wash tub. Unable to hide their tears, Megan and Em lifted Mother to her tiny cot, brought her hot broth, and tried to make her comfortable. There was no money for a doctor.

Megan stopped going to school. Instead, she took Mother's place in the soapsuds until Mother, broken in spirit and body, called Megan to her side a few months before she died. Mother's smooth, clear face now had deep creases around the eyes and mouth. In two months' time her hair had turned the color of moonlight reflected on new-fallen snow.

"I want you to get a position in the city, Megan," she wheezed, stopping often to take a breath. Her translucent hand reached out to touch Megan's cheek. "You'll ruin yourself with this backbreaking work. It's not fittin' for a pretty young thing like you to spend her life with her hands in wash water."

How courageous Mother had been through all their struggle, never thinking of herself, always thinking of Megan and Jeremy.

❧

Cold hard emptiness had filled the apartment when Mother was taken from them. The burning ache was still fresh in Megan's bosom.

Following Mother's advice, Megan took samples of her work and applied at a shop close to the center of town. She had learned to weave lace and sew fine embroidery from her governess, who had considered it a necessity for a young lady destined to join the higher ranks of society. Megan was an artist with her needle, and she loved her work. At her first stop, Mrs. Peabody, the owner of the dressmaker's shop, had hired her instantly when Megan had spread out her handiwork.

It had been enjoyable to sit in the back room of the shop and handle the beautiful threads. However, the sense of enjoyment lasted only a few months. Mother's death squeezed the last ounce of joy out of Megan's life, and when Jeremy contracted rheumatic fever a few months later, Megan felt desperation grip her. The responsibility weighed her down until she felt she would smother.

⧟

The light was beginning to fade when Megan at last set a course for home. She reached her neighborhood with her thoughts still far off. Habitually stepping around bits of broken glass and refuse, she walked on. She didn't notice the thin children huddled together in doorways and on the front steps of their homes or the starving mongrel dogs sniffing the gutters for a morsel of decaying food. When she reached High Street she stepped off the crumbling sidewalk to pass a group of ragged boys playing marbles on the corner.

" 'Lo, Megan," one urchin called.

"Hello, Joe." She smiled absently in response and walked on.

Suddenly, the chance to leave the city gave her a new awareness of her neighborhood. She awoke from her sleepwalking and looked around at the soot-covered buildings and trash-laden street. The acrid smell of unwashed bodies and rotting garbage pricked her nose. In the depths of the building nearby a man and woman raised their voices in a heated argument, while a baby wailed relentlessly. High Street had never seemed so dismal as today, the tenement houses never so dirty and depressing.

How wonderful it would be to get away from the city. To breathe fresh air, to feel free-blowing breezes in her hair, the sun on her face. To see wide, unbounded country crowned with a clear, sapphire sky.

The soothing smell of Em's thick stew welcomed Megan when she opened the apartment door. She was pulling off her gloves, adjusting her eyes to the dimness, when a tall, lean black woman came to stand in the kitchen doorway. She wore a faded gingham dress with a white apron. Her gray hair was pulled back from her face, seamed by years of hard work and sorrow. She held a dish towel in her hands.

"How is Jeremy, Em?"

"Sleepin'. I gave him some supper 'bout an hour ago." Em peered at Megan, her narrow face creased with worry. "Did you find you a new job, Miss Megan?"

"Yes, I did." Megan removed her bonnet and laid it on the shelf near the door. Hanging her jacket on a peg, she followed Em into the tiny kitchen, wondering how to tell her the rest of the news. Saying it aloud made their separation seem more real. "It pays almost twice as much as I had hoped for, Em," she said, slowly, "but there is something I didn't tell you about."

"What do you have to do?" Em asked, anxiously.

"I'm keeping house and cooking like I told you. . . ." Megan paused, avoiding Em's eyes. "But I have to go out to the Colorado Territory."

"The Colorado Territory! Lord have mercy, child, whatever for?" She stared at Megan, her lips slightly parted. The dimple in her right cheek, the one Megan called her worry mark, deepened as Megan continued.

"The gentleman has a ranch out there, and he needs a housekeeper. I've agreed to go for a year," Megan said, softly.

"A year!" Two tears slid slowly down Em's anguished face, and Megan felt her resolve bubbling away.

"Please don't cry, Em," she begged, putting arms around Em, her face on Em's shoulder. "I don't want to go. You know I don't." The tears she had been battling all afternoon finally won out. In a moment she drew back, wiping her eyes. "I have no choice. You see that, don't you?"

"Yes, child." Em's seamed, careworn face was wet also. "I know." She sank into a chair with a heavy sigh, her face a picture of misery. "It's the lonesome days ahead I'm a-thinkin' on."

"I'll make enough money so you won't have to work so hard." Megan knelt by Em's side and clasped her bony, work-hardened hands between her own. "If we can find you a place in a rooming house near the sanitarium, you can visit Jeremy every day. And you can get away from this dark, crowded tenement house. It will be better for us all." She searched Em's face for a sign of comfort.

"When you leavin'?"

"In three weeks. We have so much to do before then. I'll have to keep my job with Mrs. Peabody for another week or so. We'll have to make arrangements with the sanitarium and find you a place to stay." She looked around the kitchen. "We'll have to pack all our things, too."

"Em!" A faint call came from the bedroom.

"I'll go to Jeremy," Megan said, rising. She gave Em's hand a squeeze and ran to wash away the traces of tears.

The coal oil lamp Megan carried into Jeremy's bedroom cast a golden light over the child's hollow cheeks. His skin was almost transparent, his lips tinged a faint blue. His large nightshirt made him seem smaller than his ten years. Tousled, straw-colored hair came down to his eyes, now sunken and dulled by weeks of illness. His languid expression faded a little when he realized who it was that carried the lamp.

"How is my little soldier?" Megan asked, smiling tenderly. She set the lamp on the small table beside a chipped enamel basin. The splash of lamplight touched both walls in the narrow room.

"Megan," Jeremy murmured, a drowsy smile on his lips. "I'm glad you're home. Can you stay with me for a little while?"

"I'll stay with you as long as you'd like." She plumped his pillow, and straightened the counterpane. "I have some grown-up business to talk over with you tonight."

"What is it?" His tired eyes showed a spark of curiosity.

"Well, part of it is good, and part of it is kind of hard." She eased into the straight wooden chair by his bed. "You know what the doctor said about having to take special care of you to protect your heart?"

"Sure," he said impatiently. "That's why I have to stay in this old bed all day long."

"Today I found work that will make it possible for you to get the treatments you need to get better."

"You did?"

"Yes. I'm going next week to make the arrangements with the doctor." She hesitated, dreading the rest of her news.

"What's the hard part?" He tried to sit up by supporting himself on his elbows. "Don't worry, Meg. I can take it. I'm no baby. Did the doctor tell you something bad about me?"

"Oh, no, Jeremy," she assured him quickly. "Don't even think such a thing. He said with proper care he has good hopes you'll soon be well." She pressed her bottom lip between her teeth. "It's that the job I found is far away in Colorado. I'm going to be a housekeeper on a ranch."

"Is Em going, too?" His voice had a touch of anxiety.

"Of course not. Em will stay near you and come to visit you every day. We wouldn't leave you all alone."

"Long as Em's with me I won't mind." He lay back against the pillow, his restless hands feeling the texture of the nubby counterpane. He lay still a moment, absorbing the news until a new idea struck him. "Out West?" He raised himself on one arm again and looked more boyish than before. "Will there be Injuns and rustlers and everything?"

"I don't think so," Megan said, smiling gently. "There will be horses, though, like we had in Virginia. But what I wanted to tell you," she went on, "is that I'll have to stay there a year."

"Do you think I could go, too, when I get better?" he pleaded.

"I don't know, dear. We'll have to see." Dismayed by his flushed face and his quick, shallow breathing, she warned, "Don't get too wrought up. You must stay quiet."

"Wow, cowboys and everything!" he whispered. Reluctantly, he relaxed against the pillow. His eyes closed for a moment, then flew open to seek Megan's face in the dim light. "I'll try hard to get better, Meg, so I can come out and be with you."

She turned the lamp lower and whispered the platitudes she hoped would calm him, thankful he couldn't see her tears through the shadows. When he was dozing she padded softly back to Em in the kitchen.

"He took it like my soldier boy," she told Em who was dishing up two bowls of stew. "He wants to come out to see the Indians and the rustlers when he gets well." She filled a thick, white mug from the metal water pitcher on the table and sipped it.

"That boy's a reg'lar angel." Em shook her head, smiling sadly. "I'll take care o' him, Miss Megan. Don't you grieve yourself 'bout that."

The next week was emotionally exhausting for Megan. Like a saber-wielding duelist she beat back her fears. Her head knew that going away with Steve Chamberlin was the only answer to her predicament, but her heart moaned in torment. Each evening as she sat with Jeremy, white-hot daggers pierced her through.

I can't do it, she'd despair. *You must,* she'd argue back. *You must. You must.*

The nights she spent tossing fitfully on her hard, narrow cot. The days found her working her usual ten hours at the dressmaker's shop, making lists of things to do and take, and sorting their few possessions. The night before the wedding she didn't close her eyes until the faint gray light of dawn crept wearily through her tiny window.

three

The next morning was as tedious and long as the morning at Silverleigh when Megan broke Mother's favorite china figurine while her parents were away. She had spent four dreadful, restless hours waiting for them to return and discover her guilt. Like then, Megan couldn't concentrate on anything else except the dreaded event. This time it was her appointment with Steve Chamberlin that overshadowed all else.

She had asked Mrs. Peabody for the day off but when the day arrived she wished she had asked for only the afternoon, because her job would have filled the empty morning hours. Instead, she had to pass the time wandering from room to room, looking out windows, sitting down with a book only to put it aside five minutes later with barely a line read. She absently straightened pillows and ran errands for Jeremy. At ten-thirty she lay on her cot, feeling tired after her sleepless night and hopped up in two minutes to continue pacing. Her taut muscles must keep moving. She could not think of closing her eyes.

After forcing down three bites of lunch, she took her time changing into her best dress, a pale lavender cotton with a faint ivory swirl woven into it. She parted her waist-length hair slightly right of center and pulled it back into a wide, brown bun at the nape of the neck. Putting on her navy bonnet and coat, she left the house early to walk off some of her nervous energy.

There was a chill in the air when she reached the street. The sky over the city was dotted with small, puffy clouds, and a warm, fitful breeze toyed with the strings of her bonnet. Without any haste, she headed in the general direction of the park Steve had mentioned. She still had an hour to wait and the walk would normally take only twenty minutes.

The park, carpeted with a freshly grown crop of young grass and trees tinged with waxy, yellow-green new leaves, was almost deserted when she arrived. Mothers had their tiny charges at home for naps while older children were still in school. Megan wandered aimlessly on the path near a duck pond until she found a perch on a bench near the fish fountain Steve had told her about. With a detached attitude, she watched three mallard ducks dive for bread crumbs thrown by a grizzled old man in a tattered felt hat. Across the path a clump of daffodils swayed in the occasional breeze, bobbing their heads toward Megan.

Can I really go through with it? The question that had been battering her mind for the past week reverberated again in full force. She suddenly realized she was clenching her teeth, and she tried to force herself to relax.

Sunshine spilled over her back, slowly warming and loosening her tense muscles. Her lack of sleep from the night before took its toll, and little by little she began to feel drowsy. Her eyes were drooping when the old man with the bread crumbs carefully folded his empty sack and put it into the pocket of his faded, blue overcoat. He lingered a few moments longer before stomping down the path out of the park. Megan's gaze idly followed him until she saw something that roused her from her lethargy.

With a gray derby pulled low over his forehead, Steve Chamberlin strode past the old man, looking left then right as he came. He was dressed all in gray from overcoat to leather shoes. His face cleared when he spotted Megan, and he closed the gap between them in seconds.

"You came!" He settled down beside her. "I had almost convinced myself you would change your mind." The indecision on Megan's face stopped him. He looked at her carefully. "You're still going to do it, aren't you?"

"I can't afford to change my mind," she answered hesitantly. Seeing him again had brought a rush of panic over her.

"How is your brother?" he asked, politely.

"He's about the same, thank you." She studied the tiny stitches on the back of her gloved hand lying in her lap. Her own words echoed in her mind. Jeremy was the same, and he wouldn't get better unless she fulfilled her duty to him. When the full impact of that realization came to her, her pulse quieted. The confused, troubled thoughts fell into order.

"Did you find a sanitarium?"

"Yes. There's one on the western edge of town on Oak Street called Pinefield Nursing Home. They have an open bed and can take Jeremy as soon as I bring the first month's fee."

"We'll take care of that today. After the wedding, we'll visit my solicitor and make all the arrangements."

She rose, and they strolled to a closed carriage waiting nearby. Steve curtly called out an address to the driver, handed Megan up, and they set off at a brisk trot. Megan clasped her purse in her lap and kept her attention on the scene passing before the side window of the carriage. She felt too wrought up inside to take part in small talk. Evidently, Chamberlin either sensed or shared her mood, because he was silent for the entire journey.

The wedding was cold and mechanical. Without raising his head, a white-haired preacher read the solemn words from a small black book, his stout, red-cheeked wife looking on. Steve slid a plain gold band on her finger, and it was over. Megan's hands trembled, and she felt chilled clear through, yet she felt a bit lighter, a trifle less burdened. She breathed a deep, silent sigh. There was no turning back now. Her future was sealed.

The wedding was followed by an uncomfortable trip to Cyrus Tump's, the solicitor's office, where Steve introduced Megan and notified the ancient, spectacled gentleman of their plan to move to Colorado. Megan was afraid the steely, gray eyes of the lawyer would bore right through her, but she resolutely met his gaze and even managed a smile and nod in response to his greeting. Steve made arrangements for Jeremy's sanitarium fee and a monthly allowance for Em to be paid from Mr. Tump's office.

Back in the waiting carriage, he handed her a white envelope. "This is your first two months' pay."

"Thank you." She put the envelope in her handbag, then slid the gold band from her finger and placed it carefully into an inside pocket of the handbag for safekeeping.

"Is there any way I can help you?" he offered kindly when she pulled the drawstring tight.

"Em needs a small place to stay near the sanitarium so she can be near Jeremy. We haven't been able to find anything yet."

"I'll see to it," he said easily, and wrote it down in a small notebook he withdrew from his pocket.

"When exactly are we leaving?"

"That would be May twenty-fifth at six-thirty in the morning. We travel to Chicago, then change trains and go on to Denver. It'll take about a week."

"Only a week to go so far?" She had expected him to say twice as long.

"I want to get there in time to plant some corn, so it's none too fast. We'd leave this week if I could have gotten tickets." He returned the pad to his pocket. "Can I see you home?"

"Well, I was going to make the arrangements at the sanitarium for Jeremy. . . ."

"I'll take you there, then." He gave the order to the driver. "I don't have anything pressing this afternoon," he said, settling back on the black leather seat.

Megan was buoyed up with relief when Steve left her on High Street later that afternoon. A place in the sanitarium had been secured and a carriage engaged for Jeremy's transfer there. It was beyond marvelous to know that skilled hands would be caring for him tomorrow.

&

The next two weeks were a blur of activity. Megan and Em packed their few belongings and scrubbed the apartment. They were leaving it far cleaner than they had found it. It was heartbreaking to go through Mother's things, a task she had shied away from thus far. Mourning was momentarily replaced with excitement when she found some forgotten treasures in an old trunk. There was the forest green riding habit that had been Father's last gift to Mother before the war. She tried it on and found that with a few alterations she could wear it.

She hesitated when she found Father's old Bible, wrapped carefully in black velvet and brown paper. Never read, it had been kept by Mother as a momento. Reverently, Megan unwrapped it and ran her fingers gently over the black leather cover. Replacing the wrapping, she put it with the rest of her treasures. It would be comforting to have a few familiar things with her when she was far away.

Shopping was exhausting but also exciting. She bought blankets, feather ticking, coal oil lamps, vegetable seeds, a large cast-iron pot, needles, thread, several bolts of gaily colored fabric in check and small prints, and many other things.

She tried to concentrate totally on the task of clearing out the apartment and getting ready to go, pushing thoughts of good-byes far into the back recesses of her mind. The twenty-fourth of May soon arrived, however, and she could ignore good-byes no longer. She visited Jeremy that afternoon as she did every afternoon. Only, today it was with a sinking spirit.

At the door of the ward, she hesitated on the threshold to see what he was doing before she came closer. His eyes closed, Jeremy seemed to be asleep. Megan tiptoed toward him, studying his face, savoring the sight of him. In spite of the fact that she had not made a sound, his eyelids fluttered when she reached his side. Slowly, he focused on her.

"Hello, Meg."

"How are you feeling, Jeremy?" She pushed his hair back from his forehead, letting her hand rest near his temple.

" 'Bout the same." He paused, gazing listlessly at her face. "It's tomorrow, isn't it?"

"I'm afraid it is," Megan whispered, suddenly choked. A powerful hand gripped the core of her being. "I'm leaving in the morning."

"I'm going to miss you, Meg." A single, lonely tear slid slowly down his pale cheek. Megan gathered him in her arms and held him close. She shut her eyes hard, squeezing back the tears.

"Be my soldier, Jeremy," she said, forcing calmness into her words. "While I'm working in Colorado, you work hard on getting well. I'll try to send for you when you're better. I promise." She lay him back on the pillow and gently wiped away his tears with her handkerchief. "You keep remembering those horses and cowboys you want to see so bad, okay?" She attempted a bright smile through stiff lips.

"I will," he said bravely. His lip quivered, but he didn't cry anymore. His fingers clutched at her hand. "Will you write to me?"

"Of course. You don't think I'd forget about my best beau, do you?" she asked, lightly. "I'll write so much you'll get tired of reading."

"I'll get better as hard as I can," he promised solemnly.

"One day this will all be past, and we'll be happy again," she said softly, "but until then we'll both have to be good soldiers." She held his hand to her lips. "Always remember I love you."

"I love you, too, Meg." His lip quivered again. "Don't worry. Em will look after me."

Gently, she kissed his cheek, hugged him, and whispered a good-bye in his ear. She left the room without looking back. She couldn't endure the sight of him small and ill and alone, looking after her. But not looking back wasn't the answer, for the image of Jeremy in the sickbed was branded into her mind.

Tears coursed down her cheeks. She pressed her handkerchief to her mouth to stifle wracking sobs. Outside the door of the ward she leaned a shoulder against the cool wall, trying to get composure. In vain she drew in huge gulps of air and squeezed her sodden handkerchief tightly to her burning eyes. Finally, with tears still flowing, she straightened her shoulders, lifted her chin, and walked on.

❧

The next morning, Megan and Em rose while it was still dark to get ready for Megan's departure. The apartment had a strange, hollow quality that echoed and amplified their voices and the little noises of their moving about. Megan's trunk stood, locked and ready, near the front door. Em's was in the middle of the living room. Em would finish the transfer of her things later that morning and return the key to Mrs. Niles.

Megan couldn't swallow a bite of food. Though Em pressed her, she could force down only a few sips of hot coffee. After placing a few final things in her case, she walked through the apartment one last time to check for anything forgotten. Her shoes made a resonating clump-clump sound on the bare wood floors. The faint light of day glimmered through the curtainless windows, making vague patterns on the walls and floor.

Memories swept over her during her stroll from room to room. In this remote, dark place she had laughed and wept these past eight years. Her mother had died here. Here she had grown to womanhood.

She stared sightlessly down at the street, hazy in the new dawn, until she felt Em's hand on her arm.

"He's a-comin' soon, Miss Megan."

"I know." Megan looked up into Em's sad face. The worry mark was deep. "Oh, Em!" Her courage wavered for an instant.

"Just take it one day at a time, Miss Megan," Em said, putting a strong, loving arm around her. "That's the only way to git through the hard times. I seen a-plenty, but they always pass, child. They always pass."

The clip-clop of hooves and the squeal of iron rims on cobblestones sounded below.

"He's here." Dread put an edge on Megan's voice. She hugged Em hard and a few tears spilled over. "I'll send a telegram when we arrive."

"You in the hands o' the good Lord, Miss Megan. If prayin' ever helped anybody, you be all right, 'cause I'll sure enough be a-prayin'." Tears flowed down her dark, wrinkled cheeks.

A light tap sounded at the door. Trying futilely to dry her eyes, Megan opened it. It took but a moment for Steve's man to remove the trunk, and Steve took the case.

Moving mechanically, Megan put on her bonnet and coat against the chilly morning air. She took a step toward the door, then paused. With a sob, she threw herself into Em's arms, squeezing her hard, then she tore herself away and ran down the stairs, her heels beating a staccato tempo in her haste.

When she thought back later, all she could remember of the trip to the train station was a blur of impressions: the clop-clop of the horses pulling the carriage, the soft, steady pressure of Steve's hand on her arm guiding her through the waiting crowd, the aroma of cigar smoke in the passenger car, her wet cheeks and puffy, burning eyes.

They were in their seats less than five minutes before the train lurched ahead with a chugg-chugg-chugg that grew into a throbbing clackety-clack as it gathered speed. The sound pounded in Megan's tortured brain until it rang in her ears: *You're-not-coming-back. You're-not-coming-back.* She rested her head against the high back of the red plush seat and turned toward the window. The exhaustion of the past three weeks washed over her. The sound and sway of the train lulled her anguished mind until she fell asleep.

❧

It was near noon when next she opened her eyes. She blinked against the glare of the sun streaming through the train window and dazedly looked around. For a long second she couldn't remember where she was. It was Steve, beside her, reading a newspaper that brought her to herself. Catching a glimpse of herself in the gleaming mirror between the windows, she reached up to straighten her bonnet. She felt scruffy and had a nagging ache in her shoulder.

"Good morning," Steve said, smiling pleasantly, "though I believe it's closer to noon." He looked at her closer, realizing her discomfort. "There's a powder room near the back of the car if you'd like to refresh yourself."

"I believe I will," she said, picking up her handbag from where it had slid into the corner beside her. She avoided Steve's gaze as she passed by him, and half-stumbled down the aisle of the pitching, swaying car.

Megan bathed her red, swollen eyes and smoothed her hair back into its thick, brown bun. The cool water revived her somewhat and cleared her muddled mind. Taking advantage of the privacy, she placed the gold wedding band on her finger, this time to stay. Light though it was, it weighed heavily on her hand. She could feel it even when she replaced her glove.

On the return trip, she braced herself by holding the backs of the seats and noticed for the first time how crowded the car was. Two fat businessmen, one puffing a long, black cigar, were deep in conversation. Several coatless young men in silk pinstriped shirts with black sleeve garters were engaged in some sort of card game near the front of the car, shrilly encouraged by three gaudy young women with rouge-reddened cheeks. A fine lady in a black satin traveling suit sat alone near a window, waving a tiny square of black lace in front of her nose. Megan felt particular sympathy for the mothers. There were several of them with fussing, wriggling children. With the exception of the one next to the woman in black, every seat was occupied. The sound of many voices, the mechanical noises of the train, and the smell of box lunches, tobacco smoke, and sickly sweet perfume filled the air.

"Care for some lunch?" Steve asked, reaching under the seat for the box he had brought.

"I couldn't." Her stomach was a leaden knot.

"You'll be sick if you don't eat." He watched her thoughtfully.

"You must think I'm a crybaby," she ventured impulsively.

"On the contrary. I believe I could be a little jealous."

Surprised, she glanced at him to see if he was mocking her, but his face was serious. He met her eyes.

"When I left, no one noticed in the least," he added, soberly. "No one has noticed for a long time." He broke the mood by studying the contents of their lunch box. "There's cold chicken, rolls, a piece of cheese, and a bottle of water and two cups. Surely you can take something."

"I guess I could take a roll," she yielded, holding out her hand. She was surprised at how good it tasted after she got past the first bite.

Grassy, rolling meadows skimpily dotted with horses and cattle skimmed past the window. Megan drank in each scene. She had been in the city for so long she had almost forgotten how lovely the countryside could be.

"How long until we reach Chicago?"

"About three days. Give or take a day." He handed her a cup of water. "We'll stop for dinner in Philadelphia, then on to Ohio and Chicago. There's an overnight stay in Chicago before we can get a train to Denver."

Hour by endless hour the journey stretched on. It seemed to Megan she was in limbo. Nothing existed but the clackety-clack of the train, the continuous pain in her heart, and Steve.

four

The stagecoach waiting for them in Denver was brilliant red with shiny gold trim. Over its double doors the name *Concord* glowed proudly. Megan was surprised to see that even the wheel rims were scarlet. The team of four sleek, black horses jangled the harness impatiently.

So this is the great West, Megan thought, hungrily absorbing every detail. Men in cowboy garb were lounging at various storefronts, engaged in desultory conversation. Now and then one would break away and amble down the boardwalk, six-shooter swinging, chaps flapping with each long stride. The women were dressed much more simply than those in Baltimore. Calico and homespun were everywhere.

Some of her self-consciousness had faded during the eight-day trip to Denver. Steve was casual and kind. She found soothing support in his presence. In Chicago, there had been an embarrassed silence when they reached their hotel suite, but he had arranged his blankets in the outer room and had given Megan privacy. Only twice did she have to hide tears of homesickness, though her thoughts strayed often to Jeremy and Em.

She felt a thrill of anticipation when Steve handed her up into the stage. In a few hours she would see her new home and begin her new life. What would it be like?

As soon as the stage pulled away from the broad streets of Denver, the rough, country road jarred Megan to the core. Her already-aching muscles begged for relief but the hard leather seats were unrelenting. The four other passengers, three men and one woman, exchanged introductions with Steve.

"Coming for a visit?" asked the stout, talkative woman known as Mrs. Pleurd.

"We're going to settle on the Cunningham place," Steve said, steadying himself by holding the edge of the seat.

"The Circle C?" blurted Mrs. Pleurd. Her mouth dropped open for half an instant before she recovered herself.

All of a sudden every eye was fastened on Steve. There was an uneasy silence.

"Why, yes," Steve said, lightly. "My father bought the land about two years ago, and I've come to take possession."

No one offered any more conversation, but Megan could sense the strain. Something in these otherwise friendly people was amiss. Was it something Steve had said or done? Megan probed her mind for an answer, but none came.

The shallow, winding stream where the driver chose to stop for lunch was peaceful and cool. Megan moved apart from the rest of the party to sit in the shade of a wide cottonwood tree, her back resting against its broad, steady trunk. She closed her eyes, breathing deeply of the clear air and resting her mind in the quietness while Steve went to the stream for some water.

In a few moments, hushed voices jarred her to full attention. She sat still, her head tilted to one side, listening to Steve's voice.

"I'm much obliged for your concern, Kip," Steve was saying to the man who had introduced himself as the foreman of the Running M, "but we'll go ahead with our plans."

"I'm just thinking of the little lady," a deep voice said. "Them Harringtons are plumb mean, and you'll have yourself a whoppin' fight. I hope you know what you're doing."

"I know." Steve's voice had a deadly, still quality. "I've been down the river a ways myself. We'll go on."

The snap of a boot on a twig told Megan they had moved away. She relaxed against the rough bark once more, but the memory of those voices lingered on, and her peace of mind flew away on silent wings.

A hot, lazy June afternoon gave them a drowsy welcome when the stage rumbled into Juniper Junction. From under the brim of her gray traveling bonnet, Megan eagerly watched the town roll by. The street was deserted except for three sleepy horses standing three-legged next to various hitching rails along the dusty street and two weather-beaten wagons. At various places a tepid breeze blew the sand into small, swirling clouds.

"Whoa!" the driver bellowed as the stage lumbered to a halt. The clamor of the jouncing, jolting stage still sang in Megan's ears, and her stiff muscles complained when Steve helped her down. She stepped up onto the boardwalk and looked with interest at the shops and houses. There were one, two, yes, three saloons, and two blacksmith shops, a hotel, a bank, and a general store, as well as the stage station where she stood. Someone was building a small shop between the livery stable and the jail. It was a lonely place even compared to Denver, and wouldn't bear comparing to the crowded, pulsating streets of Baltimore.

Brushing aside a tinge of disappointment at the forsaken little place that would be their main supply point, Megan entered the stage station to send Em a telegram and ask if a letter had arrived.

"Sorry, ma'am." The boyish clerk with pock-scarred cheeks shook his head. "The mail comes through ever' Wednesday. Maybe there'll be somethin' tomorrow."

Twenty minutes later Megan sank gratefully into the wooden chair Steve held for her at the hotel restaurant. He looked anxiously at her weary face when he took his seat across from her at the small, square table.

"Do you think we should wait until morning to go on?" he asked.

"A little rest and some hot food is all I need," she replied, trying to smile. "I want to get to the ranch today. I don't think I could wake up and face another day of traveling." In her mind she pictured the wide fields and spreading trees on the ranch. She could already feel the long, refreshing bath and the bed waiting for her there.

Two thick steaks and a plateful of fried potatoes later they walked outside to see four horses hitched to a buckboard in front of the general store next door. In the wagon were their suitcases and baggage.

"Aren't they beauties?" Steve asked, a hint of pride in the words.

"Where did you find them?" Holding his arm, she stopped on the edge of the boardwalk, looking eagerly at each horse in turn. There were two blacks, a buckskin, and a strawberry roan mare.

"Man at the livery stable had the three geldings and the buckboard. I got the mare from Harper at Harper's Emporium."

Megan rubbed the neck of the strawberry mare. Memories of happy days in Virginia came back in a flood. Morning rides with Father, all but forgotten, were revived again. The mare nuzzled her hand.

"Looking for a treat?" Megan laughed happily and patted the star between the horse's eyes. "What's her name?"

"Candy. Harper tells me she loves sugar and carrots. His daughter had her until she went back East. Treated her like a baby. She married a man from Delaware a few months ago, so Harper has no need to keep the horse around anymore." He checked a strap on the harness. "The black with the star and three stockings is Star, the one with the blaze is Caesar, and the buckskin is Billy."

"Will it take four to pull the buckboard?"

"It's a steep climb to the ranch from what I hear. When the wagon is loaded down like it is now, we'll be glad to have four." Steve finished his inspection of the harness. "We'd better get our supplies and head out." He pulled his watch from his vest pocket and glanced at it. "Billy has a loose shoe that must be attended to before we set out, and we ought to get to the ranch before dark."

It was shadowy inside Harper's Emporium after the glare of the hot afternoon sun. Megan paused on the threshold while she waited for her eyes to adjust to the dimness. The inviting aroma of new leather, fresh ground coffee, and tobacco drew her inside. From that moment, the smell of a new saddle reminded her of Harper's.

In one corner on a table were two saddles with some bridles and spurs; a few leather belts hung on the wall above them. There were large, copper-banded barrels of pickles, crackers, and coffee beans near the end of the counter where the coffee grinder stood. The rows of shelves that lined the wall behind the counter were filled with bolts of fabric, shirts and pants folded in neat stacks, an assortment of guns and ammunition, and various staple food items. On the counter was a thick glass jar of peppermint candy with a small sign: Penny Candy.

"Hello." A slim young woman standing near the counter spoke to Megan. Her strawberry blond hair was pulled back into a wavy, shoulder-length ponytail. "Mr. Harper went into the back room for a minute." She had clear blue eyes, and an open, friendly smile. "I'm Susan Harrington."

"I'm Megan Wes. . .ummm, Megan Chamberlin," Megan faltered. "We came in on the stage."

"Are you going to be here long?" The woman's friendliness touched Megan's heart and made her want to reach out.

"We've come to settle on a ranch."

"Oh, good!" Susan's smile broadened. "Elaine Sanders and I are about the only young women near Juniper since Alice Harper left. Where are you going to be?"

"I believe it's called the Circle C."

Her pleasant expression froze on Susan's face. She grew pale, and her eyes opened wide.

"The Circle C?" She paused, searching Megan's face.

"Yes. I hope you'll come and visit me if you can," Megan said, offering a tremulous smile. She hoped Susan would be a friend in this friendless, far-away place.

"I will." A spark shone in the local woman's eyes. She glanced toward the curtained doorway at the rear of the shop. The noise of boots scuffling on the wood floor came from the other side of the curtain. Susan moved closer to Megan. "I will come and visit you," she hurriedly whispered on her way out.

A slim, gray-haired man with stooped shoulders stepped through the curtain-covered door.

"Can I help you folks?"

"We need supplies." Steve spoke from the corner near the leather goods. "My wife can tell you what she wants."

Megan walked to the counter. "Twenty pounds of flour, two pounds of brown sugar. . . ." She gave Mr. Harper the list of supplies, enough for a month.

"I want five hundred rounds of .45 shells and five hundred .44s," Steve added when she finished. "And I'll take those two Colts, a Winchester, and the Henry rifle." He nodded toward weapons on a shelf to the left.

Harper's bushy, gray eyebrows raised a mite. He dropped the shells into the burlap sack he was filling.

"Expectin' trouble?" he asked, his eyes still on the sack.

"We've come to settle on the Circle C," Steve said, conversationally, "and we aim to stay."

Harper looked up, startled, to meet Steve's gaze for a long moment. The storekeeper's eyes shifted, and he continued filling their order in silence.

"I'll be needing a hand."

"You'll not be finding one for the Circle C," Mr. Harper said. His face was expressionless.

"Mr. Harper, I'm not on the prod, but if a fight comes my way, I'll handle it. With or without a hand." Steve lifted a burlap sack in each hand and carried them outside. Megan followed him, her heart pounding.

"I saw a blacksmith at work near the end of the street," Steve said, picking up the reins. "He ought to be able to take care of Billy's loose shoe in short order."

The pounding of a hammer on an anvil reached Megan's ears long before she saw the giant of a man who wielded the iron. He stood inside the wide open door of his shop, shaping a red-hot horseshoe. His bulging, hairy arms were streaked with soot and sweat. When their buckboard creaked to a stop he straightened, lifted the horseshoe with a pair of tongs, and plunged it into a bucket of water, making it boil over.

He was the biggest man Megan had ever seen. At least six-feet, four-inches tall, he must have weighed close to three hundred pounds. He wore a ragged shirt, so faded and dirty that it was impossible to tell its original color. Wide suspenders made two furrows over his shoulders, and his front was covered by a blackened leather apron.

"Gud afternoon!" Nodding and wiping his hands on his apron, he lumbered toward them. His broad grin revealed a missing front tooth.

Setting the brake and winding the reins around the whip stand, Steve jumped down. "I've got a horse with a loose shoe. Can you take care of it for me right away? We have some traveling to do before nightfall."

"Five minute," the blacksmith announced in thick, German tones. He picked up Billy's foot and examined the shoe. "Two nail vill make it gud as new." He slid a hammer from a loop on his side and dug two nails from his apron pocket. Four taps and he slid the hammer back through its loop. "I never seen you before. You live here?" It was a friendly question.

"We're settling on the Circle C." Steve's voice had become defensive.

"Dat's gud. Dat's gud." The big man's round, blond head bobbed up and down. "I'm Logan Hohner. I have de Horseshoe Ranch just north of dere.

Dose be my two boys, Al and Henry." He indicated two young men in their early twenties slouching in wooden chairs in front of the gray, wind-scoured building. At the mention of their names, the one with buckteeth protruding through his lips raised his hat a fraction, then slid it over his eyes and tilted back in his chair. The other nodded sullenly. Both were of large build like their father except the father was hard and muscular, and they were soft and lethargic.

"Come by my place any time," Hohner invited.

Steve thanked him and climbed aboard. He released the brake, shook the reins, and they were off. The bouncing of the buckboard was as bone-jarring as the stage ride. Megan clenched her teeth and held on. She wondered about her strange conversation with Susan Harrington.

Susan had been frightened at the mention of the Circle C. Susan Harrington. Harrington. Hadn't that been the name she had overheard Steve and Kip use that afternoon when they were beside the stream?

"Steve?" Megan looked at his profile. "What is the problem about the Circle C?"

He looked straight ahead, studying a moment before answering.

"I guess you'd better know." Looking at her, he held the reins loosely and shifted slightly on the seat. "It seems we've bought some trouble by coming out here. The Harringtons are the big landholders, and they don't like squatters."

"But I thought you had deeded land."

"It is deeded. And that's exactly why I'm not backing down." His jaw was set in a hard line. "Evidently, Harrington has some pull around here, and he has some sort of claim on the Circle C. The problem is that the law is in Denver. A deed is only a piece of paper. Unfortunately, paper's not much protection against a loaded six-shooter."

"You think there will be shooting?"

"No doubt there will." He glanced at Megan again. "Don't fret, though. I didn't fight under Bragg for nothing. We'll get through." He glanced at the sinking sun and clucked to the horses to get along faster.

The buckboard continued across the prairie to the rolling hills at the foot of the mountains. The horses started pulling and Steve slackened the reins to give them their head. Soon, prairie grasses were replaced by wildflowers, sagebrush, and piñon pine. A clean breeze swept over them as they neared the high country.

Megan gazed at the orange and brown rocks upthrust to the sky, the scrubby, green hillsides, and the jagged cliffs. She savored the scent of sage and pine. It was rugged country but she fell in love with it at first sight. Simply being there made her feel happier than she had in a long time.

"It's not far from here," Steve said when they passed over a rise. "I believe it's through this stretch of trees and across a stream."

"There it is!" Steve pulled the horses to a stop. A sprawling, thirty-acre meadow sloped gently up until it was cut off by a stone wall. On the eastern side of the wall were a stone cabin and a smaller gray building. The two buildings were joined by a high board fence. The setting sun shone full on them, bringing life to the rock wall and house. They glowed like bronze against the darkening sky.

It was more beautiful than Megan had imagined. A cooling gust of wind bathed her face. It felt refreshing after the long, hot days of traveling.

"Giddap!" Steve called to the team, and they rode slowly down the bank. The water came a few inches below the axle of the buckboard. Megan held her breath until they were climbing up the other side. Skirting the field, Steve held the horses to an even, moderate gate. Timothy grass brushed the bottom and sides of the buckboard.

By the time they reached the house the wind had taken on a definite chill. It pulled at Megan's dress and reached down inside of her. She picked up the shawl she had draped over the back of the seat and wrapped it closely around her shoulders. Shadows filled the hollows and crannies of the dooryard, bringing with them a strange foreboding. Uneasy, Megan looked around the dooryard that was little more than an extension of the meadow, full of thigh-high grass and brush. She pushed through the grass toward the stone house while Steve rummaged for a lantern and the lamp oil.

The floor and roof of the porch sagged wearily. A few boards were missing from each. The door leaned on cracked, dry leather hinges. The smell of dampness and mold caught at her nostrils. Resting her weight cautiously on the broken porch floor, she reached a tentative hand toward the door.

"Oh!" she cried sharply, drawing back. Inches from her face an enormous spider web covered the top half of the partly open door. Cringing, she pulled her shawl tightly about her and returned to the edge of the porch. The nightly cricket chorus had begun, punctuated now and then by the ghostly "who-o-o-o" of an owl.

She shivered, and dug her nails into the palms of her hands, holding in the discouraged, exhausted tears that sprang to her eyes. How could they sleep here tonight? And she yearned for a relaxing soak in a warm tub.

"Here's a lantern," Steve called from the buckboard fifteen minutes later. "I'd better see to a fire. It's getting cold." All she could see of him now was his middle, next to the swinging lantern held high above the tall grass as he walked toward her. Never giving the spider web a thought, he pushed the groaning door open and walked inside.

With many nervous glances, Megan squeezed herself into the smallest proportions possible and followed him into the gloomy house.

five

"There's a fire already laid," Steve said when he had set the lantern down. He knelt before the fireplace and struck a match on the edge of his boot sole. The dry wood sparked into a flickering flame.

Megan hovered nearby. She was afraid to move around or look too closely at the shadowy corners of the room. The fire gnawed with gathering appetite at the kindling, so Steve added a larger piece of wood. Megan felt a hint of warmth and moved even closer to the smoldering light.

"I'll bring in some things for the night." Steve stood up, brushing off his hands. "You sit down and rest yourself. You look all in."

"I'm sure a night's rest will set me right," she replied automatically as she moved to an upholstered settee near the fireplace and sank to the seat. Without another word, Steve took the lantern and stepped into the night.

In a few moments he was back carrying Megan's trunk with several blankets stacked on top. Working quickly and efficiently, he spread out a crude bed near the fire and told her to lie down. She felt her eyes drooping as soon as her head found a resting place.

ஐ

The cabin was dusky from sunlight shining through the cloudy windows when Megan awoke. Gingerly, she sat up. She ached in every bone, and her head throbbed dully. Steve was nowhere around.

A pail of water with a metal dipper hooked on the edge stood on the dusty stone hearth. Megan drank greedily, then bathed her face. She unlocked her trunk and was searching for a fresh dress when the door hinges groaned.

"Mornin'." Steve dropped an arm load of split logs into the wood box near the fireplace and brushed off his bark-flecked arms. "I'll move your things into the bedroom yonder if you want." He nodded toward a door on the wall opposite the front door. "I laid claim to the loft last night." He added a log to the small fire. "There's a spring out back if you want to wash up."

"I'll cook breakfast first," Megan responded. "I'm starving." She grinned in spite of herself.

Steve answered with a relieved smile. "The supplies we bought at Harper's are there." He pointed to two burlap sacks beside the moth-eaten settee. "I brought them in last night. You'd better use the fireplace until we can clean up the cookstove and check for a bird's nest in the chimney."

A hot breakfast improved Megan's outlook. She armed herself with soap and towel and went in search of the spring. Opening the back door, she peered outside. A wide stream of water flowed from a crack in the rock wall behind the house to fill a stone-lined basin in the ground. Through the clear water she could see the basin had some loose stones and moss inside, but it was in good condition. She touched the stream pouring down only to jerk her hand back. The water was like liquid ice.

The bath, though not quite the long soak of her daydream, was invigorating. While she finished dressing, she noticed that when the water left the basin it continued through a stone-paved trench that led through a springhouse and drained down a bank. Megan walked to the edge and looked down. Gasping, she took a step back. It was forty feet to the bottom! The eastern side of the house was on the edge of a small cliff.

Megan looked out at a vast expanse of blue-green rolling hills that melted to meet the level prairie. The sun was a glowing yellow ball barely resting on the flat horizon. The radiant light made the prairie grass gleam like silver as it swayed in the continuous breeze. She stood spellbound, feeling like an ant on the edge of an endless wilderness. No trace of human handiwork marred the landscape. It was magnificent.

How long she stayed there, she didn't know, but finally she realized she ought to get back to the business at hand and she turned away from the panorama with a promise to visit this spot many mornings in the future.

Back in the house, she wrapped a navy kerchief around her head, tied an old work apron over her blue calico dress, and made a careful, critical inspection of the house.

The front wall of the house was built of rock, and the floor was made of smooth, flat stones. Both walls and floor were fitted together as perfectly as a piece of pottery, broken and glued back together. The walls and open-beam ceiling were swaddled with dust-laden spider webs. The windows, cracked and pocked, were covered with a thick layer of fly-specked grime. There were two wooden chairs and a three-person settee positioned in a semicircle around the fireplace. The cushions were moldy and full of holes with small tufts of gray cotton showing through.

At the western end of the house was a dining area with the kitchen branching off toward the back, making an L-shape. A thick oak table and four chairs were covered with the ever-present dust, but seemed in good condition.

Megan looked about her with an appraising eye. The marks of a craftsman were all around her. The house had definite possibilities.

She moved into the kitchen to examine the rusty range, two counters, and many cabinets. The single window revealed a small stretch of grass and one side of the gray wooden building she had seen last night. She also saw the high board fence.

The fence intrigued her. Why was it there? What did it hide? She went through the back door to find out the answer. When she had come out earlier, she was too taken up with the spring and the breathtaking view to think of looking in this direction.

The fence was six feet tall and parallel to the face of the rock wall, making a corridor about fifteen feet wide. Seeing nothing unusual behind the fence, Megan walked on until she came to the wooden building. Applying a little pressure, she lifted the reluctant door latch and was rewarded by a small shower of dirt when the door swung open.

She looked inside before she stepped over the doorsill. Six stalls stood before her with a single manger running the length of all six. The buckboard was beside the far wall, still loaded with the sacks of grain for the horses and the corn seed Steve had brought from Baltimore. On the wall near the open double doors hung a wooden bucket and a bit of chain. There was a door on the left side of the back wall, probably a ranch hand's modest quarters.

Steve stood in the second stall, a pitchfork in his hand.

"I was wondering where the fence led," she said when he looked up.

"This is a nice place, isn't it?" he asked without waiting for a reply. "I can say one thing for Cunningham, the man who built it." Steve rested his forearm on the pitchfork handle. "Besides being a craftsman, he knew how to prepare for a battle."

"A battle?"

"Sure. There's a rock wall behind the house, a cliff beside it, and no trees within shooting range. No one can approach the house unseen." He propped the pitchfork against the wall and picked up a shovel. "That fence was put there so he could get to his stock without going out in the open. And water back there, too."

"The house is well-made. I can see that."

"That's another thing. It has a stone front. The rest is made of squared logs. No bullet can get through them."

"You think he had a lot of trouble?"

Steve lifted a shovel full of hardened straw and manure from the floor and heaved it outside. "Judging from the town's reaction to us, I think it's pretty obvious," he answered, bending for another load.

"I guess I'd better get started in the house," she said in a moment and went back to the house the way she came.

It was noon when Megan walked out to the sagging front porch for a cold lunch and little rest. She was tired, but it was a satisfied feeling. The morning had been spent in the kitchen, for she couldn't tolerate the thought of no clean place in which to cook. She had scoured and scrubbed until her shoulders ached.

Steve joined her for bacon and biscuit sandwiches, leftovers from breakfast, and cold spring water. They passed the lunch break in companionable silence. In spite of the hard work, Megan was enjoying herself immensely. Those few minutes of sitting on the rickety porch, absorbing the blueness of the cloud-strewn sky and drinking in the hay-scented air, pumped life back into her tired limbs.

*

It was past dark before Megan permitted herself another rest. The windows in the house were as clean as she could make them, cracked as they were, and the four-poster bed in her room had been stripped of its rotting mattress and replaced with a fresh hay-filled one. Steve had cut the hay from the front yard.

The kindred atmosphere of Steve sitting near the fire cleaning his new guns, thick stew bubbling cheerily on the shiny black kitchen stove, gave Megan a tender, contented feeling she hadn't known for a long, long time. She ladled the soup into bowls and set them carefully on the table.

"Tomorrow I'll scout around and get acquainted with the country," Steve said, drawing a knotted string through the barrel of his Winchester. "I left word at the livery stable, the hotel, and the Emporium that I need a hand. If we can't get one I'll have to work double to get the corn crop in. It'll be late as it is. Not to mention a garden."

Megan had to school herself to wash up after supper. She moved with leaden feet and arms but somehow she managed to finish. That night she lay alone in the darkness trying to sleep in spite of her sore shoulders and aching back. She pressed the heels of her hands against her eyes to ease her throbbing head. It had been nine days since she had seen Jeremy. Was he better? Worse? How much longer would it be until she got some news? Her mind flitted from question to question. In a few minutes a soft rain started a soothing, tapping lullaby on her windowpane. The tune hushed her restless brain, and she fell asleep.

*

The next morning Steve rode out before the sun shone its face full over the prairie. Megan stood in the doorway watching until horse and rider disappeared into the stand of oaks and pines. She was about to go inside when a movement in the tall grass caught her eye. She studied the edge of the yard, expecting to pick out a rabbit frozen in its tracks, when two pointed gray ears moved slightly at the edge of the grass.

She drew in a startled breath. *A wolf,* she thought. Even as the impression touched her consciousness, she rejected it. Wolves came at night and were shy of people.

The large gray head moved higher and came into her field of vision. The shaggy face ended in a pointed nose, further confirming her first impression, but there was a nagging doubt.

"Here, boy," she called softly. She spoke more to judge the animal's reaction than in hopes he would indeed come to her. The shaggy gray head bent down out of sight and raised up again. The mouth opened and its red tongue rolled out in a wide yawn, that ended in a low whine. The black button eyes were still fastened on her face.

It was a dog.

What is a dog doing so far from anyone? she wondered. She went inside for a leftover piece of biscuit from breakfast.

She dredged the biscuit in partially hardened bacon drippings in the bottom of the frying pan. From the edge of the porch she threw the biscuit toward the dog as far as she could. It landed ten feet from him. Still watching her, he didn't move.

She waited a moment, decided she was wasting her time, and went back inside. She threw open all the windows in the house to let the clear, pine-scented air sweep through before clearing up the breakfast dishes.

That task finished, she glanced out at the spot where the biscuit had fallen. It was gone and so was the dog. Whether the dog or some other wild animal had taken the food, she couldn't tell. It was an unusual happening, but not significant and she forgot about it.

Late in the afternoon she was rubbing the wide, stone fireplace to a shine with pine oil when an odd sound stopped her in midmotion.

It was a voice as rough and rasping as a frog with laryngitis singing, "Rock of Ages, cleft for me, Let me hide myself in thee."

Half-curious and half-alarmed, Megan peered out a front window. Someone rode toward the house on a lop-eared, gray donkey.

"Let the water and the blood. . . ."

It was an old man wearing faded, dust-covered clothes and a brown Stetson with a frayed crown. He rode up to the porch and pulled up on the donkey's reins.

"Anybody home?" he shouted.

With shaking fingers, Megan lifted the latch and stepped outside. The man swung from the saddle and took off his hat.

"Howdy, ma'am." He wasn't as old as Megan had first imagined. She was relieved to see his mild blue eyes had a friendly twinkle. "I heard you folks are needin' a hand."

"Yes," Megan said, smiling in response to his polite manner. "My husband is looking over the country today. I'm expecting him around supper time." She hesitated. "I've got some water on for coffee. Could I offer you a cup?"

"I'd be much obliged." He picked up the donkey's reins from where they trailed on the ground.

"You can put your donkey in the stable. There's a spring out back." Megan went back into the house to finish making the coffee.

"My name's Megan Chamberlin," she said as she handed him a steaming cup at the dining room table. "My husband is Steve."

"Thank you, ma'am. I'm Joe Calahan, but most folks call me Banjo on account of I'm always making music." He chuckled. "It seems like there's always a song on the inside o' me that's scramblin' to get out." He sipped his coffee, and sighed appreciatively. "That's a mighty fine cup, Mrs. Chamberlin. A good cup o' coffee is a great comfort to a man." With a work-gnarled hand he smoothed the spot on his graying black hair where his hat left a crease. "What type o' hand was your husband wantin'?"

"As far as I know, he's planning to put in a corn crop as soon as possible. He says it's almost too late already. He wants to get some cattle, too."

"I've turned my hand to just about ever'thin', so I reckon it don't much matter."

That evening when Megan introduced Banjo, Steve's relief was easy to see.

"After we mow the hay in the lower meadow, we can plant it in corn," Steve said after supper. They sat around the small flame in the fireplace. The June days were warm, but the nights still had a chill. The flickering firelight made the polished stones glow. "Know much about cattle?" he asked Banjo.

"I've punched a few cows," Banjo said. Thoughtfully, he rolled the tooth-pick he was chewing to the other side of his mouth. "Ever heard of the Harringtons?"

Megan started at the name.

"Kip Morgan told me a little about them."

"I know Kip. He's a good man. As for Victor Harrington, he was one of the first ranchers to open up this country. He fought off the Indians, built a ranch, and brought in about twenty thousand head o' cattle.

"He pushed out a few small ranchers in the process, but mostly folks stayed out o' his way. The bulk of the land he claims is government land, but the law is in Denver so government land or no don't make no difference. What he can hold with a six-shooter is his."

"That's what I figured," Steve said.

"I suppose you could try to do things through the law, but that would only get Harrington to ride over to Denver and buy himself a lawyer, a judge, and a jury. You wouldn't have a Chinaman's chance.

"Well, sir." Banjo cleared his throat. "To get back to facts. Five or six years ago John Cunningham bought these four hundred acres. He came in quiet-like and had this house pretty nigh built before Harrington got wind of it. You see, Harrington only comes around this neck o' the woods once in a blue moon. But there's plenty of water coming down off that mountain behind you. If there was to come a drought, he'd need that water in the worst way."

"I found a lake just south of here, too," added Steve.

"That's on your property," Banjo said, nodding. "Cunningham dug in for a long fight, and did a good job o' holding Harrington off, too. He had to go all the way to Denver for supplies there at the last, because Harrington put the strong arm on the shopkeepers in Juniper."

"Why did he quit?" Steve asked. "He'd done so much here."

"His wife died in childbirth. It took the heart out of him, I guess. I worked for him time and agin since he come here. A little over two years ago I was passin' through, and stopped by to swap howdies. He was gone." Banjo looked at Steve. "I never heard tell what became of him."

"I don't know much myself, Banjo," Steve answered. "He sold the property to my father about two years ago. I never saw him. My father left the land to me in his will. That's all I know."

"We'll be gettin' an early start, so I'd best say good night to you," Banjo said, rising. "Thank you for the fine meal, ma'am," he said, settling his hat on his head. "I'll be gettin' to my room in the stable." After Steve's return that afternoon they had swept out the back room of the stable and cut a new mattress full of hay for one of the two bunks. The quarters seemed bare to Megan but to Banjo, who had lived in many places like it or worse, it was homey.

"You're welcome, Banjo." Megan smiled. She was glad he had come.

six

The next morning when Megan glanced out the living room window, the same gray shaggy face she had seen the day before appeared at the edge of the meadow. The dog stayed still, ears high, watching the door of the house. Megan scooped a piece of bacon and the end of a loaf of bread from the table she had been clearing and darted for the porch. When she reached the door, she slowed down and was careful not to make any sudden moves. She stepped to the edge of the porch and threw the food toward him. The dog didn't flinch or make a move toward her.

"It's okay," she said, quietly. "I want to be your friend." After a few moments she decided the creature was not going to come closer and she went back inside. She made a mental note to tell the men when they came back that afternoon. The stray dog intrigued her. She wished she could learn more about where he came from.

&

The sun was slipping down behind the mountains the next day when a group of riders appeared at the edge of the meadow and galloped toward the house. Hearing the hoofbeats, Megan came to the open doorway to watch. Steve and Banjo were on their way to the house for supper when the group reached the dooryard.

"You Chamberlin?" A wafer-thin, freckled young man with a thick crop of fiery red hair stepped his pinto horse to the front.

"I'm Chamberlin," Steve acknowledged.

"You get out," the red-haired young man ordered in a strident voice. His hard, green eyes looked down coldly at Steve. "This here's Rocking H range, and we don't cotton to squatters."

"I've got a deed for this land," replied Steve, his voice still even, "and I don't bluff." He looked around the group of five riders. "You fellows are welcome if you come peaceable. Otherwise, consider yourselves warned."

The leader edged his horse forward until it almost touched Steve. "You consider yourself warned." He dropped his hand toward his holster.

"Easy, Beau."

Beau hesitated and looked toward a tall, black-haired man with a narrow face and a deep scar running from his temple to his jaw. The man who spoke stepped his horse forward three steps. He was chewing thoughtfully on a twig.

"They'll git what's comin' to 'em if they don't go. No need to fly off the handle. Your pa don't want shootin' trouble. We can handle 'em another way."

"You heard my answer." Steve stood straight, right hand tense and ready beside his six-shooter. "Now, get off my land."

Four of the riders turned their horses, but the one with the red hair hesitated. He looked scornfully at Banjo.

"You joinin' this outfit, Banjo?"

"That's right, Harrington." Banjo's twinkle was nowhere to be seen. "I'm with 'em. And you'll get a run for your money."

Beau considered this news, then slowly turned his horse. "Get out!" he repeated and joined his friends.

Megan was shaky with relief and alarm when the group of men rode off. She went inside to set the table, but her ears were tuned to hear Banjo's comments on the incident.

"That Harrington's son?" Steve asked Banjo when he came in from washing up in the basin out back.

"In the flesh," Banjo said, pulling out a chair and sitting to the table. "He's like a banty rooster. His pa's the big rooster, and he tries to carry the same weight." He glanced at Steve. "But don't underestimate him. He's mean as a snake. I was in town one time when a stranger called him 'Red.' He bumped into Beau and said, 'Sorry, Red,' just like that. Well, sir, the young feller hauled iron and that hombre almost got hisself shot. If Clyde Turner, the feller with the scar, hadn't been there, who knows what would have happened. That boy's mighty techy about his hair."

"Who's Turner?" Steve asked, forking a piece of beef on his plate.

"He's the foreman. Been with Harrington five, six years."

"He looks familiar, but I can't place him."

"He scares me," Megan said, shivering. "Both of them do."

"Don't alarm yourself, Miss Megan," Banjo said, setting down his coffee cup and smiling kindly. "There's not many men in these parts would harm a lady."

Banjo's words were small comfort when Megan thought of all that was at stake for her in this lonesome place. What if Steve were killed, or they had to leave? What would happen to Jeremy? She brooded over those questions until she was worn out with thinking. They had to make it.

❧

Fear tightened Megan's lips and creased her brow as she watched Steve strap on his gunbelt before leaving the house the next morning. He noticed her anxious expression and paused at the door.

"A gun is a tool out here, Megan. I'm not asking for trouble by wearing it, just preparing in case it comes."

"I know," she said, tearing her gaze from the gun to meet his eyes. "But it frightens me to think of what could happen. Please be careful." Through the window she watched him cross the distance to the stable. By sheer will she forced down the fear and went about her chores.

≈

Three days after Harrington's visit Steve pulled his shiny new plow from the stable and hitched up Star before dawn. They had a long day in store for them planting their garden, and Megan would work alongside the men. The black was restless, eager to get going. He bobbed his head and blew until Steve took the reins, and they walked across the freshly cut meadow. Banjo followed him carrying a hoe over his shoulder and his old buffalo gun in the crook of his arm.

Megan finished the breakfast dishes and packed a lunch before she followed the men to the large, sunny plot near the stream at the western edge of the meadow. She carried a cloth-covered basket on her arm and many small sacks of seeds in her apron pocket. The air was sweet with the smell of newly cut timothy. A playful breeze made the wide brim of her sunbonnet flap up and down. It tugged at her full skirt, wrapping the cloth around her ankles so she almost tripped. She heard birds twittering in the woods. The beauty of the morning made her want to spread her arms wide and twirl around until she had to sit down for dizziness.

"There's power in the blood, power in the blood." Banjo's hearty voice drifted with the breeze.

What does he have to sing about? He seems so poor and alone. Like me. But he's used to it, she decided. *He's probably always lived like that.*

"Beautiful day, Miss Megan," Banjo called, cheerfully. He knocked his hat to the back of his head and wiped his brow on his sleeve. "That sun'll be mighty hot come noon, though."

Onions, carrots, green beans, and limas—she set the sacks of seeds near a cottonwood tree. She'd already put tomato, cabbage, and sweet potato seeds to sprout in a tray in the kitchen. Peas, turnips. . .she could almost taste them already.

"What should I do first?" Megan asked Steve, waiting on the edge of the plowed plot.

"Banjo will hoe you a furrow. You follow along and drop the seeds in. He'll tell you how." Calling to the horse, Steve bent over the plow handles and moved slowly away, cutting a brown strip from the edge of the meadow.

"Banjo, I've been meaning to ask you something, but I keep forgetting about it." Megan was dropping green bean seeds into a furrow three steps behind Banjo. The sun was high in the cloudless sky.

"What's that?" He didn't look up. His hoe kept chopping and pulling back the dark earth.

"A strange dog comes to the edge of the meadow every morning. When the grass was tall, he'd stay hidden, but since the meadow has been cut he sort of crawls up to the edge of the yard on his belly and crouches there. At first I thought he was a wolf, but he's got some brown and black patches on his back, and he whines sometimes when he sees me. I was wondering if he may have belonged to Cunningham."

Banjo paused to mop his brow with a splotchy handkerchief. "Now that you mention it, I believe Cunningham did have a dog. I never paid much mind." He stuffed the handkerchief into his back pocket and bent over the hoe. "If I saw the critter, I could tell you if it's the same one."

"I've been throwing food out to him but he hasn't come to get it while I'm outside. I've watched from the window. He never barks or growls, just whines."

"I'll have to get a look at him."

"Maybe Steve will be ready to break for lunch soon." She put her hands on the small of her back and leaned backward. "It will be noon shortly. I'll ask him the next time he comes close to this end of the garden."

An hour later, the men sprawled on the ground under an oak tree, and Megan spread out a blue-checkered cloth to serve sandwiches. She tried not to notice her dirt-stained hands and rough nails. They were still ugly, though she had scrubbed vigorously in the stream.

"You in Mr. Lincoln's War?" Banjo asked Steve. The sun now was glaring down upon the garden plot, and the shade of the trees was a welcome relief.

"Fortieth Mississippi." Steve lounged against a tree, chewing a long piece of grass.

"I served under Sheridan the last few years of the war," Banjo continued. "I lived in Texas then, you know." He leaned back until he was resting on one elbow. After some talk and laughter they rose and went back to work.

It was close to dusk when Megan plodded wearily back to the house. She turned to look back at Steve and Banjo finishing the last strip of rich, brown earth. Tired as she was, it was gratifying to know she belonged here. This was her own home and these were her men to care for, at least for now. If only Jeremy were here, and Em. She tried to push aside the anguish that lingered in the back of her mind ready to steal every morsel of happiness she might know here.

≥∘

During the next several weeks life on the ranch fell into a routine. Day by day Megan worked in the garden pulling out the weeds until her hands became tough and strong. Her face grew tan in spite of the sunbonnet she wore. It wasn't long before she grew to love the smell and feel of rich earth.

The morning Steve came to tell her his news, she was on hands and knees seeking out the latest interlopers among the two-inch-high sprouts. She stood and brushed the dirt from her hands when he came near.

"Banjo and I will be leaving for a few days," he said. "He tells me Jim Sanders, the owner of the Running M, may sell me some cattle. I want to get several hundred head to fatten up before winter."

"How long will you be gone?" Megan tried to hide her dismay. How would she feel being at home alone?

"It'll only be two or three days. I'd like to leave tomorrow if I can finish putting in the corn today."

Megan looked at the lower meadow, all plowed and planted except for a small patch. Steve had chosen the lower ten acres so the edge of the field would still be out of shooting range when the corn grew tall. She swallowed to ease the tightness in her throat.

"All right. I'll bake some biscuits for you to take along."

"You've done well for a city girl, Megan." He smiled down at her. Megan looked away, her cheeks burning.

His smile stayed with her when he and Banjo rode out the next morning. It warmed her inside where she couldn't reach. When the men disappeared from her sight she lingered at the open door watching for a familiar face at the edge of the yard. As usual, a shaggy gray figure came to rest just beyond her throwing range.

"Here, boy," she called again. She held out a piece of bacon rind. "Come on. I won't hurt you."

The dog moved forward a pace and sat down. He tilted his head to one side and whined.

"What are you afraid of?" She kept talking in a soothing voice. With an underhanded throw, she tossed the meat. It landed near his feet. "I won't hurt you, you know. I would like to be friends." She continued cajoling and coaxing a few moments longer. The dishes were waiting, as always, and finally she decided to go back inside and attend to them.

Before she moved, the dog crouched down and crawled to the bit of bacon. Grasping it in his teeth, he backed to the edge of the grass to eat it, always watching Megan.

"Well, you're getting braver, are you?" She went inside for a piece of bread and threw it to him. "Friends. See?" She brushed a crumb from her hand. "You could use a friend. . .and so could I." With a last wistful smile, she went inside the house.

❧

That day Megan cleaned the loft, taking advantage of Steve's absence, and made doughnuts for his return. The dog returned the next morning. Megan sat on the steps and talked to him for half an hour. He watched her closely and whined twice, but he wouldn't come near.

Early in the afternoon of the second day she was spreading out some navy gingham to make a tablecloth when movement at the edge of the meadow caught her eye. She ran to the window for a closer look. The sight filled her with horror.

Several men on horses circled the garden. One had flaming red hair and rode a piebald pinto.

Beau Harrington.

With a motion inviting the others to follow, he stepped his horse into the garden and began tramping around.

At first Megan couldn't move. She stood, mouth open, staring as they started through the garden plot. Abruptly, she came to herself. Indignation grew into outrage and she overcame her natural fear. She ran to the fireplace, tore Steve's extra rifle from its pegs above the mantel shelf, and raced outside, holding it clumsily in her arms.

"Stop! Stop!" she shouted. One time she almost stumbled on the rough ground, but she never stopped or even hesitated. She ran to the edge of the garden and awkwardly raised the rifle. "Stop, or I'll shoot!"

"Well, well," Beau Harrington was the first to speak, "what have we here? Chamberlin lettin' a woman do his fightin' for him now?"

"He's not here or he'd take on the lot of you," Megan fumed. She raised the gun higher. "But it doesn't take a man's finger to pull a trigger. You get out of here before I do."

"She means it, boss." A long-legged, skinny man with a beak nose spoke up. He watched Megan warily.

"Slim's right," Clyde Turner added. His flinty eyes sized up Megan and the long gun in her arms.

"You tell your man he can expect more of the same if he doesn't move," Beau sneered. He hesitated after the others moved away, then slowly followed them.

The closer Megan came to the house the weaker her knees became, the sicker her stomach felt. Her arms were too limp to lift the rifle back to its pegs so she propped it against the wall and sank into a chair. She realized tears were streaming down her face. Covering her face with her hands, she gave way to frustrated sobs.

Their beautiful crop was ruined. Crying relieved some of her pent-up emotions, and she stared blindly at the cold fireplace. After the first waves of despair had passed, discouragement slowly transformed into smoldering anger.

How dare those scoundrels! She wouldn't let the likes of Beau Harrington stop her. Too much was at stake.

She washed her face in the spring. Weren't there some seeds left? Yes, the sacks were in the kitchen. Armed with a hoe and the Henry, she marched out to inspect the damage. She glanced at the sun, still high above the horizon. If she hurried there may be time to make repairs before dark.

Kneeling over her injured seedlings, she discovered the damage wasn't as overwhelming as she first thought. She crept along on all fours, straightening a seedling here, planting new seeds there until the sun sank low and the seeds were spent. She stood and stretched her tired back as she looked over her work. It wasn't as large as it had once been, but there would still be fresh vegetables on their table.

Candy came to the fence and nickered when Megan walked past the corral. She propped the hoe and rifle against a post and rubbed the roan's nose. *I wonder if I can still ride,* she thought, resting her aching forehead against the mare's smooth cheek. *One of these days,* she promised herself, *I'll give it a try.*

❧

It was noon the next day when Kelsey, Banjo's lop-eared donkey, stepped out of the trees. Billy wasn't far behind. Was that a third horse with them? Megan strained her eyes but couldn't tell. Quickly, she slid her freshly risen rolls into the oven, smoothed her hair, and ran out to meet them.

"There is a fountain filled with blood, drawn from Emmanuel's veins. . . ." It was Banjo's voice, as sweet and rough as ever. "And sinners plunged beneath its flood lose all their guilty stains. Hello, Miss Megan." Banjo smiled warmly and raised his hat.

"We brought you something." Steve stepped out of the saddle on the off side and came around his horse holding a rope. Slowly, a short black and white animal followed.

"A cow!" Megan clapped her hands in delight.

"Sanders had two, and this one just weaned a heifer calf so he let me have her. For a price, you understand." He chuckled wryly. "She's a Holstein. They're supposed to be good milkers. Her name's Bess."

"She's beautiful!" Megan couldn't take her eyes off the creature. "Oh, Steve! A cow! We haven't had milk, or butter, or cheese for ages."

"We bought eight hundred head of longhorns from Sanders, too. We left them in a grassy canyon east of here. A nice looking lot, don't you think, Banjo?"

"Nice as I've ever seen." Banjo's eyes twinkled at Megan's enraptured exclamations over Bess.

"Oh, I've rolls in the oven." Megan lifted her wide skirt to free her ankles and ran lightly to the house. Banjo's chuckle followed her.

"We had some visitors while you were gone." Megan brought up the awful affair after the men had enjoyed a hot meal. They were relaxing over a second cup of coffee. "Beau Harrington and his hands."

"What did they do?" Steve sat up straight and stared at her, an unpleasant light in his eyes.

"They trampled the garden." She was worried by the thundercloud forming on Steve's face. "It wasn't as bad as I first imagined. I guess I stopped them in time."

"You what?"

"I took the rifle from over the fireplace and ran out and stopped them. I told them I'd shoot if they didn't go."

"They give you any trouble?" Steve's face matched the glowing embers in the smoldering fireplace.

"The red-haired one had his usual bluster, but the rest were ready to leave soon enough, I reckon."

"I guess they had good reason," Banjo said, dryly. "Facin' a man with a gun is one thing. Facin' a wrought-up woman with one is another'n."

Steve scraped his chair back and stood to his feet. "I'm going over there and have it out with Harrington."

His words were like a heavy millstone crushing the breath from Megan's lungs. "You'll be on their land," she protested. "There's no telling what may happen."

"This foolishness has got to stop, Megan," he insisted, clapping on his hat. "Harrington needs to learn a lesson. I reckon I'm the one elected to teach him." He flipped his gunbelt around his waist and buckled it with a quick, practiced motion.

"Please, Steve," she pleaded, following him to the door. "They'll kill you if they get a chance."

"I'm going to put a stop to this kind of thing once and for all."

She reached for his arm, but he brushed her away and strode to the stable. In a few moments he galloped away on Caesar. Megan pressed her fist to her mouth to quench a silent sob as he disappeared into the trees.

seven

Banjo joined Megan in the doorway as Caesar's hoofbeats faded into the distance. "He's got to do it you know."

"I know." Megan was still fighting tears. She was so afraid. "Are we going to win, Banjo? Do we have any chance of holding onto the Circle C against the Harringtons?"

Banjo didn't answer for a long minute. He stared across the meadow toward the setting sun. "Miss Megan," he finally answered, "I'm not a prophet like Elijah so I can't tell the future for sure, but I will tell you this. The three of us are gonna make a brass-plated effort. That's all we can do. We'll have to leave it in the hands of the good Lord after we've done our best."

Without speaking any more the old cowhand and the young wife lingered in the last light of day. Neither of them wanted to go back into the shadowy house.

"Did you have the safety off?" Banjo asked when the sky was indigo with a dull yellow glow rimming the mountains.

"The what?"

"The safety on the Henry. If you don't take the safety off, it won't shoot."

"I just picked it up and ran out, so I reckon I didn't."

"Ho, ho!" Banjo guffawed. "You chased those rascals away with the safety still on." He enjoyed a good chuckle then became serious. "You ought to learn to shoot. Most women out here do."

"Would you teach me, Banjo?"

"Well," he drawled, slowly, "you'd best ask your husband first. If he doesn't have time, I'll be happy to."

Megan flushed, realizing her slip. Confused, she chose that moment to clear away the supper dishes, hoping he hadn't noticed.

❧

Megan was pacing the floor when Steve rode in late that night. Banjo had gone to his room in the stable. Steve's step was slow and heavy on the creaky porch.

"What happened?" she asked anxiously as soon as he stepped into the light.

"No one was there. Only one I could round up was the cook, and he said everybody was in town. By the time I got there I'd cooled off some. There was no good could come of going off half-cocked." He hung his hat and gunbelt on their pegs and flung himself on the settee. "So, I came on home."

"I kept some coffee hot for you."

"That would taste mighty good." He rubbed the back of his neck and stretched out his legs. "I guess we'll have to hold on and see what happens. Banjo's right, you know. With the law all the way in Denver, we'll have to fight it out ourselves." He took the steaming mug from Megan. "Thanks. That's exactly what I needed after a day like today."

"Will you teach me to shoot?" She sat in the chair near the fireplace.

"Teach you to shoot?" He looked up. "Sure. I was figuring on putting in some practice time myself." He sipped his coffee. "You've got to get the troops in order before you can go to war."

❧

Megan tried to write a cheery letter to Jeremy the next day, but the words wouldn't come. She had been in Colorado for more than a month and still had had no word from Em. After several false starts she managed a bright description of the ranch and the garden. She described the four horses and Banjo's donkey in detail, knowing he would like to hear about them. With a heavy heart, she sealed the envelope.

Surely Jeremy wasn't worse. Could that be why Em hadn't asked someone to pen down a note for her? Tormented by doubts and fears, a dark cloud settled over Megan's spirit. Not knowing what was happening back in Baltimore was harder to bear than being there and facing the worst.

The days that followed were long and tedious. She spoke little and smiled less. Every rider that came into the meadow struck new fear in Megan's heart.

The afternoon a big palomino stepped into view she was churning butter on the porch, hoping to catch a passing breeze. Instead of riding to the house, the tall stranger rode to the corral where Banjo was stringing barbed wire around a fence post. Megan was relieved to see Banjo raise his hand in greeting and straighten to talk. The rider stayed only minutes and rode away.

Brimming with questions, she took a cup of water out to Banjo later to give herself an excuse to talk to him.

"Who rode in this afternoon, Banjo? Did you know him?"

"That was Wyatt Hammond, Harrington's horse wrangler." He smiled at Megan's alarm. "Don't fret yourself. He's a fine young man. I knowed his folks. He's a different brand than that red-topped sapling. Wyatt was on his way to town and stopped to swap howdies.

"Somethin' troublin' you I could help with, Miss Megan?" He gave her a questioning, fatherly smile, his frayed felt hat knocked to the back of his head.

"It's nothing really, Banjo." She tried to smile back at him but only half succeeded. "I haven't had any word from my little brother, that's all. He's in a sanitarium in Baltimore with rheumatic fever. I guess I've been letting my worries show too much."

"That's what friends are for, you know, helping carry burdens." He hesitated a moment before adding, "I have a Friend Who carries all my burdens."

Megan looked at him, waiting for him to continue.

"His name is Jesus. He's been carrying my burdens for almost fifteen years now."

"You don't have many burdens, Banjo. You are always so happy."

"You know what I said about being from Texas? My wife and I had a ranch a few miles south of the Red River. Purtiest little place you ever did see. We worked the land and ran some cows, kind o' like you and Steve. It was a good life. We had a son, a lively little lad. He used to foller me around like a little shadow." He cleared his throat.

"It was back in '58. I had to go away for a few days to take care of some business. While I was gone Kiowas burned the ranch. They killed Mary and took my son." His eyes filled with tears. He swallowed and went on. "Mary was a good Christian but I wasn't, then. I wandered around for a while, not sure what to do or where to go. After a few years I joined Sheridan. I figured I didn't have much more to lose.

"A young preacher came out to the troops and held some meetin's. He preached right to me. I knew Mary was in heaven, and I wasn't goin' there. After one of the meetin's, I went up and talked with that preacher. He showed me how to make my peace with God. Jesus has been my best Friend ever since." He smiled gently. "I know He'd help you, too, if you asked Him."

His words came back to her later that evening. How could he be so happy not knowing if his son was alive or dead? *He must be a strong person,* Megan decided. *I don't have that kind of courage.*

⁂

Steve spent most evenings behind the corral practicing with his six-shooter. At first Megan jumped every time he fired a shot, but eventually she became accustomed to the noise. One day she ventured out to see if he would teach her how to handle a gun.

Surprise made her hesitate when she saw him. Instead of a pistol he held a double-edged knife, poised to throw. He rose up on the balls of his feet, paused a second, and threw the knife into a straw target he had set up, a perfect hit. He walked over to pull the knife out, and stopped short when he saw her.

"So, you've discovered my secret weapon," he said, walking toward her.

"When I was in the army, we'd practice throwing to pass the time. I was pretty good at it then. I'm a little rusty now."

"I'd like to learn to shoot."

"Oh, yes. I remember you mentioning it." He looked at his guns lying on a flat rock nearby. "Which would you prefer, the pistol or the rifle?"

"I don't know."

He picked up the pistol and handed it to her. "Try this and see how it feels."

"It's awful heavy," she said, holding it with two hands.

"See if you can raise it at arm's length."

Her arm wobbled as she struggled to keep the barrel up. "Let's try the Henry." He took the pistol from her. "You can use both hands to hold it and balance it on your shoulder." The rifle was awkward. She couldn't tell where to put her hands on it. Steve adjusted her grip. "Lift it shoulder high and sight along the barrel. Aim at that tree trunk." He pointed to a pine thirty feet away. "Start at the base of the tree and follow it up."

Megan grasped the gun tightly, one hand on the trigger, one on the barrel. Taking a breath to calm herself, she lifted the rifle.

"Gently work the trigger. You feel the slack there?"

"Yes." She moistened her lips.

"Slowly take in the slack, and squeeze off a shot real gentle-like. Try for that slash in the bark about eye level. You see it?"

"I see it." Biting her bottom lip, she concentrated on that mark and squeezed gently, like he said.

BOOM!

The slam of the rifle against her shoulder made her step back. Her heel sank into a small hole, throwing her off balance. She sat down hard. Her shoulder was burning dreadfully. It must be black and blue.

"You hit it! You hit it!" He walked over to examine the tree. "A little to the left and a tad high, but you hit it."

"I think it hit me." She rubbed her sore shoulder.

He was beside her in four strides. "Are you hurt?" He knelt down beside her, concern in his eyes.

"My shoulder's bruised, but besides that it's only my pride, I guess." She looked at him accusingly. "Why didn't you warn me?"

"About the kick? I guess I forgot. I'm sure sorry." He helped her up. "Don't rest the butt on your shoulder from now on. Hold it a little away if you can, or let it rest on top of you shoulder." He brushed dirt from her arm. "Do you want to quit for today?"

"I came to learn and learn I aim to do." She straightened her skirt and picked up the rifle. "What were you saying about more to the left?"

With that, target practice became a daily ritual and, before many days passed, she could hit a leaf at fifty yards.

"You're a natural shot, Megan," Steve said after practice two weeks later. "You've got a steady hand and a keen eye. Just remember the Henry shoots a little high and to the left."

Megan thrived on these times of easy companionship with Steve. He was a patient teacher, and she liked to hear him talk. It gave her a contented, restful feeling to be with him and share things with him.

※

"I'm going to ride into town tomorrow," Steve said one evening in mid-July on their walk back to the house. "Is there anything you need?"

"You can mail a letter for me and check the post office," she replied, quickly. "Besides that, there are a few groceries. A little sugar, molasses, things like that."

"Banjo will be around if you need him. I want to get some nails to repair the porch and some glass for the windows."

But the next morning, when Steve drove the buckboard around the meadow, a strange emptiness swept over Megan. It was odd she should feel that way since Banjo was still nearby. She tried to brush it away but it kept creeping back.

Her spirits lifted later when her doggy friend crept to the porch to get a pancake lying on the ground near the steps. Megan had thrown it there to tempt him.

"Banjo," she called in the same voice she used when talking to the dog. "Banjo, come here."

Banjo appeared in the stable doorway. Megan placed a warning finger on her lips and pointed to the dog hungrily chewing the pancake. She threw down another when the animal looked up at her.

It was the first time she'd had a complete look at him. He was shaggy from his bearded cheeks to his feathery tail, a big dog, but not as large as some. His hips made bony points at his back end. He had black, brown, and white patches on his back and sides. The rest of him was the color of dirty mop water.

"Would you like a third?" she asked, holding up her last offering. The dog sat down, eyes boring into the pancake. "Here you go." She threw it to him. "I always was an easy mark for a hungry stomach."

The dog seemed to sense there was no more food to be had. He picked up the pancake and trotted away.

"That's Cunningham's dog, all right," Banjo said, walking toward her. "Used to follow him everywheres."

"What's his name?" Megan excitedly voiced the question she'd wondered every morning these past six weeks.

"I don't know." The wrinkles in his brow deepened while he searched his memory. "I can't remember Cunningham calling him. I'm sure he must have, but it didn't stick with me." He grinned at her disappointed face. "Sorry, Miss Megan. Why don't you name him yourself? He'll pick up a new name soon enough, I reckon." He took off his hat to scratch the back of his head. "Do you mind me asking why you're so interested in a stray dog?"

"I can't really say, Banjo. I guess it's because he seems so alone. And he's starving. I guess I feel sorry for him."

"Keep workin' on him. He'll get used to you in time." He adjusted his hat and clumped back to the stable. Megan took a last look at the grass where the dog disappeared. What could she name him?

ঌ

Megan was knotting a rag rug to put in front of the hearth and thinking about dog names when she heard galloping hoofbeats. Dropping her work she looked nervously out the window.

A large chestnut horse came at full tilt around the green field of knee-high corn waving gently in the breeze. A wiry man in a red plaid shirt and Levi's leaned over the saddle. Horse and rider slowed to a trot at the edge of the yard and came to a halt in front of the porch. The man swung down in an easy, lithe movement. Megan blinked her eyes and looked again.

Instead of a man, it was a tall, slim young woman wearing men's clothes, the same girl she had met in Harper's Emporium the day they arrived in Juniper Junction. Relieved and glad, Megan opened the door.

"Hello." The young woman took off her light brown Stetson, revealing her thick blond mane, full of strawberry highlights in the sun. "I'm Susan Harrington, remember?"

"Yes, of course." Megan smiled broadly. "Please come in." She was delighted to have feminine companionship. "Would you like some tea? I'll put the kettle on."

"How lovely!" Susan exclaimed when she entered the house. "I've always liked stone better than logs. And blue calico!" She gave the living room curtains a loving touch.

It was true the house had undergone a transformation under Megan's skillful hand. The floors shone with a coating of linseed oil. A blue-checked tablecloth and matching curtains made the dining room a cheery nook. The kitchen range gleamed with a fresh coating of stove blacking, all signs of rust banished. A white gauze curtain dressed the kitchen window, and the linoleum, though worn, was well-scrubbed.

"Please sit down," Megan said when she returned from the kitchen.

Susan perched on the edge of a chair, holding her hat in her hands.

"I came because. . . ," Susan avoided Megan's eyes, "because I heard about what happened to your garden. I wanted you to know how sorry I am." She glanced at Megan. "I overheard some of the men talking when I was in the stable getting ready to ride this morning." She paused and drew in a deep breath. "It was Beau's doing. I know it."

"I hope the land dispute won't affect our friendship," Megan said sincerely. "I've thought about you several times since we met in Juniper. I was hoping we could get acquainted."

Susan's troubled face brightened. She watched Megan's smooth movements while pouring tea into two cups.

"Beau's always trying to prove something," she went on impulsively. "He scares me. If it wasn't for Wyatt—" She broke off and quickly sipped her tea.

"We didn't come here to cause trouble," Megan said, resuming her seat. "My husband has a deed to this land. It's his, and he wants to keep it, that's all."

"I wish Pa wasn't so set on having this place," Susan said, wistfully. "You aren't the only ones he's been against, believe me. A year ago he accused Jim Sanders of rustling. Elaine Sanders is one of my friends. I tried to tell Pa Jim wouldn't do such a thing, but he wouldn't listen." She sighed. "Since Ma died, he won't listen to anyone." A brittle edge crept into her voice. "All he thinks about are his precious cattle." She shook her head, and smiled at Megan. "Do you ride?"

"I used to when I was a child. I haven't tried lately."

"You should. We could go riding together."

"Do you always go off alone?" Megan asked, wonderingly.

"Sure. No one will bother me. Unless I surprise some Indians or something." She laughed at Megan's alarmed expression. "We haven't had Indian trouble for a year or so. Mostly they stay on the prairie these days. Anyway, I can shoot."

"I'd like to go riding," Megan admitted. "I'll practice a little, and maybe we can go." She looked at Susan's rugged costume. "I'll have to find something to wear."

"These are my brother's clothes. Most western women don't wear citified riding clothes, but you can if you want."

"I have an old riding costume that used to be my mother's. I do want to come."

"That would be nice." Susan set down her teacup and rose. "I'd best be going. I'll come around after a while and see if you are ready to ride with me."

"All right." Megan walked to the door with the slim woman. "I'm so glad you came. I was feeling a bit lonely today."

"And thanks for understanding about Beau." Susan turned impulsively and put her hand on Megan's arm. "I wish there was more I could do."

Before Megan could answer, Susan put on her hat, stepped across the sagging porch, and was gone. Megan gazed long at the cloudless blue sky, meditating on the visit. Poor Susan, living with a negligent father and a hot-tempered brother. At that moment Megan determined that no matter what the future held, she would try to be Susan's friend.

೩

The hour drew late, and Steve did not come. Banjo sat with Megan in the light of two coal oil lamps while she read *The Pilgrim's Progress* aloud to pass the time. She forced herself not to look out the window, trusting her ears to tell her of Steve's arrival. Her nerves were frayed to a ragged edge when the hoofbeats she had been yearning to hear resounded in the dooryard.

"He's back." She dropped the book on the table and ran to the door.

"I'll take the hull off his horse." Banjo grabbed his hat from a peg near the door and was gone.

Megan stood on the porch, straining to see through the darkness. A wide, yellow crescent of light from the open door fell over Steve's face as he stepped up. The sight made her gasp.

eight

Both of Steve's eyes were black and blue, one almost swelled shut, and there was a wide, ugly gash over his left cheekbone. His lower lip was cut and puffy. He held his right arm close to his side, and that battered hand was twice its normal size. He made a rasping sound when he breathed. Like a sleepwalker, he shuffled over to the settee and sank to the seat as though the presence of the sofa was all that kept him from collapsing altogether. Several seconds passed before he could speak.

"Four or five of Harrington's men jumped me outside of Harper's." His voice was thick with pain. He grunted a little with each breath. "One of them clubbed me on the head from behind and knocked me down for the others to pound me. I couldn't see who they were, it happened so fast, but I heard that red-haired villain's voice." He stopped to take two ragged breaths. "I guess I passed out. When I came around it was almost dark. I wasn't in any shape to go looking for them, so I got the hostler to hitch the team for me and came home."

"You should have seen a doctor before you came out here." Megan stood near him, staring, shocked at the brutality of his injuries. She didn't like the sound of his breathing at all.

"Knew you'd be worried," he continued. "The doc might have wanted me to hang around and I didn't want to." He grimaced in pain and held his side. "You got a letter." Fumbling, he pulled a wrinkled envelope from his shirt pocket and handed it to her.

Megan's heart lurched as she took the letter. She smoothed it lovingly between her hands before she lay it on the table and rushed to the kitchen for hot water and a towel. Gently, she bathed Steve's face and hand, cringing at what she found under the dirt and dried blood.

"I don't think there are any broken bones," she decided as he slowly moved his fingers. "At least not in your hand." She was thinking of his ribs and the sound of his labored breathing.

"The hand won't be any good to me for a while, though." He stared at the purple, swollen flesh. "Right now I'd like to be able to use an iron mighty bad."

"That cut on your cheek has to be closed," Megan went on, ignoring his remark. "It's lying wide open. I've got some tape in the kitchen.

"Mama and I patched up many a soldier when we were in Virginia," she chattered to ease the mood when she returned with tape and bandages. "There was a lot of fighting around Fredricksburg, you know." Her hands moved steadily, efficiently, as she talked. "We changed bandages, served meals, and did anything else that was needed in the hospital after our plantation burned. I guess we bandaged as many Yanks as we did Confederates." She pressed the last piece of tape on his cheek.

"Now, let's take a look at those ribs."

"My ribs are all right," Steve protested, straightening.

"Yes, that's why you've been breathing so easily." Immovable as the rock wall behind the house, she met his eyes. "Let's have a look."

Never taking his eyes from her face, he slowly reached for his shirt buttons. In short order his ribs were bound tightly with a long, three-inch-wide strip of cloth. It was near midnight when he paused at the foot of the ladder to the loft. He put his foot on the first rung and paused, looking at her.

"Thanks."

"Get some rest," she replied lightly.

Bone tired though she was, she brought the treasured envelope close to the coal oil lamp and tore it open with shaking fingers. The words ran together when she tried to read. She squeezed her eyes shut, willing them to focus, and tried again.

Dear Miss Megan,
    Just wanted you to know we got your tellygram. Jeremy is doing good. Always talks about them horses you got. He can't git out of bed yet, tho. Doc says he'll be abed about two more months. Don't fret none. This was writ by my landlady, Mrs. Osgood.

                                     Sincerely,
                                     Em

After reading the note three times to wring every ounce of home from it that she could, she put the letter carefully in her trunk. She lay wide-eyed in the darkness thinking of Jeremy and Em, and the home they used to share. She ached to put her arms around him once more, to see him smile, to hear him laugh. The lump in her throat choked her. She turned her face into her pillow and sobbed.

ॐ

The next morning Banjo came to the house carrying a small pasteboard box. He tapped on the door and beamed at Megan when she opened it.

"Since when do you have to knock?" Megan peered curiously at the box. "What's that?"

"Look for yourself." He held out the box for her to take a look.

"Chickens."

Megan was too tired and emotionally spent to be excited at Banjo's announcement.

"Steve brought them. He brought a passel of other things, too. The wagon was loaded down." He glanced at Megan's serious face. "How is he?"

"Two cracked ribs, one of them may be broken. A horribly bruised hand, and a beat-up face. I think he'll be all right, though, as long as those ribs heal without any trouble."

"I'll put up a coop for these pullets today. By the size of 'em, they should be layin' in two months or so. Haven't had an egg for purty nigh a year." He carried the box back to the stable.

"I bought them from a woman in town," said a voice behind her.

Megan whirled in surprise to see Steve at the top of the ladder.

"I've got a hankering for eggs myself." Slowly, carefully he climbed down and eased into a chair.

"You ought to be in bed," Megan scolded mildly. She felt an almost physical pain at the sight of his swollen, shiny, purple-splotched face.

"Never stayed in bed a day in my life." He drew in a quick breath. "I don't aim to start now."

"Breakfast will be ready soon." She peeked at the biscuits in the oven and sliced some bacon. The frying pan was sizzling and popping when Steve called her.

"Come here, Megan. Banjo brought in something I bought for you in town."

Megan checked the biscuits again, wiped her hands, and wonderingly obeyed.

"I thought you might like this." He held up a large bolt of cloth. "You look mighty fetching in blue."

Stunned, Megan reached out for the powder blue fabric. She rubbed her hand over the lacy white print.

"That was kind of you," she faltered, her cheeks pink.

"I got the whole bolt so you can make a real nice one."

Her steps were light as she carried the bolt into her room, sampling the smooth weave under hand as she went. In the bedroom she draped the end of the cloth over her shoulder and looked in the mirror nailed to her bedroom wall. That shade of blue was perfect for her hair and eyes. The roses in her cheeks and glow in her eyes added to the picture. With deft movements she smoothed the fabric around the bolt and put it into her trunk. Going back to the kitchen she avoided Steve's eyes as she passed, but inside she sang a soft, lilting, wordless melody.

Steve watched from the doorway when Megan took some scraps out to the dog after breakfast.

"I'm going to call him Lobo because he look like a wolf." The object of their attention bolted down a scrap of bacon and two biscuits. "Banjo told me he used to belong to Cunningham."

"He must have been living off of field mice," Steve remarked.

"I haven't been able to get near him, yet. It's taken six weeks for him to come this close."

Lobo sat on his haunches, watching Megan's face. He whined.

"All right, boy," she laughed, throwing him a third biscuit. "You always know when I'm holding out on you."

He picked up the biscuit and trotted off.

"That's it for the day. So far I've seen him only in the morning. He's getting braver because usually he won't come near the porch if he sees one of you men around."

"He'll be protection for you when Banjo and I have to be away. I'll be glad if you can get him tamed."

"I feel sorry for him. He's been all alone for over two years. I wonder how he survived the winters."

"Probably holed up in a cave somewhere." Steve walked back into the living room and eased down on the sofa. "Hand me my gunbelt, will you? I may as well clean my guns while I'm inside."

※

It was early in August before Steve recovered enough to return to all his normal work. It took several days of painful practice to give him back his agility with a gun. Megan watched his recovery with mixed emotions. She was glad to see him strong again, but she knew each passing day brought closer another confrontation with the Harringtons. Someone was bound to be killed. Would it be Steve? She couldn't bear to voice the question even in her mind.

The hot summer seemed endless. Megan's face grew tan from long hours in the garden. She picked green beans until her arms and back groaned. She made catsup and chutney until the kitchen cabinets could hold no more jars. This in addition to her weekly chores of bread-making, butter-churning, and washing and ironing clothes made the days full indeed.

Late in the afternoons she often escaped the overheated house by doing target practice with Steve. When he hurled glass bottles into the air she could strike them four of five tries.

"You stay at it, and you'll soon be better than me," he said one evening in mid-August. They were collecting guns and shells to go inside. "I've never seen the like. Have you thought of trying live game?"

"I don't think I could kill anything," she said, shaking her head. "I couldn't stand to." They meandered in the direction of the house.

"I would like to ride Candy," Megan said.

"We don't have a sidesaddle."

"I always rode astride when I was a girl. I can do the same now. Would you teach me to saddle her?"

"A saddle may be too heavy for a little lady like you, but you can try."

The saddle was heavy. The next day Megan gritted her teeth, took a breath, and heaved. The leather hit the horse's back a bit awry, but it stayed. Candy looked around and nuzzled Megan's hand. Megan patted her nose.

"Don't worry, girl, we'll do it yet." She turned to Steve, smiling triumphantly. "Now what?"

"Make sure you didn't wrinkle the saddle blanket. Her back will get sore if it's wrinkled." He lifted one edge of the saddle and pulled the blanket. "Fasten the girth tightly." He firmly punched the mare's stomach. "A canny horse will fill his belly with air, so you can't tighten it right. Make 'em let it out before you cinch up.

"You can ride Billy or Star as well as Candy, but leave Caesar alone," he cautioned. "He's wild. He always tries to bite me when I saddle him. Don't ever turn your back on him."

Megan grasped the pommel with her left hand and stepped into the stirrup. Mother's dark green riding habit fit her to perfection after she had sewn in a few tucks. Instead of the ribboned bowler that was supposed to complete the outfit, she wore a dark green bonnet. The feel of the saddle and the movements of the horse brought back the carefree fun she had known in Virginia. With Steve on Billy they cantered shoulder to shoulder in a circle around the meadow. When they got back to the yard Megan's cheeks were flushed, her eyes shone. She felt the exhilarating urgency of a six-month-old fawn on a crisp fall morning.

"Let's do it again," she begged, "only faster."

Steve laughed out loud at her childlike enthusiasm. Without answering, he urged Billy forward, leading out at a moderate gallop this time. Candy lengthened her stride and stayed beside Billy's right hindquarters until they reached the curve in the field; then she was shoulder to shoulder with him for the rest of the ride. Megan would have gone for a third round, but it was not to be. Practicality won out. Supper must be cooked and the hour was growing late.

After that day, Steve and Megan alternated riding and shooting in the late afternoons when they both were free. It was glorious to ride in the pine-scented air enjoying the country and their companionship. She was deeply in love with Colorado.

Often they rode south to the lake and strolled along its shore, charmed by a solitude that was interrupted only by an occasional bird call or the splash of a fat trout swimming under the surface. A thick grove of spruce blocked off everything but the sky. It seemed like she and Steve were the only people in the world when they were there.

"What was it like on the riverboats?" Megan asked one day as they rambled near the water's edge.

"At first it was exciting." Steve picked up a flat, smooth stone and skimmed it across the water. It hit three times and sank, leaving a spreading series of circles. "Bright lights, plush furnishings, elegantly dressed people." He glanced at her. "But when you probed beneath the surface, the picture wasn't nearly so appealing. It was there that I learned to use a hideout knife. It was that or risk being robbed every time I won a big stake." He selected another stone.

"Don't get me wrong. I enjoyed playing cards. It was intoxicating to be able to handle them and win." He shook his head. "But I learned those cards were a two-headed serpent. One bite and you were hooked. The second bite and they destroyed you." He flicked the stone with all his might. Five skips.

Megan watched his face as he spoke. It was the first time he had spoken of his past to her since they met in the hotel in Baltimore. This time she caught a better glimpse of the person behind his handsome face.

"I saw men destroyed too often. When I felt myself withering inside, I had to get out. That's why I don't play anymore, even for fun. I don't want to give the serpent a chance to bite me again."

The sun's slanted beams sifted across the treetops. Steve measured their angle with a quick look and pitched one last stone. "It's getting late," he said, reluctantly. "We'd best get back."

In the passing days, Megan learned to read his mood by the turn of his head or the movement of his hand. His smile made the day full of sunbeams; his deep, resonant voice touched an answering chord inside of her.

❧

"What is this?" Steve's clipped words, like stones thrown at a rock wall, brought Megan up short. She dumped the last pail of oats into Candy's trough and joined him beside the mare. He stood aside for her to see an ugly sore on Candy's back.

"You left a wrinkle in the saddle blanket." The hard set of his mouth condemned her.

"I was in a hurry to go riding with Susan when I saddled up." Megan avoided his eyes. Her tongue was suddenly thick and stupid. "I'm sorry."

He turned his back to her, folding the blanket with a snap.

She stroked the horse's neck. "I'm sorry, Candy. I didn't mean to hurt you. I'll be more careful after this." The horse lifted her head out of the feed trough to nuzzle Megan's shoulder. Megan rubbed the space between Candy's eyes. She gave the roan a loving pat and walked out of the stable.

"Megan." Steve called her back.

"Yes?" Reluctantly, she retraced her steps.

"I'm sorry I was hard on you." His mouth was still a thin, straight line, but his eyes were gentler than before.

"I shouldn't have been so careless. You were right about that." She met his eyes with a serious, steady gaze.

"Let's say we both fell short." The corners of his mouth turned up little. "Care to go for a walk after supper? I'd like to look over our garden before it gets dark."

"Sure. I'll put the kettle on now, so we can get an early start." She walked slowly to the house. It had been an unusual day, first a visit from Susan and now this interchange with Steve. Seeing that side of this personality was sobering and heartwarming at the same time.

❧

Susan Harrington's visits brought sweet relief to the tedium of those days. If Megan had a few hours free they would ride together. If not, Susan lent an extra pair of hands to Megan's never-ending chores.

"Everyone's going away for six weeks," Susan remarked later that week. They were sitting at the table shredding cabbage for sauerkraut. "Except me and three hands to watch over the ranch. All the hands are going on the cattle drive to Denver. It'll be a little lonely, but at least I'll have peace for a few days."

"You're always welcome here," Megan grinned, "especially if you keep helping with all these vegetables."

"You've had a rest from their harassment, too," Susan went on, "with the roundup last month and all." She emptied her pan of shredded cabbage into the large crock on the table and picked up another cabbage. "I wish Pa would stay so busy he'd forget this land." She pushed the damp tendrils from her forehead with the back of her wrist.

"Oh," Susan broke out excitedly, "I almost forgot to tell you. The Sanderses are having a dance on September twenty-fifth. Elaine told me last week when I saw her in town. You haven't met Elaine yet, have you?"

"Not yet." Megan poured more brine into the crock. "I don't get away much."

"I can't wait. I'm having a new dress made with a huge bustle and lots of ruffles."

Megan remembered the blue dress that hung half-finished in her closet. She had been so busy with the garden's harvest she hadn't been able to touch the dress for two weeks. With a few extra touches she could make it into a party dress. Maybe she could get some blue ribbon if Steve went into town soon. Plans for the party captured their attention and the basket of cabbage was finished in short order.

What good fun a frolic will be, Megan thought after Susan said good-bye and rode off. A party seemed especially exciting because she hadn't once been away from the ranch since they arrived three months before.

She drew the unfinished dress from the closet, caressing the soft fabric, and turning it critically in her hands. An extra ruffle here, some small embroidery there, and a little more fullness in the bustle. It would make a wonderful party dress. She held the dress under her chin and watched herself in the mirror, swaying gently to the music she could already hear.

The sound of horses in the yard shattered her daydream. She swept the dress back into the closet and scurried out to meet Steve and Banjo, back from a day of moving the longhorns to a new stretch of grass. Holding her skirt up, she ran lightly across the yard.

"Howdy, Miss Megan," Banjo said. His grin relaxed the tired lines around his mouth.

"What's got you so het up?" A faint grin hovered over Steve's features, a result of Megan's red cheeks and glowing eyes. "Who was here today?"

"Susan," Megan said, breathlessly. She stood near Steve as he dismounted. "The Sanderses are having a frolic. Elaine Sanders is putting it on." The words spilled out. "Everyone's going to be there. Can we go, Steve?"

Steve stopped short, soberly regarding her hopeful face. Without answering, he pulled Billy's reins to lead him into the stable.

"Steve?" Megan took a step after him.

"We'll talk it over in the house," Steve said tersely over his shoulder.

Crestfallen, Megan looked at Banjo who, carefully keeping his eyes on Kelsey, followed Steve into the stable.

Megan stood still a moment, staring at the empty stable doorway. She was confused and hurt. Search her mind as she might she could not understand Steve's reaction, nor Banjo's.

"About the frolic," Steve said after he had washed for supper. They were alone in the kitchen. "I'm not sure we ought to go." His voice was kind.

"Not go?" Disappointment fell on Megan with a thud. "Why not?"

Steve came near her, his face troubled. Megan had to lean her head back to look up at him he stood so close to her. She noticed his lined brow, his set jaw, and she rebelled.

"Please, Steve." She raised pleading eyes to meet his. "It would be so nice to have some fun after working so hard.

It would do both of us good to forget the ranch for a few hours. It wouldn't hurt to go, would it? I do so want to go."

He ran his hand through his freshly combed hair, looked away, and looked back again.

"It's against my better judgment, Megan, but if you want to go that much, I guess we can." He looked deeply into her eyes, hesitated, and was gone.

nine

"I don't cotton to those parties much, Miss Megan," Banjo said to Megan's question the next morning. She had asked him to move a sack of chicken feed that had gotten wet on the bottom from a heavy rain the night before, seeping under the stable wall and dampening the ground. "A frolic means dancin' and likker. As a Christian I can't approve of either one." His voice was mild, but his words carried conviction.

"I can't see why Miss Susan is so worked up about goin' over there anyways." He eased the sack of cracked corn to dry ground a few feet away. "Her pa and Sanders had words a year or so ago, and Jim Sanders is one to bear a grudge. When he first came to these parts, a man tried to push Sanders off'n his own range. Sanders killed him seven years later." He pushed his hat to the back of his head and glanced at Megan. "Oh, it was a fair fight all right. But Sanders had it in his craw the whole time. When men get their reason marred with drink things start happenin'. No good can come of it."

Megan could not understand his reasoning because she had many happy memories of lively music and excitement before the war. The balls her mother had given! Megan used to stay up long past her bedtime to peer under the stair railing, hypnotized by the colorful, laughing, dancing crowd below.

Banjo is old, she decided on her way to the house. *That must be it. He's too old to enjoy those things anymore.*

That evening, Steve's offer to take her to town with him the next day topped off her anticipation. Carefully counting her change, she mentally listed the things she would buy to complete her party costume.

The sky was cloudless, the sun strong on their ride to town. Megan raised her face and basked in the clear morning air. The tall, golden-tasseled stalks of corn hid the house from view before they were halfway around the meadow. Megan watched the curling morning glory vines along the edge of the field. They made a carpet on the ground and wound around the first stalks of every row. Steve had eyes only for the promising crop. If all went well, they would reap far more than he had estimated.

With the eagerness of a six-year-old planning for a birthday party, Megan visited the only milliner's shop in Juniper Junction. After a long session of lip biting and toe tapping, she finally purchased a blue silk bonnet with fluffy, white feathers on the left side tucked under the broad blue ribbon around the brim. Some extra ribbon for her dress was her next choice. As she was about to leave, a pair of long, white gloves caught her eye. She hesitated a moment, then impulsively nodded. Surely it wouldn't hurt to be a little daring. How many frolics would she get to out here in the wilderness? A thrill of expectancy passed through her as she gathered her parcels and stepped onto the boardwalk.

A letter was waiting for her at the post office. Impatient, she tore open the envelope the moment she was outside. Like a slow leak in a hot air balloon, her spirits sank. After two months, Jeremy was still the same: no worse, but no better. He was lonely for Megan, and would Megan please write him more often.

She stuffed the letter back into the envelope on her way to the hotel to join Steve for lunch. She tried to shake off her uneasiness and enjoy the rest of her special day, but the gloom clung to her, a nagging ache at the back of her mind.

A quiet dinner at the hotel, a trip to Harper's Emporium for supplies, and they started the long journey home. They had barely topped the first rise when a group of riders came toward them on the trail. The party was led by a tall, broad man wearing a large, white hat. He sat ramrod straight in the saddle with the unmistakable air of authority. The group split when they reached Chamberlin's buckboard, half on either side, and stopped. Each man except the leader was holding a weapon. Harrington's gun stayed in his holster.

"Chamberlin," the big man said, coldly, "you're a squatter. And you're more than that. You're a dirty rustler."

"I don't take that from any man." Steve's Winchester suddenly materialized in his hands.

"You'll take it from Victor Harrington." The big man's eyes narrowed. "I've lost a lot of stock ever since you moved on my land. Get out or you'll pay the piper."

"I already gave your son my answer. I haven't changed my mind."

Megan couldn't take her eyes off Victor Harrington sitting so arrogantly on his giant black horse. This was Susan's father.

"You'll go or I'll burn you out," Harrington persisted.

"I'll tell you this." Steve's knuckles were white on the rifle stock. He spat the words at his tormentor. "If you'd show a little backbone and stop hiding behind those toughs you ride with, I'd show you who you can run off. You probably haven't fought your own battles for years, Harrington. Are you afraid? We could settle it now, the two of us."

"I don't waste my time on vermin." Keeping his gaze straight ahead, Harrington prodded his horse. One by one his men followed.

Steve and Megan rode up the mountain in heavy silence. Megan secretly watched him. She was overwhelmed by the white hot temper she had witnessed, but at the same time she was glad Steve had talked straight to the big man. Harrington had trampled men under foot for twenty years. It was time someone stood up to him.

❧

As the frolic drew near, Megan pushed aside all thoughts of the Harringtons. Daydreaming of lively music and pleasant conversation Megan stepped into the morning sunshine a week later. The glowing sun felt good after the chilly September evenings they were having. The stone house held the night coolness long into the day.

Humming softly, she took the feed pail from its peg and opened the sack of cracked corn. When she bent over the bag a strange, acrid smell made her draw back. She wrinkled her nose and peered down into the almost empty bag. Rolling down the top of the sack so she could see better she stirred the damp corn with the edge of the pail. A sticky film was over the grain.

Pulling her bottom lip between her teeth, she considered the unopened sack of feed Steve had bought on their last trip to town. He had told her to finish the old bag before using the new one. She'd better do as he said. He might be angry if she didn't. She scooped her pail into the corn and, holding it at arm's length, walked quickly to the hen yard. To her relief the six hens and two roosters attacked the feed with their usual energy.

Good, she thought. *If that's the case, why not give them the rest of the bag? Then it will be finished, and I won't have to handle the smelly stuff again.*

Holding it like an irritated mother holds a child's mud-covered shoes, she carried the offensive sack to the yard and shook it out. The greedy chickens scurried around clucking, fighting and scratching frantically.

The unpleasant job finished, she took the empty sack back to the stable. By the time she went into the henhouse to gather the eggs, her mind had wandered again to the upcoming frolic and the dress she had almost finished. Her imagination could already hear the music and the laughter-filled conversations. The henhouse became a ballroom and her gingham housedress was a elegant blue gown.

But when she returned to the henhouse door the sight of the hen yard shocked her out of her fantasy.

One hen lolled her head from side to side and made a strange squeaking noise. Another walked in circles, her beak almost touching the ground. A rooster fluttered his wings and crowed, "Gobble-gobble-goo!"

Megan stared. She gasped when a hen fell to its side kicking convulsively.

"What did you feed them chickens, Miss Megan?" Banjo asked from the front of the stable. He propped a shoulder against the stable wall and looked on with interest, a smirk hovering about his face.

"What's wrong with them, Banjo?" she cried in alarm. She made a wide circle around the crazy chickens, watching them warily. "I gave them their corn a few minutes ago."

"That wet sack I moved for you a week or so ago?"

She nodded. Her dismay grew when the rooster flapped his wings for another crow and landed in a heap.

"They'll be all right by supper time." Banjo chuckled, softly.

"What's so funny?" she demanded, eyes flashing. "They might be poisoned. We could lose our eggs. I don't think that's anything to laugh about!"

"They're not poisoned." He chuckled at her indignation, and succeeded in fueling it further. "They're drunk. Ever hear of corn likker? Home brew?"

"Drunk?"

Cluck-clucking, a hen walked head-on into the henhouse wall.

Megan's face was pink, her ears were hot, and she could hardly speak.

"This'll be a whopper of a story, Miss Megan," Banjo said, grinning widely and shaking his head. "A real whopper."

"Don't tell Steve," she begged, putting her hand on his arm. "Please, Banjo!"

"Don't tell Steve what?" a familiar voice asked.

She whirled around and there was Steve, his expression an identical twin to Banjo's. Face flaming, she looked from Steve's grin to Banjo's poorly muffled laughter and back again. Without another word she did an about-face and marched to the house, her head held high and her back board straight.

She couldn't bear to look at either of them that night at supper. The thought of what she had done set her cheeks on fire. Both men were on their best behavior. They seemed completely unaware of her lingering embarrassment. By the time she served their after-dinner coffee she was ready to believe they had forgotten all about the chickens. She breathed still easier when they rose to do the evening choring.

"Do me a favor, will you, Megan?" Steve said before following Banjo. His hand was on the latch as though he had almost forgotten to tell her something.

"Yes?" Puzzled, she looked at him. His face was expressionless except for the smallest hint of a twinkle.

"Don't ever feed the horses." With a friendly, teasing smile he closed the door quickly behind him.

Her first impulse was to fling her coffee cup after him, but her temper quickly dwindled.

"He couldn't resist," she said aloud, chuckling. For some obscure reason she kept feeling an urge to laugh as she cleared away the supper dishes that evening.

❧

The day of the frolic dawned dark and foreboding with the promise of heavy rain. With growing chagrin, Megan watched the sky. She hoped the rain would come and be done before too late in the day. She fairly skimmed through her housework that morning, wishing away the hours until time to dress, for her party gown hung in her room begging her to hurry.

With many anxious glances at the sky, she cleared away the lunch dishes and prepared to take a short nap. The dark clouds continued billowing in growing mounds, swirling menacingly. Still it did not rain.

At last the hour arrived. Megan slid into the light blue swirl of ruffles, ribbons, and lace she had spent so many hours preparing. She set to work brushing her hair into a stylish chignon she had seen in Susan's copy of *Harper's* magazine. Frowning first in concentration, then in frustration, she rested her tired arms a moment and wondered if she would ever get it right. At last, she slowly turned in front of her small mirror, satisfied.

Steve rose from his chair as the rustle of her skirt and gentle tapping of her shoes announced her arrival in the living room. His gaze lifted slowly from the wide ruffle brushing the floor in front and drawing up to join the cascade of ruffles descending from the bustle at her back, up, up to the halo of wispy ringlets that circled her face, and beyond to her rosy cheeks and starry eyes, devouring her face with his eyes. Megan was captivated by the power of his gaze. How long they stood motionless, she did not know. Suddenly, he looked down at his hat, held firmly in his hand. When he looked up his expression was closed, the same expressionless mask he wore so often these days except perhaps a little softened.

"Ready?" he asked, politely.

"Yes." She pulled her mother's white silk shawl over her arm, and swished through the door he opened for her.

ten

High above the horizon the sun peeked through a crack in the dark cloud cover when Steve and Megan left the ranch. Steve had placed a piece of tarpaulin in the back of the wagon to cover them in case it rained in earnest. Occasionally a drop fell on Megan's hand or face, and she looked anxiously at the black, billowing mass overhead, but it did not rain.

A carriage and two buckboards stood outside the Sanderses' barn when they arrived. Smiling excitedly, Susan was framed in the wide doorway when they pulled to a halt under a spreading cottonwood tree. She was lovely in a flowing, lacy, yellow gown that brought out the highlights in her strawberry blond hair.

"Megan," Susan called when they reached the door, "I'm so glad you came a little early. I want you to meet Elaine. You won't mind, will you, Mr. Chamberlin?" Assuming Steve's consent, she led Megan to the makeshift cloakroom and waited impatiently while Megan hung up her wrap and checked her hair. "There she is." Susan pointed toward a dark-haired young woman with olive skin who stood talking to a young man on the other side of the carefully swept barn. Elaine was petite and fine-featured, almost like a china doll.

After the quick introduction, Elaine said, "If we get a chance," she lowered her voice conspiratorially, "we must escape to the house for a chat. It's been ages since I've seen another woman."

"Elaine!" a man's voice called from the direction of the musicians.

"That's Ernie. He's one of the fiddlers." She put her hand on her silk skirt and lifted it slightly. "If you need anything just yell, Megan!" With a tinkling laugh she hurried away.

"Elaine's a world of fun," Susan declared. One of the fiddlers drew his bow across the strings. "They're getting ready to start. I'll see you later."

Working her way back to Steve's side, Megan wound her way through the milling crowd that had gathered since her arrival. She smiled and nodded a greeting to several people she recognized: Kip Morgan who had been with them on the stage; Wyatt Hammond, Banjo's friend; and Mr. Harper who bobbed his head absently in response to Mrs. Pleurd's chatter. Victor Harrington planted himself near the door, his henchmen nearby. The Hohner boys, Henry and Al, lounged near the refreshment table. They gawked openly at the young women, nudging each other in the ribs from time to time. Megan looked away when she passed them. Something about them made her feel unclean.

"I'm not much of a dancer," Steve said when she reached him, "but I'm willing to try if you are." Taking her hand and placing it on his bent arm, he led her to the dance floor to join the square dance that was setting up.

"I thought you said you rode the riverboats," Megan countered with a smile, "and you don't dance?" They were waiting hand in hand for the beginning chord.

"I stuck to the tables." He looked down at her with a teasing grin. "I always considered women to be trouble." His grin widened at her surprised expression, and they fell in step with the music.

"Swing your partner," the caller chanted, and they danced and danced until Megan's head reeled.

"I'd like to sit down," she said when there was a break in the music. "I'm a little tired."

"Having a good time?" Steve asked, handing her a cup of grape punch.

"Wonderful! I don't know when I've had so much fun." Still under the spell of the music, she sipped her punch and watched the dancers.

"I believe I'll check the horses."

Megan nodded to him, preoccupied with the scene before her. A deep, prolonged boom of thunder, almost like a drum roll, interrupted the gay music. In minutes, the deluge of rain hammering on the barn roof gave the fiddler competition.

"Let it pour," a man standing near her said loudly to his companion. "We can sure use it."

And pour it did. The roar on the roof made it impossible to continue the dancing. The music could scarcely be heard. For fifteen minutes it lasted until, as suddenly as it began, the rain stopped and the frolic resumed its breathtaking pace.

After a while it occurred to Megan that Steve had been away a long time. She was strolling leisurely in the direction of the door when he suddenly appeared through the crowd.

"I was beginning to wonder what became of you." Her smile froze when a woman's piercing scream shattered the gay atmosphere. Following Steve's gaze, she saw the cause of the confusion, and darkness closed in on her. For an instant she was afraid she would faint. Steve's strong arm was around her instantly, and she clung to him.

Outside the open door lay the body of a huge man. A knife was buried up to the long, black haft into the left side of his back. His out-flung hand gripped the door jamb. Megan, transfixed, stared at that strong, calloused hand. She saw it slowly relax its grip and fall limp. Horror swept over her in great, crashing waves. She buried her face in the rough cloth of Steve's coat.

"It's Harrington," a man's voice called. "Victor Harrington."

"He's pulled leather," another voice added grimly.

"Get hold of yourself, Megan." Steve pulled her away from him and looked into her face. "Susan is going to need someone. He's her pa."

Megan drew a shaky breath and turned her face away from the scene in the doorway. She knew he was right. She ought to find Susan.

"Pa!" Susan's anguished, hysterical cry struck an answering chord in Megan. Her own feelings forgotten, she rushed to her friend's side.

Susan's face was white as chalk; her eyes were wide with terror. She stared dazedly at the body of her father.

Megan put her arms around the shaking young woman and pulled her away.

"Come," Elaine said softly in her ear, "bring her to the house."

Together Megan and Elaine half-carried the grief-stricken woman into the Sanderses' living room, and Elaine ran to the kitchen for some strong, sweet tea.

"Pa," Susan groaned between deep, body-shaking sobs.

Megan stroked her hand and tried to find something consoling to say. But she felt totally helpless. Nothing would bring Susan's father back. A hot, choking sob welled up in Megan's breast. She held it down, but it grew until it fairly smothered her. She understood Susan's loss. Hadn't she lost both father and mother as Susan had? What comfort was there?

None, her soul cried out. *No comfort. No comfort anywhere.*

She sat with Susan, hardly moving or speaking until Beau Harrington's slurred speech rose to a shout outside the Sanderses' door. It was past midnight.

"I want to see Susan!"

"Your sister is sleeping," Ruth Sanders, Elaine's mother, answered flatly.

Megan drew aside the curtain a fraction of an inch to see Mrs. Sanders barring Beau from coming up the porch stairs. Even from the ground the young man was taller than the little woman, but she seemed to tower over him, so great was the strength of her determination.

"She was hysterical," Elaine's mother continued, "so I gave her a little laudanum to calm her. She'll sleep for a long while. Why don't you leave her here tonight?"

Beau blinked stupidly at the commanding figure before him, apparently deciding his next course of action.

"Megan Chamberlin is with her now." Ruth Sanders took a step forward as though to force him back.

"Chamberlin!" He bristled, spitting out the words. "Don't you let any of that lowdown, murderin' bunch near Susan." He clenched his fists. "You get that squatter's wife out of there, or I'll bust in and take Susan home now." He scowled threateningly.

"How dare you say such a thing!"

"It was her husband killed my pa," Beau insisted. "He wanted revenge for Pa trying to run him off."

Megan moved away from the window and sank into a chair. Leaning her throbbing head against the high back, she closed her eyes.

"You're drunk." Megan clearly heard Ruth Sanders's disdainful voice. "Go somewhere and sleep it off, or I'll have to call Jim from the barn."

Boots crunching on gravel was all the answer she received. Megan opened her eyes when she heard the front door open. Mrs. Sanders paused when she caught sight of Megan in the front room before deliberately closing and locking the front door. Even at this late hour, Mrs. Sanders showed no signs of strain or fatigue.

"You heard what he said?" she asked softly, coming near Megan.

Mutely, Megan nodded. After the strain of the evening, Beau's accusation was more than she could endure.

"You may as well know. Clyde Turner, Harrington's foreman, said he saw your husband outside right before the murder, and he knows your husband is good with a knife."

Megan pressed her temples.

"There wasn't enough evidence to pin Harrington's murder on your husband for sure, but there was quite a bit of arguing out there." She patted Megan's shoulder. "I'm sorry. You're new out here, and you'll have to get used to our ways. The law is a long way off in Denver, so the men have to settle these things themselves mostly. But with it being outright murder, they'll probably call in the U.S. Marshal to investigate if he has time.

"Your husband's been waiting with the buckboard for over an hour. You're done in. Maybe you'd best go on home. We'll see to Susan."

Megan sat in silence for a long moment.

"Please tell Susan I'll do anything I can to help her if she needs me," she managed at last, getting shakily to her feet.

Steve was at her side the instant she stepped off the porch. He draped her shawl about her and handed her her bonnet. Helping her into the buckboard, he clucked to the horses as he gathered the reins, and they were off into the moonlight.

When the trees had closed around them, shielding them from the watching eyes of those still at the Sanderses' ranch, Megan's control disintegrated. She sobbed into her handkerchief, her shoulders heaving with every breath. Steve put his arm about her, but she barely noticed. The sympathetic moon drew a lacy cloud handkerchief across its face, darkening the night to hide her tears.

"It's all my fault," she murmured in an agony of self-reproach.

"What's your fault?" Steve demanded.

"I. . .I shouldn't have insisted on going to the. . .to the frolic." She sniffled, wadding her soggy handkerchief. "If we hadn't gone they couldn't have accused you of. . .of. . ." A fresh storm of tears broke out.

"Wait a minute." His voice was stern. "Wait a minute. They could accuse me of coming around without attending the party, you know. Harrington was killed outside, remember. Someone could have been lurking in the darkness unbeknownst to anyone." He looked at her intently through a fresh stream of moonlight as the cloud covering passed on. "Who's been telling you things?"

"Mrs. Sanders."

Steve's gruff tone had calmed her emotional tempest somewhat. She stared at her hands, not wanting to meet his eyes, aware of the solid strength of his arm and stiffness of his coat against her shoulder. Stumbling and groping for words, she told him of her conversation with Ruth Sanders.

"In the first place," Steve said quietly when she was through, "Turner didn't make a direct accusation. He made some pointed hints, and I'm sure every man there knew what he was getting at, but they're not going to string me up on that basis.

"As a matter fact, I'm glad we were there. I had a chance to look around a bit after you left with Susan. I saw a few things that could mean somethin'." He reached inside his coat and handed her his handkerchief. "Here, take mine. Looks like yours is pretty used up."

Meekly, Megan wiped her face. She was a little ashamed of her outburst now. She felt herself relaxing as she listened to his calm voice, and she drew strength from his strength.

"It was a thrown knife," he was saying. "I went to the door after you went out with Susan. The downpour had wiped out all the footprints of people arriving. Harrington's prints were the only ones coming across the clearing in front of the barn. At one spot he stumbled. I figure that's where he was nailed. No one could have been close enough to reach him there."

"You can tell all that?"

"I learned many useful things in the Army of the Confed'racy, Miss Megan," he said, lightly. "I also located some boot prints under the shelter near the hitching rail. It had a star design in the heel. Looked like brand new boots to me." Growing animated, he said, "Harrington's back would have been toward that person as he crossed the clearing, too. It seems pretty simple to me. Find out who's knife slick and wears those boots, and we'll have the murderer."

"Did you tell the men what you saw?" Megan held her shawl closely around her. She had begun to shiver.

"They weren't over-anxious to listen to anything I had to say," he admitted, reluctantly. "They don't know for sure I'm guilty, but they don't know for sure I'm not. And I'm a stranger. That's ten counts against me to start out." He paused, guiding the horses over the bank of the stream that circled the lower meadow.

"Try not to worry, Megan," he said after they were across. His voice was tender.

eleven

Banjo was standing in the open doorway of the stable when they rode into the yard.

"Evenin', folks." He took the reins from Steve. "I'll tend the horses."

"We had some trouble," Steve said after he had helped Megan down. "Victor Harrington was murdered tonight. Stabbed in the back."

Banjo whistled softly. "You don't say. Any idea who did it?"

"Steve was accused," Megan blurted out. "Folks don't know whether to believe it or not."

"I found a couple o' clues." Steve told Banjo of his finds.

"Believe I'll ride over that way come daylight." Banjo rubbed his chin. "I'm a fair hand at readin' signs. Maybe I can come up with somethin' more."

❧

The sun shone full in Megan's face when she opened her eyes the next morning. She blinked and sat up, disgruntled at having slept so late. This, along with the heavy feeling in her head and limbs, did nothing for her disposition. She put a weak hand to her head and pressed her eyes tightly closed. The terrors of the evening before rushed over her.

She ached afresh for Susan, left alone now to cope with her explosive brother. Megan hoped Susan wouldn't believe Steve was guilty of killing her father. How could she bear to lose Susan's friendship? She had come to love Susan like a sister.

Steve was not in the house when Megan came out of her room. She didn't feel like eating. Instead she went out to her favorite haunt at the eastern side of the house. She walked off the porch to sit in the grass and look out at the rolling hills. She had been there for half an hour enjoying the breeze and the quietness of the landscape when she was startled by a stealthy movement beside her.

It was Lobo. He was lying about six feet away with his head on his paws, watching her.

"I forgot to feed you this morning, didn't I? I'm sorry, Lobo. I guess I had a lot on my mind this morning. Will you stay here if I go in for something?" She stretched her hand out toward the shaggy head. He didn't shy away. Edging a little closer, she let him sniff her hand without trying to touch him. "Wait here."

Moving quietly to keep from scaring him, she went inside and hurried back with a scrap of corn bread and a small dish of cold, congealed gravy.

She stood nearby while Lobo gobbled down the food. This time, instead of rushing away, he came to her and licked her hand. Megan knelt down in front of him. His gray face turned up to her face, his tail gave a short wag.

"Are you ready to be friends, Lobo?" she whispered. "I won't hurt you, you know." Gently, she touched his scruffy head, rubbing between his ears and long neck. "I'd like you to stay here with me and not run away every day. I'm lonely like you." She talked to him about Jeremy and how she hoped he would come to Colorado to be with them, stroking the dog all the while. His ears were pricked up, and his eyes followed her face. If she hadn't known better, she would have declared he understood every word.

They were still deep in conversation when Kelsey's lop-eared head appeared on the trail. Megan watched Banjo's progress around the meadow. When he came close, Lobo gave one short, sharp bark and ran away. Steve walked slowly from the corral to join them.

"Found a few things you'd be interested in," Banjo said, stepping from the saddle.

Steve stood without expression, waiting. Megan impatiently clenched her apron. Banjo seemed in no hurry. He ground hitched Kelsey and slowly perched on the edge of the porch.

"I found those boot marks you mentioned." He knocked his hat to the back of his head. "That feller stood there a while like he was waitin' for somethin'. The ground was tramped down a good bit with his boot prints. He was wearing California spurs. The big rowels gouged into the dirt a couple o' times. He's about six feet tall judging from his stride."

He reached into his shirt pocket.

"I found somethin' else interestin'." He stretched his hand out to Steve, a small piece of wood in the palm. "Looks to me like the man we want has a habit of chewin' short, green juniper twigs with the bark peeled off. I found two o' these. Juniper has a powerful taste. Don't care for it myself, but this hombre must have a likin' for it."

Steve turned the twig in his hand, studying it thoughtfully.

"I talked with Ruth Sanders a while this mornin'," Banjo continued. "The funeral is gonna be tomorrow at the Rockin' H. One of Harrington's hands went to Denver to get a parson. There's no parson in Juniper. A circuit ridin' preacher comes by ever' three months or so, but he's not due for another month." He accepted the twig that Steve returned to him. "What I was thinkin' on was this. If Miss Megan would like to go to this here funeral on account of bein' Miss Susan's friend, I'd be willin' to go along. That is if it's all right with you, Chamberlin."

"Megan?" Steve put the question to her.

"I'd like to go, Banjo. How is Susan? Did Mrs. Sanders say?"

"She's still with the Sanderses. Will be until the funeral. Miss Ruth says she's real quiet. Won't hardly talk to nobody, even Miss Elaine." He shook his head sadly. "I'm real sorry for the poor thing."

Megan climbed the porch steps with a tired tread. She put some soup on the stove to boil and went out back to the clothes she'd left soaking in the big tub overnight. She scrubbed and rubbed, squeezed and rinsed, puzzling over the clues Banjo had found, but her foggy mind could not make any sense out of them.

ᴥ

When Megan came outside after breakfast the next morning Lobo was lying on the ground beside the porch steps watching the door. Wagging his matted tail, he stood up and met her at the bottom step.

"Here you go. Some bones from last night's supper. If you had come last night you wouldn't have had to wait until now to get them."

The dog settled in for a long, ecstatic gnawing session.

"I've got to go out, so I can't stay to talk," she continued. "I wish you'd stay around."

He raised his head, swished his tail, and gave a short bark.

Megan laughed. "So, you're talking back to me now. We're making progress."

Megan and Banjo set out after lunch. Megan's stomach was in knots. Not only did she dread the funeral itself, but she wasn't sure how Susan would act when she saw her. Megan's face was ghostly pale against the severe black broadcloth of her dress and bonnet, the same ones she had worn to mourn her mother.

The service had barely started when they arrived. Crude benches had been set up in the yard beneath a dozen tall aspens. A slight breeze caused a faint whispering rustle among the leaves. The shiny, black coffin, a wreath of yellow flowers on the lid, was at the front. A short man with a dark complexion and a large, hook nose stood behind the coffin, a black book open in his hand.

Banjo led Megan to a seat in the rear. Without turning her head, Megan looked over the grieving congregation. Susan, darkly veiled, sat with Beau near the front. Megan could see Susan trembling even at a distance. Beau looked straight ahead like a statue, oblivious of his sister's suffering.

The minister's high-pitched nasal voice droned on and on. Megan scarcely heard what he said, so caught up was she with the violence of her own emotions. The grim congregation, the coffin, and the minister reminded her with brutal clearness of her own bereavement. She wept soundlessly, without trying to stop her tears. Occasionally she dabbed at her cheeks with a black, lace-edged handkerchief. She wept for Susan, for her own tragedies, for the feeling of utter hopelessness she felt in her soul. The parson's words were eloquent, but she found no relief in his message.

At last, the assembly moved en masse to the grave site where the minister said a prayer and threw a handful of dirt on the lowered coffin. By twos and threes the mourners left the grave. From a cool distance they bowed in Megan's direction and nodded to Banjo, eyes averted. Susan, one of the last to leave, raised her head when she caught sight of Megan. She hesitated, glanced at Beau's back as he walked toward the house, and came over to grasp Megan's clenched hands in her icy, trembling ones.

Through the black veil Megan could see Susan's hollow, red-rimmed eyes and gaunt cheeks.

"I'm so glad you came, Megan," Susan whispered quickly. A smoldering fire burned from within her. Megan glimpsed it as she leaned forward. "I don't care what they say. I don't think Steve did it."

Tears streamed afresh down Megan's face. She couldn't speak.

"I'll be over when I can." A quick squeeze of her hand and she hurried to catch up to her brother.

Banjo took Megan's arm and walked with her to the buckboard. She couldn't stop crying. On the seat of the buckboard she held her handkerchief over her mouth and bowed her head until her face was all but hidden by the brim of her bonnet. Banjo called to the horses, and they set off.

"Miss Megan, Jesus would carry the load for you if you would let Him," Banjo said after several minutes had trudged heavily by.

"How could He help me?" she asked, looking up. Her eyes were red and swollen. Her chin quivered.

"Jesus said, 'Come unto me, all ye that labour and are heavy laden, and I will give you rest.' If you know you are a sinner and need Him to wash your sins away, He'll save you. The choice is as simple as that.

"I know there's plenty o' highfalutin' preachers who would like to make it seem harder than it is, but God's love is available to everyone. Even a child can understand it. God doesn't force His love on anyone. He lets each person choose for himself."

"How do I come?"

"Just pray and tell Him you mean business. Tell Him you know what you are and you want to claim His blood to wash your sins away. You know He died on the cross for you, don't you?"

"Of course." She remembered the camp meetings she had attended long ago in Virginia. The fiery preaching had made a lasting impression.

Was she a sinner? She didn't have to think about it long before she had to admit she was. She knew she had blamed God for her problems. She had never tried to live her life to please Him.

"Remember, God loves you," Banjo said, softly. "He wants to help you."

Megan squeezed her eyes shut. She poured out her tortured soul before the Almighty. There was no lightning bolt, no crash of thunder, no audible voice from heaven, yet surely, definitely, Jesus calmed the churning, frothing sea that was inside her. Some sadness still lingered, but for the first time in her life she was at peace.

"I did it, Banjo," she said softly when she looked up. "And God heard me. I know He did. I feel so quiet inside." She gazed into the distance examining the change within her like a mother examines her newborn child.

"That's the peace of God," Banjo said, nodding. "It's one of the greatest blessings of being a Christian. As long as you obey Him, that peace will stay with you.

"Do you have a Bible?" he asked.

"Yes. I have one in my trunk." She thought of the old black Bible that had been a gift to her father from a beloved teacher. How glad she was she had brought it along.

"Read it every day," Banjo advised. "You'll get strength from it."

"I will read it," she promised. "I surely will."

And read she did. The words in that old Bible came alive as she read each morning, often before dawn. She grew to love its delicate ivory pages. It was marvelous the way its message met her heart's need every time. She never forgot the day she found the verse in 1 Peter, "Casting all your care upon him; for he careth for you." Knowing God cared for her gave her new strength.

It was well she had found new strength, for only a week later Banjo brought her a letter that caused her to cry out for still more.

twelve

The letter read:

Dear Megan,
I thought you should know Jeremy is having a time of it. The doctor says he has to go back to his bed agin. His heart does git to racing when he sits up a while. I visit him every day but he misses you powerful. He loves your letters. Reads 'em till he has 'em down by heart.
Love,
Em

Megan sat on the edge of her bed, rereading the letter. How bad Jeremy really was she couldn't tell. She felt sick with longing to be with him, to hold him close and tell him she loved him. She knelt by the big bed and rested her head on the quilt to give her fears and heartaches to the One Who had promised to care for her. An hour later a tender, sweet calmness replaced the fear and anguish. She washed the tears from her cheeks. Surely God would take care of Jeremy.

An idea came clearly as she patted her face dry with a towel. Jeremy had never heard that he could have his sins forgiven. She must write to him immediately and tell him about how she had found Jesus. And Em, yes, Em.

The letter was hard to begin, but once she found a starting place, her pen flew. There was so much to share of the joy and peace she had found and wished for her loved ones to find, also. Jesus was the answer to their devastating loss. He gave hope, blessed hope.

The letter was lying on top of her trunk ready for mailing the next morning when she went out to the henhouse. Steve and Banjo were working frantically to get the corn crop harvested for fear of a frost destroying it. When she finished her chores she would help pick the fat ears while the men chopped the stalks for cattle feed.

The sound of the birds twittering in the branches of the oaks, the soft breeze flowing down from the mountain, even the familiar barnyard smells of earth and straw lifted her spirits. Something brushed against her skirt making her turn around. It was Lobo walking behind her.

"Well, hello." Megan knelt down to rub his neck. He leaned into her hand a little, his head cocked to one side. "I hate to tell you this but you do need a bath. I wonder what color you really are under all that dirt." She stood up. "I have to hurry. Steve needs me to help get in the corn." She continued across the yard, followed by Lobo. He went into the stable with her while she drew a pail of grain from the burlap sack.

"Chook! Chook! Chook!" she called to the clucking, scratching hens while she threw handfuls of cracked corn to the ground. Suddenly she stopped in midmotion, staring at the side of the stable, the side not seen from the house. Scrawled on the weathered gray boards in large, white letters was one word: Murderer.

For a full ten seconds she stood there. She clenched her fists, pressing her lips so tightly they were all but invisible. Beau Harrington! It had to be Beau Harrington who did such a ghastly thing! She glared at the wall as though it were a living thing mocking her, mocking Steve, mocking their cause. Hadn't they done only what was right? Wasn't Victor Harrington wrong in trying to force them away? The pail of corn fell to the ground, forgotten.

"Well," she fumed, "he won't have the satisfaction of upsetting Steve with his malicious pranks. I'll scrub that wall before he sees it."

Shuffling her way through the mob of chickens looting the pail at her feet, she went through the rear door of the stable to fill a pail with water and get a broom. She scoured ferociously, until the whitewash was nothing more than a gray smear.

Satisfied, she retrieved her empty feed pail and walked slowly to the corral to give Candy the carrot in her apron pocket and rest a minute to calm her shaken nerves. It wasn't until she got back to the house that she realized Lobo still followed her.

"Here, Lobo," she called holding out her hand. He trotted up and licked her hand. "You're a good fella." She scratched the ruff behind his neck. "Steve's probably wondering what became of me." She gave him a parting pat and then scurried inside to get a lunch packed and put on her bonnet.

After dark that evening the men had barely reached the house to wash up for supper, when a wide, powerfully built man cantered in. He had a square face with a thick neck that seemed to be one with his wide chest. His silver badge reflected the lamplight streaming from the open doorway.

"Evenin', gentlemen," he said, holding his reins loosely on the pommel. "Is one of you Steve Chamberlin?"

"I am." Steve stepped forward from the porch. "What can I do for you?"

"I'm Ben Walker, the U.S. Marshal. I'd like to ask you a few questions."

"Certainly. Come in and set a spell. We were just about to sit up to the table. You're welcome to join us."

"I'd be much obliged." The lawman dismounted. "Don't get much chance to eat home cooking in my business."

Megan, watching from the door, couldn't believe Steve's unconcern. How could he act so naturally when the marshal could be here to arrest him? She clasped her hands tightly together across her waist.

"We've a guest for supper, Megan," Steve called. "Set another place."

The fork and knife rattled against the enamel plate as Megan set them down. Taking a deep breath and biting her lip, she willed herself to calm down. Quickly, she set out a jar of her own bread-and-butter pickles for good measure.

"This is my wife, Megan," Steve said when they came inside.

"Ma'am." Walker took off his big hat and offered a polite smile.

"Hello." She smiled, but her cheeks felt stiff and heavy.

The man wearing the silver star was generous in his praise of the steaks and new potatoes baked with butter. He also commented on the bread while he was buttering his third piece.

"You're a blessed man, Chamberlin," he said, pushing back his chair. "I haven't had a finer meal in a coon's age."

Steve gave Megan that slow smile that made her glow inside. "I can't but agree with you, Mr. Walker," he said.

"What's on your mind?" Steve asked when the men were seated in the living room around the crackling fire. Megan, still clearing away the dishes, strained her ears to hear. Her hands moved automatically, for her mind was far from the chore at hand.

"I'm investigating the Harrington murder. I'm sure you know you've been accused in so many words. I must say there doesn't seem to be an overabundance of evidence against you, but four different people have told me you're an ace with a knife. I thought I'd come out and see what you had to say."

"I'll tell you all I know," Steve said, easily. "Banjo can tell you some, too. He picked up some signs over at the Running M."

"What was your relationship to Harrington?"

Systematically, the marshal directed the questions until the entire story was told. Megan finished the dishes and quietly joined the men in the living room.

"What's your opinion of the folks around here, Banjo?" the marshal continued. "You've been in these parts long enough to know the lay of the land. Being from Denver puts me at a disadvantage. Who had a grudge against Harrington?"

"Most folks hereabouts," Banjo said after considering a minute or two. "Harrington pushed folks around to suit him. Offhand I'd say Jim Sanders, because of an old dispute, and Wyatt Hammond, because of Harrington's daughter. Then there's Logan Hohner, one of the blacksmiths in town.

German man with two grown, no-account sons. He has a rawhide outfit north of here."

"What was Harrington's beef with him?" Walker asked.

"Accused him of rustlin'.'"

"He had a real imagination about rustlers, didn't he?" Steve asked quickly. "That's what he accused me of on the trail."

"I guess he's been losing cattle for four, five years from what Wyatt tells me. Never has been able to catch the rascals," Banjo said. His chair creaked as he changed position. "Then there's his son.

"I have my doubts Beau would have the gumption to do it, but he sure is a rebellious one. He could have gotten impatient to have the reins on the Rocking H himself." He paused. "I'm talking through my hat, Mr. Walker. I don't have any proof for that."

"I'm not saying I'm sorry Harrington's out of the picture," Steve admitted. "But I think it could have been handled better. You know, a fair fight. Whoever did it is a coyote. Not fit to live among decent folk."

It was late when the marshal left. Banjo went on to the stable when the big man rode away.

"Do you think Walker believes you did it?" Megan asked, anxiously.

"Can't say for sure." Steve sat on a chair near her. "All we can do is wait for his decision. But he did say he'd be interested to hear of anything else we may learn in the meantime." He leaned slightly toward Megan. "I don't want you to make yourself sick by worrying over this thing. When a man's in the right he shouldn't have anything to fear. Folks hereabouts are basically honest. They don't want to punish the wrong man any more than you or I do."

"It's hard not to worry, though." Megan looked down at her hands folded tightly in her lap. "There's so much at stake."

"You've been a real trooper, Megan. I'm glad you were the one I brought out here with me."

Megan glanced at him. He was watching her closely. She felt her face warm.

"I believe God will work everything out for the best." She wanted to tell him about her new faith but wasn't sure how to go about it.

"God?" Steve's eyebrows rose higher.

"I trusted Jesus as my Savior a few days ago." Once she had found an opening she spoke with assurance. "The Bible says that He will give rest to people who carry heavy burdens. Since I trusted Him, I know there's a difference. You may not be able to see it outside, but I know it's there deep inside."

"If that makes you feel better, I'm all for it," he said, awkwardly.

"Have you thought much about God?"

"Not much." He slammed the door on that subject and opened another. "The corn crop is excellent," he said abruptly. "I'm sure I'll be able to make four or five times what I spent for seed. If the frost holds off tonight, we'll finish getting it in tomorrow, and I'll take it to the mill the next day."

"I hope the other people around here don't convince the marshal you're guilty," she returned to the subject uppermost in her mind.

"I'm not worried about that." Steve relaxed, stretching his legs in front of him. "There is something that does bother me, though."

"What?"

"I've never held a knife around anyone in Colorado to my knowledge, except Banjo and you." He looked at his boots thoughtfully, pursing his lips.

"So?" His silence was maddening.

"So how does everyone know that I can handle one?"

thirteen

October days were busy indeed. With Lobo trailing after her like a gray shadow, Megan followed the buckboard through the woods, picking up deadfall to fuel the stove and fireplace through the winter. Banjo butchered a fat young cow, and showed them how to jerk the beef and store it for the time when game was scarce.

Megan continued her target practice though her rides with Steve became less frequent. There simply wasn't time for both.

She held her rifle by the stock and gave it an excited shake the day she overlapped three shots in the center of a tin can lid at two hundred feet. Steve chuckled and shook his head when he retrieved the lid and examined it.

"I haven't seen many men who could do that," he said, giving her a wide approving grin. She glowed under his praise.

Megan had conflicting emotions the day she watched Susan's boyish figure ride in. She was glad to see her friend, but she dreaded hearing the news Susan carried. Megan lay the heavy iron on the kitchen stove, hung up the shirt she had been ironing, and went out to greet her.

"Morning!" Megan called with a cheerfulness she didn't feel.

Susan waved a greeting and ground hitched the chestnut on the edge of the meadow where he could reach the rich grass, and came to the house. She seemed like a vacant shell of the vivacious, quick-smiling young woman she had been such a short time ago. Always slender, she was now gossamer-thin and pale to the lips.

"I had to get away from the ranch for a while," she said when they sat down. "I had to talk to somebody." Her face contorted, and Megan was afraid she was going to cry.

"I've been missing you, too," Megan said, trying to ease the tension.

"I'm so worried. I haven't been able to sleep or eat much the past two weeks. It's about Wyatt." Tears spilled over her cheeks and fell to her shirt. She pulled a handkerchief from her pocket and pressed it against her face. Her sobs were soundless but they came from deep inside.

Megan didn't know what to say.

"Tell me about Wyatt," Megan prompted when the other woman's sobs had almost subsided. "You never have, you know."

Susan looked up from behind her handkerchief. "How do you know about Wyatt?"

"Banjo told me."

"Oh." Susan wiped her eyes. "That's right, Banjo would know." She drew a shaky breath, and kept her eyes on her fingers twisting and wadding her wet, wrinkled handkerchief. "There's not that much to tell, really. He came to work at the ranch about two years ago. He works Pa's horses." She cleared her throat. "I like to ride, and I spend quite a lot of time at the stable. One thing led to another, and. . ."

"You love him, don't you?"

Susan nodded, tears falling afresh. "Pa said, 'No' when Wyatt asked his blessing," she continued in a moment. "He said no cowhand would ever marry his daughter. Wyatt was awful mad. He comes from a good family. Banjo can tell you that. They don't have much, like the Harringtons do." A bitter expression marred her pretty features for an instant. "Wyatt said he would have killed Pa if it wasn't for me."

"What?" Megan stared at Susan, instantly alert.

"He said he would have killed him," Susan repeated, defiantly. She stared at the low embers in the fireplace. "That's what's got me so upset, Megan. Wyatt was at the party, and he's good with a knife. I've seen him."

"You think he did it?" Megan could scarcely believe what she heard.

"I don't know," she said in a small, tortured voice. "I don't know." She fell silent, staring at the floor, still absently snarling her handkerchief.

"Let me get you a cup of tea."

Susan had regained some composure when Megan returned.

"I'm not accusing Wyatt," Susan said after taking a sip. "I don't know what to think."

"I can understand that."

"Things have been awful since Pa's funeral. I don't know how I can bear to stay there much longer. Beau is more arrogant than ever, bullying me, trying his best to irritate me. And that Clyde Turner, the foreman. He doesn't seem to know his place anymore. I heard him talking to Beau last night, and it sounded like he was giving orders, not taking them." She shivered.

"Then yesterday the marshal. . .what's his name? Oh, yes, Walker. . .came to the ranch. He was there all morning looking around and talking to the men. He spent a long time talking to Wyatt before he left. It scared me something fierce."

"Have you talked to Wyatt?"

"No, I've been afraid to. I guess I'm being foolish, but I can't help it." Susan set her teacup on the small table beside her chair.

"Why don't you lie down in my room for a while?" Megan suggested. "You're all in. A quiet rest would do you a world of good."

"I ought to be getting back," Susan protested weakly.

"For what? There's nothing for you to do there except mope. Come along." She took Susan's arm. "Steve probably won't be home until shortly before dark, so everything will be quiet."

"I guess you're right." She allowed Megan to lead her to the wide, quilt-covered bed.

"If you need anything, call out. I'm going to finish the ironing in the kitchen." Megan let down the curtain from its tie, dimming the room, and quietly went out.

Lifting the hot iron from its resting place on the stove, she thought about what Susan had told her. That Wyatt would murder the father of the woman he loved was inconceivable to Megan. If Wyatt killed Susan's father, Susan would turn against him, and he would lose the very thing he wanted.

Unless he lost his reason in a fit of rage.

She considered the possibility and rejected it. Maybe at the time Victor Harrington had humiliated him, but not months later. The problem weighed heavily on her mind long after Susan had returned home.

❧

"I think a few strays have wandered out of the canyon," Banjo said when they sat around the fireplace after dinner that evening. "I saw some tracks leading toward Hohner's piece. I'd estimate there are probably less than ten cows, but I think it bears lookin' into. I didn't have time to do it today."

"Want to ride over that way tomorrow?" Steve looked up at Banjo from where he sat on the hearth plaiting a horsehair hackamore.

"Sure thing. It shouldn't take more'n half a day."

"Can I ride with you?" Megan asked impulsively. "It's been ages since I've been riding, and I'd like to get away from the house for a while."

"I guess it wouldn't hurt anything." Steve looked back down at his plaiting. "We'll leave at sunup."

Megan tingled with anticipation as she donned her riding habit the next morning. She could already feel the crisp autumn air and smell the pines. After all the heavy work of harvest time and the anxiety over the Harrington murder, she was ready for a change. She had been digging up vegetables, picking vegetables, canning vegetables, and jerking beef. She wanted to stretch her muscles, shake off the doldrums, and enjoy the day.

She packed a small tin with lunch, tied on her bonnet, and set off for the stable, Lobo close behind her. Whenever she stepped outdoors, he was always nearby.

Ears forward, head bobbing high, Candy was as eager to set off as Megan was. The strawberry roan nickered and nosed over Megan's clothes in search of a treat while Megan slid her Henry rifle into the saddle scabbard.

She put her lunch tin in the saddlebag as she stood beside the mare to scratch under her mane before mounting up.

"Here's what you're looking for." Megan held out her palm, exposing a tiny mound of brown sugar. "You're a big baby," she said, patting Candy's nose affectionately. She stepped into the saddle with ease, enjoying the feel of the horse's movements beneath her, listening for the creak of leather.

"All set?" Steve called from the yard.

"Let's go!" Megan smiled happily and lightly squeezed her knees on the mare's sides. When she reached Steve they set off together at an easy canter around the meadow with Banjo close behind.

They were halfway around when a rider came through the trees and trotted toward them. In the dim light of dawn it didn't take long to recognize Beau Harrington. He was alone.

"You still here, Chamberlin?" Beau shouted menacingly. He drew his pinto horse to a halt near Steve. "I thought you'd have tucked your tail between your legs and run by now."

"Innocent men don't run," Steve said mildly, his hand resting on his thigh near his pistol. "What's your business, Harrington?"

"Thought I'd give you some friendly advice." He stared at Steve, hatred burning in his eyes. "The tin star had to go back to Denver. Seems he couldn't stay long enough to hang you. But don't you worry, the Rocking H can handle that job. You hang around asking for trouble, and we'll take care of you."

"That's the difference between you and me, Beau," Steve said. There was deadly stillness in his voice. "I don't ask for trouble. You came here looking for a fight. I'd hate to disappoint you."

Steve's hand shot out and grabbed Beau's shirt at the neck. He kicked the smaller man's boot from the stirrup and pushed him to the ground, falling on top of him. Caught off guard, Beau clutched frantically at the ironlike fist holding him.

Steve sat down across the smaller man's middle, drew back his free hand, and slapped Beau's freckled cheeks, back and forth again and again. Beau's red hair, now hatless, rolled in the dirt. A crimson drop oozed from the corner of his mouth.

Breathing heavily, Steve pulled the young Harrington to his feet and backed away from him.

"You'd best get back where you belong before I decide to fight you like a man."

Beau's bruised lips drew back into a snarl of rage. Livid streaks adorned both cheeks. He clawed for his gun.

Beside Megan's horse, Lobo growled deep in his chest.

"I wouldn't do that if I were you, Harrington," Banjo said in a conversational voice.

Megan turned around to see the big buffalo gun lying in the old man's hands like it had been carved to fit.

"This here's a Sharps .56. It takes soft nose bullets. It ain't purty what they'll do to a man."

Harrington stiffened and slowly turned his eyes toward Banjo. At the sight of that wide, black bore pointed at him, he raised his hands. Slowly, keeping his hands wide, he reached down and picked up his hat, set it on his head, and scrambled for his horse. He missed the stirrup on the first try then mounted up. He jerked his horse around.

"We ain't done, Chamberlin!" he screeched. His face was the color of raw beefsteak. He gouged his spurs into the pinto's sides and galloped away.

When he had gone, Megan was shocked when she looked down to find that her rifle was in her hands, cocked and ready. She couldn't remember pulling it from the scabbard. She turned it wonderingly in her hands as though seeing it for the first time. Would she have used it? Her hands started shaking. The ague traveled up her arms until her shoulders were trembling. She slid the Henry rifle back into the scabbard and clenched her hands on the pommel. Sensing the change in Megan's attitude, Candy side-stepped a little.

"Are you all right?" Steve moved his mount close beside her. "Do you want to stay at the house?"

"No. I'll be okay." She moistened her lips, fighting for control. "I don't want to stay behind. Especially now. I'd spend the whole day doing nothing but worrying."

"If you say so," Steve said uncertainly. "If you feel too tired let me know, and we'll turn back."

"I'll be okay," she repeated, as much to convince herself as to assure him. She gathered the reins tighter and straightened in the saddle. Steve gave her another searching look before leading out. Megan stayed beside him.

When they entered the woods, Megan fell behind Steve at the narrow spots, Banjo bringing up the rear. She studied her husband, with new eyes. He could have drawn a gun on Beau Harrington and killed him. It would have been called a fair fight. She knew Steve had the coolness that comes with maturity. Beau was hot-headed, too rash. He would have probably spoiled his first shot and been easy pickings for Steve. But Steve hadn't taken advantage of the younger man's temper in spite of the trouble Beau had caused him. An icy hand squeezed Megan's heart. She knew Beau would be back for revenge.

"Would you really have shot Beau this morning?" she asked Banjo later as they rode together on the trail. "I thought Christians were supposed to be peaceful."

"Christians shouldn't hunt trouble," Banjo replied, "but the Bible teaches that folks are supposed to obey the law. There's no lawman here to make sure that they do, so it's up to us law-abidin' folks to see the law is kept. Otherwise, the outlaws would soon run the rest of us off." His mild, blue eyes had that fatherly look again. "This is still a wild land, Miss Megan. When a peace officer comes to these parts, it'll be our Christian duty to let him do the keepin' of the law. Until then, we'll have to see to it."

"It scares me to think of what Beau will do next."

"Don't fret yourself," Banjo said. "Steve handled the situation this morning. He can handle it again." He drifted behind her. "Rock of Ages," he sang softly, and Megan urged Candy forward.

With Lobo still on their trail, they picked their way across rocky slopes and skirted huge boulders. Though it was only midafternoon, Megan's dress felt like it was pasted to her back. Her forehead and neck were clammy. When they reached the canyon where their cattle were pastured, Banjo moved around her and Steve to take the lead. Megan kept her eyes on Banjo when he leaned over Kelsey's gray shoulder to study the ground. Fifteen minutes of searching and he found the trail.

fourteen

The trail was easy to follow, and they moved along at a steady gait. They rode north over sagebrush-flecked hills, in and out of spruce and piñon pine, talking rarely, for almost an hour. The sky, full of great, billowing clouds when they left the house, had darkened to a muddy purple.

When they reached a large rock-strewn clearing, Banjo pulled up and dismounted. He knelt down, examining something in the dirt. In a moment Steve bent beside him. Megan came near enough to hear but kept her mount.

"The tracks join some others," Banjo remarked. "It appears some other cattle were drove through here sometime yesterday."

"Other cattle?" Steve asked.

"Not ours. They're coming from the wrong direction." He continued scouting around, his eyes examining every mound of dirt, every chipped stone.

"Well, looky here," he said at last.

Megan walked her horse closer and stepped down. Her curiosity grew by the minute. She looked over Banjo's shoulder. Lobo sniffed all around the tracks.

"See these horseshoes?" he said, softly. "They have an *X* carved into them." Megan could see the print plainly. "That's the mark Logan Hohner puts on his own shoes."

"Logan Hohner? Whose range is this?"

"We're heading into a corner where the Circle C, the Rocking H, and Hohner's outfit meet up. I think we're at the edge of Harrington's range. If not, we're close to it.

"It wouldn't have been Hohner himself that came through here. He's always at the blacksmith shop in town. Must have been his boys." Banjo stood and knocked his hat to the back of his head. "I wonder what they was doin'."

A few drops of rain hit Megan's hand, and she looked toward the gray, swirling sky. Another drop hit her chin and another her cheek.

"There's a hollowed out spot in that boulder yonder." Banjo pointed to a rock face twenty feet high with a large stand of brush in front of it. "I've camped there a time or two."

Megan was surprised to see that behind the brush was an indentation in the rock about six feet by eight feet. They hadn't reached shelter any too soon. In seconds the rain was coming down like a heavy wind-blown curtain of water. From time to time a heavy gust blew some spray into the shelter.

Megan stood near the front watching the rain. Steve and Banjo moved inside to look around.

The remains of many campfires lay on one side with a little dry wood stacked not far away.

"Look at this." Steve picked up something from the ground.

"What is it?" Banjo asked.

"It's a twig." He held it out between thumb and finger for Banjo to see. "See how the bark is stripped halfway off, and one end has been chewed? It's not that old, either." He peeled a small piece of bark off. "See how much lighter the wood is under the bark? It hasn't completely dried out yet."

"Let me see that." Banjo stretched out his hand. "It looks mighty like the one I found at the Running M." He sniffed it. "It's juniper, too. It has a strong, sweet smell. It's a twin to the one I found after Harrington's murder."

"That's what I was thinking."

"Can I see it?" Megan asked, excitedly.

"Here." Banjo lightly tossed it to her. "Put it someplace safe." He turned back to the area he had been studying. "Let's look close. We may have hit pay dirt."

"This fire is only a day or two old," Banjo said, kneeling beside it. "Some of the coals are smooth, and some are jagged. The jagged coals are new."

"Let's quarter the area," Steve suggested. "I'll take the right side, Banjo." He held up a warning hand. "Don't come too close, Megan. You may ruin some good sign without knowing it. Stay where you are until we have a chance to look the place over real carefullike."

Leaning her shoulder against the rock, Megan fell into watchful silence. Lobo finally came in out of the rain. He sat by Megan's skirt, and she absently put her hand on his ruff. His fur was wet and foul. Disgusted, she looked at her grimy hand. It had a repulsive, wet doggy smell. She scrubbed at it with her handkerchief and made herself—and Lobo—an unspoken promise.

"Well, what do you know?" Banjo said in a half-whisper a few minutes later. "Here's a boot print. A clear one, not scuffed out like the rest. It looks like the ground was soft when he stepped here and it dried without being disturbed." He knelt on one knee. "Old boots, I'd say. Run-down at the heel. And a big man. Two hundred pounds at least."

"Any idea who it may be?" Steve asked.

"There's quite a few big men hereabouts." Banjo shook his head. "I wouldn't want to venture a guess. You got anything else?"

"No, can't say I do." Steve carefully searched the ground at his feet.

Megan placed the twig in the pocket of her riding habit. She resolved again to watch for a man who chewed twigs. Many men she had seen chewed straws. She couldn't remember anyone chewing a twig.

The rain had let up a little when Megan's stomach reminded her it was lunch time.

"I'm hungry." Megan's voice sounded small. The men turned quickly. They had almost forgotten she was along.

"Let's eat." Steve walked toward her. "I could use a bite myself." He ran through the rain to retrieve the lunch tin from Megan's saddlebag.

"That Harrington boy won't soon forget the whoppin' you gave him this morning," Banjo said, helping himself to a second piece of corn bread.

Megan, already finished, idly twirled a yellow cottonwood leaf with brown edges, holding the stem between her thumb and forefinger. She glanced at Steve who was wiping his mouth with the back of his hand, and waited tensely for his answer.

"I know it." He took a sip from his canteen. "He's a bully, but I don't want to kill him if I can help it, Banjo."

"I respect you for it, Chamberlin, but you'll have to be on your guard. I wouldn't put it past the young pup to burn the house around your ears if he happened to think of it."

The old panicky feeling came back to Megan in full force. "What are you going to do?" she asked Steve. "Even Susan's afraid of Beau. He may do something terrible."

"You don't have to be afraid of the house burning. The sides and back are wood, but they're solid logs." Steve lay back, an arm under his head. "It would take a mighty big match to get them going. Now the stable would be a different story altogether."

"Maybe Banjo should start sleeping in the house—" Megan stopped in midsentence. She suddenly realized what that would mean to her and Steve's arrangement. She bowed her head, pretending to examine the leaf in her hand to hide the redness she could feel warming her cheeks.

"No, Miss Megan," Banjo said. "I need to stay in the stable to keep watch. Who will warn you otherwise?"

"If we do have trouble at night," Steve added, "come to the house through the back door. Just bust in and get us up."

"I'll surely do that." Banjo rose stiffly to his feet. "That was good, Miss Megan. I sure am glad I don't have to live with my own cookin' anymore. And there's always plenty. I appreciate that, too. There was times when I was so poor and hungry I had to cut my corn bread in half so I could get enough to eat."

"Cut it in half?"

"Yeah, so I could have two pieces instead of one." Chuckling, he peered outside. "Rain's stopped. We may as well move on."

Shaking her head, Megan smiled at the joke. She picked up the lunch tin and followed the men.

The shower had wiped away the tracks, but Steve led out in the direction they had been following before the storm. Ten minutes later they came on six young Circle C cows bunched together by a stream. It was short work to drive them back to the herd.

❧

No one came to the clearing during the next week, not even Susan. The last of the canning was finished. The turnips were covered with straw so they wouldn't freeze in the ground and could be dug during the winter. Megan looked over her full cupboards with a deep sigh of satisfaction. The work had been hard, but now she was thankful.

She was pinning a last pair of jeans to the clothesline beside the house when she caught sight of Lobo lying on his back, legs spread-eagle, napping in the sun. Lobo was basking in the warmth, because the nights were windy and cold. The warm sunshine chased the gripping chill from his doggy bones. The smell of wood smoke from the fireplace and Banjo's potbelly stove in the stable made the air smell, as well as feel, like autumn.

Clothes basket in hand, Megan marveled at the change in the wolf-faced dog. His hipbones were no longer easy to see. He was quick to wag his tail and give short, happy barks when she played with him. He had lost his fear of Steve and Banjo, but barked ferociously when a stranger rode in.

She set the laundry basket in the kitchen and went out by the spring to dump out the dirty wash water. She wished Jeremy could see Lobo. They would love each other. The warm, soapy water sloshed as she raised the edge of the tub. She was about to give the final heave, but suddenly stopped.

Eyes on the few remaining soapsuds, she thought some more about Lobo.

"Lobo, my boy," she said aloud, "today is a red letter day for you."

She opened the back door of the stable and called the unsuspecting dog. Tail wagging, tongue lolling, he trotted into the stable. He licked her hand once before sniffing her skirt, the ground, the doorway.

"Come on, boy." She led the way through the door with Lobo close behind. "I know you think I have something for you to eat. . .get down! I don't want your dirty paws on my skirt." She looked at the spot. "Oh, well, I guess it doesn't matter. Who knows what I'll look like by the time this project is over."

She led him to the edge of the tub. How to go about getting him into the tub was the next problem, after that how to keep him there. She put her forearms under his middle near his front and back legs. He licked her face and uncertainly waved his thick tail. Megan gasped when she hoisted him into the water.

"You certainly have put on weight," she panted, her hands holding him firmly. There was marked doubt in Lobo's eyes now. He sniffed the surface of the water and looked longingly at the stable door he had just come through.

"Be still, Lobo," Megan said, soothingly. "It'll all be over in a minute. Make that five or ten minutes. I promise to hurry." She picked up the bar of soap and rubbed it over his back.

The transformation took fifteen minutes. In that short space of time Lobo's gray, matted fur turned ivory, the brown was rust-colored, the black dark gray instead of soot. Megan, on the other hand, changed from a neat, albeit slightly damp, housewife to a dirt-smudged, gray-flecked, dog-smelling woman. When she set Lobo free, he gave his shaggy coat a healthy shake to further adorn his mistress.

"What happened to Lobo?" Steve asked her that afternoon on their way to shoot targets. "He have a fight with a scrubbing brush?"

"You could say that," Megan laughed. "I stuck him in my wash tub after I finished the clothes." She looked lovingly at the fluffy animal at her side. It was hard to see a wolf resemblance now. She reached down to scratch behind a pointed ear.

"Do you want to go with me to Juniper tomorrow?"

"That would be nice," Megan answered, happily. "I have a letter to mail. I hope there will be one waiting for me, too." She broke open her rifle to check the load and then snapped it shut. "What are we shooting today?"

Her hopes were fulfilled the next morning when the young postmaster handed her a small, white envelope. She tore it open and scanned the contents. When she finished, the hand holding the letter fell limply to her side. She stepped outside and stood motionless on the boardwalk with the letter still crumpled in her hand. Jeremy had taken a turn for the worse. He was weak. The doctor was anxious.

Sheer willpower forced the tears back. Where could she hide to have a good cry?

"Megan!" Susan's voice startled her.

"Oh, hello." Megan shoved the letter into her skirt pocket.

"Bad news?" Susan asked, looking at her friend's strained face.

"Not really bad, just disappointing," Megan managed. "How are you?" She steered the conversation away from herself. If she had to talk about Jeremy now she would burst into tears.

"Not too good." Susan stepped close to the wall of the postal station, away from easy view. "I saw what Steve did to Beau's face." She held up a hand against Megan's reply. "I'm glad, Megan. He needed someone to bring him down a notch. He wouldn't show himself outside the ranch until yesterday. I got him to bring me into town today." She glanced up the street. "I can't let him see me talking to you.

"Be careful." Susan was in dead earnest. "Beau says he's going to settle accounts with Steve, and he doesn't have any scruples. Tell your husband."

"Thank you, Susan." Megan clasped Susan's hand.

Tears shone brightly in Susan's eyes. She gave Megan's hand an answering squeeze and hurried away.

The letter in Megan's pocket had drained all the pleasure out of the outing. She was all in before Steve was ready to leave. The buckboard was parked in the shade of Harper's Emporium so she put her few packages into the back and climbed heavily to the seat. Sitting in the shadow was much better than plaguing her shoe-pinched feet any longer. She lay her hand on her skirt and felt the paper crackle.

Poor little Jeremy. If only he could come to Colorado and play in the clear sunshine. She pictured him running free and strong in the meadow romping with Lobo. Another crackle of the letter in her pocket and the picture shattered, leaving a painful emptiness in the pit of her stomach.

Did I make the right decision? In trying to give him more than I could afford, did I take away what he needed most: love, security. . .myself?

"Bad news?" Steve asked when he joined her.

"Jeremy is worse." She tried to say it without betraying her agitation, but her voice cracked. She pressed her arms against her sides and smoothed her skirt with small movements.

"Is there anything I can do for him? Does he have the best doctors?"

"The best the sanitarium has to offer, I guess."

"Let me get him the best one in Baltimore."

"Do you know how much that would cost?"

"I know. But it doesn't matter. I'll go to the telegraph office and send Tump my instructions."

"I appreciate what you're trying to do, but the doctor alone will take up more than all my wages."

"Consider it a gift. No strings attached." He jumped to the ground. "No more arguments," he said, firmly. "It's settled."

She was relieved Jeremy would be getting better care, yet she wasn't sure how to take Steve's offer. Or his insistence. Why was he doing this? In all their struggles against poverty, her mother had never taken charity. She didn't want charity, either. Was that what Steve's gift was?

A flash of sunlight on silver caught her eye. It came from Clyde Turner, the Rocking H foreman, who was standing in front of the Red Rooster

Saloon. He was wearing black pants with silver studs down the sides. On his black boots were huge silver spurs. The pants were topped by a silky black shirt with a gray kerchief. Fascinated, Megan watched him. She had never seen a cowhand turned out like that before.

Arms folded, Turner loafed against the hitching rail. He kept looking down the street like he was waiting for someone. Henry and Al Hohner shambled down the dusty street and walked up to talk to him. Glancing around secretively, he spoke a few words to them and strode into the saloon, causing the doors to swing to and fro several times after he passed. Al and Henry continued down the street in the direction of their father's shop.

"All set." Steve was at her side before she saw him. "I left instructions that we are to be wired of his condition within the week."

Megan drew a deep breath. There was nothing more to say.

Scraping the hoof of a horse, Logan Hohner stood outside his black-smith's shop on the edge of town. He straightened and waved for them to stop when the buckboard drew near. Steve pulled up, and Hohner shuffled over to them.

"Gud afternoon, Mr. Chamberlin. Ma'am." The gap in his teeth was con-spicuous when he smiled. His jaw was coarse with a thick patch of stubble. "I vanted to tell ye that I doan mind de gossips und all de slander dey be speakin' about ye. Ye can come to me any time to have work done." He leaned forward, speaking in a loud whisper. "Dey lie about my boys, too. My boys is gud boys. Dey never did no rustlin' in dere lifes." He leaned back and stuck his thumbs under his over-stretched suspenders. "So you cum to Logan Hohner if ye need someding."

Megan absently watched the Rocking H hands ride out of town.

"Thank you, Mr. Hohner. I'll be sure to do that." Steve clucked to the horses and the buckboard jostled ahead.

When they were on the trail out of town, Steve cleared his throat. "I had an interesting conversation while we were in town. I saw Jim Sanders out-side the Emporium shortly before you came. As Banjo would say, he was as jumpy as a June bug at a poultry convention. He said not to worry, the gos-sip about Harrington's murder would die down before long. He thought Harrington deserved what he got. Whoever did it did a service to the com-munity, so to speak. Then he left at almost a dead run." He shrugged. "I can't figure out why he was telling me all that."

"I saw something interesting, too." She told him about the incident between Clyde Turner and the Hohner boys.

"Most cowhands couldn't afford that getup," Steve agreed.

"He's the foreman, though," Megan reasoned. "And the Harringtons prob-ably pay a pretty good wage."

"That Turner definitely reminds me of someone," Steve said. "The more I see of him, the more it strikes me. But for the life of me I can't put a name to him."

Suddenly, a shot shattered the afternoon stillness. The four horses pulling the buckboard instantly bolted. They charged down the rough trail as though driven by an insane wagon master. Bracing her feet against the front of the wagon, Megan gripped the seat, her knuckles white, trying to stay aboard.

"Whoa!" Steve shouted frantically. "Whoa!" Raising the reins high, he leaned back on the lines with all his might, but still the horses ran. The rushing wind caught Steve's hat, sending it sailing. The plain was a brown blur. On and on the buckboard flew, bouncing, swaying, careening down the trail.

Frothing at the mouth, eyes wild, the horses bounded on. Megan's arms ached from clinging to the seat. She knew she couldn't hold on much longer.

The front wheel on her side slid into a small gully, and she felt the wagon tilt. Scrambling, clawing for a hold, she heard the splinter of cracking wood and the terrified scream of a horse. The buckboard fell heavily on its side, throwing her to the stony ground. She had the sensation of falling, felt a stabbing pain in her right shoulder, and everything went black.

fifteen

"Megan? Megan?" A gentle hand touched her face. She raised her arm to touch the hand. The movement brought another stabbing pain to her shoulder, and she moaned.

"Megan?" It was Steve.

She opened her eyes to see him kneeling beside her, bending close to her face.

"My shoulder hurts when I move it."

"Don't try to move until I check it out." He rubbed gentle fingers over her upper arm and shoulder. "Tell me when it hurts."

"Now." She winced.

"Move your fingers. Okay, now your lower arm."

She had to force herself to obey, clenching her teeth against the pain.

"I don't think it's broken, but it may be out of joint. I'm taking you back to the doctor in Juniper."

She looked at his scraped, dirt-covered face so full of concern for her.

"You're hurt yourself," she breathed.

"Just a few scrapes." His jaw grew hard. "I wish I had the scoundrel who did this!"

"What?" His words frightened her.

"Someone burned Caesar's back with a bullet. That's what set the horses to running. You could have been killed."

He ran his hand through his wind-blown hair. "I've been a fool, Megan, thinking I could win against that Harrington outfit. We're bucking a stacked deck. I had no right to bring a woman out here in the first place." His eyes were windows to a tormented soul. "I think we ought to catch the next train back to Baltimore."

"But—" She tried to sit up, but the ache in her shoulder made her lie back. "We can't! Do you know what you're saying?"

"I can't stand to have them hurt you. Why can't they face me and fight like a man?" He slammed an iron fist into his callused palm.

❧

Dr. Leatherwood, the new doctor in Juniper Junction, told them the shoulder was only badly sprained. He bound it up and put her right arm in a sling.

"Wrap the shoulder in brown paper soaked in vinegar twice a day," he instructed as Megan prepared to go. "Leave it on for half an hour and then replace this binding." He was a young man, probably not much older than Steve. He was prematurely bald and his nose looked like it had been broken more than once. In fact, he looked more like a boxer than a doctor.

"You'll have to rest the arm for at least a week. Ten days if it still pains you." He handed Steve a small, brown envelope when they came out of the examination room. "Give her a little of this if she can't rest because of pain. And feel free to call on me again if you have any problems."

"Thank you, Doctor." Steve gave Megan a relieved smile and opened the door for her.

"You've already got it fixed." Megan looked at the front rigging of the buckboard where it had cracked.

"I took it over to the blacksmith while the doc was looking at you. He did a smart job."

"I'll say." She supported the sling with her left hand. "I wasn't looking forward to limping home like we did to get back to town." Her arm ached frightfully from her elbow to her shoulder and neck.

"You think you ought to lie down in the back?" He looked anxiously at her wan expression.

"I think the jarring of the wagon would be worse that way than if I sat up."

"I'll try to take it easy on the ruts."

"Just get us there as fast as you can," Megan said through tense lips.

It was an endless, grueling journey. Every jostle was an irritation, every jolt an agony. Darkness fell before they had reached the stand of pines and oaks around the meadow. The pain was nauseating. White to the lips, she clamped her arm against her middle to keep it still.

"Why don't you lean against me?" Steve asked, sliding close to her.

Weakly, Megan lay her head against his shoulder and closed her eyes. The change of position did ease her arm some. She was weary beyond endurance.

"You were right back there when I was spouting off. I don't want to leave the ranch," he said at length. "It's more than my father's inheritance. I've come to love the place."

"I know," Megan said, softly. "It's so good to have open spaces and fresh air after living in the city. If it weren't for Jeremy, I wouldn't ever want to go back."

"You know what I said about putting down roots here?"

"Yes," she said, wincing as the buckboard bounced into a dry puddle.

"I want do to that. Stay here and work the land, raise some beef. . . ." His voice drifted off, and they rode in silence the rest of the way home.

"Megan's been hurt," Steve told Banjo when they arrived at the stone house. "Ride over to the Rocking H and see if you can talk to Susan without anyone knowing. I don't want to cause her more trouble. Just tell her

Megan could use her help for a few days."

Ignoring her feeble protests, Steve carried Megan to the house and lay her on the bed. Tears of pain and exhaustion trickled down the sides of her face toward her ears.

"Here, take this powder. It'll help you sleep." He handed her a full spoon of powder stirred into a glass of water.

Raising her head off the pillow, she swallowed the medicine and shivered at the bitter taste. Steve took the glass from her hand.

"Thank you for looking after me," she said weakly.

"Don't talk." He turned down the lamp beside her bed until it was a dull glow. "I'll check in on you in a while."

The lamp was still glowing dimly when she awakened. A blanket covered her to the chin. She touched it, wondering how it got there. Sleepily pulling it aside, she sat up. She was thirsty. Thinking of the pitcher of water in the kitchen, she put her toes on the cold floor and realized for the first time that her shoes had been removed. She must have been sleeping like the dead to have stayed asleep when they were taken off.

Her shoulder still ached, but not as sharply as before. Moving slowly through the gloomy room, she reached the open door of her room and paused. In the fireplace hot coals glowed brilliant orange, casting an eerie light over the room. When her eyes adjusted she recognized Steve's figure rolled in a blanket on the floor in front of the hearth. His back was toward her, but she could tell from his position that he was asleep.

Putting her hand out before her like a blind person, she started across the room. She had taken only three steps when Steve rolled over and came to his feet in one move.

"What are you doing up?" He blinked and peered at her through sleep-dulled eyes. "You should have called me."

"I wanted a drink." She felt like a schoolgirl caught passing a note.

"Go back and lie down. I'll fetch it for you."

"Banjo left a message for Susan with Wyatt," he said as he gave her a glass of cold spring water. "Hopefully she'll be here in the morning."

Megan drank long and deep. The cold water felt good on her parched throat.

"You shouldn't take on about me so." She handed him the empty glass. "I'll be all right. There's nothing terribly wrong with my arm. It won't hurt me to move around some."

"Tomorrow you'll be sore in places you didn't even know you had. Take it from one who knows. You'll be glad I sent for Susan." He pulled the cover over her. "You need any more of that powder to get back to sleep?"

"I don't think so." She yawned.

"Well, if you need anything else give a holler. I'll be right outside."

&

The gray light of morning made a segmented square on the wall of her room. Half-asleep, she tried to roll over and felt a stab in her shoulder. The accident came back to her in the same instant. The creak of the opening front door had awakened her.

"How is she?" It was Susan's voice.

Steve replied, "She's sleeping. Seemed to rest fairly well through the night."

"What happened?"

Megan heard Susan's light steps cross the stone floor, and Steve told the story in five sentences. Susan, dressed in her black silk mourning clothes, was standing in the bedroom doorway moments later.

"Good morning." Megan tried to sound cheerful.

"I'm so sorry." Susan came to the bed and bent over her. "Does it hurt much?" She looked anxiously at the sling.

"Not so much now. It's a dull ache." She shifted her position on the bed. "Steve was right. I do ache all over this morning."

"You relax." Susan pulled off her black gloves. "I'll have you a nice, hot breakfast in no time." She was tugging at her bonnet strings as she went out.

"I've got some things to attend to on the range." Steve stepped into her room when Susan was gone. "I'll be back at supper time." He came a step closer. "You be good and stay quiet."

"The way I feel I can't do anything else." She tried to say it flippantly, but the words fell a little flat. Steve's expression unnerved her so much she couldn't think of anything else to say.

His face was full of compassion, but behind his eyes was something alive. He picked up her hand and held it between both of his. He didn't speak anymore, either, just stood there looking down at her. Megan felt strength in his gentle touch. She sensed fire beneath his tender concern. It gave her a sweet, warm feeling, but frightened her a little, too.

He replaced her hand on the quilt like a collector setting down a rare piece of crystalware; he took a step backward and went out.

She wanted to analyze his expression, relive the sensation of his hand holding hers, but it was too tiring. She nestled her head deeper into the pillow.

Brilliant light cascaded over the bed when Susan tied up the curtain. Megan squinted against the glare. She must have fallen asleep.

"I've brought you some hot biscuits and tea," Susan said, placing a tray over her knees.

"Thanks." Megan slowly and painfully eased up into a sitting position and adjusted the sling around her neck. "I don't know what I would have done if you hadn't come over."

Susan's smile matched the sunbeams spilling through the window. "Wyatt woke me up last night. He threw pebbles at my window. It was very romantic."

"Really?" Megan came to life. "Did he say anything else besides Banjo's message?"

"That would be tellin'." Susan laughed lightly and Megan noticed that though it was September, for Susan roses were back in season. "He said he'd come over here if he got a chance."

"What did you tell your brother? About coming over, I mean." Megan took a small bite of a buttered biscuit.

"I left a note saying that a friend of mine wasn't feeling well, and I'd be away helping her for a few days. What he doesn't know won't hurt him in this case."

"I hope you don't have any trouble because of me." The worried look returned to Megan's face.

"Never mind." Susan took the tray from Megan's lap. "Rest. You'll never get better if you lie there and fret. I'll have your brown paper and vinegar in a few minutes."

The stench of the vinegar was stifling but it did seem to help the pain as it soaked into her sore muscles. Slowly, Megan moved her lower arm up and down.

"It's a miracle it wasn't broken!" Susan exclaimed when she saw the dark blue bruise on Megan's shoulder and upper arm.

"I've never seen a runaway horse before." Megan shuddered. "And when the wagon started tipping. . ."

"Don't dwell on it," Susan interrupted. "Let's get the dressing back on now and you can have a rest.

"Would you like me to read to you or do you want to sleep?" she asked when Megan was lying down again.

"I'll sleep. I'm worn out. I can't believe how something so small can make me feel so tired."

Sometime later, the sound of the front door opening awakened Megan for the second time that day.

"Susan." It was a young man's deep voice.

"Hello, Wyatt."

"How's Mrs. Chamberlin?"

"She's resting." Light footsteps sounded on the stone floor. "Would you like to sit down?"

"I need to talk to you, Susan," he said, urgently. "Things are bad with you and Beau, aren't they?" Pause. "You don't have to tell me. I know they are. Why don't you come away with me? We can go to Montana or Oregon and start a life for ourselves. There's nothing left for us here."

"I wish I could, Wyatt, but it's impossible." There was a frustrated longing in her words.

"What's the holdup?" he demanded impatiently. "There's nothing to stand between us now."

"I can't leave Colorado without knowing who killed Pa. After the murderer is caught and punished I may consider it, but right now it's out of the question." She hesitated, then plunged on. "I've got to ask you something. Please don't be angry with me. I think I already know the answer, but I have to hear you say it."

"What is it?"

"Did you do it?"

"Kill your pa? Of course not!"

"I didn't think you did, Wyatt. I had to hear you say it." She sounded on the verge of tears.

Megan sank deeper into her pillow and closed her eyes. She didn't like overhearing their conversation.

"He was a scoundrel," Wyatt went on, "and I have to admit I hated him, but I didn't kill him. I was tempted to the night he turned me down, but I knew you loved him. Not that I could understand why you did. I would never do such a lowdown thing to you as that."

"You don't know how relieved I am. I've wanted to talk to you a hundred times since the funeral, but I was too afraid of being overheard."

"To tell you the truth, I think a rustler killed your pa. While we were on the cattle drive, I heard him talking to his foreman and one of the hands. He said he thought one of the hands must be in on the rustling, because it's been going on so long. This was the fourth year the count was low. And this year it was the worst of all."

"Do you have any idea who it could be?"

"It's hard to tell. There's quite a few of the hands may have done some underhanded things in their time. A person don't ask about those things. You know that." He paused. "Things are getting pretty rough at the ranch. Some of the hands are talking about asking for their wages. If it weren't for you, Susan, I'd pull out, too."

"Don't. Please, don't leave me there all alone."

"I was sort of hoping you'd see it that way." His voice surged with a strong undercurrent. "You haven't given me much encouragement the last while. I was starting to fear you'd changed your mind about us."

"I could never change my mind, Wyatt." Susan spoke softly, intensely.

Boots scraped against the floor, and a chair creaked. Then silence.

"I can't stay too long. Turner'll miss me and ask me a lot of questions I don't want to answer. He sure has been on the prod lately. He's about as easy to work with as an irritated porcupine."

After a few minutes of silence the door opened and the clumping of heavy boots on the porch told Megan he was gone. Megan lay still, feigning sleep when Susan came in. She was happy for Susan, but even as she rejoiced, she wrestled another emotion: a strange, deep yearning. It was the sweet agony of discovering a deep, pure vein of gold at the bottom of a craggy cliff, a cliff so loosely seamed that one blow with a pick would bring the mountain crashing down on the miner's head.

It was the knowledge of something precious with no hope of having it for her own. She savored the new sensation, and tried to understand it.

sixteen

"How are you comin' on, Miss Megan?" Banjo asked the next evening. He and Steve sat by Megan's bed for a chat after supper while Susan finished the dishes.

"Restless." Megan sat propped against some pillows. Her arm was still too sore to move freely.

"I rode back to the place where the horses stampeded," Steve said, "but I couldn't find a clue."

"Who would do such a terrible thing?" Megan asked, cradling her sling in her strong arm.

"Someone who wants to get rid of you folks mighty bad," Banjo offered.

"Wyatt was here today," Megan said. "He thinks Harrington had an idea that one of his own hands had a part in the cattle rustling."

"The Rocking H hands are a hard bunch, but I've my doubts that any of them would be a thief," Banjo said, thoughtfully. "'Course, there are a couple new ones I don't know so good."

"Wyatt said they've had cattle missing for four years now," Megan continued. "It would have to be someone who has been with them longer than that."

"I'd have to study on it a while, I reckon." He shifted in his chair. "With your permission, Chamberlin, I'll ride over toward that corner of the range we were on a few days ago and have another look-see. I believe the man who stood under that shelter the night Harrington was killed is the same man who was in that cave."

"Shoo, you men," Susan scolded from the door. "Can't you see Megan's tired?"

"Susan's making herself right to home," Banjo said to Steve with an unusually serious expression. "Reminds me of a sergeant I knew in the Confederate army."

"Don't pay him any mind, Susan," Megan advised, smiling. "He's like a toothless lion, a big roar with nothing to back it up."

"Everybody around here knows Banjo," Susan countered, "and we make allowances for the aged and infirmed."

"All right." Banjo chuckled. "I know when I'm bested."

Later that night Steve came into her room, closed the door, and made up his bed on the floor where he'd been sleeping since Susan came. He paused, blanket in hand.

"Still hurt bad?" he asked, referring to her arm.

"Not as much as at first, but it's still sore. I expect Susan will be able to go home day after tomorrow."

"I don't think she's in any hurry." He spread out the blanket and sat on it. "I feel for her, living with that hot-headed brother of hers."

"So do I." Megan turned her face toward the wall and closed her eyes. She lay a long while half-asleep, missing Jeremy and Em, thinking of Susan and Wyatt, listening to Steve's deep, regular breathing as he slept on the floor at her feet.

≥≥

"I found it," Banjo announced the next day. The three of them sat around the table after Megan's first lunch outside her room. Susan had ridden home for some fresh clothing. "The purtiest little box canyon you ever did see."

"Where?" Steve asked.

"A little north of where we found the camp. It's Hohner's range. I'm sure of it. A hundred acres of nice grazing and a stream running through one end. Had maybe two hundred head of cattle. Good lookin', young stuff. I'd say they're all two years old or less.

"I scouted around and found another camp near the stream. And get this," he leaned forward, "it had the same marked horseshoe tracks and the same juniper twigs."

Steve whistled softly.

"Most of the cattle were too young to hold a brand, but I saw a couple steers with a doctored Circle R. The top half of the brand was new, hadn't healed proper yet. It's my guess they're Rocking H cattle."

"What are you going to do?" Megan asked.

"Sit tight," Steve answered. "We don't know who's doing it yet."

"But it must be Logan Hohner," Megan persisted.

"Not necessarily," Banjo said. "I think someone is using Hohner's land without him knowing it." He paused and shifted his toothpick to the other side of his mouth. "Knowing Logan Hohner, he hasn't seen that canyon for a couple o' years." He shook his head. "His boys are probably in on it in some way, but I think we need to look a little further before we can find the person behind it, the rottenness at the core."

"You think someone is putting Hohner's boys up to it?" Steve asked.

"That's about it. Those Hohner boys aren't smart enough for a long-term operation like this'n. Their boss has to make a slip-up sometime, and with us knowing what to look for, we should be able to catch him."

≥≥

In a few days, Megan's arm was in working order again. It was weak, and she had to rest often, but she was able to carry out her household chores.

The promised telegram from the new sanitarium made Megan cry from glad relief. Jeremy was responding to the more expensive treatment. The doctor was encouraged by his progress in the few days he had been there. She hugged the news to her like a woolly blanket on a cold, wintry night.

"The circuit riding preacher is coming through next Sunday," Banjo said, pausing after breakfast. "I wondered if you were feeling up to attending. I plan on going myself. A body don't get much chance to hear real preaching in these parts."

"I'd love to go," Megan said. "I'm sure Steve'll let us use the buckboard. Maybe he'll want to go himself. I'll ask him."

Steve shook his head doubtfully when she brought up the subject that evening.

"That's all right. You and Banjo take the buckboard and go," he replied. "I'll stay here and look after things."

She was disappointed by Steve's blunt refusal to join them, but the feeling was short-lived. She was too excited to let anything dampen her spirits. This would be the first church service she would attend as a Christian. She was looking forward to it even more than she had the frolic.

The buckboard rattled over the leaf-strewn trail on that fine, hope-filled Sunday morning. Only Billy and Star were hitched up today since they weren't going for supplies. It was a cool, crisp day. Megan pulled her white, knotted shawl closer around her pink dress with the starched white collar. She took a deep breath of the tingly breeze. Beside her, Banjo looked like a stranger in his carefully brushed black suit and black string tie. Without its usual growth of stubble, his face looked like a freshly skinned squirrel.

"Preacher Tyler is a young feller, but he can really preach." Banjo tugged at his celluloid collar. "He's been traveling through these parts for purty nigh three years. Don't have no real home. He keeps moving from place to place. Goes all the way from Montana to Texas, I hear." He glanced at Megan. "Don't expect no fancy sermonizing like that city feller from Denver who preached at Harrington's funeral. But you'll carry something home with you to hide in your heart against the hard places in life."

"Do many people come to the meetings?"

"Quite a few. Most of them because they go to every social gathering that comes along. But there are a few real saints in Juniper. I'll be proud to introduce you to 'em."

"I'm looking forward to it, Banjo."

The schoolhouse was half-filled when they arrived. The desks had been removed and long, backless benches filled the room. They were crammed so closely together that Megan could barely get her skirts though the aisle.

Banjo found seats for them near the center of the room. The seats near the windows were already taken, and the air felt stuffy. A hushed buzzing hovered over the group as folks chatted before the service. Megan recognized Mr. and Mrs. Harper coming in. They nodded, unsmiling, in her direction and found places on the far left. Elaine Sanders gave her a small, noncommittal wave from across the room where she chatted gaily with a blond young man Megan didn't know.

A steady stream of people poured in until the room was packed shoulder to shoulder, knee to back. Megan's light, cotton dress, so cool this morning, was becoming itchy with its high collar and long sleeves. Megan tried not to fidget, but she was impatient for the service to begin.

The sermon was simple and direct. In spite of the warmness of the room and the closeness of the congregation, Megan forgot all but the power of the message. The preacher's dark suit was shiny at the elbows and knees, and there was little to draw the eye to his rawboned, pock-scarred face. But Megan had never seen a man so completely absorbed in his message. She could tell he really believed what he preached.

"You must be born again," he urged, his voice quiet, intense, as he pleaded with the lost. And on he spoke, "Why call on the Lord and then not do the things He commands you to do?"

Megan's spirit was gripped. At the end of the message, she stood with others who wanted to surrender to God's will for their lives. Yet even as she stood, there was confusion and anxiety inside her soul. What of her marriage to Steve? What of her future?

She brushed her anxious thoughts aside to nod and smile in response to Banjo's introductions after the service. She especially liked Mrs. Stowe, a small middle-aged widow with wavy, chestnut brown hair and a motherly smile.

"Be sure to stop and have a cup of tea with me when you're in town," Mrs. Stowe urged. "I'd love to hear about Baltimore and the East. I'll pray for your brother, too," she promised when Megan told her about Jeremy.

Megan was touched by Mrs. Stowe's sincere kindness and promised to stop and visit the widow when she came to town.

The preacher's quick smile and friendly handshake were also encouraging.

"I'm glad to see you take your stand for Christ, Mrs. Chamberlin," he said. "I'll be sure to pray for you in the days to come. Satan would like to discourage you, but God is a strong tower. When you feel temptation, run to God and He'll keep you safe." He gave Banjo a friendly punch in the shoulder. "You can depend on Banjo to give you good advice if you need it. We go back a long way together. He prays for me. It's folks like him keep me on the circuit."

It was an hour past noon when they set off on the trail out of town. They had barely passed the last frame building when Banjo untied his string tie and pulled off his collar.

"Excuse me, Miss Megan, but I can't abide this contraption any longer. Puts me in mind of being tied with a rope halter." He stuffed the black string and bit of celluloid into his shirt pocket.

Megan picked up the basket of food she had packed for their lunch and handed Banjo a thick beef sandwich.

"Much obliged," he said, taking a bite.

Lost in thought, she finished her lunch and packed away the leftovers. What about her marriage to Steve? What of the future?

seventeen

"There's power in the blood, power in the blood. . . ." Banjo's song reached far across the brown, evergreen-spotted hills. When they started to climb the mountain trail, he stopped singing. "I don't want to be buttin' in where I don't belong, but it appears to me something's troublin' you, Miss Megan," he said. "I don't want to know your business, but you know I'd do anything I can to help."

"I know you would, Banjo," Megan replied, carefully. "I'm thinking of the decision I made this morning and wondering what the future holds for me." She looked at her hands, clasping and unclasping them in her lap.

"It's Chamberlin, ain't it?"

Megan pressed her lips together and nodded. "You see, we don't have the usual relationship." She turned her head away from him, gazing out over the bare trees and rocks. Feeling a chilly breeze, she tightened the shawl around her shoulders. "We're really married, and all, but we're not. . . ." She sighed. "It's hard to explain."

"I knowed it. I knowed it all along."

"You knew? How?"

"You told me yourself." He smiled at her doubtful expression. "Oh, not in so many words. But you didn't act like a young newly married couple. I'm no spring chick. I've been down the pike and across the river, you know. And one morning I came to the house early for breakfast and I saw him coming down from the loft. It didn't take much figuring to work it out."

"I met him only a few weeks before we came here. He had to have a wife to fulfill his father's will. We have to live on the ranch for a year in order to collect his inheritance. He actually hired me to do it." She pressed her lower lip between her teeth, unable to go on.

"You did it for Jeremy, didn't you?"

Looking down at her restless hands, she nodded.

"He had to go to a sanitarium, and I didn't have the money. It is legal. The marriage, I mean. We didn't cheat on that."

"So what's got you so wrought up? You and Chamberlin seem to hit it off all right."

"Next May he's going to have the marriage dissolved, and I'll go back to Baltimore. I g–guess it shouldn't matter to me." She dabbed at the tears, blinking others back. "Jeremy is getting better, the doctor said. It's just that when I think of having to leave someday, I get all scared inside. I don't know what will happen to me."

"You're in love with him, aren't you?"

Megan stared at him. She wanted to cry out, "No, I'm not!" but her lips were silent. Was she in love with Steve? She couldn't say no. If she had said the words they would have been a lie.

Like a priceless gem, she held the knowledge at arm's length and examined it against the light, marveling at its sparkling facets. It was too brilliant. Her eyes couldn't stand the brightness. She pushed the thought aside. Her future was too uncertain.

"I shouldn't have told you about the marriage," she said in a moment.

"You didn't tell me, remember? I already knew." The wagon paused on the edge of the stream. He clucked to the horses, and the buckboard rattled down the bank. "There's a verse in Proverbs says, 'Trust in the Lord with all thine heart; and lean not unto thine own understanding. In all thy ways acknowledge him, and he shall direct thy paths.' You've been trying to carry the load your ownself, Miss Megan. Give the problem to Jesus. The Lord will take care of the future."

෨

Letting the Lord take care of the future wasn't always easy as windy and cold October became icy November. True, Jeremy was better. With the help of a kind nurse, Em sent glowing letters that thrilled Megan. Jeremy was able to sit in chair for an hour at a time now. He gained strength by the day.

In spite of the good news, the feeling of emptiness lingered. Since her talk with Banjo, Megan was intensely aware of Steve. It was exhilarating torture. Secretly she scrutinized his every word, every expression hoping vainly for a sign that he cared for her. He was polite, even deferential, but no more.

When the feeble light of a frigid November morning crept into the kitchen, she parted the curtain to see snow silently sifting down from a steel sky. The roof of the stable was covered in downy white, and little mounds were forming on top of each aspen post of the corral. Excited, she dropped the curtain and ran to the front windows to look at the meadow, fast disappearing under a fluffy, cold blanket.

"It's snowing!" she called to Steve when she heard the scuffling of his boots overhead. "It's snowing!" Happy as a child on Christmas morning she skipped about the kitchen, popping a pan of biscuits into the oven, stirring the oatmeal with flourish.

The snow fell for three days, filling the meadow until not one nubby corn stalk could be seen and forming white winter blossoms on the trees. The house was tolerably warm as long as the fireplace blazed and the kitchen stove glowed. Megan despaired of ever being able to keep the kitchen linoleum clean with the constant tracking in of snow-laden boots from the stack of wood behind the house.

Because of the bitter cold Lobo stayed in the stable with the horses and Banjo's potbelly stove, but every day Megan disappeared under wool wraps, scarves, and mittens to walk with him in the yard. She scattered crumbs for the ravenous birds and then knelt down to study their star-shaped tracks in the snow, wishing there was some way to preserve such a pristine art. She and Lobo played and ran until numb feet and chattering teeth forced her back to the throbbing, aching warmth of the roaring fireplace.

On the morning of the second day Megan was surprised when Steve came into the kitchen while she was washing the breakfast dishes.

"I want to make a built-in sideboard in the dining room. I was wondering where you thought would be the best place to put it."

She stood on the edge of the room taking stock of the oak table and the two windows.

"Why don't you put it in the corner? The depth of the corner would make extra storage space without taking so much space from the room."

"Good idea." He walked to the corner and spread his hands. "From here to here?" He nodded, considering. "And a small cabinet overhead with glassed-in doors for pretty dishes would be nice, too, wouldn't it?"

"That would be nice."

"I've been saving some wood for the project. It's in the stable. We may as well use up all this empty time doing something useful." Shrugging into their heavy coats, he and Banjo went out the back door and came back carrying some wide pine boards. They moved the table into the living room and soon the air was filled with the rasping noise of sawing interrupted by loud pounding.

"Never use nails on furniture," Banjo said philosophically as he whittled a peg. "Like the Good Book advises, you don't put new wine in old bottles. Well, you don't put iron nails in good furniture."

"That your interpretation?" Steve asked, smiling.

"Sure, from the book of Banjo Calahan." Banjo chuckled. "You know, Chamberlin, the Good Book does have plenty to say about life that's for our good. It's not just for women and old folks. Like in Isaiah, 'Though your sins be as scarlet, they shall be as white as snow,' or in Matthew 'I am not come to call the righteous, but sinners to repentance.' "

Steve picked up the saw and drew it loudly across a board. Smiling to himself, Banjo picked up another scrap of wood to whittle.

"Haven't you ever thought about your soul?" Banjo continued when Steve lay down the saw.

"Not much." Steve gave Banjo a calculating look.

"You ought to. Young fellow like you has a long future ahead of him. Jesus can make all the difference as to how things come out."

"That your sermon for today?" Steve asked, mildly, picking up the hand drill.

Megan heard their conversation from the kitchen. "Please, God," she prayed, "convince him that he needs You."

If only Steve were a Christian. Maybe then things would be different.

The men were still working on the cabinet when she sat down to write a letter to Jeremy. She wanted to tell him about the snow. If he were able to be here he'd be rolling in the cold whiteness with Lobo, his cheeks ruddy with good health and a happy, secure life.

What would happen to them when she went back to Baltimore? Another squalid tenement house? She shuddered. How could she go back to the city now? "Oh God," she prayed, "help me to trust and leave the rest to You."

❧

The weather warmed up a little after two weeks of near-zero temperatures. The snow melted, leaving the ground soggy. Great puddle lakes lay across the meadow. Cold, damp, and miserable, Steve and Banjo slogged back to the house after the evening choring.

"I believe I like the snow better than the slush," Steve remarked, warming his hands before the fireplace. "This dampness goes plumb through a body."

"Soup's ready," Megan called from the kitchen. Hot food warmed their insides and cheered the men considerably. They were lingering over steaming cups of black coffee, enjoying the peacefulness of the evening when a commotion in the stable broke off the conversation. Lobo was barking frantically, loud, angry barks with no letup. A horse gave a piercing whinny and there was the scuffling noise of pawing hoofs.

"Smoke!" An acrid smell and the scream of a horse reached Megan the same time as Banjo's cry.

"The stable! The stable's on fire!" Banjo overturned his chair in his hurry to reach the back door.

On the run, Steve grabbed his gunbelt from its peg and followed him.

"Get the stock behind the house," Steve called as they banged out the back door. "And if Harrington's men are out there, heaven help 'em if I get my sights on one of 'em." The back door crashed closed, and they were gone.

From the kitchen window Megan could see smoke billowing from the far side of the stable. She grabbed the water bucket from the counter and ran to the back door in time to see Steve struggling to get panic-stricken Candy out of the stable.

"Steady, girl," Megan called, soothingly. "Steady, girl." She set down the bucket and walked slowly toward the horse.

Candy turned her head in Megan's direction and nickered. Holding her hand out, Megan walked on until she held the horse's bridle.

"Tie her to the side of the spring house," Steve called and ran back inside the stable. Banjo led Kelsey and Bess out as Megan drew Candy along. The presence of the other stock calmed the mare, and Megan was able to tie her without any difficulty.

Billy and Star bounded from the smoke-filled stable, their eyes rolling in terror, making it hard for Steve to keep them from rearing up. Tying them with hasty fingers, Steve raced back to the stable as Caesar's screams rose to a crescendo. Banjo held the horse's halter. He had to step nimbly to avoid the gelding's flying hooves.

"Megan, get in the house!" Steve yelled. He grabbed the halter on the other side so he and Banjo could force the horse into the fenced-in corridor. Thrashing and heaving, Caesar fought them. His front hoof caught Banjo on the leg, throwing him to the ground. Steve held on with both hands, talking, pleading with the horse. The fire roared higher behind them. Rearing high, Caesar raised Steve off the ground then bolted, dragging Steve along.

"Let him go!" Banjo shouted. "He'll kill you!"

Throwing himself clear, Steve fell into the freezing water of the stone basin. Caesar bounded forward toward the only opening he could see, and he galloped headlong over the cliff. His terrified scream turned Megan's blood to ice.

Teeth chattering, limbs shaking, Steve walked to the edge of the house and looked down. He stayed there only an instant.

"It's as b–black as p–pitch down there," he stuttered, coming back. "I c–can't see a thing." He walked past Megan to where Banjo lay. The air was thick with heavy smoke and the hissing and popping of burning wood. Inside the stable a heavy timber crashed to the ground.

"You've got to get into some dry clothes or you'll freeze," Megan cried after him. She raised an arm to shield her eyes from the smoke, blinking as she peered after Steve.

"The f–fire will keep me from freezing. We've got to s–stop the flames from reaching the house."

"I'll help you tear down the fence." Banjo struggled to his feet.

"Chamberlin!" Beau Harrington's adolescent voice called from the darkness. "This is just the beginning, Chamberlin. Next it'll be the house. Or better yet, we'll string you up to the highest cottonwood around. Won't we, Turner?"

"Turner!" Steve's voice bellowed above the roar of the inferno. "I know you, Turner. Come out in the open, you yellow dog, and fight like a man!"

"It would be your funeral, Chamberlin." A second voice called back. "No two-bit riverboat gambler could hold a candle to me!"

"Keep talking, Turner. I've almost got it."

"Got what?" The voice was edgy.

"Your real name. It'll come to me sooner or later."

The only answer he received was the volley of pounding hoofbeats retreating across the meadow.

eighteen

With strength that came from desperation, they tugged and tore at the smoldering wooden fence until there was a sizable gap between the house and the stable. Without a thought for her bruised, scraped hands, Megan worked on. Hauling bucket after bucket of water, they drenched the fence and the side of the house, praying all the while the wind would not blow in their direction.

"The chickens!" Megan cried. "What about the chickens?"

"I think the coop is far enough from the stable to be out of danger," Steve said, wiping his smoke-bleary eyes with his sleeve, "but I'll go open the door so they can get out just in case."

The roof of the stable collapsed with a jarring, scraping crash, sending a shower of sparks into the black sky. It startled Megan and broke the last thread of her endurance. She walked over to Candy and leaned forward, resting her head on the mare's neck. She didn't want Steve to see her, but she couldn't hold in tears any longer.

"Come." Steve's hand was on her arm. "Let's go inside. You're all in."

Megan washed the smeary soot from her face and set on the coffeepot. Steve climbed to the loft in search of dry clothes while Banjo hobbled in, painfully favoring his right leg, and sat down at the table.

"Is your leg okay?" Megan asked, worried.

"It will be in a day or two. It's just bruised. We can thank the good Lord no one was hurt any worse tonight. Trying to get a spooked horse out of a burning building is dangerous work. Your husband is a brave man."

Megan felt tears welling up again, hot, furious, revengeful tears. The hay and fodder they had carefully stored were gone as well as the buckboard and saddles. With six animals to feed through the winter the loss was devastating.

"I could find it in myself to hate Beau Harrington," she said as she brought the coffeepot and three cups to the table. She sank into a chair and put her hands over her face.

"I know how you feel, Miss Megan," Banjo replied. "Just you remember, the Lord doesn't play any favorites when it comes to sin. Our sin is just as wicked in His sight as Beau's."

"I can't understand how anyone could be so vicious. We have a deed to this property. We've never done anything to hurt the Harringtons. We're right and they're wrong. So why are we the ones suffering?"

"I don't claim to understand it myself. All I know is that boy needs the Lord. Just the same as you and me."

"I guess you'll have to take the loft, Banjo," Steve said later. "No doubt it'll be more comfortable than the stable was."

"I'm much obliged." Banjo said slowly. He bent over to rub a spot below the knee. "But I don't know if I can climb the ladder." He took two steps, testing his leg. "I'd best bed down in front of the fireplace tonight." He looked at Megan. "That is if you have an extra blanket."

"Oh, Banjo," Megan cried, "all your things were in the stable. You didn't even mention it. Of course I have a blanket. And anything else you need."

"Beggin' your pardon, ma'am, my Sharps was in the house, and Kelsey's safe out back. Long as I've got them and the Lord that's all I need. The only thing I regret is my Bible. It's been with me since I got out of the army. I rode nigh two hundred miles to get it. But I'll get another'n one day." He sank to a chair, his face tense as he eased his leg.

"I'll get the blanket right away." Megan hurried to her room for the blanket, wondering at Banjo's matter-of-fact attitude through this entire ordeal.

"Why don't you let me have a look at the leg?" she asked as she arranged the blanket on the couch. "I may be able to do something for it, you know."

"Just let it rest tonight, Miss Megan."

"Megan's a hand when it comes to doctorin'," Steve said, coming to stand near her, close enough for his arm to brush hers.

"Tomorrow," Banjo insisted. "All I want now is a little rest." He lay down, rolled up in the blanket, and was still.

Megan rinsed out the coffee cups. Her mind was fuzzy with fatigue, her body weary beyond the point of exhaustion. She traced her way to her room hardly aware of her surroundings, but she turned around, startled, when she heard Steve follow her inside.

"How are we going to handle having Banjo in here?" he whispered after firmly shutting the door. He glanced at the floor. "I don't relish the thought of sleeping on the floor for the duration of the winter."

"I'm afraid I have something to confess." Megan avoided his gaze. She was afraid what she had to tell him would make him angry. "Banjo knows. About us, I mean."

"What?" His brows drew together.

"He's all right. He won't tell anyone. I was upset one day and he asked me about it. I guess I just blurted it all out." She turned away from his frown. "I know I shouldn't have. If it was anyone else, even Susan, I wouldn't have told. But Banjo's different."

Steve studied her a moment before his expression relaxed.

"I guess it's just as well under the circumstances. You're right on two counts. You shouldn't have told. And Banjo is different. I've never met anyone like him." He pulled his gun from its holster and checked the load. "I've got to see about Caesar. I can't let him lie down there with a broken leg or worse to suffer through the night." He put his hand on the door latch. "I couldn't rest if I did."

Megan crawled between the stiff, cold sheets and lay back with a deep sigh. Her eyes were so heavy she expected to drop off to sleep right away. Her eyes stayed closed but sleep didn't come, for her ears were straining, her mind wondering what Steve would find at the bottom of the cliff.

She must have dozed, because the sound of a single shot jerked her awake, and made her heart race. When the awful reality came to her, she turned her face into her pillow and wept.

❧

Shivering with cold, Megan hurried into her clothes before dawn the next morning. With shaking hands she added small logs to the glowing orange coals in the kitchen stove and put on the coffeepot. Banjo hadn't moved when she tiptoed past, so she worked quietly, trying not to waken him.

She mixed the pancake batter, set it aside for frying when the men were ready, and sliced bacon into a pan. A quick glance out the kitchen window stopped her in midmotion and made her go back for a longer look. Before her lay the blackened, still—smoldering remains of the stable. It was nothing more than a flattened heap of rubble with the old potbelly stove standing toward the back. Across the yard the chickens hopped in and out of the open door of the henhouse scratching and pecking about.

Megan tore herself away from the window when she heard Steve's tread on the loft ladder. She added coffee grounds to the boiling pot and set the cast-iron skillet on the stove.

"Sleep okay?" Steve pulled a chair from the table and sat down. Dark circles rimmed his bloodshot eyes.

"Well enough." She greased the skillet with a piece of bacon and poured on some pancake batter.

"I had to put Caesar away." He ran his hand through his hair. "Both front legs were broken."

"I heard." When the first pancake was done she added a little cold water to the brewing coffee. Filling a thick, white mug to the brim, she set it on the table in front of Steve.

"I've got to ride over to Hohner's spread to see if he'll loan me a wagon and if he can sell me some hay for the stock. Buying feed is going to take most of our profit from the corn crop," he added bitterly.

"What about making a profit to meet the terms of the will?"

"We still have the cattle. If I have to I'll sell them all in the spring. We'll still get by." He hit a hard fist on the table top. "If I had that Beau Harrington where I could get at him. . . ." His eyes narrowed. "Not only him. That Turner fellow. I was awake most of the night trying to remember how I know him. I finally figured it out.

"He was in the Confederate army. But his name wasn't Turner, it was Taylor. Charlie Taylor.

"He joined our outfit outside of Chattanooga. We used to pass the time playing poker for pennies when we had them, or else we used match sticks. Anyway, we were having a friendly game and my friend, Ted Miller, was winning. The boys used to kid me about being a riverboat gambler and losing to Ted, who was a farm boy." He stared into space, absently running his forefinger along the rim of his coffee cup.

"Ted and Charlie were the only two left in the game when Ted showed three aces. Charlie was mad as hops. Stood up and called Ted a cheat. Well, Ted pulled a knife and they set to. Like magic, Charlie had a knife in his hand, too. I never did figure out where he got it from.

"They came at each other and Ted cut Charlie a bad one on his cheek. Ted stepped back and about that time Charlie flipped that shiv to where he held it by the tip and threw it right into Ted's heart. Ted dropped like a stone. I don't think he even knew what hit him."

"What happened to Charlie?"

"They took him to the hospital. We pulled out shortly after that, and I never saw him again."

"Did he know you could use a knife?" She piled three pancakes on a plate and brought them to the table with a jar of sorghum.

"Come to think of it, he probably did. We used to practice pitching sometimes. He could have seen me. Offhand I can't remember ever holding a conversation with the man. That's why it took me so long to place him." He poured a generous amount of sorghum on the pancakes and ate like a man with an appetite.

"I'll ride Billy bareback to Hohner's," Steve said later as he set a pail of Bess's milk on the counter. "Should be back well before noon."

"Please be careful," Megan pleaded. "They'd have no scruples about ambushing you if they could."

"You watch yourself," Banjo called from the table where he was finishing a piece of bacon.

Later, Megan was wrapping Banjo's bruised shin in brown paper and vinegar when the drumming of a running horse drew her to the front window. Riding a horse Megan had never seen before, Susan raced into the dooryard. She wore a brown coat and her Sunday bonnet.

Megan threw open the door to catch the panting young woman by the arm and draw her inside.

"What's happened?" Megan demanded, fear overtaking her.

"It's Beau," Susan gasped. "He's getting the men in town stirred up about Pa's murder. They're organizing a lynching party to come after Steve."

"Sit down, child," Banjo commanded. "Get hold of yourself, so you can tell us the rest."

Susan pulled at the buttons on her coat until she managed to get it off and hand it to Megan. Her hands trembled as she struggled to untie the strings on her bonnet. She sat in a chair near the blazing fireplace. Her breathing was more regular, but panic lingered beneath the surface.

"Beau took some of the hands into town this morning. They kept laughing and saying they were going to celebrate. I couldn't understand it all." She clenched her white hands in her lap.

"I went along to see Mrs. Mullins, who has a new baby. I think the men had already been drinking a little from the way they were acting." She shuddered. "When I came out of the Mullins's house I saw a commotion in front of the Gold Mine Saloon. Beau was standing on a barrel in front of the crowd. I walked close enough to hear him call out that Steve Chamberlin had killed Pa. Clyde Turner got a rope off his saddle horn and held it up." She squeezed her eyes shut. "It was awful. When I saw what they were up to I ran to the telegraph office and asked Tom to wire Denver for the marshal, then I ran back to Mrs. Mullins and borrowed a horse. I had come in with Beau in the buckboard."

"What are we going to do?" Megan asked Banjo.

"Sit tight until Steve gets back. He'll be here directly." He pulled the paper off his leg. "In the meantime, bring me my Sharps." He pulled down his pants leg and stood holding the back of the chair. "I'll set by the window and keep an eye on things."

"Mrs. Mullins loaned me a Winchester," Susan said.

"You wouldn't fight against your own brother!" Megan was horrified.

"Don't count on it." Susan's mouth was set in a hard line. "After all I've been through with him in the past few months, I'd be likely to do just about anything."

Megan dug every bit of ammunition from the kitchen cabinet and set the boxes on the sideboard. She took the Henry from the wall and lay it beside the bullets.

"May as well put on some more coffee and fix some vittles," Banjo said. "It's hard tellin' how long it'll take them to get here." Holding the rifle across his lap he stared out the window. "They'll probably stop at the saloon and drink to their plan before headin' out. Bunch of coyotes."

"Here comes Steve in a buckboard full of hay," he announced an hour later. "Looks like he did right well for hisself. Hohner let him have another horse to help pull it."

Steve pulled the buckboard behind the standing length of fence. He climbed into the back of the wagon to throw hay to the stock before coming in the back door.

"Beau Harrington is stirring up a lynch mob in Juniper to come after you. Susan rode out to warn us," Megan blurted out from the back door.

"How many?" Steve asked, stepping past her into the house. He walked to the sideboard and looked at the weaponry spread there.

"Twenty-five or thirty if they all come," Susan said, quietly.

"She wired for the marshal," Banjo said, "but it'll take him a day to get here."

"We'll have to stand them off." He loaded the empty chamber in his six-shooter, snapped the magazine shut, and replaced it in his holster. Striding to the ladder, he brought his other pistol down and loaded it. A strained, suspenseful silence saturated the room. Megan, preparing lunch, wondered how long she could stand the tension. Had the fire been only yesterday?

nineteen

"Here they come!" Banjo's words late that afternoon brought everyone to their feet. Clutching her rifle, Megan took up her post by the living room window, heart racing, mouth dry. She looked past the edge of the window to see a small group of riders enter the clearing. They rode close together. Beau's pinto was in the lead.

"When they get in range, dust them," Steve ordered calmly.

Raising the window a small crack, Megan knelt and rested her rifle on the sill. To her, the men outside were no longer fellow human beings; they had become the enemy who wanted to destroy what she loved. Swallowing hard, she took up the slack under the trigger and waited. She heard Lobo's excited bark near the front of the house.

"Now!" A volley of shots rang out at Steve's command.

As one man, the group wheeled and ran for the shelter of the trees. There were a few answering shots then all was still.

"Don't let them fool you; they're still there." Banjo eased his leg as he leaned forward. "I wonder how cold they'll have to get before they give up."

But they didn't give up. After an hour of waiting, a thin plume of gray smoke rose above the trees.

"They've built themselves a fire," Steve commented. "Looks like they'll be staying a while."

"Long's we've got food and ammunition, we'll be all right. The law will be here directly," Banjo said, dryly.

"What if the marshal won't listen to us?" Megan spoke for the first time.

"He'll listen," Steve answered. "That Walker's a square dealer. He doesn't want to hang the wrong man."

"I hope you're right," Megan answered doubtfully.

"Let's take turns watching, Banjo," Steve said, stretching. "No need for all of us to watch all night. I don't think they'll be doing anything drastic right away."

Shortly after dark, Lobo's barking intensified. He was behind the house now.

"Call off the dog!" A young man's voice called from the stable ruins. "I'm coming to join you."

"It's Wyatt!" Susan cried, running for the back door. Megan was closer. She unbolted the door and called, "Down, Lobo!" Lobo growled softly, the fur on his back standing up. "It's okay. Wyatt's a friend." The canine trotted to Megan and put his wet nose under her hand.

Susan slipped past Megan and raced to Wyatt. She threw herself at him with such force he stepped back, off balance.

"Now that's what I call a welcome!" He put his arm around Susan's shoulder. "And what, may I ask, are you doing here?" He guided her inside the house.

"I came to warn them this morning when I saw what Beau was up to."

"So that's where you went off to." He squeezed her gently. "I was powerful worried about you when you disappeared.

"Chamberlin," he turned to Steve, "I ride for the brand, but there comes a time when a man has to stand for what's right. What Harrington's doing is right lowdown, and I can't abide it any longer." He looked down at Susan. "Are you with me?"

"I've always been with you." She smiled tremulously up at him.

"What are they planning to do?" Steve asked.

"The gang? They don't really have no plan. Just starve you out as far as I know. Beau and some of the hands were pretty bad off for liquor when I left. And the rest were getting tired. They'll probably sleep it off until early morning unless someone gets a bright idea before then.

"This place is a fortress. It's almost impossible to get within shooting range without getting shot first. I slid in on my belly right next to the rock face, but I doubt any of them are that determined. Might ought to keep a watch thataway, though."

"Lobo will keep watch," Steve replied.

Wyatt and Susan settled on the sofa in the flickering glow of the fireplace, the only light in the room. Steve relieved Banjo at the window, and Megan tried to keep from nodding as the heat from the fire relaxed her weary muscles. Hands clasped under his head, Banjo stretched out on his back before the hearth.

"This is cozy as a goose in a corncrib," Banjo drawled. "It'll be good havin' another man to spell us with the watching." He looked over at Wyatt. "Feel up to takin' the next round?" Suddenly, his expression changed. He stared at Wyatt's feet stretched out, ankles crossed, before him.

"Sure. I can take it." Wyatt noticed Banjo's wrinkled brow. "What's the matter?"

"Where'd you get those boots?"

"Bought them in Cheyenne this spring. There's an old timer up there who makes them." He looked down at the feathery pattern stamped on the light brown leather. "Why?"

"Were you wearin' 'em the night Harrington was killed?"

"I reckon." He sat up straighter. "I've worn 'em to all the occasions since I got them." He stopped. "Wait a minute. Wait. . .a. . .minute." He stared overhead. "I didn't wear them that night. I hadn't intended on going because I was sick all day. Clyde Turner broke the heel off his good boots. We're about the same size, so I told him to go ahead and wear mine. Then I got to feeling better. I hated to disappoint Susan so I shined up my old black boots and went anyway. I let Clyde have my new ones. I didn't want to take them back after I told him he could have them."

"I found those boot prints at the edge of the clearing where Harrington was killed," Banjo explained. "More than likely the man who wore them killed Harrington. The murderer stood there a while, dropped a green juniper twig he'd been chewing, and stepped out like you do if you're throwing a knife."

"You mean Clyde Turner was wearing those boots that night?" Steve spoke from the window.

"Does he chew green juniper twigs?" Megan asked, now wide awake.

"He chews some kind of wood. I don't rightly know if it's juniper or not. I never looked close." Wyatt looked around. "You think Clyde did it? Why would he do a fool thing like that?"

"We haven't put it all together yet," Steve said, "but I think we're finally barking up the right tree."

"Well, I'll be." Wyatt propped his right ankle on his left knee. "You may have a loop on the right steer at that. He sure has been coming off all high and mighty since Harrington died. Especially with the hands."

"He makes me feel creepy inside." Susan moved even closer to Wyatt.

❧

Before daylight the next morning Megan broke the thin layer of ice on her wash basin and bathed her face to drive sleep from her eyes. She had left Susan sleeping in the bedroom to stir up the fire in the kitchen stove, add a few small logs, and set on the coffeepot.

"Been a long night," Steve commented from his post. His face was grizzled, his hair tousled. Only his keen eyes seemed the same as they had been last night when she had finally gone to bed. Wyatt was stretched out on the floor, and Banjo snored softly on the sofa.

"Coffee'll be ready soon." She pulled the flour bin from under the counter. "If that'll help." She smiled in his direction.

"Having someone to talk to helps." He leaned back, resting an elbow on the back of his chair. "I took over for Banjo about two hours ago. Nothing's moving out there as far as I can tell."

"I hope we don't have to pass another night like last night." She scooped some flour into a large bowl. "What are we going to do?"

"I'm not planning on being the main attraction at any neck stretching party. I can tell you that." He rotated his shoulders, working out the kinks. "If we have to fight, we'll fight. If the marshal comes, and we can convince him I'm innocent, we'll do that."

It was a haggard crew that gathered at the breakfast table at dawn. Susan's face was strained, her eyes seemed too large for her thin face. She hovered near Wyatt, speaking little and glancing often toward the front windows. Megan bustled about setting on the oatmeal, biscuits, and bacon more from the need to stay busy than from any need to hurry.

"With your permission, Chamberlin," Banjo said as they sat to the table, "I feel the need to ask the good Lord's help during this day. Would you mind if I said a short prayer before we ate?"

"Help yourself, Banjo. We can use all the help we can get."

Megan watched Steve closely to see if he was making light of Banjo's request, but his face was expressionless, his eyes serious. He bowed his head, studying the edge of the table while Banjo prayed.

"Dear Lord, we know You have a reason for everythin' that comes into our lives. I pray that You would watch over us today. Protect us from harm and teach us all to trust in You. Amen."

A dreadful lethargy caused by weariness and anxiety hovered over the stone house that morning. Conversation lagged. Everyone was too consumed with his own thoughts and fears for small talk. The sun was high above the horizon before the long-awaited something happened.

"Chamberlin! Come on out. I want to talk to you. It's Ben Walker, the marshal."

"It may be a trick." Megan took a step in Steve's direction.

"That's Walker's voice all right." Steve peered out the window, keeping his body behind the stone wall. "I can see him. He's astride his horse to the north of the meadow. The gang is behind him."

"Yes, sir, Mr. Walker," Steve called back. "But I'm keeping my guns."

"Keep them. I only want to talk to you."

Megan could scarcely breathe as she watched Steve check his guns, slide them loosely in their holsters, and walk to the door. Putting on his hat and buffalo coat, he went out. Swiftly putting on her wrap and picking up her Henry, she shoved a handful of shells into her pocket and followed him. Banjo had already stepped through the door ahead of her, buffalo gun in hand.

Banjo stopped five yards behind and to the right of Steve at the edge of the dooryard. Megan stood a few feet from Banjo. She could feel her pulse pounding in her neck. Her eyes were riveted to the men in front of them.

Megan sensed someone walking up behind her. She turned to see Wyatt pass by her and stand a few feet to her left, his shooting iron ready. Susan stood on the edge of the porch huddled in her coat, looking small and helpless. But the rifle she held was neither small nor helpless.

twenty

"There he is, Marshal! Take him!" His breath billowing out in white clouds as he spoke, Beau stepped his horse ahead of the ten to fifteen men behind the lawman. Their number had diminished considerably during the freezing night.

"That's high-handed talk comin' from a fellow whose sister stands with the other side," Banjo remarked, dryly. His voice, though not loud, carried far in the icy air.

"The rest of you brave hombres are hangin' far back for men acting in the cause of justice," Banjo continued. His voice was thick with sarcasm. "You, Harper." The storekeeper jerked his head around at the sound of his name. "Are you here because you think Chamberlin's guilty, or because it's Harrington money that keeps you in business?

"And Jim Sanders. If Chamberlin were hung for the murder of Harrington it would take suspicion off you, wouldn't it?" Sanders studied the ground. "Everyone remembers the old score you had with Harrington." Banjo's eyes shifted to the two hulking figures in the rear.

"I can't say I'm surprised to see you, Henry. Al. You know where your bread's buttered, don't you?" As each man heard his name, there was a marked change of attitude. The thought uppermost in each man's mind was how to bow out without losing face.

"Marshal, I'd like to swear out a warrant," Steve said.

"You'd like to swear out a warrant?" Beau's look was lethal enough to kill a rabbit at twenty yards.

"Quiet, Harrington," Walker ordered. "Let him have his say."

"I'd like to swear out a warrant on Clyde Turner, otherwise known as Charlie Taylor, on suspicion of the murder of Victor Harrington."

Turner stiffened. He slowly took from his mouth the twig he was chewing.

"He's talking through his hat, Marshal," Turner said easily, back on balance again.

"Check that twig he has in his hand," Steve countered. "How many men do you know that chew juniper?" He reminded Walker of the twig found at the Running M after the murder and told him of the matching twig found at the campsite near the Hohner range.

In a furtive movement, Turner flicked the twig he held away from him.

Sanders saw what Turner was up to and slid from the saddle to pick up the twig. He handed it to Walker.

"You've got to be crazy," Turner said, angrily. "Why would I want to kill my own boss?"

"Maybe because he was getting too close to catching you rustling his cattle," Steve said. "Right, Henry?" Henry Hohner's jaw dropped open, his buckteeth sticking out. Seeing his reaction, Steve plowed on. "We found that pretty little box canyon on the Hohner range. The perfect place to hide stolen cattle until time to take them to the railroad. You boys had a real nice setup, didn't you?"

"It wasn't us!" Panic-stricken, Al spoke up. His eyes turned toward Turner. "All we did was pick up a few cows and keep them hid away. He did all the rest," he babbled, jerking his horse's head back as he sawed the reins.

"You idiot!" Furious, Turner railed at Al, the scar twitching as he spoke. "Don't you know what he's doing? He's trying to trap you into admitting something."

"Turner's knife-slick, Walker," Steve continued. "I knew him in the war. His real name's Charlie Taylor. I saw him throw a knife and kill a man. It took me a while to place him because of that scar. But I know him all right. If you look a little deeper I believe you'll find he's been prodding young Harrington and fomenting the trouble we've had between us."

"He's right, Marshal." It was Curly, the bald, Rocking H hand that spoke up this time. "I've heard Turner making hints and pushing young Harrington. Us boys have had about all we kin take. I say he's your man." He walked his horse across the field to Steve and turned around, watching Clyde Turner carefully.

Slowly, thoughtfully, Slim and two others joined him.

"I don't know about the rest of you folks," Sanders said, turning his horse, "but I'm heading home. I can smell a polecat when I get next to one."

Turner cast an ugly glance in his direction.

Pointedly ignoring him, Sanders prodded his horse to a trot. The rest of the townsfolk followed, leaving Beau and Turner alone with Marshal Walker in the meadow.

"Stay where you are, Turner." The lawman's revolver was in his hand. "You're riding back with me. I'll get your accomplices, by and by. Right now I want you." He took Turner's guns, pulled two pigging strings from his saddle, and tied Turner's hands to the pommel.

"I should have killed you, Chamberlin!" Stark hatred glared from Turner's weasel face. "I should have killed you when I first recognized you. You are the only one who knew who I was. I tried on the trail, but I missed. All I did was burn your horse and see if he'd do the job. If I had made that shot I could have had it all. The Rocking H and everything that goes with it."

"Your days are over, Turner." Steve spoke without rancor. "There's no place here for your kind."

Beau had not uttered a sound throughout the unfolding of the facts about his father's death. He watched the marshal take Turner away as though he couldn't quite understand what was happening.

"Kill him, Beau!" Clyde Turner yelled in a desperate try for revenge. "Kill Chamberlin! He's the cause of all your trouble! Kill him!"

Marshal Walker silenced Turner with a lash of his quirt. He grabbed the reins of Turner's horse, and they trotted into the trees.

Absently looking at the spot where they disappeared, Beau was as still as though carved in marble. The four Rocking H hands slowly followed the marshal. Wyatt returned to Susan on the steps. Their footsteps and the creak of the door told Megan they had gone inside. Banjo relaxed, resting his rifle in the crook of his arm, barrel down. He stepped forward to meet Steve as they broke ranks. Megan, too, stepped forward. But a movement caught her eye. Looking back she stopped dead in her tracks, horror gripping her.

It happened in an instant, a split second. There was no time to cry out, no time to warn Steve. There was only time for action. Totally by reflex, Megan raised her rifle to her shoulder as Beau Harrington sighted his Winchester at Steve. Their shots, only a fraction of a second apart, sounded as one.

But Megan was too late.

Beau dropped his rifle and grabbed his right biceps, but Megan had already forgotten him. She had eyes only for Steve sprawled on the snowy ground before her, a thick red stain spreading from a point just above the knee of his left leg. Banjo already knelt beside him.

"Get a cloth to tie around his leg to stop the bleeding!" he ordered.

Megan pulled her handkerchief from her sleeve. Quickly Banjo tore the thin white cloth in half, tied the ends together, and wrapped it tightly around Steve's thigh. He and Wyatt carried him, half-conscious, to Megan's room where they put him on the bed.

Steve's eyelids fluttered. He opened them wide and tried to sit up.

He fell back with a groan. "What happened?"

"That fool boy Harrington shot you in the leg," Banjo said between tense lips. He stepped aside so Megan could cut away Steve's trouser leg with a small pair of scissors. "Wyatt's going for Doc Leatherwood." He laid his hand gently on Megan's arm. "You know what to do. I'd best go have a look at the boy out yonder."

Megan didn't answer. She was only conscious that the bleeding must be stopped. She was terrified that the bone might be broken. She raced for a bowl full of flour from the bin. Taking a handful of flour, she packed the wounds, front and back, and wrapped the leg tightly with a wide strip hurriedly cut from a sheet. Susan's sobs reached her from the living room, but she paid no mind. There would be time for Susan later.

Rushing to the closet, she found the paper of powder given her by the doctor for the pain in her shoulder. She poured a generous portion into a glass, mixed it with a little water, and held it to Steve's lips.

"What's that?" he grimaced, then shivered.

"For the pain." She smoothed his hair back from his pain-creased brow. *There's so little I can do,* she agonized. *If something happens to him, how can I go on without him?*

She remembered the sound of his anxious voice calling her name when she was lying on the ground beside the overturned buckboard. She thought about his strong arm around her, supporting her on that torturous journey home. His insistence on getting Jeremy better care. Their quiet walks and talks beside the lake. He was security, comfort, and happiness to her as she had never known before.

With unspeakable dread she watched the crimson stain spreading over the bandage.

"Please, God," she begged with all her being, "stop the bleeding and let him get well. I know it may be selfish, but I can't face life without him."

Yet, even as she prayed she knew she would face life without him next spring.

She walked into the living room when she heard the front door close.

It was Banjo. "How is he?"

"Dozing off and on. I gave him some of the pain powder I had left." She wrung her hands. "How long until the doctor can get here?"

"It could be another two hours, it could be tonight. There's no way of tellin'." He pulled off his coat and hung it on a peg. "Your brother's not hurt bad, Miss Susan." On the sofa, leaning against the back, Susan lifted a red, puffy face from her arm. Her breath came in ragged sobs. "He only got a flesh wound in his upper arm," Banjo told her.

"I didn't intend on killing him," Megan said, reasonably. "I figured if I shot his gun arm it would stop him."

Eyebrows raised, Banjo stared.

"You intended on shootin' his arm?"

"Yes. Why?"

"Well, I'll be a jackrabbit's hind leg. It must have been a hundred yards."

"Where is he?" Susan stood and leaned to look out the window.

"He was on the ground trying to get a grip on his Winchester when I went out. He was whining like a baby. Somehow he'd managed to get his bandanna tied around the wound. I tried to help him, but he swore at me and knocked my hand away. Didn't say where he was headed, but he was in a big hurry to get there."

"I'm sorry, Susan." Megan put her hand on her friend's shoulder.

"I'm not upset about that. Beau got what he's been asking for. It's hearing about Pa's murder that's got me upset. To think that Clyde Turner was the one. Just remembering all the times I was near him makes my insides turn over."

The doctor arrived shortly after noon. With haunted eyes Megan watched him unwrap the wounded leg.

"How bad is it, Doc?" Steve asked through thin, white lips.

"I've seen worse." After cleansing the wounds, Dr. Leatherwood made a close inspection. "I doubt that the bone is broken, but you'll have to take it real easy on the leg for a month or so." He smiled at Megan. "It's a good thing your wife knew how to stop the bleeding so soon. If she follows my instructions as well as that you should be up and around before long." He rebandaged the leg, gave Steve another dose of powder, and stepped outside for a word with Megan.

"You did fine." He nodded appreciatively to Megan as Banjo looked on. "I'm glad the bullet passed clean through. The wound will drain better, and we won't have to go through the ordeal of digging out a bullet. Change the bandage and put on antiseptic twice a day to try to ward off any infection. That's the biggest danger. Infection. Here's some more of that powder. Don't give it to him unless he needs it, but he'll be needing it for the next two or three days." He put on his hat. "I'll be back around to see him day after tomorrow."

The doctor's words eased Megan's fears a little, but the possibility of infection was an ugly specter hovering over the sick man's bed. Megan had to force herself to leave him long enough to do a minimum of cooking and washing. She wanted to be with him every second.

⁂

"I've been a fool," Steve said tersely through the pain the next day.

Concerned, Megan felt his forehead before answering.

"No, I'm not delirious," he said, ruefully. "I'm thinking more clearly than I have for years." Beads of sweat stood out on his forehead. Megan wiped them away with a cool cloth. "A few inches higher and I'd have been a goner, Megan. It's put me to thinking about what my life means. If it's really important." He took a sip from the glass she offered him.

"You're tiring yourself by talking so much," she cautioned.

"I've got to tell you this," he insisted with an impatient wave of his hand, "so don't stop me." He paused while she pulled a chair close to his bed. "I guess I've been turning it over in my mind for a long time, but it never struck me as so important until now. I'm talking about my standing with God. Like you and Banjo have been trying to tell me. I want to make peace with God and let Him have what's left of my life."

Megan's hand crept to his brow again. It was cool and clammy.

"I don't think I'm going to die, if that's what you're thinking." He attempted a weak smile. "I want to be ready to live."

"I'll get Banjo." Forgetting her coat, Megan flew from the house to where Banjo and Wyatt were building a makeshift stable. "Steve wants you, Banjo," she panted. "Please come."

Banjo dropped the board he held and followed Megan. When they reached the house, she caught his sleeve.

"He says he wants to make his peace with God."

"What? Is he worse?"

"I don't think so. He says he wants to get ready to live, not to die, and he wants to live his life for the Lord."

"Thank God," he breathed. "If you'll get me your Bible, I'll go in."

Megan fetched the sacred book from her trunk and handed it to Banjo. She listened as Banjo explained the story of salvation in the same simple way he had told her.

"Just tell God you're a sinner, and you want to claim the blood of Jesus to wash away your sin," he concluded.

Pain-wracked as he was, Steve's voice was strong.

"Lord, I want You to save me. I'm a rotten sinner. I know Jesus died for me, and I want You to take my life and make something useful from it. Amen."

Megan's eyes were misty when she looked up. She was surprised to see tears streaming down Banjo's face.

"I believe I could use some of that powder, Megan." Steve's face was ashen. His eyes closed as Megan scurried to bring him what he had asked for. He swallowed the medicine without opening his eyes, and sank back to the pillow.

Outside the bedroom door, Banjo drew a large red handkerchief from his pocket and loudly blew his nose.

"I tell you seein' someone born into the family of God is almost as good as bein' born again yourself," he said, wiping his eyes.

"God sent you here, Banjo," Megan said with conviction, love welling up inside of her. "I'm so glad He did." Her voice quavered.

"Thank Him, not me." His voice was husky. "All I did was tell you. God made it real in your hearts."

❧

The next evening Steve felt well enough to have Banjo visit for a few minutes.

"You wouldn't believe the shootin' that little lady did that morning," Banjo declared. "She saw Harrington draw and in one motion sighted and shot him in the arm. She hit what she shot at. Dead center."

"Is that right?" Steve looked over at Megan's faint blush.

"I did it before I thought." She was almost apologetic. "All I knew is that for some insane reason Beau had decided to kill you and I had to stop him."

Steve grinned at Banjo. "I'm glad she's on my side." He shifted to a more comfortable position. "What happened to Beau?"

"He lit a shuck. Took some stuff from the ranch and they haven't seen hide nor hair of him since. Miss Susan's takin' it pretty good, considerin'. I guess she's glad to have some peace after all the trouble. She's got spunk, that one. She made Curly foreman and had to talk with the men, Wyatt tells me. They're all staying on."

≈

The next long week, Megan nursed the man who was her husband in name only. It was gratifying to feel the closeness she sensed between them since he accepted Christ. They had quiet chats when he felt up to it, and she shared with him how God had given her a peace she could not explain through the past months of hardship.

She was with him every available minute of the day, feeding him hot soup when he could swallow it, boiling water for preparing fresh bandages, changing linen, and doling out pain powder until she fought collapse.

"Megan." Steve caught her hand as she passed by. "You're pushing yourself too hard. It'll be no help to me if you wear yourself out to the point where you have to be cared for yourself." He had shown encouraging signs of improvement the last two days. "Go up to the loft and lie down. Banjo can get me anything I need when he comes in from choring."

"But—"

He waved aside her protest.

"Go. That's an order."

It took her last bit of strength to climb the ladder and lie down on Steve's cot. Her head hurt. Her eyes closed before she touched the pillow. The house had a tomblike silence and it was fifteen hours before she opened her eyes again.

≈

"It looks good," Dr. Leatherwood said a few days later as he replaced the bandage. "We want it to heal from the inside out, not close over too soon or the wounds will fester." He winked at Steve. "You've got a good nurse there."

"I know it." Steve smiled at Megan. "She's done everything but pass her hand over the place and say, 'Be healed.'" Some of his original color had returned, though he still had spasms of pain now and then.

"How soon can I walk on it?"

"If you had a crutch you could get up now." The doctor buttoned his buffalo coat around his thick neck. "But under no circumstances are you to put any weight on it." He picked up his bag. "And take it slow at first. Fifteen minutes, then twenty, and so on."

"Will do." Steve shook Leatherwood's hand. "And thanks.

"Thanks to you, too," Steve said to Megan when the doctor had gone.

"You're getting better. That's thanks enough." Confused, Megan picked up his water pitcher and carried it to the spring to refill it. She yearned to be near him, but she wanted to run away from him at the same time. She was afraid. Afraid he might not care, afraid she was reading things into his words that didn't exist.

❧

"When Susan was here today she told me she and Wyatt are planning a December wedding," Megan remarked to Steve as she sat by his bed the next afternoon. She was cutting bandages from a large piece of white cloth.

"So soon?" He looked up from the newspaper Banjo had brought from town.

"It's long enough, after all they've been through. I know it hasn't been a year since her father died, but she's all alone with Beau leaving her like he did. Folks should understand." She avoided his eyes, so probing and somehow close these days. "I got a letter from Em, too."

"How's Jeremy?"

"Out of the woods, thank the Lord. I can't tell you how relieved I am. Em says he may be able to leave the sanitarium in the early spring." A clammy hand squeezed her heart at the thought of returning to Baltimore. "I'll be back sometime around then."

"Will you?" Something in his voice forced her to look at him. His gaze pierced to the core of her being.

She didn't know how to answer his question. She knew she must go back East no matter how much she longed to stay. She must look after Jeremy. Tormented thoughts cascaded over her as she stared at him, her throat too tight to make a sound. She looked away, cutting blindly at the cloth, wishing she could hide from him. He was torturing her by looking at her like that.

"Megan." He laid the paper aside and sat up. "Megan, don't run away from me. I can't stand it any longer. Please."

Against her will, she raised her head and met those eyes again.

"I don't want you to go, Megan. I want you to stay." He searched her troubled face for the answer. "I know I'm not the greatest fellow that ever came along, but I love you, Megan. With all my heart and soul, I love you. All this," a wide sweep of his hand included all that lay around them, "would be worthless to me if you weren't here."

Her lip began to quiver, and her eyes filled with tears. She pressed her eyes tight and looked down as the tears spilled down her cheeks.

"My dear." Anxiety clouded his features. "I'm sorry if I've upset you."

"No. It's not that." She shook her head, fumbling for her handkerchief. "I just. . .don't know what to. . .it's what I've been asking the Lord for ever since I've been saved. Of course I'll stay."

Sunbeams broke through the clouds like the first bright rays after a storm. He reached out and grasped her wrist, pulling her to him. Her scissors clattered to the floor, but no one heard.

"I can't believe it's true," Megan whispered in a moment. A lone tear trickled down her cheek, inconsistent with her glorious smile.

Steve took her handkerchief and dabbed at the spot.

"If you're happy, why do you keep crying?"

"I don't know," she said with a little laugh. "I can't help it."

"We'll send for Jeremy as soon as he's released."

"And Em," Megan added. "Don't forget Em." She nestled her head on his strong shoulder.

"Certainly Em. When you answered my ad, you were so scared and brave at the same time that it changed something inside me. I wanted to help you, to protect you from all the trouble you were having. That's why I was so anxious for you to come with me."

"Why didn't you tell me before this? There were times when I thought I'd die if you didn't care."

"When I got to know you I saw what a conscientious, uncorrupted person you are, Megan. I'm nothing but a riverboat gambler. I couldn't ask you to stay with the likes of me."

Megan shook her head. "I never felt that way."

"Back then that possibility never occurred to me, but when I turned my life over to God all those guilty feelings disappeared. I began to wonder if I may have a chance with you now that we share the same faith." He gave her a loving squeeze. "I want to build a new life, Megan. With you."

He tilted her chin up so he could look into her eyes. "There's only one thing I regret."

"There is?" Flickering doubt crossed her face.

"Yes. I can't ask you to marry me."

"Oh." The smile reappeared. "Well, you could say it anyway."

"Will you be my wife, Megan?" Infinite tenderness was in the question.

"Yes."

The fear, the empty longing, the anguish were rooted out and washed away by a flood tide of joy.

ત

Whistling softly to himself, Banjo came into the house intending to ask Steve how he wanted the stable door set. When he reached the open door of Megan's room, he drew back. It took only a fraction of a second for him to realize how matters stood. Without hesitating he tiptoed out of the house and quietly closed the door behind him.

When he reached the middle of the yard he couldn't hold the joy in any longer. He let out a thundering, "Eee–hah!" and raised his hat in salute. A song gushed out with all his strength behind it.

"I will praise Him!
I will praise Him!
Praise the Lamb for sinners slain;
Give Him glory all ye people,
For His blood can wash away each stain!"*

Megan heard his words, and her spirit joined in the benediction. She wanted to shout.

---

*Great Hymns of the Faith, ed. John W. Peterson (Grand Rapids: Singspiration Music, 1980), p. 464.

Her Father's
Love

Nancy Lavo

NANCY LAVO
Nancy is a gifted author from the big state of Texas where she lives with her husband and three children. She authored three complete novels for the **Heartsong Presents** series. *Her Father's Love* was her first historical title. She wants to write stories in which the spiritual aspect gets equal time with the physical aspect of romance. The message of salvation through Jesus Christ is a very important part of Nancy's life and she tries to share that through her characters.

one

Seth,

I will be brief. Yesterday, I received an offer of marriage on behalf of Elise from Mr. Percival Bennett, of the Boston Bennetts. Mr. Bennett is a solid, dependable gentleman of excellent family and, at twenty-two, Elise is certainly of marriageable age.

I consider it a good match and plan to accept his offer on her behalf.

Due to the increased expenses that I will undoubtedly incur in the upcoming months, I must insist on a significant increase in my monthly allowance.

Claudia

"Rosa!" Seth Garver stormed across the library and threw open the heavy paneled door with a crash. "Rosa!"

A honey-skinned woman emerged from the kitchen, calmly drying her hands in her apron.

"What are you shouting about?" She tossed her long braid over her shoulder. "You sure got yourself worked up—" She stopped in midsentence to study the expression on his reddened face. "Señor Garver, are you all right?"

"It's the old crab. She's done it again." Seth began to pace across the polished plank floor, his boots pounding an agitated rhythm. "But this time she's gone too far."

"Old crab?" Understanding dawned slowly across Rosa's face. "You must mean Claudia's at it again." Her concerned frown melted into a laugh. "What does she want this time? By the look on your face, it must be more money."

Seth stopped in midstride. His voice was a strangled whisper. "It's Elise. She's gonna marry off my Elise." He resumed his frantic pacing. "I've got to stop her."

Rosa stepped into his path, hands planted firmly on her hips. "What do you mean she's gonna marry off Elise?" she demanded. "What are you talking about?"

"This!" Seth shook the paper he clutched in his fist. "Some fella wants to marry Elise, and Claudia's going to let him." He paused briefly to scan the missive then read aloud, "Mr. Percival Bennett. . .a solid, dependable gentleman." He glared at Rosa. "What kind of description is that? Sounds more like my mule than a suitor!" He waved the offending letter in the air. "And what kind of name is Percival, anyway? Sounds uppity, if you ask me."

"Never mind the name," Rosa snapped impatiently. "Can she do it, Seth? Can Claudia really do it?"

Seth said nothing as he ran trembling fingers through his salt-and-pepper hair. "I've got to get her home," he mumbled finally. "I've got to see her. Twenty-two years old. . .it's been too long." He sidestepped Rosa to pace more rapidly.

Rosa raised a skeptical brow. "Señor Garver, if I'm recalling correctly, Claudia said she'd never send Elise here." As an afterthought she added, "Unless you were dying, of course."

"Dying." Seth halted his pacing. "Dying?" he repeated. A hint of a smile touched his lips. "Dying! Now why didn't I think of that?"

"Señor Garver," Rosa warned, alarmed by the glimmer she saw in his eyes. "You're as healthy as a horse; you and I both know that."

"But Claudia doesn't."

Rosa tried again. "Señor, I can see trouble in those eyes of yours. It's lying you're talking about. And lying's a sin."

Seth was grinning broadly now. "Desperate times call for desperate measures."

⁊⦁

"Do you mind if I take this seat beside you?"

Elise looked up from her well-worn copy of *Mrs. Rhoades's Complete Handbook of Courteous Behavior and Social Graces for Young Women* and smiled politely at the ruddy-faced woman standing beside her. "Not at all. Please, sit down."

With a groan, the woman eased her bulky frame into the seat. "I always look for someone to talk to when I travel. Seems to make the time pass faster." She offered her chubby hand in greeting. "I'm Mrs. Mavis Teekle, from Fort Worth."

Elise hesitated for a split second, nibbling her lower lip with uncertainty. Aunt Claudia had been most insistent that she was not to speak to anyone while traveling, citing endless examples of the treachery that awaited unsuspecting women travelers.

She slanted a gaze toward her companion. The woman did not look dangerous and it had been such a long, tedious trip. Perhaps one short conversation would not hurt anything.

Still, she vacillated. To defy Aunt Claudia would be unthinkable.

Her next thought settled the matter once and for all. Decorum. Hadn't Aunt Claudia drilled into her the importance of showing respect to elders by speaking when spoken to? Dangerous or not, Elise would converse with

Mavis Teekle. After all, it was the proper thing to do.

With a warm smile, Elise accepted the older woman's hand. "How do you do. I'm Elise Garver, from Boston."

Mavis's small eyes opened wide. "I should have guessed," she clucked admiringly. "You city girls are always at the height of fashion, aren't you?"

"Ma'am?"

"Just look at you. All gussied up in that pretty, pink-colored suit with a red blouse and a bright blue hat to match. Country folks like me would never have the sense to put them colors together."

Elise felt the blush creep across her face. "Actually—"

"From Boston you say?" Mavis interrupted. "That's a long way from home for a pretty young woman like you. Now don't tell me; let me guess." She studied Elise momentarily. "I know. You've come to Texas to meet your betrothed. How exciting!" She clasped her hands together gleefully, obviously enraptured with the romantic notion.

Elise shook her head. "Oh, no ma'am, nothing like that. I'm on my way to Crossroads to meet my father."

"Oh." Disappointed with Elise's answer, Mavis slumped back against the seat.

"But it really is quite exciting," Elise insisted. She leaned toward the woman and added in a whisper, "You see, I haven't seen him since I was three years old."

"Mercy!" Mavis was on the edge of her seat once more, her attention riveted on Elise. "You haven't seen your own father since you were three?"

Elise nodded. "My mother died then, and my father sent me to Aunt Claudia's in Boston—that's my mother's only sister—to raise me. I've been there ever since."

Mavis laid a consoling hand on Elise's arm. "Poor man. Must have been out of his head with grief to send his little girl away."

Elise smiled brightly and nodded. "You know, that's exactly what I've always thought." Her smile faded slightly. "Aunt Claudia said it was because he didn't want me." Elise's tone was matter-of-fact as she continued, "She says my father is a barbarian who killed my mother then shipped me off, like an orphan."

She did not miss the shocked look on her companion's face and was quick to add, "Oh, Mrs. Teekle, he didn't kill her, of course. My mother died of the fever. But there weren't any doctors for her when she died. According to Aunt Claudia, that's as good as murdering her."

"You poor darlin'." Mavis's expression was tragic. "That's about the saddest thing I've ever heard. It must be so painful for you to think about it."

"To tell the truth, I'm used to it by now. I'll bet Aunt Claudia's told the story at least a hundred times. Do you know it's the all-time favorite topic at our Ladies Literary Society meetings? She's gotten so good at telling it now that by the time she's finished there's rarely a dry eye in the room." Elise flashed a wry smile. "My father is practically a legend."

Mavis was silent for a moment, trying to digest all she had heard. "Why don't you tell me about him, dear? Tell me about your father."

Elise warmed to the topic. "He's a wonderful man, Mrs. Teekle. Kind and gentle and very strong. The kind of father every girl dreams of." Her green eyes sparkled with enthusiasm. "He's handsome, too. Real tall, with broad shoulders and strong hands." Her voice grew more animated. "His skin is deeply tanned from all the time he spends in the sun. . .he's a cowboy, you see, and he has tiny little crinkles at the corners of his eyes when he smiles, which is almost all the time."

"I just can't imagine where your Aunt Claudia gets the idea that the man has abandoned you. It's obvious to me that you two have stayed in close contact over the years, with lots of letters and photographs, I'll bet."

"Well, no." Elise cleared her throat uncomfortably. "Not actually."

Mavis nodded her understanding. "Well, as busy as a cowboy's life is, he's probably doing the best he can, just getting a letter or two off to you each year."

"There haven't been any letters, Mrs. Teekle." Elise felt the warm color stain her cheeks.

"None at all?" Mavis's voice rose to an astonished squeak. She seemed to note Elise's discomfort and added quickly, "Aw honey, that's nothing to be ashamed of. There's lots of cowboys that can't write. Running cattle doesn't leave much time for schooling. Besides, just a photograph can tell you plenty about a person."

"I've never seen a single photograph of my father."

Mavis had to strain to hear Elise's whispered confession. "Aunt Claudia forbade me to even mention his name."

"But the way you described him. . . ."

Elise raised an earnest gaze to her companion. "I hope you don't think I've misled you. It sounds odd I suppose, but I don't need a photograph of him to know what he looks like." She studied her hands resting in her lap. "I've dreamed of him so often, I have a very clear picture of him in my heart."

For the first time in her life, Mavis found herself speechless. When at long last her voice returned, she asked softly, "Child, after all this time, why are you going to him now?"

"He's dying," Elise replied with renewed cheerfulness. "At least, that's what the doctor says." She turned a dazzling smile to Mrs. Teekle. "Isn't it nice to know they've got a doctor in Crossroads now?"

Mavis's mouth dropped open in surprise. She tried to speak, but could only sputter.

Elise saw her concern. "Oh, he won't really die. Don't you see? All these years, I've been hoping my father would want me to come home. This is it. His doctor sent me a letter, saying Father was dying and asking me to come to Texas." Her voice faded to a whisper and tears glittered in her eyes. "He wants me to come home." She cleared her throat self-consciously. "Once we're together, I'm sure he'll be fine. Good as new."

Mavis opened her mouth to reply, then seemed to think the better of it. Instead, she shook her head and turned to stare out the window across the aisle.

Elise caught the look of disbelief on Mavis's face as she turned away. It was obvious she did not share Elise's optimism. An embarrassed flush warmed her face as she realized she'd practically talked the woman's ear off. She wasn't certain why she had poured out her heart like that. Must be nerves.

Thankfully Aunt Claudia had not been here to witness her appalling lack of restraint. This was just the sort of behavior that had earned Elise many a stern lecture over the years on the merits of propriety.

"Don't be such a magpie," Aunt Claudia would say. "Gentle women of breeding do not run on so. It's that bad blood of your father's showing through. Heaven knows what a trial it is for me to try to make something of you."

Elise brushed the unpleasant memory aside as she checked the timepiece attached to her bodice for the umpteenth time. According to her calculations, she had another hour before she would reach the station. She sighed impatiently and settled back into her seat to study the rugged Texas landscape through the soot-streaked window.

Texas. Elise could not believe she was actually seeing Texas again. It was lovely, she mused. Everything looked green and alive. Not at all what she expected. She'd been so young when she left the last time, too young to remember the endless, flat, wide open spaces or the life she had had there with her father.

Her heart soared. Her father. She had to pinch herself as a reminder that it was not a dream. She was finally going to be with him. Excitement bubbled up within her.

Ever since she'd been a young child, her father had been foremost in her mind. Over the years, she had spent countless hours comforting herself with thoughts of him. It was her father who whispered endearments to her when she felt the sting of Aunt Claudia's sharp tongue. He was the one by her side when she faced the terrors of a lonely, dark night. His was the willing ear with which she shared her innermost secrets.

Until today, Elise never mentioned these dreams to anyone. Aunt Claudia was not interested in what she termed "the fanciful products of Elise's over-active imagination." In fact, she had forbidden her to mention his name. Elise couldn't hold it against her. After all, Aunt Claudia had been terribly hurt when her sister had died and, in her frustration, she blamed the only person she could—Seth Garver. But Elise didn't blame him. She loved him and she knew he loved her.

There was one wrinkle in her perfect dream: Father and daughter were separated. Elise had struggled long with the matter of why her father had never sent for her. After all, a man who loved his daughter like her father loved her would most certainly want her by his side. Yet she had never heard from him, not once in all those years.

Elise was eleven or twelve years old when the answer had finally dawned on her. She had been reading the story of a family separated through poverty when she found a plausible explanation. The father and mother went to a workhouse and the children were sent to an orphanage.

Her father was poor. That explained everything perfectly. Seth Garver must be poor, so poor that he did not want to bring his daughter to Texas until he could afford to take care of her. He was a proud man, of that she was certain. After all, he was a Texan and she knew from reading any book she could find about the state, that Texans, especially cowboys, were very proud.

With that discovery, the nagging question was settled once and for all in Elise's mind. And it stirred within her a deep desire to help her father in any way she could.

The recent letter saying her father wanted to see her was the long-awaited culmination of all her dreams. True, there was the matter of his dying, but Elise did not take it too seriously. God would not go to all the trouble to get them together, just to tear them apart.

The conductor stepped into the car. "Crossroads. Next stop, Crossroads." Elise checked her timepiece again. The train was right on time.

Mavis pressed a crumpled piece of paper into Elise's hand. "Honey, this is my name and address. I'd like you to have it, just in case you need me."

Elise smiled politely at Mrs. Teekle's kindness and tucked the paper into her reticule. It was obvious the woman thought she was making a mistake. Elise couldn't blame her; she knew the evidence leaned heavily against her dreams. She, too, struggled with doubts. But even then, deep in her heart, she knew her father loved her.

When the train finally screeched to a noisy stop, Elise stepped quickly over Mavis and her bags. In her excitement, she was halfway down the aisle before she remembered her manners. She turned and waved. "Good-bye

Mrs. Teekle. It was a pleasure meeting you." Etiquette satisfied, she turned and ran.

She paused momentarily on the top step of the train to breathe deeply of the warm spring air. Happiness surged through her. She was here at long last. Texas. Home.

Elise descended lightly to the planked platform to survey the tiny station. Two rough benches, both empty, leaned against the wall. There was none of the customary hustle and bustle one usually found at a depot. In fact, the place appeared deserted.

She caught her lower lip in her teeth as a tiny doubt nibbled at her confidence. Could her father have forgotten she was coming?

The dire warning that Aunt Claudia had delivered just days ago as they stood waiting for the train in Boston, rang in her ears. "I can't very well forbid you to go." She had raised her chin a notch as she addressed Elise in her haughtiest tone. "It's my Christian duty to fulfill a dying man's request. But," her steely eyes grew hard as she continued, "mark my words, you're making a mistake. The man's a barbarian. He's not interested in you, Elise. Never has been."

Having delivered her cruelest barb, Aunt Claudia had folded her arms across her chest triumphantly, waiting for Elise to change her mind about the trip and stay home.

Elise had surprised them both by getting on the train.

Now she suffered a momentary qualm, one of many she had fought to suppress during the long trip. Had she misjudged him? Was her father truly a barbarian? After all, what did she really know about the man?

Nonsense, she reassured herself. Surely even a barbarian would know to send someone to the station to pick up his daughter. Anyway, it was too late for second thoughts. She was here now and she had come too far to lose heart.

She glanced over her shoulder to see Mavis's round face pressed against the window, worry etched in her plump features. Elise mustered a brave smile for her and waved before turning again to the vacant station.

She took a deep, fortifying breath. "It's going to be all right," she whispered aloud. She smoothed the jacket of her traveling suit, adjusted her bonnet, squared her slim shoulders, and marched resolutely into the station.

Once inside, she paused, blinking hard, waiting for her eyes to adjust from the bright sunlight to the darkened interior.

With the exception of the man seated behind the ticket window on the far side of the room, the station appeared to be deserted as well. Elise ignored the niggling fear tormenting her and decided her first course of action should be to check with him. Perhaps he knew of her father.

She started toward him when a movement to her right caught her attention. A tall man wearing a dark cowboy hat emerged from the shadows.

"Your name Garver?" It was not a question, but rather an accusation.

"Yes, I'm Miss Garver." She hoped her voice didn't reflect the intimidation she felt as the cowboy loomed over her. She studied his face, her efforts hampered by the poor lighting. He had dark hair and a mustache, that much she could make out. And, judging from the harsh line of his mouth, he seemed to be angry with her. "Are. . .are you here to take me home?"

"I'm here to take you to Seth's place," he growled, placing extra emphasis on the word Seth.

It was obvious to Elise that she had gotten off on the wrong foot with the man, although she could not figure out why. She decided to start over. She took a tentative step toward him and extended a small, gloved hand. "I'm so glad to meet you. I'm Elise Garver."

The man simply glared. He pointedly ignored the outstretched hand, choosing instead to brush past her and stalk out of the station.

Elise stood immobilized, the smile still frozen on her face, an embarrassed flush creeping over her cheeks. She could not remember a time in all of her twenty-two years of ever being treated so rudely. In her sheltered existence in Boston, even sworn enemies hated one another with propriety and decorum.

Her slight shoulders sagged with disappointment. The meeting was nothing of the warm homecoming she had envisioned. The doubts that had plagued her across the country crowded in. Perhaps she had made a mistake, after all.

A sudden thought brought a genuine smile to her lips. The man was obviously a cowboy, that much she could surmise from his attire. According to Aunt Claudia, cowboys were uneducated barbarians. Elise's smile grew wide. He hadn't intended to slight her, he simply had not known any better.

Her heart went out to him immediately. Poor man. No wonder he was so cross. She knew firsthand how painful it could be to be socially inept. Maybe she could help him. Perhaps during the course of her stay, she could teach him some basic etiquette.

Endlessly relieved, she followed him outside to a wagon where he was loading her trunks. A huge black dog of questionable parentage yapped excitedly from his perch on the wagon bench. Maybe she'd have better luck with the dog.

"Hello there, fella." Elise reached up to pat the dog's shaggy head. "What's your name?"

"*Her* name's Becky." The cowboy's mocking voice was low and velvety smooth.

Elise gasped. She hadn't heard him come up behind her. Before she could turn around to respond, two large hands grasped her around the waist and carelessly tossed her up onto the wooden bench.

"Ooof!" She landed with a surprised thud. Her emerald green eyes flashed as she whirled around to enlighten him of her opinion of being man-handled. Cowboy or not, his behavior was highly improper.

Elise hadn't fully recovered when the wagon dipped slightly as he took his place on the bench beside her. For a big man, he certainly moved quietly.

She faced him, ready to begin his education with a lesson as to the proper way to assist a lady, when she noticed the expression in his dark eyes. The cold challenge she found there silenced her complaint. The cowboy looked positively ferocious. She didn't doubt that with the slightest provocation, he'd leave her there stranded.

Never mind the lesson, she thought, smoothing her skirts. It wasn't worth it. Cowboys probably had few dealings with ladies, anyway. *My father won't be like that,* she reassured herself. *He will be gentle and polite.*

Her father. Elise relaxed visibly at the thought. Her trip was almost complete. In no time at all she'd be reunited with her father. Her pulse began to race. It wasn't a dream. Seth Garver had asked her to come to Texas. He loved her, just as she had always imagined.

"I can't wait to see my father," Elise voiced her thoughts aloud.

"You don't sound too worried about him. I mean the fact that Doc Kalina says he's dyin'." The cowboy's voice was hard.

"I'm not," she replied brightly. She wouldn't try to explain to the irritable cowboy that she knew beyond a shadow of a doubt that her father would be all right. She remembered too clearly the look Mavis Teekle had given her when she had tried to explain it to her.

Elise heard his sharp intake of breath at her reply, but she refused to meet the piercing eyes that burned into her. She couldn't expect him to understand.

"What a lovely town," Elise said as she studied the graying, wooden buildings lining the dirt street. A few people, mostly men, strolled the planked sidewalks. While it lacked the sophistication of New England, Elise found it charming and exciting.

She longed to ask questions about the town and its inhabitants but, with a quick glance toward the stony countenance of her formidable escort, she elected to wait and ask her father.

The wagon rattled through the center of Crossroads, then set a course due west. Wide open stretches of land flanked the well-traveled dirt road. Elise studied the gently rolling landscape with interest. It was so unlike Boston.

Unfettered by civilization, it seemed to promise freedom and opportunity.

She began to understand the strange draw that the West offered. Here there was the chance to begin again.

Overhead, the sky was a sweeping canopy of clearest blue. A warm breeze danced across the land, carrying with it the sweet scent of spring. The swaying vegetation was bright green with the advent of a new season. Scrubby trees and cactus dotted the grassy fields.

The warmth of the late afternoon sun and the rhythmic rocking of the wagon had a sedating effect on Elise. With Becky wedged between herself and the cowboy to provide a buffer, the two rode in silence.

Elise studied the primitive shanties, built of mud or wood, that were scattered randomly across the open terrain. Each time the wagon came within view of one, she held her breath in anticipation. Any one of these could house her beloved father.

A smile stole across her lips. She knew his home would be crude, not the luxurious surroundings she had shared with Aunt Claudia in Boston, but that didn't matter. They would be together. She would be there for him, to nurse him back to health. That had been her fondest dream. To be useful to him. To provide for him. To be wanted by him.

Gradually the landscape changed. The once-open fields on either side of the road were now enclosed with endless stretches of barbed wire fence. When half an hour had passed since Elise had last sighted a house, her patience waned. "How much longer?" Her question broke the long silence.

The cowboy's eyes never left the road. "This is Garver land now. We ought to be at the house in a few minutes." His deep voice was expressionless.

Elise roused from her comfortable lethargy at the mention of Garver land. She sat up ramrod straight on the bench, giving him her full attention. "I beg your pardon, I'm afraid I don't understand."

The cowboy turned to face her, his dark hat pulled low over his brow. He spoke slowly, enunciating each word as though addressing a small child. "We passed the Garver marker a while back. Won't be long till we can see the main house."

For a moment, Elise was still, her mind racing as she tried to digest the information. This was Garver land? How could a poor man own so much land? There had to be a mistake.

The cowboy's deep voice pierced the silence. "There's the house now." He pointed to the horizon.

Suddenly, she didn't want to see. The sight of the house might confirm the gnawing fear growing inside her. She didn't want to know. The cowboy kept his hand extended, waiting for her to respond. Elise forced herself to look.

It was a large, white, two-story structure with a long porch stretching across the front, an impressive home even by Boston standards. Several smaller buildings and enclosures were scattered beside it.

Elise tore her eyes away, a stricken look on her face. "There's got to be a mistake," she said weakly. She reached a tentative hand to rest on his arm. Imploring green eyes met steely dark ones. "This is some kind of mistake. I am looking for Seth Garver."

"No mistake."

"How long. . . ?" The tortured whisper caught in her throat. "How long has he lived here?"

"Long time." The cowboy's dark eyes held hers. "Is there a problem?" There was no kindness in his voice.

No sound would come from her throat. She shook her head mutely as she drew her hand back to her lap. There was no problem at all. She had all the facts. It was just that the facts did not line up with her long-cherished dream.

Her father owned a huge home and all the land as far as the eye could see. He wasn't poor, too poor to raise his only daughter. He was rich.

She'd been wrong. All those years, clutching tenaciously to the hope that he would send for her as soon as he could, believing doggedly in his devotion and love, she'd been terribly wrong.

"Why? Why did he wait to send for me now?"

The cowboy seemed impatient with her. "Isn't it obvious? The man is dying. He's trying to tie up loose ends."

"Loose ends," she repeated mindlessly.

Suddenly, Elise felt hollow inside, completely void of any emotion. Her beautiful dream had died.

two

A slight woman in a bright red dress and white apron stood on the porch, waving frantically as the cowboy maneuvered the wagon around to the front of the house.

"Hola!" The woman shouted. "Welcome!"

Elise sat atop the wagon bench, unmoving. Her usually quick mind felt sluggish, her though processes dulled. The joyful anticipation of meeting her father had evaporated, leaving her limp.

The cowboy appeared noiselessly at her side to help her down from the wagon. Elise offered no protest. Again, large hands encompassed her waist as he lowered her to the ground. He was gentler this time. *Probably for the benefit of the woman on the porch,* Elise thought wryly. Not that it mattered to Elise. Nothing mattered now.

Face to face, she took the opportunity to study him at close range. The cowboy was younger than she had thought, surely no more than thirty years old, and handsome. Her eyes widened as her heart gave an uncharacteristic flutter. Really handsome. With his hat pulled down so far on his face, she hadn't noticed his strong, ruggedly chiseled features or dark wavy hair.

Their eyes met briefly. His were dark, she noted, almost black. His expression was grim as he released her.

"You're here! You're here!" The strange woman from the porch pounced upon her, first hugging Elise to her chest, then drawing her back to study her face, finally pulling her back into an enthusiastic embrace. "We've waited so long to see you."

"Thank you." Elise's reply was somewhat muffled because her face remained compressed against the woman's shoulder. She was completely rattled. No one in Boston had ever hugged her like that. In truth, no one had ever hugged her at all. This open display of affection was so foreign to Elise, she had no idea as to the proper response.

Elise's entire life had been dictated by the strict adherence to *Mrs. Rhoades's Complete Handbook of Courteous Behavior and Social Graces for Young Women and,* as she racked her brain, she was quite certain that nowhere in the handbook was it explained how one greeted affectionate strangers. So what should she do now?

Mrs. Rhoades often advocated taking a deep breath to clear one's head.

Perhaps with some air, something would come to her. Two deep breaths later, Elise was still uninspired. Not wishing to commit a social blunder, Elise gently disengaged herself and extended her hand in the formal greeting to which she was accustomed. "I'm Elise Garver."

Rosa smiled warmly. "Sí, of course you are. I can see it in those green eyes. You've got your father's eyes, you do."

At the mention of her father, Elise self-consciously dropped her gaze to the floor, the corner of her lower lip caught between her teeth.

"I've forgotten my manners. I am Rosa Viegas, your father's housekeeper." She offered a broad, white smile, a striking contrast to her golden skin. "Speaking of which, I am certain he is anxious to see you. Come, I'll lead you to him."

Elise followed obediently in Rosa's wake, dread weighing down her slender limbs. She briefly considered delaying the encounter by pleading exhaustion, but thought better of it. It would not be correct to keep her father waiting.

She stole a quick look around as they stepped inside. It was a lovely home, tastefully appointed with handsome furnishings. She found no pleasure in that fact. A mud hut would have suited her just fine. The obvious wealth displayed in her father's home served only to remind Elise of the foolishness of her dream. A lost dream.

The women climbed a long flight of stairs, walked to the end of the hall, and paused before a polished oak door. Rosa knocked softly.

"Come in."

Elise's knees felt weak and her stomach churned. At last, the moment she had been waiting for—the realization of her life's dreams. But with the information now in her possession, she was not at all certain how she would react to the man inside. He was a complete stranger to her now. And she was a "loose end."

Rosa swung the door open and stepped aside for Elise to pass. Heavy draperies at the windows blocked the afternoon sun, bathing the room in shadows. Elise took several hesitant steps toward the bed. Propped up against a wall of pillows was a huge man with an unruly crop of dark hair threaded with silver.

They studied each other in silence.

"Elise. It's really you." His voice faltered. "Come closer and let me see you."

Elise stepped closer to the bed, her hands clasped tightly before her. Her heart beat wildly in her chest. This was surely her father. She'd have known him anywhere.

He looked just as she imagined he would, ruggedly handsome with warm, compassionate eyes. She was relieved to see that his illness had not yet sapped the vitality from him.

Face to face with the man of her dreams, a tiny spark of hope ignited within her. Maybe the cowboy was wrong. Maybe she was more than a "loose end" to her father.

She moved to the side of his bed, pulse pounding in her ears, waiting to hear him declare how much he loved her and had missed her. And how much he had wanted her home.

He simply stared. An awkward silence stretched between them. Elise could hear the ticking of a clock.

"You are lovely," Seth whispered finally. "How proud your mother would be to see you now."

The polite compliment was a far cry from the pledge of love she longed to hear. It only seemed to confirm what the cowboy had spoken. Elise felt as though her heart would break. "Thank you, sir," she responded stiffly as she tried to mask her disappointment. "Aunt Claudia did her best."

"Claudia!" her father barked. "That woman's never done a good thing in her life."

Elise's wide eyes reflected her astonishment at his outburst. "Sir?"

He was silenced from further comment by Rosa who began to fluff his pillows vigorously while pinning him with a censorious stare. "It's nothing, dear." Rosa smiled soothingly at Elise, then turned her gaze back to Seth. "Your father's thinking has been somewhat clouded by his illness." She placed special emphasis on the last word.

"I'm sorry. I was distressed to hear of your illness, sir." Actually, Elise had been delighted when she received his letter saying he was dying and wished to see her.

She never believed he would die. She thought the sickness would signal a beginning for their lives together as father and daughter. How could she have been so wrong?

A sharp rap at the door caught her attention. She was surprised to see the cowboy stride across the room and stand on the opposite side of her father's bed. "I'm sorry, Seth. I needed to talk to you. Trouble with some of the fences. Am I interrupting anything?" He fixed Elise with a dark stare.

"Tanner, my boy, I guess you've had the chance to meet my daughter, Elise."

"We—" Elise began.

"Yes. We've met." Tanner's curt reply cut her off.

Elise cleared her throat in acute embarrassment. "I fear I've detained you long enough, sir. I'll leave you two alone to your discussion." She turned and left the room with all the dignity she could muster. Was there no end to the rudeness of that cowboy?

Rosa appeared at her side. "I'll bet you're tired after all your traveling. Let's get you settled in your room. You can freshen up and take a nice nap before supper."

She guided Elise to a room at the top of the stairs, down the hall from her father's. "Do you like it?" she asked anxiously.

Elise nodded her approval. "It's lovely." The room had obviously been decorated with a woman in mind. An elegant paper of trailing green vines blooming with pale pink roses covered the walls. Delicate lace curtains hung in the windows. The large bed heaped with soft coverlets looked especially inviting.

Rosa kept up a steady stream of comforting chatter while she bustled through the room. "I see Tanner has brought your trunks up. I'll put your things away later. Why don't you lie down and try to rest for a while. Traveling can be so tiring."

Elise sat at the dressing table and took the pins from her hair. With the silver brush she'd carried in her valise, she began to work through the tangled waves.

Rosa paused behind her. "What beautiful hair you have. Reminds me of my own daughter's." She addressed Elise's reflection in the mirror. "She used to love it when I brushed it for her. Do you mind?" Rosa gestured for Elise to hand her the brush.

Again Elise was startled by the easy, affectionate manner of Rosa. She was even more surprised to find she liked it. With a shy smile, she relinquished the brush to Rosa. "No one's brushed my hair for me since I was a little girl. Aunt Claudia said I could do it myself."

At the grunt of disapproval from Rosa, she added, "I hope I haven't made her sound callous. It's nothing like that. It's just that Aunt Claudia was always very careful not to spoil me with too much affection."

Rosa chose to keep her opinion of Aunt Claudia to herself as she continued to brush Elise's thick, mahogany tresses with gentle strokes. "It's nice to have someone here to look after. My daughter got married last year. She and her husband have gone to El Paso to start a ranch." Tears filled Rosa's eyes. "It was so hard to let her go. El Paso's so faraway."

Elise felt Rosa's sorrow keenly. She knew how hard it was to be alone. With unaccustomed boldness, she laid a comforting hand on Rosa's hand that rested on her shoulder.

Rosa smiled as she brushed away an errant tear. "You'll have to forgive the ramblings of an old woman." She stopped brushing to meet Elise's gaze. "I guess in my own way I'm telling you that if you ever need someone, you know, someone to talk to, well, I'm an experienced mother who's looking for someone to take care of."

"Thank you, Rosa." Tears glistened in her eyes as she whispered, "Your daughter is a very lucky woman."

Rosa paused from her brushing. "You know—" She stopped in midsentence and laid the brush on the dressing table. "Never mind. We'll have plenty of time to talk later, but for now, I think a nap would be best."

Elise slipped out of her traveling suit and burrowed gratefully between the crisp sheets that smelled of spring and sunshine. She hadn't realized how truly tired she was.

"Rest now, little one." Rosa pulled the covers up over Elise's shoulders then bent and kissed her forehead before slipping noiselessly from the room.

ஃ

Several hours later, Rosa peeked in to study the still slumbering form. She intended to call Elise to dinner, but it was obvious that what the exhausted young woman needed most was rest. . .and lots of love.

Rosa shook her head in frustration as she pulled the door closed behind her. It was inconceivable that a child could be raised without tenderness. In her own demonstrative family, hugs and kisses were a big part of every day.

Yet, she knew after meeting Elise that afternoon, the young woman had received neither. Rosa vowed to God she wouldn't let her go until she'd gotten all the love she had missed.

ஃ

Tanner pounded his pillow viciously before dropping back against it to stare at the ceiling. His temper was still boiling, and he knew it would be a long time till he found sleep.

"Conniving, scheming little brat. Never in my life have I ever seen a bolder woman than our little Miss Garver." He rolled over onto his side, his head propped against his hand. "You should have seen her, Becky, arriving here just as fancy as you please. She might think she's fooling us with those slick city ways, but I've got her figured out real good."

Becky moved to the rug beside his bed and whimpered softly.

"Sure, she's pretty. I'm not blind. But trust me, Becky, behind those great big green eyes and pretty smile is a greedy woman."

She whimpered again, this time scratching lightly on the bed.

Tanner's large hand dropped down to scratch her behind the ears. "Yeah, she did smell real sweet, didn't she." He smiled briefly at the memory of lifting her from the wagon, his hands easily spanning her tiny waist. She smelled heavenly to him, like a whole field of flowers. He could almost smell her now.

His smile disappeared abruptly. "That doesn't change anything. Elise Garver is trouble, and the sooner we send her packin' to Boston, the better."

three

The tantalizing aroma of coffee wafted under Elise's nose, causing her to stir slightly. *No need to hurry,* she told herself, *Aunt Claudia won't be up until noon.* She burrowed more deeply into the covers.

The coffee was relentless in its assault. Elise's eyes flickered open reluctantly. For a moment, she was confused. Where was she?

Bright sunlight filtered through the lace-covered windows, bathing her face in its warmth. Elise sat up with a start. "This isn't Boston. This is home!" Initially crushed by yesterday's disappointing meeting with her father, the new day brought with it new hope. She was out of the bed in a flash.

She found to her surprise that her trunks were empty and her clothes were already hung in the wardrobe, everything neatly pressed. *Rosa,* Elise thought with a smile. She studied the garments carefully, finally selecting a day dress of emerald silk. She wanted to look just right for her father. If only she could remember what color of shoes to wear.

Suppose Tanner's right, Elise thought as she buttoned up her dress. *Suppose my father's only interest in me is to tie up loose ends. Should I give up now?* She shook her head. *Of course not. I'm not giving up the one chance I have for a real father.* She chewed her lip thoughtfully. *I just can't. So my only option is to change his mind.*

As she sat at the dressing table, putting the finishing touches on her hair, Elise continued to ponder the situation. She needed a plan of action; one in which she could earn her father's love. She balked slightly at the thought. It seemed a bit improper, scheming to win his affection. She doubted that either Aunt Claudia or Mrs. Rhoades would approve, but she could see no other alternative. She shrugged at her reflection. Desperate times called for desperate measures.

Elise followed the fragrant path of coffee to the kitchen where she found Rosa and Tanner seated at the table. "Good morning," she called from the doorway as she paused to scratch Becky behind the ears. "Do you mind if I join you?"

"You're up. Bueno, good." Rosa was on her feet instantly. "Come sit down, let me get you a cup of coffee and some breakfast. You must be starving."

"Famished. Thank you, Rosa." Elise smiled hesitantly at Tanner as she took the seat across the table from him. He said nothing as his dark gaze raked over her.

Rosa placed a cup of coffee and a filled plate in front of Elise. "I'm sorry you didn't get dinner last night. I came up to wake you, but you were sleeping so soundly, I hated to disturb you."

Elise flashed her a grateful smile before taking a long draught from her cup. "I was more tired than I realized. It was kind of you to let me sleep." She placed her cup on the table. "And thank you so much for pressing all my things and putting them away."

"It was my pleasure. It's wonderful to have a woman to look after." Rosa's dark eyes glowed. "And didn't I have fun looking at all your fancy dresses. I've gotta say, you've got the finest clothes I've ever laid eyes on. Such pretty colors."

"Too many colors," Elise muttered under her breath.

Belatedly remembering her manners, she added, "Thank you. They are lovely, aren't they? Aunt Claudia has always been quite emphatic about the importance of correct attire. She's spent a fortune on them, I'm afraid."

Tanner gave a snort of disgust and rose to his feet. "Thanks for breakfast, Rosa."

"You're not leaving, are you? I was hoping you could show Elise around the place this morning."

Tanner scooped his hat off the table and dropped it onto his head. "Sorry, Rosa." He patted her shoulder affectionately. "Too busy." Without so much as a glance toward Elise, he disappeared through the door.

Rosa clucked disapprovingly. "Wonder what's got into the man?"

"It's me, I'm afraid," Elise confessed, "although I'm not quite certain what I've done."

Rosa patted her hand. "Nonsense. He's just got himself worked up about the fences, that's all."

"The fences?"

Rosa nodded, rising to her feet. "He and Seth are both worried. Thieving rustlers been cutting 'em." She began to clear away the empty plates.

Elise made a mental note to find out more about the fences. If they were of interest to her father, then she would be interested, too. Any common ground would help her earn a place in his heart.

"Rosa, when can I see my father?"

"He said he'd see you this afternoon." Rosa missed the look of disappointment on Elise's face. "He thought you would like to see the ranch this morning."

Elise chafed at the delay. Her time was so limited, she wanted to see her father so she could get started on her plan right away.

Rosa seemed to sense her agitation. She sat down at the table. "Maybe you'd like to ride?"

"Ride?" Elise's eyes grew wide. "Do you mean ride, as in ride horses?"

Rosa laughed and nodded.

"I'd love to ride!" Elise was on her feet in an instant, her face flushed with excitement. "I've never ridden before. But I've read all about it. Hundreds of books." She clasped her hands together. "It sounds so wonderful."

"Bueno. Run upstairs and change your clothes. I'll take you over to the stables. I'm sure James will be glad to help you. Next to Tanner, he's the best horseman I know."

Elise was halfway through the door when she whirled around, a deep frown marring her face. "Rosa, I'm afraid I don't have a riding costume."

Rosa dried her hands on her towel. "Don't you fret. I've got a skirt or two of my daughter's we can use." She paused to study Elise's trim figure. "They'll fit just fine after we take a tuck or two."

An hour later, Elise emerged from her room, swishing her newly acquired skirt with delight. She paused at the top of the stairs to twirl gracefully on her toes.

"My, don't you look lovely," Rosa called from the foot of the staircase.

"Oh, Rosa!" Elise exclaimed with a start as she clapped a hand over her heart. "I didn't see you down there." She smoothed the front of her skirt self-consciously. "I hope you won't think I'm silly for dancing around. I suppose it's quite improper, but I couldn't resist." She hesitated a moment before explaining. "The skirt is so light, not at all like the mountains of fabric I'm usually wearing. I feel as though I could fly."

"I don't think it's silly at all," Rosa reassured her. "I'm glad you like it."

"It's lovely. Such a pretty shade of orange. I hope your daughter won't mind my borrowing it." Elise descended the stairs while tying the ribbons of her straw bonnet beneath her chin. She could see Rosa staring at her hat. A bright crimson warmed her cheeks. "Is something wrong? Is it my bonnet? Wrong color? I have an awful time with colors. I like pink and turquoise and orange together, so I hoped it would be acceptable." She nibbled her lip in embarrassed uncertainty.

Rosa dragged her eyes from the pink, flower-strewn confection perched on top of Elise's elaborate coiffure to meet her troubled gaze. "Sure, honey, it'll be just fine. This isn't Boston. The folks up there got rules about everything. Texans are more concerned with what's practical. As long as its got a brim to keep the sun off your face, it'll be great."

In truth she thought the ensemble looked a bit on the bright side, but wild horses wouldn't drag it out of her. Poor child seemed insecure enough. Thanks to Aunt Claudia no doubt. "Come on now, honey. James is awaiting you."

Elise followed her through the house and out the back toward the stables. A tall young man, who she guessed to be in his early twenties, appeared at the doorway.

"Hello, James." Rosa made the introductions. "This is Miss Garver, your new student."

James gave a low whistle of appreciation as his eyes roamed over Elise. "Rosa, you didn't tell me how purty she is."

Elise felt herself flush hotly and she studied the ground in embarrassment.

"James has always been one to speak his mind, Elise. Doesn't have a clue as to what's proper with the ladies. You'll have to forgive him." Rosa turned to James. "Now you take good care of her, you hear?"

James gave a broad grin. "It'll be my pleasure." He slid an arm around Elise and guided her toward the stalls. "Ever ridden before?"

She shook her head.

"Then what we need is a real gentle mount." He stroked his chin thoughtfully as he considered the horses, finally coming to a stop in front of a chestnut mare. "I think Miss Sadie will do nicely."

Elise reached up cautiously to stroke the velvety nose of the horse. "She's beautiful."

"You and her's a fine match, Miss Garver. Two beautiful women with hair the color of chestnuts."

Elise smiled at the unusual compliment. She'd never been compared to a horse before. James glowed at her reaction, obviously proud of his prowess with women.

She stood back to watch in fascination as James saddled Miss Sadie and led her from the stall. "Are you ready?" he asked finally.

Elise's eyes opened wide. "Already?" she gulped.

James gave a hearty laugh. "Don't you worry. She's as gentle as a baby." He moved closer to Elise to confide, "And I'm not going to let anything happen to you."

Elise nodded solemnly.

"Ordinarily, folks use a stool to get their foot up in the stirrup, but," he smiled broadly, "in your case, I think it best if I lift you up."

Elise backed up a step. "Oh, I'm not sure that would be at all seemly."

Before she could protest further, James grasped her around the waist and swung her up high into the saddle.

Elise gasped. Sitting atop the horse was unlike anything she'd ever done, and no amount of reading could convey the awesome feeling of towering in the air on the back of a magnificent beast.

"Now relax," James coached. "Hold the horn there in front of you and get your balance." He steadied her until she felt stable. "You okay?"

Elise nodded, her lower lip tucked between her teeth.

"Good. I'm gonna take the reins and lead you around the corral a time or two. When you're ready, I'll give you the reins and you can ride alone."

Elise took a deep breath and nodded again.

The first circle around the corral, Elise clung to the horse for dear life, her knuckles white on the horn. Gradually, she began to relax as her body adjusted to the rhythm of the horse's gait. After a second pass, she mustered enough confidence to signal James she was ready to go it alone.

"Here are the reins. Hold them like this." James placed the leather straps into her hands, lingering a bit longer than necessary. "That's good, now relax your grip. You don't want to hold them quite so tight."

Elise complied, her body tense with concentration.

"Okay, take her around once. And Miss Garver?"

Elise looked up.

"It's okay to smile."

Elise grinned self-consciously. "Thank you, James. I'll try to remember that."

At his command, Miss Sadie obediently began to walk with her pupil around the corral. It was wonderful. Elise reveled in the freedom of sitting up so high, and the knowledge that she was in control. Riding into the cool spring breezes, she'd never felt so alive. With each pass, her confidence grew stronger. Perhaps it would be easier for her father to love her if she could ride well.

She was disappointed to see James finally climb down off the fence where he'd been sitting and move into the ring to join her. She didn't know how long she'd been riding, but she was certain she could have ridden the same path for hours.

"Miss Garver, I think you've had enough for today." He didn't miss the sad little sigh that escaped or the disappointment in her eyes. "I can see that you're having a fine time. Why, I can tell that you have the makings for a real fine horsewoman, but another minute in the saddle and you'll regret it tomorrow."

James took the reins and led them back to the stables. "We'll handle the gettin' off same as the gettin' on."

Elise obediently turned to face him, allowing him to gently lift her from the saddle and place her on her feet. To her astonishment, her legs felt like jelly beneath her and she began to collapse. James came to her rescue by scooping her up against himself.

"That looks like enough lessons for today, James," Tanner thundered from behind them. "I'm sure you have plenty of work to do."

James grinned unabashedly into the scowling face of his boss. "Yessir, you're right. Plenty of work, but nothing that smells this sweet."

Elise disengaged herself from James's supporting arms and struggled to stand alone. She smiled brightly as she tried to adjust her bonnet that now listed heavily to the left.

"Good morning, Tanner." She pushed a stray lock of hair from her eyes. "I hope you won't take Mr. uh, James to task for the time spent on my instruction. I requested it, you see." Her trembling hands overadjusted the bonnet, which now hung precariously over her right ear. "I was in need of a tutor. Up until now, my only experience with horses has been in books and while I have done extensive reading on the subject, I must say that reading about it simply doesn't compare. Do you know—"

"Miss Garver," Tanner growled, "I know that we're running a ranch here, not a baby-sitting service for Boston socialites. So why don't you get yourself up to the house and out of my way."

Elise's eyes flew open in astonishment at the animosity she heard in his voice. For a moment she was speechless.

"Thank you, Tanner." Her voice was politely cool. "I'll do just that."

She remained only a moment more, to bestow a warm smile on the man standing beside him. "James, I thank you so much for the lovely morning." With those words, Elise turned and staggered to the house with as much dignity as her wobbly legs would allow.

four

Elise's heart fluttered wildly as she knocked on her father's door late that afternoon. Here was her chance to put her plan in action. She wasn't certain how, but one way or another, she was going to earn his love.

"Good afternoon, sir."

"Good afternoon, Elise." Seth smiled broadly. "Come in and sit down, won't you?"

She moved into the room and took the chair he indicated by the bed. "How are you feeling today?"

"Just fine, thank you. And you? Did you rest well last night?"

"Yes, thank you. My room is very comfortable."

"That's fine."

Father and daughter sat regarding one another, each waiting for the other to speak. Silence stretched between them.

It was Seth that finally spoke. "Rosa tells me you went riding today."

Elise's eyes lit up with the memory. "Oh yes, it was wonderful. I rode Miss Sadie, the chestnut mare. James said she was very gentle." Her voice grew more animated as she continued, "I've read about riding in books, but the written word simply doesn't do justice to actually riding a horse. It gives such a feeling of power. Of course, I didn't go very far, just around the corral, but it was so exciting. Back in Boston—" Elise stopped abruptly. She was rambling again.

Aunt Claudia had warned her time and again that her rambling was annoying and unbecoming to a lady. Not at all proper. Now here she was with her father, trying to win his affection, and instead she was repelling him with her bad manners. Elise stared dejectedly at her hands folded primly in her lap, her lower lip trapped between her teeth.

Seth was puzzled by the sudden change in his daughter. She seemed so happy and then, with the mention of Boston, she became quiet. A fleeting thought saddened him. She must be homesick already. Ready to get back to her life in Boston, her life without him. His smile dissolved into a worried frown.

Elise looked up into the stern face of her father, thinking it was disapproval she saw mirrored there. Her heart sank. Why couldn't she be quiet, like a proper young lady? Hadn't she learned one thing from Mrs. Rhoades's handbook?

Tanner stuck his head inside the door. "Seth, have you got a minute?"

"Sure. Find out anything about the fences?"

"The ones by the south spring were completely destroyed."

"Any clue as to who did it?"

Tanner strode into the room, shaking his head. "None. Must be pretty organized, whoever they are, cuz the rustling problem is countywide. Word is, the Texas Rangers have been called in. Figure they'll have it under control in no time. Meanwhile, I've sent a couple of the boys out to repair—" He stopped as he seemed to notice Elise for the first time. His dark eyes held hers.

Elise recognized the hostile glare from earlier. She rose quickly to her feet, hoping to avoid another confrontation with Tanner, this one in front of her father. She did not need another strike against her. "Will you two excuse me? I need to help Rosa with dinner."

"That's fine, Elise," her father said, nodding to her as she paused in the doorway. "I enjoyed our visit."

❧

"So, Tanner my boy," Seth asked as soon as the door closed behind her, "what do you think of my little girl? She's a real beauty, isn't she?"

"Yes, sir, she is."

Seth's brow raised slightly at the begrudging tone of Tanner's voice. Something wasn't quite right here. He pressed on, hoping to get an answer. "She's been riding today. James had her on Miss Sadie. Wished I coulda been there."

Actually, Seth had watched the whole thing from the window of his room, after Rosa had alerted him to the fact that Elise was to ride. His heart had swelled with pride as he watched his precious daughter circle the ring on the back of Miss Sadie. She was nervous, he could see that in her posture, but he could also see a natural grace as she handled the horse. She'd be a fine rider someday.

From his vantage point, he had also seen Tanner watching Elise's progress from the shadows of the stable where he thought he was undetected. "Sure was nice of James to work with her. I figured you musta been busy, otherwise you'd have been the one teaching her. Not a finer horseman than you anywhere."

Tanner refused to meet Seth's gaze as he mumbled something unintelligible, confirming in Seth's mind the fact that something wasn't quite right between Tanner and his daughter. It was also obvious Tanner wasn't ready to talk about it yet. Seth elected to hold his peace for the time being.

❧

Elise wandered downstairs thoroughly disheartened. Rosa met her at the door of the kitchen.

"Why the long face, honey? I thought you were visiting with your father."

"He and Tanner had business to discuss, so I left. I thought maybe there was something I could do for you."

Rosa gave her a warm smile. "You can keep me company over a cup of tea while I peel these potatoes for dinner."

Elise sat down at the table, resting her chin on her hands. "May I ask you a question? It's about Tanner."

"Sure, honey." Rosa put two cups on the table then sat down to join her. "What do you want to know?"

"What exactly does he do for my father?"

Rosa chuckled. "Better question would be what doesn't he do. Officially, Tanner's our foreman, but actually, he's much more than that. He's Seth's right-hand man."

"My father seems to like him very much," Elise said, absently tracing the rim of the cup with her finger.

"Tanner's been like a son to Seth, ever since we found him."

Elise quirked a delicate brow. "Found him?"

"That's right," Rosa nodded. "Indians had attacked his family's wagon. Everything was burning when Seth arrived. Seth was able to save Tanner. I'm afraid the rest of the family was lost."

"Oh, Rosa, how awful. He has no one." Elise felt a familiar pang, knowing the pain of being alone.

"That's right, honey, although he and Seth hit it off together real quick. The two of them's inseparable. Seth raised him, and together they built this place."

Elise brushed aside a momentary stab of jealousy.

Tanner had found a place where he belonged and someone to care for him. It hurt to know he held the place in her father's heart that she had wanted for herself. Was there room for both? She wondered if she would ever know the peace of belonging and the love and approval of a family.

A dreadful thought occurred to Elise. If she wanted to earn her father's love, it was likely she'd have to gain friendship with Tanner, his right-hand man. She smiled to herself at the incongruity of them being friends. Perhaps a more realistic goal would be securing his tolerance.

The plan was becoming more complex by the hour. And yet it was so simple. Elise would not go back to Boston without knowing her father loved her.

Elise stood up. "Rosa, is there something I can help you with before dinner?"

"No, honey." Rosa smiled up at her. "It's all done."

"Well then, if it's all right with you, I think I'll go on upstairs. I've got lots to do before dinner." *Lots of scheming,* she added silently.

٭

Elise arrived at dinner, ready to implement her recently amended plan of action to earn Tanner's approval as well as her father's love. She stared in dismay at the table set for two.

Rosa bustled into the room behind her. "There you are. Dinner's all ready. We may as well get started." She took her place at the table and signaled Elise to join her.

"But my father. . . ?"

"Must take his meals in his room," Rosa finished for her.

Elise's face fell. "Oh, I didn't know. Is he that weak?"

Only in his head, Rosa thought. Aloud she said, "The way I figure it, him having to eat in his room might be the strongest medicine for what ails him."

Elise turned an earnest gaze upon her. "Rosa, exactly what is it that ails him?"

Rosa bit her tongue to keep the word "foolishness" from escaping. Instead she merely shook her head. "You'll have to ask him about that."

Elise was thoroughly confused and more than a bit curious. The letter she had received from the doctor had been vague, no specific diagnosis given for her father and now Rosa refused to elaborate. She hoped they weren't merely sheltering her from the truth to protect her.

"Tanner won't be joining us, either?"

"No. He said he's got work to do." Rosa clucked softly as she shook her head. "It's not like him to miss a meal. Must be real worried about the rustling." She noticed the concerned look on Elise's face and decided to change the subject.

"Listen to me chatter while the food's getting cold. I'll ask the blessing and then we can eat." Rosa took Elise's hand in hers and began to pray, "Heavenly Father, I thank You for the food You have provided for us out of Your abundance. Bless it to the nourishment of our bodies. And Father," Rosa continued, "take care of the troubles we're having with the rustlers and our fences so that Seth and Tanner can quit worrying about them. Finally, Father, I thank You for Elise. Thank You for bringing her here to us. I ask You to guide and direct us in all that we do and say so that You will be glorified. In Jesus' name, Amen."

Rosa looked up to find Elise staring at her in wide-eyed amazement. "Is something wrong?"

Elise shook her head. "No, nothing's wrong. It's just that I've never heard anyone pray like that before."

"Like what?"

"Well," Elise hesitated, searching for the right words, "so conversationally for one thing, like you were actually talking to God."

Rosa giggled. "I was actually talking to God."

Elise blushed. "Well, yes, that's true I guess. Do you always talk to Him about the things going on in your life, like rustlers and fences?"

"Certainly." Rosa studied the awed expression on her companion's face. "Don't you?"

"No," Elise answered matter-of-factly. "I don't pray at all. Except at church, of course. We have prayer books to read out of on Sunday."

Rosa was clearly shocked. "You don't pray?" she managed to squeak out.

"Not anymore." Elise shook her head. "I used to pray a lot, but God never seemed to answer my prayers." *At least the ones about my father,* she thought. "When I asked Aunt Claudia about it, she said it was because God isn't interested in the minor details of our lives. He has more important things to concern Himself with, like saving sinners and judgment. You know, really big things. She said that's why He gave us minds, to take care of the everyday things."

Rosa was speechless. She had always gone to God about everything. She couldn't imagine being deprived of the peace of mind she had knowing her Heavenly Father was deeply concerned with every area of her life.

With a new resolve in her heart, Rosa passed the heaping plate of fried chicken. Along with the love and affection she was going to shower on Elise, she'd have the privilege of introducing her to the loving care of her Heavenly Father.

❧

Becky scratched her tin plate and gave a plaintive whine.

Tanner looked up from his place at the table and frowned. "Quit your complainin'. That's all you're getting tonight. Fact is, you're looking a little hefty, anyway. A little less food won't hurt you a bit."

She ambled over to the door and barked.

"Forget it. I'm not eating over at the house and neither are you. No way. Not with that Garver woman."

Becky cocked her head slightly, her liquid brown eyes locked on Tanner's face.

"Don't give me that look. I know what you're thinking. That I'm scared of softening. Well, don't give it a second thought. She's trouble and I won't rest until she's gone." Tanner rubbed his lightly stubbled chin. "I owe it to Seth, Becky. Fact is, I scared her off good today—"

A knock at the front door interrupted his discourse. Becky was on her hind legs instantly, yapping excitedly to greet the new arrival.

"Now what?" Tanner muttered ill-naturedly as he swung the door open. He stopped and stared, unable to believe his eyes.

"Good evening, Tanner." Elise smiled tremulously.

"I hope I'm not interrupting anything. We had lots of food left over from dinner and I thought, well, we thought you might be hungry. Rosa said fried chicken was your favorite."

Becky gave a soft bark. Elise smiled. "And yours, too, Becky." She looked back to Tanner who continued to stare at her without speaking. He didn't look nearly so fierce without his black hat, she thought with relief. Perhaps he wasn't quite so angry with her anymore.

When she had mentioned fixing a plate up for him to Rosa, she hadn't intended to be the one to deliver it.

"That's a wonderful idea, Elise," Rosa had said. "I'll fix up a couple of plates, and you can carry them over real quick while I clean up the dishes."

Elise couldn't very well deny her. How could she explain the problem between her and Tanner when she didn't understand it herself. She tried to refuse on the grounds that it was improper for a lady to visit a man at his home without a suitable chaperone, but her protests fell on deaf ears. Rosa would not be swayed. Mrs. Rhoades and her rules of propriety didn't seem to hold the same importance here in Texas as they did in Boston.

Fortunately, her fear of facing him appeared unfounded. Though he continued to stare at her with a look of disbelief, he had not berated her or sent her away. Her hopes raised slightly. Maybe one day they'd be friends, after all.

"If it's all right, I'll just leave the plates here and let you get back to work."

Tanner found his voice. "Work? Oh, yeah, work." He ran a hand through his hair. "Had lots to do tonight. Didn't feel like I could get away."

Elise smiled and nodded. "I understand completely." She waited for him to step aside so she could pass. He seemed rooted to the floor. "May I come in?"

"In? Sure, that's fine." Tanner frantically scanned the room, trying to see it through the eyes of a stranger. His eyes fell upon the pair of boots he had deposited in the middle of the floor. He walked over to them and bent casually to retrieve them, quickly stashing them out of sight behind the sofa.

"You have a lovely home," Elise said as she followed him inside.

"Thanks. Seth built it for your mother."

"My mother? Lived here?" Elise's voice was reverent. She laid the plates on the table and turned to survey the room more carefully.

It was more of a cottage than a house, with one large, general purpose room, one half serving as a kitchen and the other as a living room. She guessed that the door in the back led to the sleeping area. The furnishings were simple, as befitting a man, but comfortable.

"It's just lovely." Elise heard her voice break slightly. It was so special to be in the very home where her mother had once lived. She wanted to sit down and close her eyes, to let her imagination fill the house with the family she never knew.

Becky barked, startling Elise back to the present. "Oh, I really must be going. I hadn't intended to detain you." She pulled the towels off the plates. "Come, sit down and eat before it gets cold." Elise stepped toward the door. "I can let myself out. Enjoy your dinner. Good night."

Tanner said nothing as she pulled the door closed behind her. He continued to stare at the doorway for a long time until Becky's insistent scratching at his leg caught his attention.

"You can just wipe that silly grin off your face, fool dog. Nothin's changed. I couldn't hardly throw her out after she was so nice to bring us dinner." He placed Becky's plate on the floor, shaking his head in mild frustration. "I gotta admit, it would be a whole lot easier if she was mean and ugly."

five

Elise sat on the edge of her bed in complete misery. Yesterday's ride had taken its toll just as James had predicted. Her legs and backside were so stiff and sore; she couldn't decide what hurt worse, sitting or standing.

She managed to dress herself, but she was not altogether certain that she could navigate the flight of stairs. She knew she'd have to come down eventually; Rosa would worry if she didn't make it to breakfast and Elise was mortified at the idea of being discovered. Her soreness was proof positive that she was nothing more than a Boston socialite.

Summoning all her strength, she maneuvered slowly and painfully down the stairs to the kitchen where Becky's familiar black form reclined by the door, indicating that her master was present.

"Good morning," she called with forced cheerfulness. "Sorry I'm late."

"Come sit down, honey." Rosa hopped up and headed to the stove. "I've got your breakfast all ready."

Elise hoped they wouldn't notice her stiff-legged gait as she hobbled to the table. "Smells delicious, Rosa." She pasted a smile on her face as she gingerly lowered herself to the chair, but she couldn't help wincing as the hard wood connected with her wounded flesh.

She fought back the hot tears that stung in her eyes, knowing instinctively that Tanner's dark gaze was following her every movement. She couldn't let him see that she was hurting. It would simply confirm all the bad things he thought of her.

Rosa placed a full plate in front of her, completely unaware of her discomfort. "Bet you're anxious to get out there riding again this morning. James was bragging to me what a fine rider you are. Says you show a lot of promise."

Elise nibbled her lower lip. "Well, uh. . ."

"No, she won't be riding today," Tanner pronounced. Elise jerked her head up with a start and stared into his face. Their eyes locked as he continued, "I need James to help me with the fences."

Elise rewarded him with a dazzling smile. Without knowing it, he had just saved her hide, literally.

Rosa however, didn't share Elise's enthusiasm. "Now Tanner, surely you could spare him for an hour or so." Her dark eyes were pleading. "James says she's a natural."

"I'm sorry, Rosa." Tanner got to his feet, hat in hand. "I can't spare him today. Too much work to do."

"I guess I can find someone else to work with her."

Tanner shook his head. "Seth would skin me if I let her ride without James or myself. Miss Garver doesn't ride today."

"Well," Rosa answered a bit huffily, "if you insist."

Rosa missed the wink Tanner directed at Elise before he disappeared through the doorway. "Maybe tomorrow," he called over his shoulder. "If she's up to it."

Elise blushed furiously, partially because it was painfully obvious that Tanner had discovered her secret.

But a portion of the warmth she felt diffuse through her was directly attributable to the handsome man himself. Had he actually forbidden her to ride in order to protect her? Was it possible he might like her just a little bit, after all? And why did that thought hold so much appeal?

"He can be so stubborn when he wants to be," Rosa complained. "I'm sorry about the riding, honey. Maybe you'd like to help me plant my kitchen garden this morning instead?"

Elise was still in a daze. "Sure, Rosa, that sounds just fine."

≈

Several hours later, after having spent the morning in the garden, Elise slowly ascended the stairs. Her back and head now ached along with the rest of her anatomy; her only thought was to make it to her comfortable bed where she could collapse and die.

She pulled the bedroom door closed behind her and dropped, fully clothed, onto the bed. In a matter of minutes, she drifted off into an exhausted slumber.

≈

"Good afternoon, Father," said Elise.

"Oh, Elise, come in." Seth closed the ledger he was reading. "I didn't hear you."

Elise paused in the doorway. "Am I interrupting something? Perhaps I should come back later."

"No, no indeed. Just looking over the books." Seth smiled up at his daughter. "Sit down."

Elise eyed the chair warily. "I think I'd prefer to stand if you don't mind."

Seth shrugged. "Fine with me. So tell me, did you have a nice day?"

"Yes, sir. Rosa and I put in her kitchen garden."

"Good, good. Nice weather for planting, not too warm."

"Yes, sir, very nice. Quite comfortable, actually."

Seth nodded and smiled. Elise nodded and smiled. Then silence.

The clock, ticking in the background, reminded her of how quickly her time with her father was fleeing. If she didn't implement her plan soon, all would be lost. How could she make him love her if they didn't speak? The proper thing to do would be to wait until he spoke, to let him initiate the conversation. But being proper was getting her nowhere. Perhaps she should risk taking a chance.

"So, you were looking over the books," she began hesitantly. "Is there a lot of bookkeeping involved with ranching?"

She was delighted to see he did not seem annoyed by the question. On the contrary, he appeared to be pleased.

"Depends on the rancher, I suppose. I like to keep up with the expenses, of course, and I keep close tabs on how many head of cattle I've got."

Elise's heart soared. She could tell by the sparkle in his eyes that this subject was something in which he was interested. Since horses had become a painful subject, perhaps the operations of the ranch could be their common ground. "How many head of cattle do you have?"

A brisk knock on the door interrupted his answer.

Tanner strolled across the floor to Seth's side. "I got those numbers you were looking for. Cattle prices look better than ever."

Elise was crestfallen. She and her father were actually talking, not just exchanging meaningless pleasantries. She didn't want to leave. Perhaps she could stay and listen to the men talk business.

She nibbled her lower lip while studying the two men in conversation. Suppose in the course of the discussion, Tanner decided to share with her father the fact that she was practically incapacitated by her ride yesterday. She couldn't bear it. She didn't want her father to think she was just a Boston socialite. She wanted him to be proud of her. She wanted him to love her.

Maybe if she disappeared, her name wouldn't come up. "If you will excuse me." Elise walked stiffly to the door. "I need to get ready for dinner."

"Fine, Elise, thank you for coming."

Both men watched as she closed the door behind her.

❧

"Evenin', Rosa." Tanner strode into the kitchen with Becky following close on his heels. He wrapped his arms around Rosa, squeezing her in a bone-crushing embrace. "Dinner smells delicious. We're starved."

Rosa beamed up into his handsome face. "Go on and sit down. I'll get it on the table right away."

He sat down at the empty table and asked casually, "Where's our little city kid tonight?"

Rosa laid a full plate in front of him. "She's not coming down. Says she's not hungry." She sat down with a worried sigh. "The child hasn't been herself today."

"What do you mean?" Tanner's dark eyes met hers, his brows suddenly furrowed with concern.

Rosa shrugged. "I don't know exactly. She just seemed real sluggish. Almost like it pained her to move."

Tanner thought of Elise's behavior at breakfast. He recognized clearly the signs that she had spent a bit too much time in the saddle. The thought was actually amusing to him at the time. Fact is, he figured, she deserved it. *She doesn't belong here, anyway.*

Tonight, however, he found himself strangely disappointed that she wouldn't be joining them for dinner. For a city kid, she had a lot of gumption. She must be in more pain than he had realized.

Seeing that Elise hadn't explained the source of her discomfort to Rosa, Tanner opted not to mention it, either.

"Rosa, I wouldn't worry if I were you. It just takes city folks a few days to settle in. That's all."

"Do you think so?" Rosa's voice was hopeful. "I wish I could help her."

"I'll bet a hot bath would fix her up just fine."

"A hot bath?"

Tanner grinned broadly. "Trust me on this one."

"If you really think so." She studied Tanner's face to be certain he was serious. Satisfied that he was, she got up from the table. "I'll start heating the water up right away."

ॐ

After dinner, Tanner left the house and Rosa continued to prepare Elise's bath. "Elise, honey," Rosa called softly into Elise's darkened bedroom, "I've got a nice hot bath ready for you downstairs."

Elise pushed herself up into a sitting position on the bed to look at Rosa. "A hot bath?" If it wouldn't have been so painful, she'd have jumped for joy. "That sounds wonderful. I'll be right down."

She gathered her soap and powder and a dressing gown from the wardrobe, and descended the stairs as quickly as she could on her stiff legs. Rosa led her to a small room off the kitchen with a huge tub in the center. Elise could see steam rising from the water.

In no time at all, Elise undressed, pinned her long hair up on top of her head, and lowered herself slowly into the tub with a delighted sigh. Submerged in the steamy liquid, she could feel her stiffness melting away.

For a long time, she was absolutely still, savoring the delicious warmth. Finally, as the water began to cool, she reached for the bar of soap. She hummed a happy tune while working it into a frothy lather, its flowery fragrance filling the air.

Tanner swung open the back door and stepped into the house. He had forgotten his hat at dinner and had come to retrieve it. A familiar fragrance wafting down the hall stopped him in his tracks—flowers, a whole field of flowers. He breathed deeply of the heady aroma.

Even though the door was closed, he could hear Elise humming cheerfully as she splashed around in the next room. He paused for a minute or two, enchanted by the sound of her voice. Finally, he forced himself to move down the hall to the dining room, his heart inexplicably lighter with the knowledge that the little socialite felt better.

After Elise had dried herself off and dressed in her robe, she padded into the kitchen where Rosa was seated at the table. "Rosa, I can't thank you enough for fixing the bath for me. It was exactly what I needed."

Rosa smiled up at her. "I'm so glad, *querido*. But I'm afraid the thanks should go to Tanner. The bath was his idea."

"Tanner?" Elise squeaked, wrapping her dressing gown around herself more tightly. "It was Tanner's idea?"

Rosa nodded, oblivious to Elise's distress. "He seemed to think it would be a real tonic for you. And I can see that he was right." She pointed to the stove. "Are you hungry? Can I fix you a piece of pie?"

"No, I think not." Elise shook her head. "I'm awfully sleepy. I'll just go on up to bed."

"Fine, honey. Oh, by the way, do you remember our conversation last night, about talking to God about all the little details in our lives?"

Elise nodded.

"I was reading in my Bible tonight, and I found a couple of verses that helped me to see that God cares about all the details in our lives." She picked up the worn book resting on the table in front of her. "I wrote them on a piece of paper. Maybe if you get a chance, you can look them up."

"Thank you." With a smile, Elise accepted the Bible from her. "That was very kind of you."

Rosa got to her feet and pressed a kiss onto Elise's cheek. "Sleep well, *querido*." Rosa breathed a silent prayer as she watched the young woman leave. *Heavenly Father, I've shown her the truth. It's up to You to help her believe it.*

Elise lay back against the cool sheets, up in her bed, wondering if she should be elated or mortified. That a man should suggest she take a bath was truly beyond the bounds of propriety. Poor Aunt Claudia would be apoplectic if she knew.

On the other hand, the bath had truly worked miracles on her abused flesh. How thoughtful of him to be concerned. Elise pulled the covers up under her chin. Was it possible? Was Tanner concerned about her?

Not likely, she told herself. Yesterday's tongue-lashing was still fresh on her mind. He made it clear that he wanted her as far away from him as possible.

However, she argued, hadn't he prevented her from riding this morning? And wasn't he the one who suggested a bath for her tonight? She was no expert, but that sounded like concern to her.

Elise drifted off to sleep, smiling at the thought.

six

Elise's long dark lashes flickered against her cheeks. The sun peeked through the lace curtains, beckoning her to awaken to a new day. Her first thought was about her stiffness. Would she spend another day in agony?

Ever so carefully, she gave a tiny stretch, testing her arms. To her relief, they felt fine. Next, she flexed her legs. Again, no pain. She pulled back the covers and sat up. Other than an awareness of her backside, she felt completely normal.

She stood up with the intention of getting dressed when the Bible that Rosa had given her last night caught her eye. She picked it up off the bedstand and flipped to one of the passages that Rosa had marked.

The first one was Matthew 10:29–30, and Jesus was speaking. " 'Are not two sparrows sold for a farthing? and one of them shall not fall on the ground without your Father. But the very hairs of your head are all numbered.' "

Elise read the passage again. She'd been attending church every Sunday of her life and yet she had never heard this Scripture. God knew the number of hairs on her head? She absently twirled a silky lock on her finger. That sure sounded like He was interested in little details about her. And the part about the sparrows. She had no idea God kept up with birds, too.

For a moment, Elise disputed the truth of what she had read. After all, if it was true, wouldn't she have heard it before now? Why hadn't their minister told them? Her eyes were drawn back to the Scripture. It was Jesus speaking: God's Son. She knew He did not lie. And Who better than He to tell just exactly what God was interested in.

The second passage Rosa had written down was found in Philippians. Elise fumbled through the pages until she found the fourth chapter. "Be careful for nothing; but in every thing by prayer and supplication with thanksgiving let your requests be made known unto God." Rosa had scribbled a note in the margin: *Paul tells us if it is important enough for you to care about, it is important enough to share with God. He wants to bear all our burdens, nothing is too small, so turn your cares into prayers.*

Elise sat down on the edge of the bed. Paul, too, seemed to be convinced that God was interested in the day-to-day details of His children's lives. Paul didn't say that God takes care of salvation and judgment and you take care of the rest. It sounded to her as though God wanted to hear about it all.

It was late, and Elise's stomach rumbled, urging her to get downstairs for breakfast, but she delayed a moment longer to read a final verse in 1 Peter 5:7. "Casting all your care upon him; for he careth for you." Here it was again. Another directive to place all of one's burdens on God. The verse even explained why—because God cares. She sighed as she closed the book, replacing it on the table. What a thought. *God cares.*

Rosa was clearing away the dishes when Elise finally arrived in the kitchen.

"There you are! I was afraid you weren't feeling well this morning."

Elise smiled. "I feel fine. I got interested reading in your Bible and lost track of the time." She eyed the stove hopefully. "Any more coffee?"

"Sure is. And biscuits, too. They're warming in the oven."

Elise placed two fluffy biscuits on a plate and sat at the table. Rosa joined her with a cup of coffee for each of them.

"So what did you think? I mean about the Bible verses?"

"It's all right there, just as you said." Elise spread a liberal dollop of butter on one of her biscuits. "Each one of them seemed to point clearly to the fact that God is indeed concerned with every area of our lives."

She bit into the biscuit and chewed thoughtfully. "But you know, Rosa, I used to pray. I prayed faithfully, every single day about something very important thing to me, and yet He never answered my prayer."

Rosa was at a loss for words as she studied the intense, emerald gaze directed at her. James's sudden appearance in the kitchen made it impossible for her to continue.

"Good morning," he began, beaming at Elise. "Is my student ready for another day in the saddle?"

"James," Rosa intervened, "I haven't had a chance to tell her you called for her already this morning. She just now got downstairs. Maybe you can come back later."

Elise popped the last of the biscuit into her mouth. "Oh, no, don't go. I'm ready now. I just need to get my hat." She hopped up from the table. "Thanks for breakfast, Rosa." She was halfway down the hall when she called out, "I'll only be just a minute, James."

Minutes later the two of them crossed the yard to the stables, Elise skipping alongside him in her excitement. "I'm looking forward to my ride this morning. Will it be Miss Sadie again? We worked so well together, I thought. I don't think I'll be quite so nervous."

James laughed at her enthusiastic chatter. "I figured you'd be wantin' Miss Sadie. I got her all saddled and ready for ya." He stopped for a moment, licking his lips nervously. "May I say, Miss Garver, you're looking mighty colorful this morning."

Elise smiled self-consciously. "Thank you. I hoped I wouldn't look silly. I have the most difficult time knowing which colors to wear together. My Aunt Claudia always says I'm as thick as a post when it comes to colors."

"Tain't true, Miss Garver. Why, God Himself puts all them colors together in the rainbow."

Elise couldn't resist a smile. "I never thought about it that way before. I guess you're right."

Encouraged by his success, James pressed on. "And that's a right fine bonnet yer wearin'. Why I bet every bee in the county will be plum delighted over all them flowers. It's like a regular garden, just sittin' on your head."

She smiled again. James, immeasurably pleased with himself, puffed out his chest and strutted into the darkened stable with Elise following close behind. She stepped aside to allow him to lead Miss Sadie from the stall.

"Here she is. Lemme give you a lift up and we'll get started." He stepped toward Elise with his arms extended.

"Thank you, James." Tanner's deep voice rang out from the entrance. "I'll be taking care of Miss Garver's instruction today." He and Becky joined them in front of the stall.

James's face fell at the interruption. "Aw, Tanner, why did ya have to come in now? This here's the best part."

Elise was unable to see the exchange between the two men, but she suspected Tanner of applying his chillingly dark glare to James. Whatever it was, James decided not to protest further. "Okay, boss, I've got lots to do, anyway." He shrugged his shoulders. "See you later, Miss Garver."

"Tanner, I'm. . .surprised. . . ," Elise stammered once they were alone. "I mean, I didn't expect. . . ."

"I had some extra time today." Tanner refused to meet her gaze as he fumbled for an explanation. "Besides, James has plenty to do."

Honestly, he didn't have a clue as to why he volunteered to help her. He certainly had not planned to. He had more than enough to do without wasting time on a frivolous socialite. But here he was.

"I brought something I thought might help," he said quietly, producing a small suede object from behind his back.

"How nice," she answered politely as she studied it with interest. "What is it?"

"A pillow. For your uh. . .uh, well, you know." Tanner dropped his glance to the floor of the stable. "For sitting on."

Elise felt the crimson stain scorch her skin as it swept across her body. This new infraction was positively unthinkable. No one in polite society ever discussed, even alluded to this sort of thing. And yet. . . She looked over to Tanner, the ferocious, towering cowboy whose dark gaze struck fear in her heart.

He didn't look too fearsome right now. He was staring at his boots in what looked to Elise to be mortification. Something deep within Elise began to stir and she began to laugh. It started small with a breathless giggle, then blossomed into a full-blown laugh that brought tears to her eyes.

Tanner regretted his words the minute they escaped from his lips. He knew it wasn't the sort of thing one mentioned in front of a lady. What was he thinking, anyway, bringing a pillow for Elise? He had never felt like such an idiot in his life. He was formulating an apology when he heard the lilting sound of her laughter.

He looked up to stare at her in complete disbelief. She was actually laughing. . .hard. Tears glistened in her eyes and one or two were rolling down her silken cheeks.

Tanner was so relieved at her totally unexpected response that he smiled. Her mirth proved infectious and he found himself joining in the laughter. Becky added to the merriment of the twosome with shrill barks of delight.

"What's goin' on in here?" James called from the doorway of the stables. "You two sound like a pack of coyotes. What's so funny, anyway?"

Both Elise and Tanner sobered instantly with his appearance. Elise's hand flew over her mouth in alarm at their discovery. She would rather die than reveal the source of their amusement.

Tanner seemed to sense her concern. "It's nothin'," he called back.

"Didn't sound like nothin' to me," James grumbled as he went back to work.

Elise exhaled loudly, releasing the breath she'd been holding.

Tanner smiled down at her, his dark eyes still glittering with mirth. "Perhaps we should get on with the lesson then?"

Elise nodded.

He placed his hands at her waist and lifted her as though she were weightless, positioning her gently on the pillow-topped saddle. Elise drew a sharp breath. Partially with the pleasure of being atop the horse and partially with the pleasure of being held in Tanner's strong arms.

Tanner heard her draw the breath and mistook it for pain. "Are you all right?" His eyes reflected genuine concern as they searched hers for the answer.

Elise was mesmerized, held captive by their inky depths. For a long moment she could neither think nor speak.

Finally, with a small shake of her head, she broke from the spell. "I. . .I'm fine." Her voice sounded shaky to her own ears.

Tanner, too, seemed strangely disturbed. "Good. That's good," he said absently. "Now, what were we talking about?" He pushed his hat back farther on his head. "Oh yeah. Lessons. I think for today, you should stay in the corral and work on form and control. Tomorrow you can start taking Sadie out on the ranch."

"Sounds fine to me."

Tanner took the reins and guided Miss Sadie into the corral. "You need to use your legs when you ride," he instructed. "It's their job to keep you in the saddle, instead of bouncing up and down. I'm afraid you are familiar with the results of bouncing."

Elise nodded sheepishly.

He folded his arms across his chest as he circled the horse to consider his student. "Your posture looks good. You have good tension on the reins. I think you're ready. Remember, use your legs." With that final directive, he inclined his head slightly, signaling her to ride.

Elise and Miss Sadie went through the paces with Tanner standing in the center of the ring to offer his suggestions. She was elated at the end of the hour of walking and trotting, starting and stopping, when Tanner pronounced her ready to ride around the ranch.

"That sounds wonderful." She was beaming as she reined in the horse beside him. "It's a beautiful day for it."

Tanner shook his head. "No, I'm afraid you misunderstand. You're finished for the day. An hour in the saddle, even with padding, is more than enough for a city girl. Tomorrow's plenty soon enough."

Elise was too delighted by the way he referred to her as a city girl to offer any protest for the delay. It wasn't the words, but rather the way he said them, as though she were a fragile prize. "Tomorrow sounds just fine."

He reached up for her, and their eyes met and held as she leaned forward, her hands resting lightly on his broad shoulders. Ever so slowly he lowered her to the ground, their eye contact unbroken.

She knew she should remove her hands from him once she felt her feet touch the ground, but she could not. Tanner's hands remained fastened around her waist. For a long silent moment, they stood there, eyes locked, unmoving. His dark gaze drifted to her lips. Elise's heart began to thunder wildly in her chest and her mouth suddenly went dry.

"Hey, boss man! You want me to put Miss Sadie away for ya?"

James's sudden appearance had the effect of an icy shower. Instantly, the couple separated. Elise dusted the front of her skirt, while Tanner shoved his hands deep into his pockets and kicked at the dirt with his boot.

"That's fine, James." Tanner's deep voice cracked slightly. "We were just finishing up."

James laughed. "Yes, sir. I could see that real plain."

Elise felt the familiar rush of warmth spread across her face. "I need to get on inside." She studied her hands clasped before her, refusing to meet Tanner's eyes as she continued, "Thank you so much for the lessons, Tanner. I've learned a great deal today." With that, she turned heel and practically ran for the house.

"Look, Tanner, I'm real sorry about Miss Garver. I had no idea that you two were, uh. . .sweethearts. I hope you don't take offense to me riding with her the other day. It was nothing, really."

"No offense taken." Tanner watched as James led Miss Sadie toward the stable. Becky moved over to take her place beside him, rubbing against his leg.

He swept the hat from his head and ran his hands through the dark waves. "Don't bother to ask me what I'm doing, Becky, cuz I don't have any idea."

seven

"Good afternoon, Father." Elise let herself into the room. Her father was in his customary position, propped up against a wall of pillows. "You're looking fit."

"Thank you, Elise. And may I say that you are looking particularly lovely today. Texas must agree with you."

"Thank you, sir." She settled primly into the chair by his bed. "I believe it does."

"Did you enjoy your ride today? Rosa tells me you had another lesson."

Elise stared off into space. "Tanner was wonderful," she said with a dreamy sigh. Her eyes flew open when she realized what she'd said. "What I mean to say is, Tanner is a wonderful instructor." She stared dismally into her lap and tried again. "That is, he seems to be very knowledgeable about horses."

Seth suppressed a chuckle. This morning, he had been at the window, watching with interest as his daughter and Tanner talked together. He hadn't detected the usual animosity. In fact, from where he was sitting, it looked like the opposite. He only wondered if things were truly as they appeared from one story up. Elise's discomfort had given him his answer.

"Yes, he is. Very capable man. I place you in his hands with complete confidence." He wanted to snicker at his little joke, but held his tongue. At that moment, he looked up to see Tanner, standing in the doorway. "Well, speaking of Tanner, here he is. Come on in, son, we were just talking about you."

"Afternoon Seth, Miss Garver." Tanner nodded to both of them as he crossed the room with several long strides. "Rosa told me you wanted to see me."

Seth nodded. "That's true. I want you to look over some of my projected figures for cattle sales. But first, I'd like to thank you for helping Elise with her riding today. She was just telling me what an excellent instructor you are."

Elise had already determined that no matter what the interruption, she would not be driven from her father's room today. In the time she'd spent in Texas, she was no closer to her goal of earning her father's love. She hadn't even had a good conversation with him.

But the sight of Tanner evaporated her resolve. Just looking at him gave her the queerest feeling in her stomach. She actually felt a bit giddy. She had no doubt that if she opened her mouth to speak, something inane would spill out. She couldn't take the chance. She would have to catch her father alone.

"I'll be running along then." She stood up and offered a smile to her father. "I'll be back, same time tomorrow."

"I'm looking forward to it, Elise."

૨ે

By the time Elise arrived downstairs for dinner, she had time to analyze her strange reaction to Tanner. It was obvious, she decided, that the lightheadedness and butterflies were nothing more than elation over securing his friendship, the first step toward the realization of her dream. It seemed reasonable. After all, hadn't that been part of her plan? To secure Tanner's approval as well as her father's.

She suspected that his dark, ruggedly handsome good looks might be responsible in part for the giddiness; after all, she was only human. But then she reassured herself that it was largely the pleasure of his friendship that left her feeling somewhat addled in his presence.

Fortified with the knowledge that she and Tanner were indeed becoming friends, she faced dinner with complete confidence. The food Rosa prepared was delicious, and the conversation between the three of them was light, making the evening a success.

There was only one awkward moment, when Elise's fingers accidentally met Tanner's as she passed him the platter of beef, and a flash of energy coursed through her. Her surprised reaction had been to withdraw her hand immediately, as though she'd been burned, and the platter would have fallen, had not Tanner caught it. Fortunately for her, no one seemed to notice her blunder.

After everyone had eaten their fill of pie and coffee, Tanner pushed back in his chair. "It's gettin' late."

His voice sounded reluctant. "Guess Becky and I better get back to the house, and let you ladies get some rest."

At the signal, both Rosa and Elise got to their feet.

"I surely had a nice time, surrounded by you young people," Rosa said as she scooped several plates off the table and headed for the kitchen. "It was good to have the both of you at dinner for a change." She called over her shoulder, "*Buenas noches,* Tanner. We'll be seeing you in the morning."

"I want to thank you again for my riding lesson today," Elise said once they were alone. She lowered her eyes to add, "I enjoyed it very much."

"It was my pleasure." He dropped his hat onto his head and added with a wicked grin, "And if the pillow did the trick, we'll have you riding out on the ranch tomorrow."

Elise couldn't help but return the smile. "Good night, Tanner."

"Good night, Miss Garver. Sleep well."

She watched as he and Becky walked down the hall to the back door. Once they were out of sight, she picked up several dishes from the table and carried them into the kitchen.

"Thank you for dinner, Rosa. It was delicious."

"I'm so glad you liked it, honey." The two women moved back to the dining room together to collect the remainder of the dishes. "You know, Elise," Rosa said as they worked, "I was thinking about what you told me this morning, about not having your prayers answered, and I wanted to ask you a question."

"Certainly."

"Are you a Christian?"

Elise stopped, frozen in her tracks, her green eyes flashing with shocked indignation. "Of course I am," she huffed. "I have attended church every Sunday of my life for as long as I can remember, and," she raised her chin a fraction, "I was elected the recording secretary of the Ladies Missionary Society." Suddenly, she didn't look quite so self-assured. "Is there something about my conduct that would lead you to believe otherwise?"

"No indeed, your conduct is just fine," Rosa soothed. "I can see that you are a fine young woman. But some good folks, even those that are members of a church and go every Sunday aren't Christians at all."

Elise was somewhat mollified. She followed Rosa back into the kitchen. "I'm not sure I know what you mean."

"Take yourself for example. You went into the stables today, didn't you?"

"Well, yes."

"Did it make you a horse?"

Elise giggled. "Rosa, that's silly."

"Yes it is, but it makes a point. Just going to church doesn't make you a Christian any more than going to a stable makes you a horse."

Elise looked puzzled. "Then how do you become a Christian?"

"Simple, really," Rosa said as she plunged a plate into the tubful of soapy water. "By making a personal commitment to Jesus."

Elise took the plate that Rosa had washed and rinsed, and dried it with a towel. A worried frown troubled her features. For the first time in the conversation, she wondered if she were, indeed, a Christian.

She couldn't recall ever making a personal commitment, not to Jesus, not to anything. Fact was, Aunt Claudia made most of her commitments for her. Aunt Claudia had chosen the church they attended, the friends that she kept; Aunt Claudia was even the one to choose the position of recording secretary for Elise. Elise merely did as she was told.

"I wonder if you could be more specific," Elise suggested as she took another dripping plate.

"I'll try." Rosa's dark eyes darted around the room, as she sought inspiration. Her gaze came to rest on the stack of dirty dishes in front of her and she smiled. "You see this plate?" She held up a dinner plate that was streaked with leftover food and gravy. "This is like our lives, all dirty and messy with sin."

Elise giggled at the illustration.

"God wants us to be all pure and clean, so we can be His children. And we want to be His children, because the Bible is full of the many wonderful promises God makes to His children. One of those promises is that He hears their prayers.

"So, we try to clean ourselves up to be worthy of God; like trying to be real good, or attending church regularly, but it doesn't work. We can't make ourselves clean." Rosa took a rag and swished it over the face of the plate, smearing the mess even worse.

"So God sent His only Son, Jesus, to wash away our sins. But our cleanliness came at a very high price. It cost Jesus His life, a sinless life He offered on the cross."

Rosa caught the look of distress on Elise's face. "Jesus was glad to do it, though, because He knew that by taking the punishment we deserved for our sins, we would be cleansed, and we could be God's children." Rosa dipped the plate into the sudsy water and scrubbed it. Then she poured clear water over the plate, rinsing it sparkling clean.

"I've heard all that before, I mean the part about Jesus being crucified for our sins and then being raised from the dead three days later. But I still don't see where the personal commitment part comes in."

"Just knowing the facts isn't enough. You've got to believe them. You have got to believe that Jesus is God's Son and that He died on the cross for your sins. You have to accept His sacrifice on your behalf and confess Jesus as your Savior."

For a long moment, Elise was silent. She finished drying the plates Rosa handed her, and then stacked them with the others. While she worked, she replayed the conversation over in her mind. She had not known her need for a Savior until now, but once exposed, she felt it acutely. She couldn't wait another minute. In a very small voice, she said, "Rosa, I'd like to make that commitment to Jesus. I want to be one of God's children."

Rosa beamed. "Then let's pray." She must have noticed the crimson blush on Elise's cheeks because she added, "Why don't I pray and you can pray along with me?"

Elise's face mirrored her relief.

Rosa took Elise's hands in hers and bowed her head to pray. "Lord Jesus, I know that I'm a sinner. I thank You for dying on the cross for me, taking my punishment so that I could be forgiven. I ask You to forgive me now. I accept Your sacrifice on my behalf and confess You as my Savior. Thank You for making me a child of God."

A comforting warmth spread through Elise as she whispered the heartfelt prayer. She knew instantly that God had heard. The warmth changed quickly to an unspeakable joy that flooded her from head to toe, dazzling her with its intensity.

Elise was horrified at her own impropriety. Joy? Religion was no place for frivolous emotions. She learned early that church was a place for solemnity and one's spirituality could be accurately gauged by the degree of dourness reflected in one's face. Elise secretly suspected that Aunt Claudia's reputation as a pillar of the church was largely based on her ability to scowl.

She squeezed her eyes closed more tightly, trying to suppress the errant feeling. She'd best carefully school her expression to one of cheerlessness before opening them to meet those of Rosa. She didn't want Rosa to see her grinning like a fool; she might think her prayer had not been sincere.

Finally satisfied that her own expression was one of appropriate gloom, Elise opened her eyes a crack to steal a glance at Rosa. Rosa positively glowed. Her smile was so wide and bright it almost hurt to look at it.

A giggle escaped before Elise could catch it. Another followed, and then another until the two women fell into each other's arms, laughing and crying tears of joy.

❧

Tanner lay in bed, his arms folded behind his head. As was customary since the arrival of the Garver woman, he found it difficult to sleep.

"I got it figured out!" he suddenly exclaimed into the darkness. "Becky, old girl, I know what I was doing this afternoon. I was switching strategies!"

At the sound of her name, Becky stopped scratching and looked over toward the bed.

"Sure, that's exactly what I was doing." He rolled over onto his side to face the dog. "What's the best way to get to know the enemy? To spend time with them, right? Well, that's what I was doing. By riding with Miss Garver, I was able to study her at close range, to see what she is really all about."

Seeing he had nothing for her, Becky went back to scratching at the flea that was annoying her.

"You don't believe me, do you? You think I'm falling for her. Well, don't you worry, Becky. I'm no fool. Those green eyes and the smell of flowers lay a pretty fine trap, but it would take more than that to turn my head. I'm going in with my eyes wide open."

Becky shifted positions in order to reach the flea now lurking on her hind leg.

Tanner was silent for a minute before he spoke again. "I wonder, Becky, while we're on the subject of Miss Garver, did you happen to notice what a fine sense of humor she has? I mean, it takes a big person to be able to laugh at herself."

Becky got to her feet and ambled off into the other room.

"And gumption," he called after her retreating figure. "For a city kid, she's got gumption."

He rolled onto his back. "Don't worry, though. I've got my eyes wide open."

eight

Elise could scarcely wait to get to breakfast. She raced down the stairs with what she knew to be indecent haste and burst breathlessly into the kitchen. "Good morning, Rosa."

Rosa gathered her into her arms for a hug. "Good morning. And how's the new Christian this morning?"

Elise beamed. "Wonderful, thank you." Her eyes darted around the room. "Where's Tanner?"

"He and a couple of the hands went to check out the cattle. He ought to be back around lunch."

"Oh." Elise was strangely disappointed.

"Something wrong?"

"Oh, no, it's just that I thought he was going to teach me to ride today. He said I could go out on the ranch."

Rosa grinned. "That must be why he told me to pack up a picnic. He's figuring on you two getting hungry during the lesson."

"A picnic?" Elise squealed as her heart gave a little jump. "Oh, Rosa!" Her hands flew to her face. "I need to get ready."

Rosa laughed and shook her head as the girl bolted excitedly from the room. "Tanner and Elise? That's something I won't believe till I see it," she declared to the empty room.

The morning dragged on interminably for Elise. She wrote another letter to Aunt Claudia, though she'd already written and mailed one during the course of her short stay. Since little had happened, the letter was quickly written and Elise was again at a loss for something to do.

She thought she might read a bit from Rosa's Bible, but her eyes and mind refused to cooperate.

Even sewing seemed to be beyond Elise. She tried to pick up her much-neglected needlework, but her mind was so far from the fabric that nearly every stitch had to be ripped out and done again.

She'd almost given up hope when she heard the sound of the back door closing and the heavy footfalls of booted feet. With a quick glance in the mirror, she grabbed a bonnet and flew down the stairs, colliding abruptly with the solid wall of Tanner's broad chest.

"Oh, Tanner, I'm so sorry," she stammered as she backed up a step. "I guess I wasn't looking where I was going."

Tanner stared down into her face, her green eyes sparkling and her smooth cheeks flushed with excitement, and he felt his heart give an unfamiliar twist. He had the oddest sensation, as though the breath had been knocked from him, yet he knew the slight impact from her tiny form hadn't been nearly enough to do so.

"Good morning, Miss Garver," he said as he pulled the hat from his head. "I was just on my way up to call you. Are you ready for your lesson?"

"I've been ready!" she pronounced with an impish pout. "I didn't think you'd ever get here."

Tanner chuckled at her candid reply. He couldn't say why, but it pleased him to know she'd been looking forward to seeing him. "Rosa's got lunch all packed. We'll get the horses, and we'll be on our way."

Elise placed her bonnet on top of her head and began to tie the ribbons. She missed Tanner's upraised brow as he considered this latest outfit.

He'd grown accustomed to her odd color combinations, so the mint green blouse and red skirt looked completely normal to him. It was the hat that held his attention.

He wasn't certain he'd ever seen anything quite like it. It extended some six inches above her head and appeared to be covered with tiny clusters of fruit and bits of gauzy lace. It was pretty enough for a tea party, he supposed, but on the range? He had no doubt that during the course of their ride they'd be attacked by a flock of hungry birds. "Have you got something a little less, uh, fancy?" he asked tactfully.

Elise dropped her hands from the yellow ribbon and stared wide-eyed into his dark gaze. "Don't you like it?"

"Well, sure, I like it. It's just that I'm afraid uh, well, I'm afraid it might get messed up somehow."

She placed a hand on his arm and smiled warmly. "Aren't you sweet to be concerned. You mustn't worry, though. It's really quite sturdy." She gave the bow under her chin a final pat. "Shall we go?"

The sun was high overhead as the two of them crossed the yard toward the stables, with Elise practically running to keep up with Tanner's long strides. The now-familiar smell of freshly cut hay welcomed Elise as she stepped inside the cool shade of the building.

Elise watched as Tanner effortlessly saddled Miss Sadie. She couldn't help admiring his muscles straining beneath the fabric of his shirt as he lifted the heavy saddle into place. She leaned against the wooden stall to study him more carefully. Again she was reminded of how attractive he was. His ruggedly chiseled features and dark wavy hair were enough to make her weak-kneed.

"All set," he said as he turned to place the reins in Elise's hands. He must have felt her staring, because he quirked an inquisitive brow.

She felt herself blush to her toes. What would he think of such a bold woman? "Which horse will you be riding?" she asked, trying to divert attention from herself.

"Gypsy is tied up outside." He inclined his head toward Miss Sadie. "You ready?"

She nodded and Tanner lifted her high, placing her gently upon the pillow-topped saddle. Elise was relieved that he failed to mention the pillow, and even more relieved that he remembered to bring it.

He guided the horse out into the sunlight and around to the side of the stable where his horse was tethered.

Elise gasped her admiration. If James thought Elise and Miss Sadie were made for each other, so much more this horse and Tanner. She was an immense creature with a silky black coat that glistened in the late-morning sun. With her regal head held high, she stomped her hooves impatiently as she awaited her master. Becky was dwarfed standing beside it.

Tanner swung easily into the saddle. "Okay, Miss Garver, let's ride."

They took the horses out at a leisurely pace, stopping frequently to discuss some point of interest. Elise was fascinated by everything. "What is that long building over there?" she asked, pointing toward a structure well behind her father's house.

"That's the bunkhouse. For the hands."

"I never noticed it before. Is that where James lives?"

Tanner couldn't imagine why he felt a sharp jab of jealousy at the mention of James's name. His response was less than enthusiastic. "Yeah."

Elise didn't seem to notice. "It's lovely. Funny that I've never seen it before." She leaned forward in the saddle, looking from side to side, studying the panorama. "There's just so much to see. And it's all so beautiful."

She was truly enraptured by the ranch. The untamed beauty was breathtaking, but there was more. It was her father's. He'd carved out this prosperous business with his own two hands. Her heart swelled with pride. What a wonderful man he was.

Tanner was watching the unabashed delight on her face when a sudden jolt of inspiration struck. He reined his horse around and called back to her, "Follow me."

They rode due south through the swaying green grasses, slowly enough for Elise to stop and admire each bird or wildflower that caught her fancy. Becky would run off on her own to chase anything she could find and then reappear minutes later at their sides.

The wind picked up as they traveled, replacing the morning's fluffy white clouds with more substantial gray ones.

When they finally reached their destination, the crest of a tree-topped hill, Tanner reined his horse to a halt. He extended his arm before him, indicating that Elise should look.

She gasped with pure delight. Below her for as far as she could see, the valley was a sea of bright blue flowers waving merrily in the gusting winds. "Oh, Tanner!" she exclaimed without taking her eyes from the spectacle. "I've never seen anything so beautiful. What are they?"

"Texas bluebonnets." A wide grin spread across his face as he watched her enthusiastic response. He'd wanted to surprise her, and it was obvious he had done just that.

"They grow wild?"

"Yup. Come back every year."

She turned in the saddle to face him. "Do you suppose I could go down and pick some?"

"Sure. We'll come back on our way home." He checked the darkening sky. "We may have to cut our tour short today. Looks like a storm comin' in."

"And miss our picnic?" Elise sounded crushed. Her expression was so forlorn, he almost laughed.

Tanner glanced up at the threatening clouds. He knew the storm was imminent. He wanted to tell her the smartest thing they could do would be to ride back to the safety of the ranch, but one glance at the pleading look in her emerald eyes and he relented. "No, we'll have our picnic. And I know just the place. Come on."

He thought of the spring-filled pond back toward the house. There was even a cluster of trees they could sit under. It would be the perfect location. Elise would get her picnic, and he would have moved them closer to home before the storm hit.

Elise was obviously reluctant to leave the bluebonnets behind. With a heavy sigh, she tugged at Miss Sadie's reins, falling in behind Tanner. Becky obediently brought up the rear.

The sky grew more ominous by the minute. Thick black clouds roiled overhead. The gusting wind had transformed into a steady gale. They were less than halfway to the picnic site, still three-quarters of an hour from the main house, when the first raindrops began to fall.

Tanner glanced toward Elise. He was relieved to see she didn't look fearful. Quite the opposite, in fact. She appeared to think the whole rain-splattered excursion was a lark. He noticed that her ridiculous fruit basket hat was doing an admirable job of keeping her dry. He supposed he ought to be thankful for small blessings.

He quickly revised his original plan. There would be no picnic today, that much was certain. But as long as the rain held slow, he'd head them back toward the house. With any luck, they'd beat the downpour.

No sooner had his brain registered the thought than the heavens opened up, and the rain began to come down in driving sheets.

"Ready to try a gallop?" he shouted, to be heard above the wind.

Elise smiled brightly as raindrops coursed down her cheeks. "I'd love it."

"Use your legs and hold on tight!"

Tanner kicked his horse up and took off like a shot. Miss Sadie needed no encouragement to follow suit and they raced across the field side by side, with Becky keeping pace at their heels.

A bolt of lightning zigzagged across the sky, followed by a deafening crash. Miss Sadie balked slightly at the sound. Tanner knew they couldn't continue on toward the ranch now. It was too dangerous.

"This way," he shouted, signaling toward his left. He knew of a small abandoned shack a few minutes to the west. They could stop there until the storm slacked off.

Minutes later the rain-drenched travelers thundered up to the cabin. Tanner dismounted quickly and lifted Elise from the saddle.

"Go on inside. You, too, Becky." Rivulets of water ran down his face as he spoke. "I'll take care of the horses and be in right behind you."

After tethering the horses securely inside the crude shelter behind the building, Tanner dashed to the door of the cabin and ducked inside.

Elise was waiting for him, standing in the center of the room, with her slender arms wrapped across her rain-soaked middle. She had removed her bonnet and he could see that her hair was drenched. So much for the fruity hat.

Becky was exploring, busily sniffing out the room, totally unconcerned about her own rain-plastered coat.

"I'm sorry about the mess," he apologized, surveying the dilapidated interior.

"It's dry," Elise said cheerfully, flashing him a shivery smile.

He couldn't help but grin. For a city kid, she sure had spunk.

"There's some wood in the fireplace. Let me get a fire started, and we'll see if we can get you dried out."

Elise nodded gratefully.

The well-seasoned wood caught fire instantly and Tanner had a crackling blaze going in no time. Once satisfied it would burn, he stood up to study their meager accommodations.

An old, scarred table was pushed up against the wall near the door. Beside it lay the fractured remains of the only chair in the room. No help there. A small cot along the far wall caught his attention and Tanner walked over to have a closer look. The mattress was patched and worn, but apparently clean.

He picked the mattress up, dusted it off, and carried it across the room, positioning it in front of the fire.

"Come sit here," he instructed Elise who stood watching him from the door.

She hesitated, nibbling her lower lip. Sitting on a mattress with a man was most unseemly. Aunt Claudia would certainly not approve of this. And Mrs. Rhoades's handbook was replete with warnings about just such an arrangement. Not that there was an alternative. She, too, had noticed the lack of seating in the room.

Tanner seemed to sense her reluctance. "You've got to sit down," he coaxed. "This is the spot where we'll have our picnic."

Elise didn't need a second invitation. It might be a bit unorthodox, but surely there was nothing improper about a picnic. She took the place he indicated on his left and faced the roaring fire. Almost immediately the warmth began to penetrate her rain-soaked skirt and shoes, and she breathed a sigh of pure contentment. She hadn't realized how cold she was.

Tanner retrieved his leather saddlebag from the doorway and joined her on the mattress. Sensing there was food to be had, Becky traipsed over and plopped down between them. She was not disappointed. Inside the bag, still dry, was the picnic lunch that Rosa had packed earlier. They ate without speaking, quickly devouring the tasty food.

Outside, the storm raged on, but inside, a cheerful quiet pervaded with only the crackling flames to disturb the silence.

Becky gobbled her food in several greedy bites. Once filled, she wasted no time in finding a comfortable spot on the mattress to nap.

"She's a wonderful dog, Tanner. I've always wanted a pet," Elise said as she popped the last crumbs of her cookie into her mouth. "Have you had her long?"

"About four years. I took her in after her mother was killed. She'd been shot. Some greenhorn must have mistaken her for a wolf. Left old Becky all alone."

"How horrible. I bet that was especially painful for you, being an orphan yourself." She clapped a hand over her mouth as soon as the careless words escaped. "Oh, Tanner, I'm so sorry." Her eyes reflected her heartfelt remorse. "How rude of me to mention that."

Tanner shrugged. "You're right. In a way, Becky and I are a lot alike. Both of us were all alone and lucky enough to have someone take us in. If it weren't for Seth, I'm sure I'd be dead with the rest of my family."

"Don't even suggest such a thing."

"It's true. Seth saved my life that night." His dark eyes held hers. Something compelled him to continue. "We were coming West, a couple of families together, to make a new start. None of them made it. Indians attacked the wagons shortly after nightfall. The adults were sitting around the campfire, laughing and telling jokes. I was in the wagon with my kid brother. He had just fallen asleep when I heard the noise. I figured he was safe enough, so I slipped out for a minute to check things out."

Tanner stared into the leaping flames, his face a blank mask. "I crawled around to some bushes behind the campfire." He was silent for a moment, and his gaze dropped to his hands. When he spoke again, his voice was a low whisper. "What I saw was so horrible, I couldn't move.

I just sat there. There wasn't any moon that night and things were dark so I couldn't make much out, but I could tell they were all dead. Every one of them."

Tears filled her eyes as Elise reached up and laid a cool hand against his cheek. "Don't, Tanner. Don't think about it anymore."

He stared at her in silence, the emotion in his dark eyes unreadable. After a long moment, he returned his gaze to the fire. "The Indians started screaming then, a noise that would make your skin crawl. The screams seemed to get me moving, and I remembered my brother.

I crawled back through the bushes to the wagon. I remember it seemed to take forever. I was so scared, I could hardly move. That's when I saw the flames. Everything was burning." His voice broke. "Nobody could have survived it. Seth saw me and pulled me away before the Indians got me, too. He'd been riding by when he saw the fire and moved in for a closer look."

Tanner shook his head slightly, as if to clear his thoughts. His voice was stronger when he spoke again. "Your father is the finest man I've ever known." His eyes locked onto hers. "I owe him my life, and I'd do anything to protect him."

Elise attributed the fierceness of his oath to the emotion of the moment. She appreciated his loyalty to her father. He loved him as she did. And her father obviously loved Tanner. She only wished that there was room in her father's heart for them both.

It seemed the most natural thing in the world when she inched over beside Tanner, her shoulder brushing his, and slipped her hand into his. "My father's a lucky man to have a friend like you."

Neither spoke again as they sat side by side, mesmerized by the dancing golden flames. Elise could hear the rain falling against the roof. An occasional clap of thunder rattled the dilapidated building, but she felt safe from the violence of nature's fury. The warmth of the fire made her sleepy and her eyelids grew so heavy it became an effort just to keep them open. *Perhaps,* she thought, *if I close them for a moment, the sinking spell will pass.*

Tanner's thoughts were jumbled as he stared into the flames. He didn't know why he had poured out his heart to her. He'd kept his past closely guarded from others. After all these years, the memories were still too painful and the guilt he bore for his brother's death too fresh. Yet, he hadn't been able to stop the rush of words.

Interestingly enough, he felt better. He dropped a glance to the slender hand resting on his and smiled. He'd seen the tears in her eyes as she tried to comfort him. Tears of compassion.

Tanner's brow furrowed slightly. "Compassionate" didn't fit in with his initial appraisal of Elise. He had her pegged as a gold digger, pure and simple. A greedy opportunist out to collect her dying father's fortune to support her extravagant lifestyle.

He'd seen the evidence. Why, the price of her hats alone would put an average guy in the poorhouse. The thought of her hats brought a grimace to his face.

He didn't know how she and her aunt had been supporting themselves all these years, but the way he figured it, they had been biding their time, waiting for the news that Seth was dying. No doubt they knew the value of his holdings and were anxious to get their hands on it. The fact that Elise never communicated with her father until his illness seemed to validate his assumptions.

Tanner heard a yawn escape from Elise. He looked down at the top of her head, her mahogany tresses shimmering in the firelight. After spending time with her, it was becoming more and more difficult to imagine her as the enemy.

Suddenly, he knew he had to ask her, point blank, why she'd waited so long to see her father. What did she hope to gain by coming back after all these years? He had to know. Was she a conniving gold digger or a gentle woman of compassion? And he had to know now.

"Elise?" he began softly. "We need to talk." He turned slightly to see her face better. To his surprise, she didn't look up at him as he expected; instead, her head slumped against his chest. Closer inspection revealed that she'd fallen sound asleep.

Tanner grinned. Poor soul, she was no doubt exhausted by the afternoon's ordeal.

He settled back to allow himself the luxury of studying her at his leisure. Long, coal-black lashes fanned out against her creamy cheeks. Her lips, the color of roses, were parted slightly in slumber. A long, bronzed finger stole up to stroke her skin. It was just as soft as he had imagined.

He shifted slightly to wrap her in the protective circle of his arms, and the scent of fresh flowers assailed him. As he cradled her more closely to his chest, Elise sighed contentedly in her sleep.

Tanner was aware of a change deep within himself that afternoon as he stared into the glowing embers. The barrier of suspicion coiled around his heart melted, leaving him free to listen to its direction.

Becky looked up at him from her place by the fire and cocked her ears. He chuckled. "Okay, okay," he whispered, "so you were right. I admit it, I fell for her. Now give it a rest."

&

"Rosa! Where's Elise?" Seth demanded crossly from his bed. "I haven't seen her yet today."

Rosa placed his supper tray before him. "She and Tanner went out riding. I 'spect with this storm they had to stop someplace and wait it out. You'll just have to wait till tomorrow to visit with her."

"Tomorrow?" he wailed.

Rosa wagged a finger at him. "If you're looking for sympathy from me, you're barking up the wrong tree." She turned to walk from the room. "Far as I can see, it's your own fault you aren't with her." She stopped at the door to ask, "Hasn't this dying business gone far enough?"

Seth shrugged helplessly. "What choice do I have?"

"How about the truth?"

"We've been through this before," Seth said with a sigh of resignation. "The truth wouldn't get Elise here. You yourself admitted that Claudia would settle for nothing less than death."

Rosa stalked back over to the bed. "Sí, that's true, Seth. But the child's here now. Must we continue with the lie?"

"She wouldn't stay, Rosa. If she knew the truth, that I'm as healthy as she is, she'd run back to Boston so fast, it would make my head spin."

"Oh, Seth, be reasonable. She's your daughter."

Seth's eyes met Rosa's. "I haven't been completely honest with you. I never told you why Elise stayed in Boston."

"Certainly you did. You thought Claudia was better equipped to raise a young lady."

He shook his head. "The truth is, I wanted her back. She hadn't been gone a month when I realized my mistake." His voice was a whisper. "A father should raise his own daughter."

He stared past Rosa for a moment before he continued, "Anyway, I went to Boston to tell Claudia I wanted Elise to come home. Claudia wouldn't hear of it. She told me I was selfish, and that if I was any kind of a father at all, I'd think of the child's well-being.

"I foolishly agreed to give her a year. No longer." He raked his fingers through his hair. "With the war and all, the year stretched to two, then three. I couldn't have risked her life, trying to travel across the states, so I waited longer, till things settled down.

"Finally, I went back to Boston. Elise was nearly eight by then. I was desperate to bring her home. I wasn't going to take 'no' for an answer." Seth fell silent.

"Well, go on," Rosa urged. "Did you see the child? Why didn't you bring her home?"

"I got there late in the morning, and Elise had already gone to school. That's when Claudia told me."

"Told you what, Seth? You're not making a lick of sense."

"She told me Elise hated me. She said Elise blamed me for the death of her mother." His voice wavered. "Claudia said the very thought of me gave the child nightmares." He raised pain-filled eyes to Rosa. "I couldn't take her then."

"You believed her?" Rosa was incredulous. "You believed the old crab?"

"I had to. She had nothing to gain by keeping Elise. Why would she lie?"

Rosa was quiet for a moment as she sorted through what she had heard. "But Seth," she said finally, "Elise came to you. Doesn't that mean anything?"

He shook his head. "Claudia made it clear that Elise was coming only out of her sense of duty. Fulfilling a dying man's request. Nothing more."

"I for one don't believe it. Elise is a lovely young woman. I can't imagine her hating anyone."

Seth nodded his agreement.

"Ask her. Ask her how she feels."

"I can't. Claudia made me agree not to talk about it. She said Elise would come only on the condition that I would not discuss our relationship. Not one word."

Rosa threw her hands up in disgust. "Then what do we do? Continue this ridiculous pretending? And for how long?"

"For as long as it takes to make her love me."

"And just how do you propose to do that?"

"Slowly, little by little. We're strangers now and I hardly know what to say to her. So I'm going real slow. We'll start out with short visits in the afternoon, like we're doing now. I don't want to rush her. When I notice she's enjoying our time together, then I'll get better, you know, healthier, so that I can have meals with her and spend more time together."

He looked over to see Rosa shaking her head in disapproval. "This is my only chance, Rosa. If I offend her and she leaves, I may never see her again."

nine

Elise stood just inside her bedroom door, her ears trained on the sound of familiar booted feet traveling across the wooden floors toward the back of the house. She breathed a sigh of relief a moment later when she heard the hinges of the back door squeak as it swung open and closed.

She was much later than usual for breakfast this morning and her stomach growled a complaint. She paid it no heed. A little hunger was a small price to pay for the assurance of not facing Tanner this morning. After her unfortunate behavior yesterday, she doubted she'd ever have the courage to face him again.

As a precaution, she tiptoed ever so carefully across the hall and began a silent descent of the stairs, her ears alert for any sound of his return.

She smiled triumphantly as she stepped from the last stair, having successfully made it down without a sound. Her eyes remained on her feet as she rounded the corner toward the kitchen. Elise was so intent upon stealth, she failed to notice the man, dressed in black, leaning negligently against the kitchen door frame, until she was practically upon him.

"Oh, Tanner!" she cried, clapping a hand over her heart, "I thought I heard you leave; uh, what I mean is I didn't think you'd still be here."

"Good morning to you, too," he drawled, a lazy grin on his face. "You weren't thinking to avoid me this morning, were you?"

Elise dropped her gaze. She felt the heat of the blush on her cheeks as she replied, "No, not exactly." It was true. The plan was to avoid him for the rest of her life.

"Good." His lips pulled into a roguish smile. "You and I have some unfinished business to attend to this morning."

"We do?" Elise barely recognized the squeak as her own voice.

He nodded solemnly. "Matter of honor, actually."

Elise didn't think it was possible to blush any harder. Her face felt so hot that at any moment she expected to smell smoke. Honor could mean only one thing. He was referring to yesterday's fiasco.

Tanner appeared unmoved by her plight. He took her elbow and propelled her through the back door to the yard where Gypsy was waiting.

"Are we going somewhere?" Elise managed a tremulous smile.

He nodded.

"I'll run get my hat while you saddle Miss Sadie for me." *Or perhaps just keep on running,* she thought grimly.

Tanner tightened his grip on her arm. "We won't be gone long, so you don't need a hat, and since I'm running short on time, you can ride with me."

He swung up easily behind the saddle, then motioned for Elise to give him her hands. She did so obediently and he scooped her up, settling her on the saddle in front of him.

Elise did her best to remain rigid, so that her shoulder wouldn't come in contact with Tanner's broad chest. She wouldn't make the same mistake as yesterday.

Just thinking about it now was as embarrassing as it was yesterday when she awakened in his arms. True, it felt wonderful, cradled against his strong chest, the fresh, clean scent of him surrounding her. And, yes, he had been the perfect gentlemen, releasing her as soon as she was awake. But just the same, it was no way for a proper young lady to act.

She had tried to apologize well over a hundred times. Elise swallowed hard. Evidently, it hadn't been enough. Unfinished business could mean only one thing. He meant to tell her just what he thought of such a brazen woman. Of course, it was no less than she deserved. Aunt Claudia had been right—bad blood would tell.

Elise tried to look on the bright side. The fact that he was taking her away from the house to scold her meant that her father would not hear. She couldn't bear to think that he would find out about her impropriety. He would never love her then.

Gypsy's long legs ate up the range as she galloped into the breeze. Elise's valiant struggle to remain upright made the ride most uncomfortable.

Tanner seemed to sense her discomfort. He leaned forward to whisper, "It's all right, Miss Garver, you can lean against me."

She sank gratefully against him, his two strong arms flanking her sides. As her cheek pressed against his crisp cotton shirt, Elise closed her eyes and smiled to herself. This time snuggled beside him somehow made the coming punishment well-worth it.

Elise did not know how far they had traveled before Gypsy climbed a rise and Tanner reined her to a halt. "Here we are," he announced.

And here it comes, Elise added silently. She reluctantly raised her head from its resting place on his chest and stared up expectantly into his dark eyes.

"Well, go on." His deep voice held a smile. "Get busy."

"Busy?" Elise was totally perplexed.

"Didn't you say you wanted to pick bluebonnets?"

Elise's green eyes opened wide. Slowly she turned away from him to gaze out across the field of blue. "Oh, Tanner!" she squealed in delight as she slid from the horse and raced out into the sea of bluebonnets.

Tanner remained atop Gypsy to watch Elise gambol through the flowers. The sunlight danced off her hair and he was glad he hadn't given her time to find a bonnet.

He resisted a twinge of guilt over the high-handed way he got her out here this morning. True, he didn't have much time, but he certainly could have waited the short time it would have taken to saddle Miss Sadie. The fact was, he didn't want Elise to ride her own horse. He wanted her next to him, in his arms, just as she had been the day before.

He leaned forward atop Gypsy to watch her bend gracefully to pluck another bluebonnet. He was relieved to see she was in good spirits after yesterday's adventure. The way she had kept apologizing and blushing, he was afraid she'd never speak to him again.

He dismounted as she approached, her face wreathed in smiles. "Oh look, Tanner," she held up her bouquet for his inspection. "Aren't they lovely?"

His eyes never left her face. "Very."

Elise's smile faded as she broached the subject she dreaded. "Was there some other reason you wanted to see me this morning?"

"No." Tanner shrugged. "Should there be?"

She shook her head, blushing furiously in spite of herself.

Suddenly, he seemed to understand. "This is about yesterday, isn't it? Did you think I was angry with you? That you did something wrong?"

She bit her bottom lip and nodded. "I fell asleep on you," came her strangled confession.

He struggled not to smile at the memory. "Guess it does sound kinda incriminating, but it was completely innocent. It's just one of those things that sounds bad when you try to explain it."

"But—"

"No, Elise," Tanner cut her off before she could continue, "you did nothing wrong. The fact is, the blame is mine that we were there in the first place. Mine and the storm's." He took her hands in his. "You were the picture of propriety."

Her face brightened with his words.

"I brought you here today only because I promised you could pick flowers. You looked so disappointed when we left yesterday." He took her chin in his hand and tilted her face to his. "I brought you back because I love to see you smile."

Tears welled in Elise's eyes. "You know, this is one of the nicest things anyone has ever done for me." She continued earnestly, "Next to Rosa, you must be the kindest person I know."

"Rosa, huh?" he teased.

She gave a solemn nod. "Do you know the entire time I've been here, she's never once mentioned my awful taste in colors or the fact that my behavior frequently falls short of proper." Elise's voice was awed as she said, "I think she really cares for me. She even taught me how to become a Christian." Concern suddenly marred her brow. "Tanner, are you a Christian?"

He nodded.

"Are you sure? I mean, there's more to becoming a Christian than just attending church. You have to make a personal decision to accept Jesus as your Savior."

Tanner laughed. "I can tell Rosa's been after you, and yes, I am absolutely certain that I am a Christian."

"I'm so glad." Elise sighed contentedly. The matter resolved, and her heart lighter, she turned back toward the field of flowers. "It's so lovely; I believe I could stay here for hours."

"Not today, I'm afraid. I've got to get back. The boys are waiting on me for the branding." He hated to see her bright smile fade. "Tell you what. We'll come back another time. For a picnic."

Elise beamed. "I'll hold you to it. Matter of honor."

Tanner put his foot into the stirrup and climbed onto Gypsy, then leaned over to pick up Elise. He gently placed her before him, careful not to crush her flowers.

She turned slightly, so she could look up into his face. "Thank y—" The words caught in her throat when she realized his handsome face was just inches from hers. All rational thought fled as she stared up into his dark eyes.

It took sheer strength of will to drag her eyes away. She stared down at the bouquet on her lap. "Thank you, Tanner. For everything."

His response was a husky whisper. "No, Miss Garver, thank you."

Elise settled comfortably against his chest to make the trip home.

ten

"Elise, *querido,* I've got a great idea," Rosa said.

Elise dropped the heavy basket of wet laundry on the ground and with the back of her hand, wiped the beads of perspiration from her forehead.

"I hope it doesn't involve any more cleaning," she laughed weakly.

"Oh, no, much better," Rosa assured her as she joined Elise at the basket and the women began to hang out the clothes on the line. "We're going swimming."

Elise wasn't sure she had heard correctly. "Swimming?" she repeated.

"Sí." Rosa nodded enthusiastically.

"No, Rosa, I don't think so." Elise shook her head.

"Sure, we will. It's really hot out here today and we've worked up a sweat. A swim is just what we need to cool off."

"No, no, I don't think so. I'll have to pass," Elise persisted. "Aunt Claudia has always insisted that swimming isn't proper." She paused, trying to find a more solid argument. "And besides, I don't have a thing to wear."

Rosa laughed mischievously. "Oh, yes you do."

Elise was still protesting an hour later when Rosa pulled the buggy to a stop under a stand of oaks. She hopped down from the buggy and followed Rosa through the copse of trees, toward the pond. "But I don't even know how to swim."

"That's fine, honey," Rosa dismissed her argument with a wave of her hand. "The water's pretty shallow for swimming, anyway."

They reached a pile of large rocks that stood in a semicircle in front the pond. Elise gasped as Rosa casually slipped off her dress and folded it neatly on top of the rocks, before proceeding around the pile and into the water wearing only her camisole and petticoat.

"Rosa!" she exclaimed in true horror. "What if someone should see you?"

"Who's gonna see me out here? Nobody's around except you and me and old Seth up at the house, and he sure can't see this far. I don't expect the boys back from branding for at least another day."

"Oh," Elise said in a very small voice. She had hoped they'd be back sooner. In the week since she and Tanner had taken refuge from the storm in the old abandoned shack, she'd barely seen him, much less talked to him. She'd never had a friend like him, and she found she missed him very much.

"The water feels wonderful," Rosa cajoled as she paddled around. "It's so cool and refreshing."

Elise's thoughts whirled back to the present dilemma. Rosa was a hard woman to refuse. *But then, what harm could there be in a little wading?* she asked herself. Claudia never actually expressed her disapproval of wading; it was swimming she considered immoral. Since her own conscience didn't convict her of any wrongdoing, perhaps she could give it a try. Besides, she rationalized, *Who would ever know?*

After removing her shoes and stockings, she took a tentative step toward the pond and dipped her toe into the crystal-clear water. It was refreshingly cool, just as Rosa had said. Somewhat heartened, Elise stepped in, holding her skirts above the ankle-deep water.

"You might as well take the skirt off," Rosa called from the middle of the pond where she floated on her back. "It's just gonna get wet, and we'll have more laundry to do."

Elise groaned. That argument was highly effective in light of the grueling morning they had spent washing clothes.

"You win," she said with a sigh of resignation. She climbed out of the water and slowly removed her skirt and blouse. The layers of fabric that comprised her camisole and petticoat provided more than modest coverage, but she couldn't help feeling a bit sheepish about being outdoors in her undergarments. She glanced nervously from side to side as she folded her clothes and added them to the pile with Rosa's.

Satisfied that she and Rosa were alone, she scampered into the pond, walking out to where the water came up to her waist. A sudden movement from behind caught her eye and before she could react, Rosa popped up from under the water and drenched her with a splash.

Elise laughed and retaliated with a splash and the battle was on.

&

Tanner pushed his hat back off his forehead and mopped the perspiration from his brow. "What a scorcher, Becky. I don't remember the heat ever being this bad in April."

Becky flopped down at the feet of his horse, her tongue lolling from her mouth.

"Tell you what. We've got time for a quick swim before we ride in to surprise the women. Why don't we stop at the spring?"

Becky was on her feet in an instant, running around the horse and yapping excitedly. Tanner grinned as the threesome loped through the grass toward the pond. He couldn't wait to see the look on Miss Garver's face when he showed up for dinner tonight.

He hadn't realized how much he would miss her while he was tied up with the spring branding. He'd actually been counting the hours till he could get back to see her. He could hardly wait for tonight.

Tanner was still a long way off when he spotted the familiar black buggy parked under the trees. His brows furrowed slightly. "Now what do you suppose Rosa's doing out here in the middle of the day?"

He kicked up the horse to a gallop, sending clods of dirt flying behind him as he covered the distance in record time. Concern replaced curiosity when he pulled up beside the buggy and heard the screams. His heart lurched sickeningly within his chest. Somebody had Rosa! Tanner sprang from the saddle, hitting the ground at a dead run. He kept low, dodging from tree to tree, finally taking cover behind the rock pile.

Blood hammered in his brain as he checked his gun. Who would be on Garver land? Somebody must have been watching the place to know the men were gone. But why was Rosa out here, away from the house? He looked up suddenly. He had a gut feeling something was wrong. The screams had stopped. He didn't want to think of what had happened.

Tanner cocked his gun and stood, legs braced, ready to open fire, when he noticed the pile of neatly folded clothes. At that same moment, a high-pitched squeal pierced the air, followed by a riotous burst of giggles. Elise. Elise and Rosa. Tanner slumped against the rocks with relief. They weren't hurt. From the sound of things, they were playing.

Becky started toward the pond at the sound of familiar voices. Tanner reached out and grabbed her, crouching down beside her. "Not so fast," he whispered. "I owe them a good scare."

He waited for a lull in the giggling before getting to his feet. In a loud voice he called, "Here we are, Becky, ready to go swimming. Sure hope the water's cold. Won't take me but just a second to get these clothes off."

Piercing screams rent the air. Tanner chuckled at his success.

"Tanner?" Rosa's voice was unsteady. "Is that you?"

Tanner stayed behind the rock, his voice the picture of innocence. "Rosa? What are you doing out here?"

"Stay where you are!" she warned. "Better yet, why don't you walk on over to the buggy. . .it's parked under the trees. . .and wait. Elise and I need to get our clothes."

"Your clothes?" Tanner feigned shock. "Do you mean to tell me that you ladies have been skinny dipping?"

"Never mind that, Mr. Smarty. Just get on over to the buggy," Rosa snapped. "And be quick about it."

Tanner took his time sauntering over to the buggy, careful not to look back toward the water. He leaned against it to wait, his arms folded over his chest, his ankles crossed.

Minutes later, the women emerged through the trees. Any thought he had had of teasing them died as he spotted Elise. Her face was the picture of mortification and she refused to look at him, choosing instead to study the ground.

"Thought I'd surprise you by coming in early. Looks like I was real successful." He winked at Rosa, but Elise's gaze remained downcast. "Would you like an escort back to the house?"

Rosa took one look at Elise and shook her head. "No, I think we'll go on ahead. You and Becky can clean up here, and we'll see you for dinner."

"Sounds fair. See you then."

ॐ

"Why don't you young people carry yourselves out to the front porch, while I clean up these dishes?" Rosa asked, picking up several plates from the table.

Elise, who'd been conspicuously quiet all evening, spoke up quickly, "Oh, no, I'd like to help."

"Wouldn't hear of it, *querido*." She dismissed her offer with a wave of her hand. "There's too little here for the two of us. Besides," she glanced meaningfully toward Tanner, "there's a cool breeze out there tonight and a beautiful full moon. You haven't lived till you've seen a Texas moon."

"But. . . ."

"Rosa's right," Tanner's deep voice chimed in. "You haven't really seen Texas until you've sat out on the porch under a full moon." He walked over to stand behind her chair. "Rosa can join us when she's finished."

Seeing the futility of further argument, Elise conceded, reluctantly following Tanner's tall frame down the hall and out through the front door with Becky close on her heels. After this afternoon's humiliation at the pond, he was the very last person with whom she wanted to be alone.

She sat stiffly in one of the high-back rocking chairs, her hands folded primly in her lap. Tanner took the seat beside her, crossing his long legs at the ankles. For a long time, neither spoke.

"Tanner?"

"Miss Garver?"

They each chose the exact same moment to break the silence. Elise giggled in spite of herself. "Go ahead."

Tanner shook his dark head. "You first."

"I. . .I wanted to apologize about this afternoon."

"For what?" Tanner was obviously baffled.

Elise was glad for the cover of darkness to shroud her flaming cheeks. "I behaved badly, I'm afraid." She dropped her gaze to her lap and nibbled the corner of her lip. "I knew swimming, especially in my uh. . .well um, especially dressed the way I was, was completely improper." She raised her eyes to his. "I just hope you won't judge me too harshly."

"Judge you for swimming?" Tanner's voice was incredulous.

Elise nodded. "You said it yourself. We were skinny dipping." She hung her head and mused aloud. "Why is it do you suppose that someone who spends as much time studying proper behavior as I do, has so much trouble applying it? It seems I'm continually entrenched in compromising situations."

Tanner suppressed a laugh. "Have you struggled with this problem long?"

"No." She frowned, trying to pinpoint the exact time the problem began. "Just since I arrived in Texas."

Tanner grinned unsympathetically. "Maybe it's the climate."

"My father will be so ashamed."

Tanner was confused. "Now wait a minute. How will he find out? Do you think I'm going to tell your father?"

Elise nodded again. "Well, yes, aren't you? I mean, you two are the best of friends, and I'm sure you discuss everything. I know you carry a strong influence with him."

Tanner captured her hands in his. "Miss Garver, 'round here folks don't go in big for swimming clothes. Fact is, swimming in your underwear is normal. Since it was just you and Rosa that saw each other, I can't find a thing for you to be ashamed of. I was just teasing you when I said that about skinny dipping."

"You were?" Her voice was hopeful. "You mean you're not offended? You won't mention it to my father?"

Tanner nodded, a smile playing at the corner of his mouth. "I think this falls under the category of one of those things that sounds bad when you try to explain it."

"Oh, Tanner!" She squeezed his hands that still held hers. "I'm so glad. I was afraid I'd ruined everything. I guess I'm not doing a very good job as a new Christian."

"Speaking as an old Christian, I think you're doing just fine."

Elise sighed her relief. "I'm happy you think so." She paused to study his handsome face. "You've been a Christian a while, so you must already know what it's like to have God answer your prayers."

"Well, uh, sorta," he hedged.

She tilted her head to one side in question.

"Honestly, I'm not too big on praying," he admitted sheepishly.

She gave his hand a comforting pat. "Don't feel bad. You can start fresh with me. Rosa has me reading the book of John. She says it's a great place for new Christians to start." Her voice became more animated with her enthusiasm. "Maybe we could read the same chapters and discuss them." She stopped herself in midsentence. "You do have a Bible, don't you?"

"Yeah."

"Good. Read the first two chapters and if you have time tomorrow, maybe we can discuss what we've read."

Tanner grinned. "I'll try." He paused for a moment before adding, "Say, I've got to go into town tomorrow for a few supplies. Why don't you ride in with me? We can talk then."

With enthusiastic abandon, Elise threw her arms around his neck and hugged him tightly. "It sounds wonderful. I can't wait." She suddenly realized what she was doing and quickly withdrew her arms. She cleared her throat self-consciously and stood up, walking over to the porch railing. "The sky is so lovely in Texas," she said in an obvious attempt to change the subject. "I don't think I've ever seen so many stars."

Tanner strode over to join her. "It's a beautiful, clear night."

Elise sighed wistfully. "It's so peaceful and lovely here. Heavenly, don't you think?"

Tanner ignored the sky, choosing instead to move closer, concentrating his full attention on her upturned face.

The light from inside the house cast a golden glow on her delicate features. An errant breeze carried with it her sweet scent of flowers, and he was reminded of how soft her skin felt to his touch. "Definitely heavenly." His whispered words were almost a caress.

Elise startled at the proximity of his voice; she hadn't heard him move so close. She glanced hesitantly in his direction and their eyes met. Elise's heart hammered wildly within her chest as Tanner placed his hands on her shoulders, gently turning her toward him. He brushed a wispy strand of hair from her face. "Elise," he whispered huskily, "I. . ."

The hinges of the front door creaked. "See now, I told you it wouldn't take long—" Rosa began as she stepped onto the porch. "Oh!" she exclaimed as she saw the two of them. "Looks like you were planning on a little more time alone."

Tanner dropped his hands to his sides, and Elise backed away guiltily. "No, Rosa, come on out. We were just about to say good night. Isn't that right, Tanner?"

"Something like that," he answered wryly.

"Anyway, it's getting late. I think I'll go on in and get a good night's rest before tomorrow's trip into town." Elise flashed a nervous smile over her shoulder before ducking through the front doorway. "Good night. See you both in the morning," she called. "And Tanner, don't forget your assignment."

Rosa was puzzled. "What assignment is that, Tanner?"

"Hmmmmm?"

She caught sight of the silly grin on his face as he stared after Elise and she shook her head in disbelief. *Tanner and Elise? I'm seeing it, and I still don't believe it.*

eleven

"Elise, have you got my list?" Rosa asked.

Elise patted the pocket of her skirt. "Right here."

"Good enough." Rosa stepped back from the wagon. "Be careful, you two. And have fun."

Tanner nodded and slapped the reins, directing the horses toward the town.

The late-April morning was bright with promise. Golden sunlight glittered magically on the crystalline dewdrops carpeting the endless fields. Elise settled back on the bench, content for a time to sit quietly at Tanner's side, watching with interest as he handled the horses. "Is it proper for a woman to drive a team?" she blurted out at last.

Tanner's teeth flashed in a grin. "Sure, it's proper. Downright necessary for Texans." His dark eyes sparkled. "You wanna try?"

Elise's eyes grew wide. "Me? Really?"

Tanner chuckled at her enthusiasm over the simplest things. "Really." He slid over closer to her on the bench and placed the reins in her hands, wrapping his hands around hers to steady them.

"The horses are trained to respond to your commands and the tension you keep in the reins," he began the instruction. "It's similar to how you handle Miss Sadie."

With her hands clasped in his, Elise had difficulty concentrating on what he was saying. His clean, masculine scent and handsome face captured her attention. She actually felt breathless.

"I think you'll be more successful if you keep your eyes on the road."

Elise jerked her eyes from his face to the road in front of her. She hadn't meant to stare, and she certainly hadn't meant to get caught. She chewed her lower lip in mortification. The man had the most peculiar effect on her senses.

"I'm disappointed in you, Miss Garver," Tanner said, breaking the embarrassed silence as the wagon rattled down the dirt road. "You haven't asked me about my assignment."

Elise's eyes lit with delight. "Tanner, you did read the chapters from John!" Having her hands on the reins restrained her from hugging him. "I'm so glad. I want you to tell me which verse was your favorite. But first, I must ask a favor of you."

He raised his brow.

"Would you please call me Elise?"

"Elise." Tanner repeated her name softly before favoring her with a warm smile. "I think I can handle that."

Elise felt her heart give an inexplicable jump. Her name had never sounded that good coming from anyone else's lips. "Uh, yes, well then," she fumbled around, trying to remember what it was she was saying, "which verse did you like best?"

"I liked the part where it says anybody can be a child of God, just by believing in Jesus."

Elise handed him back the reins so she could pull her Bible out of the basket at her feet. She flipped through the pages to the book of John and skimmed the the first chapter. "Here it is, verse twelve: "But as many as received him, to them gave he power to become the sons of God, even to them that believe on his name." She looked over at Tanner. "That's mine, too. What a wonderful promise. It makes us part of a family."

"Family?" He shook his dark head. "I never thought of it that way before. I just like it 'cuz it shows how simple it is to be saved."

"That's true, of course, but there's so much more. That verse is a promise. I think it's a special promise to people like you and me who have lost our family or have been separated from them. It assures us that even in the loneliest times, we belong to God. We're His family, and He cares for us. The best part is that because we are His children, He'll answer our prayers."

Tanner shoved his hat back as he studied her for a moment. "You know, you amaze me. For someone who's just become a Christian, you're heads above me already."

She shook her head. "You're being too hard on yourself."

"No, I mean it. I was saved a long time ago and haven't honestly given God much thought since then."

"Why not?"

He shrugged his broad shoulders. "I don't know. I guess I didn't figure I needed to. Fact is, I've been handling things pretty well without God."

Their discussion came to an abrupt halt as Tanner pulled the wagon up in front of the store. Elise was disappointed to see it end.

"Where to first?" she asked after Tanner secured the team and lifted her to the ground.

"I've got to head over to the livery for some supplies. Why don't you go on into the general store and pick up the things on Rosa's list. I'll probably finish first, so I'll be back here to meet you."

Before proceeding into the store, Elise lingered on the sidewalk for a moment to watch him cross the street. The shopkeeper nodded politely to acknowledge her presence then returned his attention to his customer.

Elise was mesmerized by the sights and smells of the store. Unlike the specialty shops of Boston, this store seemed to carry an endless range of products. She wandered to each corner, stopping to study the rows of canned goods or to finger the bolts of fabric.

"Can I help you, ma'am?"

Elise smiled up at the shopkeeper. "Yes, please. I've got a list here, from Rosa Viegas."

He grinned. "You must be Seth's daughter. I can tell by them green eyes. I heard tell you were coming. Fact is, I got a letter here for you. From Boston, I think."

"A letter?" Elise was distracted as the door swung open to admit Tanner.

"Howdy, Mr. Dalton." The shopkeeper stepped forward to shake Tanner's hand. "How's things at the ranch?"

"Just fine, Nathan. Herd's looking better than ever this year."

"Glad to hear it. Anything I can get for you today?"

Tanner shook his head. "Nothing for me, thanks. Miss Garver's got the list." Tanner's gaze strayed over to Elise and fell on her hat. "Say, wait, there is one thing." He looked back at Nathan. "What have you got in the way of hats?"

"Got a new box in last week." He pointed toward the front of the store. "They're over there, by the window. Help yourself."

Tanner took Elise's arm, guiding her through the cluttered aisles and toward the window. "Come on, we're going to find you a decent. . . ," his gaze rested on her bonnet, this one boasting an enormous pink satin bow and a tuft of pheasant feathers, "uh, I mean a sturdy hat to wear while you're riding."

He located the boxes and began rummaging through the contents, finally selecting a plain, black felt hat similar to his own. He held it up for her inspection. "What about something like this?"

Elise doubted seriously that Mrs. Rhoades would approve. "I don't know, Tanner," she said, her hesitant smile revealing her misgivings. "It looks awfully masculine, don't you think?"

Tanner grinned as he studied the bundle of femininity before him. "Trust me, that shouldn't be a problem on you."

Elise obediently removed her bonnet and placed the black hat on her head. "Well?"

Tanner chuckled. "Let's get it at the correct angle." He stood in front of her, tilting the hat slightly forward. She stared up at him, waiting patiently for him to finish the adjustments.

He smiled with satisfaction as he gave it a final quick pat. Slowly his dark gaze traveled down to meet hers. His smile suddenly melted and the look in his eyes became serious. Elise was powerless to look away, totally enchanted by the ebony depths. Ever so slowly, he lowered his head toward hers. Instinctively, she slanted her head backwards and her eyes fluttered closed.

His lips gently brushed hers, sending shock waves through her body. The kiss lasted only a fraction of a second, yet it rendered Elise breathless. Tanner, too, seemed shaken by the brief contact.

"Does that mean it looks all right?" Elise asked with an unsteady voice.

"What? Oh yeah, the hat." Tanner stepped back to consider her. "Just perfect."

"This everything, Mr. Dalton?" Nathan called from the counter.

Tanner pointed to the hat on Elise's head. "We'll take this, too."

They were loaded in the wagon, with the packages neatly stowed away when Nathan popped out from the store, waving an envelope. "I nearly forgot your letter, Miss Garver!" He handed it up to her. "Regards to your father and Rosa."

"Thank you." Elise tucked the letter into the basket along with the Bible. "Goodbye."

&

"So what'd you think of Crossroads?" Tanner asked as he headed the wagon home.

"It's wonderful." Elise saw the look of amused disbelief on his face. "No, really, I mean it. There's such a comfortable feeling here in Crossroads, and Texas, too. Almost like I belong here."

Tanner's eyes were warm as they held hers. "Maybe you do."

Elise shook her head sadly. "If only that were true. But there's Boston and Aunt Claudia and. . .oh! I almost forgot her letter. I suppose I ought to see what she has to say."

She plucked the envelope from the basket and settled back against the bench to read.

Dear Elise,

It was evident from the tone of your letter that you are enjoying your visit to Texas. I must remind you that your obligations lie here in Boston. There's Percival to consider; he's quite anxious to be married.

By the time this letter reaches you, I will be on my way to join you in Texas. It is time for you to return to Boston to resume your duties, and I have grave misgivings about allowing you to travel alone.

Percival will be accompanying me. He is most interested in seeing Texas and your father's holdings.

Elise couldn't believe her eyes. This couldn't be happening. Aunt Claudia coming to bring her home? Her heart twisted in her chest. She couldn't leave now. She hadn't earned her father's love. And what about Tanner? She read the letter again, hoping that somehow she was mistaken.

"Oh, no," Elise wailed dismally and slumped against the bench as the words of the letter sank in.

Tanner's brows furrowed with concern. "What's the matter, Elise? Is something wrong with your aunt?"

"No. She's fine," Elise replied gloomily. "In fact, she's coming here."

"To Texas?"

Elise nodded her dismay. "That's not the worst of it. She's bringing my fiancé."

Tanner reined the horses to an abrupt halt. "Your what?"

Elise continued to stare at the letter in her hands. "My fiancé."

Tanner's voice was dangerously calm as he asked, "You're engaged?"

"Uh–huh."

"You never mentioned you're going to be married."

Something in his tone of voice alerted Elise to his displeasure. She glanced up from the paper to see the dark fury in his eyes, and she blanched when she realized he was angry with her. "I guess I forgot." She tried to laugh, but the sound was more of a nervous squeak.

"You forgot?" Tanner's voice remained quiet. . .deadly quiet.

"That sounds silly I suppose. I mean, one shouldn't forget something as important as that, but you see," Elise stammered, "it happened so suddenly, just before I left to come here, actually, and with everything else that's happened, it just slipped my mind." She gave a helpless shrug of her shoulders. "It's not like it seems—"

Tanner raised a hand to silence her. "It's all becoming very clear to me." A muscle in his cheek twitched as he struggled to control his anger. "I've been such a fool. You really are here because you want something from your father. Guess you figure that since you're his daughter you deserve it."

Elise nodded her head very slowly. After all, what Tanner said was true, to a point. She had come to Texas to gain something from her father—his love.

"You've been waiting all this time to get what you think is coming to you, and now that Seth is sick you've decided it's time to collect."

Elise stared at him in wide-eyed amazement. He didn't understand her motivation, but he did seem to see through her plan. "Well, yes, that's true I guess, but it's not what you think. . ."

Tanner wouldn't let her finish. "Just how long have you been planning this little scheme?"

Elise flushed scarlet at his choice of words. Scheme. Hadn't her own heart warned her that scheming for her father's affection was wrong?

"I didn't want to scheme." She wrung her hands as she spoke. How humiliating to have to explain how naive she'd been, that she had actually believed her father loved her. "I never knew I'd need to. But after I got here and saw the situation for myself. . . ."

Tanner laughed bitterly at the sight of her red-stained cheeks, seeing them as further proof of her guilt. "What an idiot I've been," he berated himself. "I actually believed you cared for me."

"But I do care for you." Elise's green eyes glittered with tears as she blurted out, "Don't you see, Tanner? I. . .I love you."

"You love me?" Tanner's face grew white with fury. "Enough of this game, Miss Garver," he shouted. "You're engaged! It's your father you're after. I'm just a convenient way to get to him. A 'strong influence' is the way you put it, I believe." He turned an accusing glare on her, daring her to contradict him. "Go ahead. Tell me I'm not just a part of your plan."

"Maybe at first," Elise admitted reluctantly, "but if you'll just let me explain—"

"Spare me your explanations, Miss Garver," he gritted out. "If you're very quiet, maybe I'll forget you're here and allow you to ride back to the ranch."

"But—"

"It's a long walk." Tanner growled the warning.

Elise lowered her head, accepting defeat. They rode home in silence.

twelve

Elise paused at her father's door and rested her cheek against the cool, oak panel. Her heart ached within her. She'd never felt so defeated in her life. It was over. Her one chance to earn her father's love was gone. Aunt Claudia was on her way to whisk Elise back to her responsibilities in Boston, away from her father forever.

She had failed. Her vow to have her father's love before she left would go unfulfilled. Hot tears of disappointment welled up in her eyes. She'd counted on more time. She needed more time. She knew now that love couldn't be rushed.

Except in my own case, she amended with a sad little sigh. A lone tear strayed down her cheek as Tanner's face flashed through her memory. It was true. She was in love with Tanner. Elise shook her head with dismay. Her own heart hadn't been slow. In the course of a few short weeks, it found its deepest desire in the form of a tall, dark cowboy. And she wasn't even looking!

A second tear trailed the first. How could things have gotten so bad? The two men she loved didn't love her back. Her father was polite enough, of course, but it was time to face the truth. Her father didn't want or need her. She was here as a loose end, nothing more.

And Tanner hated her. Elise winced at the memory of this afternoon's confrontation. She could still see the murderous look in his dark eyes as she proclaimed her love for him. Elise sighed again.

"Elise? Is that you?" her father called from inside the room.

Elise wiped the tears from her face and took a deep breath before pushing open the door.

As it had every day since she arrived, Elise's heart swelled with pride as she spied her handsome father propped against his pillow. She marveled at how strong he looked, even in the midst of his illness. He actually appeared to be thriving.

She paused in the doorway, wishing she had the courage to throw her arms around him and tell him how much she loved him. Her feet and arms remained frozen in place. It was no use. She was a coward. She would rather return to Boston carrying the fragile hope of one day returning to earn his love, than bear forever the pain and burden of his rejection.

"How was your trip to town this morning? Rosa tells me you and Tanner went into Crossroads to do some shopping."

Elise flinched at the mention of Tanner's name. "It was fine, sir."

Seth didn't miss the unhappiness in her voice. It was just as he feared. She didn't like it. What was he thinking anyway? Did he honestly believe that Crossroads could measure up to Boston?

"I received a letter from Aunt Claudia today."

Seth held his tongue. Rosa warned him about disparaging her aunt in front of Elise. That was no way to endear himself to his daughter.

Elise, however, mistook his lack of response for a lack of interest. Though her heart sagged with disappointment, she tried to sound cheerful as she continued, "Both she and Mr. Bennett are coming to take me home."

The color drained slowly from Seth's face as her words registered in his mind and drove a dagger through his heart. Going home? No! She couldn't go back to Boston. Not now, not yet. She didn't love him yet.

Tanner entered the room before Seth could respond to his daughter. "Seth, I need to talk to you. Alone."

Seth heard the urgency in Tanner's voice and yet the desperation in his own heart refused to give way. His little girl was going to leave. Nothing was more important than that. "Later, Tanner," Seth dismissed him without looking up. "Elise and I are talking right now."

"It won't wait."

Seth's brows raised in astonishment at the grave tone in Tanner's voice. He knew it must be something serious. Reluctantly, he gave in. "Elise, would you excuse us for a moment?"

Elise knew the reason for Tanner's visit. He was reporting her duplicity to her father. She didn't hold it against him. In fact, it made her love him all the more. After all, Tanner was just protecting the one he loved. She would have done the same thing had the situation been reversed.

She left without protest, too ashamed to face her father. She couldn't bear to see his face when he heard what she had done.

Tanner stood silently before Seth, shifting his weight uncomfortably as he searched for the right words to say. His heart ached so badly right now, he could hardly think. He knew what he had to do, but it hurt so much. How could he repeat vile things about the woman he loved? He felt like a traitor.

But what about Seth? Tanner owed him his life. The decision was made. No matter the cost, Tanner had to protect him.

"Well?" Seth prodded. "What is it?"

"Sir, it's about your daughter." Tanner hesitated for a moment. "What I've got to say isn't pretty, sir. I just want you to know I wouldn't say it if there were any other way."

"Say what, Tanner?" Seth snapped impatiently. "I've never known you to mince words. Tell me what it is you've got to say."

"She's deceived you, sir."

"Deceived me?" Seth repeated for clarification. "Deceived me?"

The words cut deeply through Tanner as he spoke them. "Seth, doesn't it seem a bit odd that you've heard nothing from her all these years and she suddenly shows up at your door when she hears you're dying?"

Seth narrowed his gaze. "What are you getting at?"

"That the reason she's here is not concern for your health." He swallowed hard before continuing, "That she's only here for your money."

Tanner braced himself for an explosive response, but Seth said nothing. He simply stared.

"I'm sorry, Seth. You'll never know how sorry." Tanner dragged his long fingers through his dark hair. "I know it's hard to believe, I can hardly believe it myself, but I talked to her. I confronted her with my suspicions and she didn't deny them. She's fooled us both, sir." Tanner shoved his hands into his pockets and stared at the polished floor. "You've always been like a father to me. I just can't stand by and watch you get hurt."

"Then don't."

Tanner thought at first he imagined the voice. No one, upon hearing of such cruel betrayal, could respond so coolly. He looked up and his eyes locked with the emerald green ones of his employer. He'd never seen the look of raw determination that now glittered in his eyes.

"Seth?"

"I mean it." Seth's voice was emotionless. "Go on. We've got plenty of business to tie up over in Fort Worth. You can ride out tomorrow morning. By the time you finish the cattle negotiations and get back, she'll be gone."

Tanner was completely astonished by his cool demeanor. "Seth, did you understand what I said? Elise is only after your money."

"I understand perfectly. You ride out at first light."

Tanner shook his head in protest. "I'm sorry, sir, I can't do that. You might need—"

"I don't need anything!" Seth pounded his fists into the mattress as he shouted, "I especially don't need you, so get out!"

Elise had returned to wait outside her father's door in hopes that after Tanner finished, she would muster the courage to explain everything. She arrived just in time to hear her father throw Tanner out, to reject the man he loved as a son.

Hot tears bathed her face as she ran blindly to her room. She pulled the door closed and slumped wearily against it. To know that she'd failed to win her father's love was painful, but to think she'd driven a wedge between the two men she loved was unbearable.

thirteen

Unmindful of the turmoil that rocked the Garver ranch, the morning dawned brightly, ushering in a beautiful new day. Yet even the sight of bright golden sunlight, streaming through her bedroom window, failed to dislodge the heaviness of Elise's heart.

She lay motionless under the blankets, staring up at the ceiling. She had never known such despair in her life. It finally happened. Her seemingly endless reserve of optimism had dried up.

She needed to get away, to think things out someplace away from distraction. That shouldn't be too difficult. After all, Texas was a pretty big state. She sat up with new determination, and swung her feet over the side of the bed.

She dressed quickly, slipping into the pumpkin orange calico riding skirt hanging from a hook in the wardrobe. The lavender blouse she donned was chosen solely because it hung closest to the front of the cabinet. She was too depressed to care whether it matched or not.

She bent to select a bonnet for her ride, when the black felt hat that Tanner had chosen for her caught her eye. She picked it up, gently caressing the brim. If she closed her eyes tightly she could remember the look on Tanner's face when he had placed it on her head. For that brief moment, he had loved her, she had seen it in his dark eyes. She hugged the hat to her chest. She would wear it today.

Elise decided not to take the time to pile her mass of dark hair on top of her head in its usual elaborate coiffure, opting instead to wear it in one long braid as she had seen Rosa do. She knew it wasn't a proper hairstyle—Mrs. Rhoades would certainly not approve—but for once, Elise didn't care. Who would see her, anyway?

She finished tying off the braid as she stepped off the bottom stair. The empty place in the hall where Becky usually reclined indicated her master wasn't present. Elise slipped into the kitchen. "Has he left already?"

"Who?"

"Tanner. Has Tanner gone?" Her voice was tinged with despair.

"Sure, honey, he left at first light. Says he's got business in Fort Worth he needs to clear up." Rosa's smile faded at the sight of Elise's downcast face. "Is there a problem, *querido*?"

Elise's shoulders slumped in disappointment. "No, I only hoped I could see him before he left." She started to turn back toward the door.

"Don't worry, honey, he's never gone more than a couple of days. He'll be back in no time."

"No time will be too late," Elise whispered as she stepped into the hall.

"Wait, where are you going?" Rosa bustled after her, wringing her hands. "You can't go yet. You haven't had any breakfast."

"I'm not hungry. I thought I'd do a little riding this morning."

"What is it? Is there a problem? Can I fix it?"

Elise's lips curved upward as she shook her head. "No, I'm afraid not. I've got to handle this one alone."

Rosa placed a comforting hand on her shoulder. "Never alone, *querido*. Remember, you are a Christian now. You are never alone."

"I guess I'd forgotten." She opened the back door and stepped outside. "Don't hold lunch for me. I won't be back till later."

Rosa watched from the doorway as Elise made her way across the yard and disappeared into the stables. *It looks bad, Father,* she prayed with a shake of her head. *Poor girl's hurting. I don't know what the problem is, but I'm thankful You do. Help her, Lord. Help her to see You. Amen.*

Elise found James working in the stables and he was more than happy to saddle Miss Sadie for her. In a matter of minutes, she was directing the mare out into the bright sunlight.

She bent over to whisper in Miss Sadie's ear. "I need some time alone. How about you?"

Miss Sadie seemed to sense her rider's mood and, with a burst of speed, the twosome was galloping across the yard toward the wide-open range.

❧

Rosa swung the heavy wooden panel open with a crash. "Okay, Señor Garver," she demanded, "just what is going on around here?"

"Rosa!" Seth shouted, "You 'bout scared me out of my wits."

"Then it couldn't have been much of a scare," Rosa quipped. She could see the beginning of a protest on Seth's lips and she raised a hand to silence him. "What's going on with Elise and Tanner?"

Seth folded his arms across his chest and looked out the window, refusing to meet her penetrating stare. "I don't know what you mean."

"You most certainly do," she accused. She strode over to stand beside his bed. "Why did Tanner ride out of here this morning looking like he'd lost his best friend, and why is Elise so upset she won't eat?"

Seth shrugged noncommittally. "Maybe a little tiff?"

"Seth, I am at the end of my patience with you. I've stood back, watching you play the invalid, hoping you knew what you were doing. I can see now that you've made a complete mess of things, and I need to step in and fix them up."

He looked at her then, his eyes filled with pain. "It's too late, Rosa. She's going home."

Rosa dropped into the chair beside his bed. "Elise is going home?" she repeated for confirmation. "To Boston?"

Seth nodded. "She got a letter from Claudia. The old crab is on her way to Texas right now. With that Bennett fella."

"Bennett fella? Where have I heard that name?" Rosa racked her memory for his identity. "Oh, no, the man Claudia mentioned in her letter. What a mess!" she exclaimed as the full import of Seth's words sunk in. "I forgot all about Elise being engaged. No wonder Tanner looked so bad."

"That's only part of it. Tanner's upset with me, too. I practically threw him out."

Rosa's dark eyes flashed angrily. "You did what?"

"I had to, Rosa. He knows why Elise is here. He was going to protect me from her." Seth laughed bitterly at the irony of his words. "I couldn't let him come between us. I had to send him away. There's so little time left."

"Slow down, Seth, you lost me somewhere. Why would Tanner think you need to be protected from Elise?"

"He's talked to her. I'm not sure how it came up, but he asked her why she came to see me, and she told him it was for my money."

Rosa gasped. "That can't be true. Elise isn't like that. Besides, she already has your money. Claudia's been living on your money for years. Elise too. Why would she have to come here?"

"I don't know." Seth shrugged his broad shoulders. "Maybe Claudia was afraid I didn't have everything written out, you know, to make it legal that they get everything when I die."

"The very idea of it makes me sick. I just can't believe it of Elise."

"Don't hold it against her. After all, think of who raised her. As greedy as old Claudia is, it's no wonder she's trained Elise to think the same way. The way I figure it, it's my own fault for giving the child away."

Rosa's mind was reeling. Elise had told Tanner she was only here for her father's money? Something was not right. "Look, Seth, I don't know what's going on, but the Lord does. Let's take this to Him."

To her surprise, Seth didn't argue. "That's a good idea, Rosa. Let's pray."

❧

Horse and rider appeared as one as they sailed effortlessly across the grassy fields. Elise leaned into the horse, rolling comfortably with the now-familiar gait. Riding never failed to exhilarate her and this morning was no exception. The breeze and sunlight had a healing effect on her aching heart.

Upon sighting the circle of trees marking the pond on the horizon, Elise slowed Miss Sadie. "There it is, girl." She pointed straight ahead. "There's the spot we're looking for."

Again, she picked up the pace, not stopping until they reached the cool shade of the spreading oaks. Elise slid out of the saddle and secured Miss Sadie's reins around a low-hanging branch of a tree. "You rest here. I'll be back later," she promised, patting the horse's velvety nose.

The sight of the pond brought a rush of memories flooding back to Elise. It seemed like ages ago that she and Rosa had spent a carefree afternoon here. Her life was so full of promise then. What a difference a few days could make.

She gave her head a shake, dismissing the melancholy thought. No point in reliving the past. Better to concentrate on the future.

Without Rosa to coax her, Elise felt no draw to the crystalline water. Instead, she crawled up on the wall of rocks, settled back against a sun-warmed boulder, and closed her eyes.

Myriad thoughts vied for her attention. Was it wrong to come to Texas? Was it pure selfishness to want her father's love? If only she'd been satisfied with what she had, none of this mess would have happened. If she hadn't come to Texas, there would be no rift between the two men she loved.

If she had been content to settle for dreams, she wouldn't have this heart-break now of never hearing her father tell her he loved her.

Yet, no dream was as sweet as seeing him, really seeing him, had been. And perhaps the pleasure of talking with him face to face was worth the price of not hearing the words she needed so badly to hear.

If she'd stayed in Boston, she'd probably be married by now. She'd never have met tall, handsome Tanner nor felt the pain of his rejection.

But perhaps the joy of being in love, the giddy head-over-heels feeling she'd known when he kissed her was worth the pain she was suffering. After all, she might never feel that alive again.

She didn't know Mr. Bennett very well; they'd met only once or twice before, but she knew it would be a marriage of convenience. She doubted she would ever have the strong feelings for him that she had for Tanner.

So what should she do? Should she take the memories she'd gathered back with her to Boston to live and relive for the rest of her life, and leave Tanner and her father to their lives? Or should she take what little time she had left and press for their love, possibly at the cost of their relationship?

Elise sighed heavily. She felt so very alone.

Suddenly, Rosa's words came back to her. "Not alone. You're a Christian now. Never alone."

Elise bowed her head. "Oh, God, I know it's awfully late to ask You, but what do I do now?"

રજ

The sun had begun its slow descent when Elise galloped up to the stables. James met her at the door. "Good, you're back! You've got company up at the house. I was gonna ride out looking for you."

"Company?" Elise squealed with delight. Could it be? She kicked the horse up and raced around to the front door. Her face fell at the sight that greeted her.

Aunt Claudia stood grim-faced on the porch with Mr. Bennett close at her side.

"There she is now!" Rosa called, pointing out Elise as she rounded the corner.

"Look at you!" Claudia's steely gray eyes nearly bulged from their sockets.

Astonished and pleased that Aunt Claudia was impressed by something she'd done, Elise smiled as she patted the horse's neck. "Oh yes, ma'am, I ride all the time. Are you surprised?"

Claudia dismissed her with a curt wave of her hand. "Don't be such a simpleton. I'm not talking about your riding. Look at your clothes! That color combination is horrible, even for your pitiful standards." She looked to her companion. "She's a trial, Percival. Positively hopeless."

Percival snickered.

"Elise is a fine rider," Rosa pointed out in her defense. "She shows a lot of promise."

"I don't recall asking for your opinion. And I can't believe that you've already finished with our unpacking. Get busy." She turned her imperious glare toward Elise. "Elise, is it too much to ask for you to get down off that beast and join us?" she barked impatiently. "Mr. Bennett and I have come an awfully long way to see you. How rude of you to keep us waiting."

Elise kept her gaze downcast. "Yes, ma'am, I'll be right there." Slowly she reined Miss Sadie around and headed to the stables.

"Did you see your people?" James asked eagerly. "Bet they were proud to see what a fine horsewoman you've become."

Elise shrugged. "I don't think so, James."

He did not miss the disappointment in her voice. "Aw, Miss Garver. They just don't know any better, being city folks and all."

"Thank you," Elise said with a half-hearted smile. "Would you take care of Miss Sadie for me? I need to hurry back up to the house."

"Sure will. And did I mention how purty you're looking? Just like a flower."

She brightened momentarily, flashing him a grateful smile. "I'm glad you think so. Good night."

&

Elise closed the back door behind her without a sound and tiptoed down the hall, hoping to get up to her room undetected. No such luck. Aunt Claudia met her at the top of the stairs.

"Elise, did you or did you not bring your copy of *Mrs. Rhoades's Complete Handbook of Courteous Behavior and Social Graces for Young Women* with you like I told you to?"

"Yes, ma'am, I did."

"And did you consult the book before you selected that. . .that ensemble?" she demanded disdainfully.

"No, ma'am. I did not."

"Of course not!" she snapped. "I am certain Mrs. Rhoades would never advocate a young woman going out so poorly attired. Your hair and clothes are a disgrace. What will Mr. Bennett think? And that hat." Claudia's arm snaked out as if to grab it, and Elise backed up quickly, pulling the hat from her head and wrapping her arms around it. Claudia was seething. "Well? What do you have to say for yourself?"

"I'm quite thankful Mrs. Rhoades isn't here to see me."

Aunt Claudia was not amused. She fixed Elise with a condemning glare. "Bad blood will always tell."

Elise was familiar with the accusation. She heard it all the time. She learned it was best to say nothing in her own defense. "I'm certain you are correct, Aunt Claudia. Now, if you will excuse me, I need to change before I see Mr. Bennett."

"Mr. Bennett and I are exhausted from our travel. He told me to tell you he has retired for the evening. Since you haven't a civil tongue in your head, I will retire as well." With that, she turned and stalked down the hall in a huff.

&

It was late when with a sigh of resignation, Elise crawled between the crisp white sheets. She would not cry or complain. After all, it was in God's hands now.

This afternoon, when she'd prayed, she finally decided to cast all her cares upon Him. She would trust God for her future. She hadn't received immediate direction. The clouds did not part as she breathed her "Amen;" no words appeared on the glossy surface of the water telling her what to do, yet she knew she could trust Him. She would let Him lead.

When James had met her with the news of her company, her heart skipped a beat. She'd thought that God's answer was Tanner, that somehow, miraculously, he'd come home.

When instead she saw her aunt's disapproving scowl, she took that to be

God's answer. She belonged in Boston. Her memories would have to be enough.

≈

Tanner smoothed out the corner of his bedroll, then lay back with his arms folded behind his head to stare up into the starlit sky. There was little breeze tonight, nothing to disturb the silence that settled comfortably over the land.

Becky nuzzled up beside him. "Made good time today, Becky. We'd be halfway to Fort Worth by now if I hadn't. . . ." He paused. "Just what would you call what I did? Reconsidered? Saw the light? Changed my mind or just lost it?" Tanner chuckled at his little joke. "Guess there's a little truth in all those things."

This morning there had been no softening of his resolve. He rode out at first light, just as Seth had commanded. That hurt, no doubt about it. He loved Seth like a father and it was painful to feel the sting of his rejection. He'd wanted to protect him, and was thrown out for his efforts.

Fact was, he had tried to tell himself it suited him just fine, he didn't want to be around that Garver woman, anyway. She'd shown her true colors. Despite the fact she looked and smelled like an angel, she was a gold digger, pure and simple. How could he have been such a fool to fall in love with her? The bitterness of her betrayal had fueled his ride most of the morning.

But, without warning, sometime during the course of the day, a doubt had taken seed in his mind. Was it really that simple?

As he made his trek east, he had continued to replay all the events. He could remember clearly the bright blush on her creamy white cheeks when he'd confronted her with his accusations. That was proof, wasn't it?

Perhaps, but a blush was hardly conclusive evidence. After all, didn't those same smooth cheeks flame with the slightest provocation?

She had wanted to explain herself. Tanner had tried to erase from his memory the pleading look in her green eyes as she tried to offer an explanation. He had refused. He was hurting so badly, he didn't want to hear anymore. Now, from somewhere deep within himself the realization emerged— *You should have heard her out.*

She lied to me—she doesn't love me—she's engaged, he had argued. *But,* came the rebuttal, *you love her anyway.*

It was a little past four in the afternoon when Tanner had stopped. He'd bowed his head and prayed. "Lord God, I don't know what to do. Seems like I'm slow to learn to bring things to You in prayer, but I'm here now. I only hope it's not too late. Please show me what to do."

Tanner grinned at the memory. There he'd sat, stock-still, in the middle of a deserted road, waiting to hear from God. The amazing thing was, he did!

Not audibly, of course, but the leading was so clear, he didn't hesitate.

Without a second's delay, he had reined Gypsy around and galloped toward home. He'd trust God to know what to do when he got there.

Tanner shifted, pulling the blanket up under his chin for protection against the cool night air. "I don't know, Becky. I'd be lying if I said I wasn't mixed up. But this much I know. I love her. And I've got to go home."

fourteen

Elise rose early and slipped quietly down the stairs and into the kitchen.

"Good morning, Rosa."

Rosa met her at the door and enveloped Elise in her arms. She didn't know what was going on, but she knew she loved Elise—that was enough. She'd trust God to take care of the details. "Good morning, *querido*." She held Elise at arm's length, her dark eyes studying the younger woman's face. "Did you sleep well? I was afraid you'd be starving, so I fixed a big breakfast for you. Don't tell Rosa you're not hungry; it would break my heart."

Elise laughed. "I'm famished."

"Bueno, good." Rosa walked to the stove and returned to the table, carrying a full plate. She motioned for Elise to sit down. "You eat every bite."

Elise slid into the chair. "You are too good to me, Rosa."

"Nonsense. You and I are part of the same family, God's family, and I always take care of my family."

Elise bit into a fluffy biscuit and chewed thoughtfully. "What did you think about my other family? Aunt Claudia and Mr. Bennett, I mean."

Rosa took a long draught of her coffee to give herself time to fashion an acceptable answer. "Your aunt is exactly as I expected," she said with a forced smile, "and Mr. Bennett, well, he's uh, he's. . .here!" Rosa was on her feet instantly.

Elise turned to look up at the man standing behind her. "Good morning, Mr. Bennett. I am surprised to see you up so early."

"Couldn't sleep," he grumbled. "Too quiet here. Don't know how you've been able to stand it so long." He took the seat Rosa vacated and studied Elise's breakfast with interest. "Get me a plate, too," he instructed Rosa.

Bennett lowered his voice only slightly as he leaned over to confide in Elise, "This country cooking is terrible. I can hardly get it past my lips. Of course, a man's got to keep up his strength." He patted the elaborate brocade vest covering his stomach. "At least it's filling."

Her emerald eyes flashed indignantly as she enunciated, "Rosa is an excellent cook, Mr. Bennett. And a dear friend. Please be careful how you address her."

Bennett was momentarily stunned into silence. "Never known you to contradict me, Elise." He wagged a finger at her. "It's most unladylike of you. And frankly, the idea of you, fraternizing with the domestic help is scandalous. I can see there are many things we will have to work on once we are married."

Rosa stomped over to the table and slapped a plate in front of him. Sensing an impending storm, Elise sent her a beseeching look, and Rosa reluctantly turned away without comment.

Bennett didn't seem to notice anything amiss as he dug into his breakfast with gusto. "After breakfast, I'd like to see the place. Quite a ranch here. Very profitable, I'd say."

"Are you interested in ranching, Mr. Bennett?" Elise found her appetite was gone, so she busied herself moving the food around the plate.

"Not particularly, but I'm very interested in seeing what I bargained for."

Elise lowered her fork to her plate and looked over to give him her full attention. "I'm not certain I know what you mean, Mr. Bennett."

"Just as well." He dismissed the topic with a wave of his fork before stuffing a huge bite of steak into his mouth. "Anyway," he managed between bites, "after breakfast we'll mount up and tour the place."

"Do you ride?"

"Yes, my dear. I know it's difficult to believe a man of my refinement would take an interest in equestrian diversion but, in truth, I've spent many a pleasant hour astride a fine thoroughbred."

Elise found her first genuine smile since Mr. Bennett had joined her at the table. He liked to ride. She knew it would be important for them as husband and wife to share some common interest, and until now she was unaware of any similarities between them. This was great. They could share a love of riding. She smiled broadly. God had been listening to her prayers.

"If you'll excuse me, Mr. Bennett, I'd like to go change for our ride."

"Good enough," he said with a nod, cramming an entire biscuit into his mouth. "I'll meet you at the stables in one hour. And be prompt, Elise. Remember, a Bennett is always punctual."

Rosa followed Elise out into the hall with a bundle in her arms. "Wait, *querido*. Take this for your ride. I made it for you."

Elise accepted it with a protest. "But I have the skirts of your daughter's."

"Sí, that is true," Rosa nodded, "but I want you to have one of your very own." Tears glittered in her dark eyes and her voice broke as she whispered, "Maybe you'll think of me when you wear it."

Elise's eyes widened with understanding. The riding outfit was a farewell gift from Rosa. Elise threw her arms around the older woman and hugged her tightly. "Oh Rosa, I don't know if I can bear it. I'll miss you so." Tears rolled down her cheeks. "You're my dearest friend, and I'll never ever forget you."

Rosa backed away, brushing the tears from her eyes. "Get upstairs now.

Remember," she teased, "a Bennett is always punctual."

Elise climbed the stairs slowly, her troubles momentarily forgotten as she studied the garment, her brow furrowed. From behind her Rosa called quietly, "It's navy. Any color blouse would match nicely."

"How did you know what I. . . ?" Elise turned around and smiled sheepishly. "Thanks, Rosa. Thank you for everything."

After a quick change, Elise hurried to the stables. "Good morning, James. Would you saddle Miss Sadie for me please? And Mr. Bennett will need a mount as well."

James turned around and his mouth gaped open at the sight. "Miss Garver, is it you?"

She felt the blush burn all the way to her feet. She nodded shyly.

"Why yer. . .yer. . . ," he struggled to find the right word, "elegant! That's it. Yer elegant. Like one of them ladies in the magazines. Boy howdy, I wish Tanner was here to see you right now."

A wistful sigh escaped as Elise nodded again. "Me, too."

✦

"If you'll notice, Mr. Bennett, that's the bunkhouse up ahead," Elise extended her gloved hand to indicate the structure, "which means we've come full circle. That's the end of our tour. What did you think?"

Silence. "Mr. Bennett?" Upon getting no response, she turned around in her saddle to see what he was up to.

She had to bite her tongue to keep from laughing out loud at the sight that met her eyes.

Percival Bennett's horse trailed Miss Sadie by a good five yards, with her disheveled rider clinging to the saddle horn for dear life. To say he sat atop the horse would be overly optimistic, for in truth the man listed so heavily to one side, Elise was uncertain what it was that kept him in his saddle.

"Oh, Mr. Bennett!" she cried, quickly riding to his aid. "Are you all right?"

The glazed look in his blue eyes evaporated at the sound of her voice. "Of course, I'm all right," he snapped indignantly. "Just resting, that's all."

Elise couldn't resist goading him a bit. "How sensible of you. Are you ready to ride out to see the cattle? My father's herd is very impressive."

"No!" he answered quickly, then amended, "What I mean is, uh, this horse is winded. That's it. The horse is winded. Wouldn't be right to take the old nag out again. Most humane thing would be to take her back to the stall."

"Oh, no, Mr. Bennett, Baby is not a nag. She's one of my father's prize mares." She turned her sweetest smile on him. "And don't you worry; I'm certain she'd enjoy the ride out to the far pasture."

"Are you contradicting me, Elise?" Bennett was incredulous. "Highly improper for a woman aspiring to be a Bennett. I expected better of you."

Elise's cheeks burned brightly with shame. He was right. She'd been deliberately perverse with him. For what purpose? Did she want him to withdraw his offer of marriage? No, indeed. Aunt Claudia would be livid. How many times had she reminded Elise of her duty to marry well. "Mr. Bennett is the epitome of all that is desirable in a man, Elise," she would say, "and you are fortunate that he would even consider you."

She knew Aunt Claudia was right, and yet, she didn't feel too fortunate right now. He might be the height of desirability, but her tastes lately seemed to run a bit more rugged. Someone tall and dark perhaps. . . .

Nonsense, she upbraided herself for her wayward thoughts. *You've prayed about it. It's in God's hands. And if God thinks Mr. Bennett is right, then so be it.*

"I'm sorry, Mr. Bennett. How thoughtless of me."

"Never mind the apology, my dear," his tone softened slightly, "you're obviously overwrought. I have that effect on women." He smiled magnanimously. "It's forgotten. Let's press on to the stables, shall we?"

≈

"You two finished already?" James asked as they walked up to the stable.

"Yes, we are," Bennett said as he slid unceremoniously from his saddle and hit the ground with a dull thud. He pulled a small mirror from the pocket of his coat and studied himself. "But my hair's a fright. Young man?"

James finished lifting Elise from the saddle and placed her gently on the ground before responding, "Sir?"

"You need to go into town for me. I'm out of my pomade for my hair, and this awful Texas wind has ruined me. I must have a jar right away."

James shook his head. "Sorry, sir, can't do that. Short-handed around here today. I'll be glad to run in for you first thing tomorrow morning."

"Tomorrow? Tomorrow?" Bennett repeated imperiously. "Do you know who you are addressing? Percival Bennett, of the Boston Bennetts. If you value your job, you'll head for town right away."

"Look, Mr. Bennett," James gritted out between his teeth, "work here is priority one. . .not baby-sitting city folks."

"Why you impertinent. . . !" Bennett's face mottled with rage.

Elise slipped between the men and raised her hands for silence. "Please gentlemen. May I make a suggestion? I need to run into town for some ribbon, and I would be happy to purchase Mr. Bennett's hair tonic while I'm there."

"No fiancée of mine will be traipsing around the country unescorted. Think of the disgrace!"

"Then you'll have to make the trip," James said, glaring his challenge, 'cuz I can't spare anyone else today."

The tension between the men in the stables was thick enough to cut with a knife, and it wasn't until after James harnessed the horses to the wagon and Elise was, at last, heading the team toward town, that she could release the breath she had been holding.

She stole a sidelong glance at her companion on the bench who was mumbling under his breath about the inconvenience of the trip. An alarming thought gripped her. *As soon as we get back to Boston, this man is going to be my husband.* She tried to ignore the hollow feeling in the pit of her stomach.

Try to look on the bright side, she told herself. Marriage, even to Mr. Bennett would provide her with the family she so desperately wanted. It wouldn't be the same as her father's love, she knew, but she'd be a Bennett. She'd have someplace to belong and maybe even children to love.

And, she continued to encourage herself, it would be nice to be out from under Aunt Claudia's critical eye. She chewed the corner of her lip. Of course, she wasn't too certain she wouldn't be jumping out of the frying pan and into the fire. Mother Bennett, a rather dour matron and a pinnacle of propriety would be sharing a home with Elise and her husband.

She closed her eyes for a second, shutting out the fearful thought. She tried to replace it with something positive by imagining married life. She could picture herself strolling hand in hand with her husband, with several children scampering around them. She imagined herself saying something to her husband that pleased him and he bent to favor her with a loving smile. His ebony eyes met hers. . . .

Elise started, accidentally jerking the reins. Mr. Bennett stared at her with wide eyes. "What is it, Elise? Trouble with the wagon?"

"Oh, no, everything is fine." She gave an embarrassed shrug. "I'm afraid I was just daydreaming."

"A Bennett is always alert, Miss Garver," he scolded. "Please remember that."

"Yes, Mr. Bennett, I'll try."

Satisfied that she would be more careful, Bennett slumped back against the bench to continue his grumbling, leaving Elise to consider her daydreams. Mr. Bennett's eyes were a peculiar shade of pale blue, not ebony like the man in her imagination. Those were Tanner's dark orbs infiltrating her dreams.

Forget him, she told herself. *He hates you. I can't,* she argued back. *I love him.*

❧

Tanner galloped to the door of the stables just as James stepped out into the sunlight. "Hey, Tanner! What're you doing home? Thought you were in Fort Worth."

"Change of plans. You seen Elise?"

James nodded. "Yep. She and some city fella rode into town. Left here about ten minutes ago."

"Thanks." Tanner pushed his dark hat lower on his brow and kicked up his horse, galloping off in a cloud of dust.

He and Gypsy made good time by cutting across a field, and they closed in undetected on the wagon in a matter of minutes. From his vantage point, he could see Elise at the reins and a man beside her on the bench.

Tanner swallowed hard. In spite of his confidence that he was doing exactly what God wanted him to do, he suddenly felt nervous. As he galloped up to the wagon, he steeled himself for his meeting with the competition.

He reined the horse up on Elise's left side. "Morning, Miss Garver," he said, tipping his hat casually as if his appearance were an everyday thing.

"Tanner?" Elise squeaked, nearly dropping the reins. She had to blink twice to make certain the smiling man riding beside her was not a figment of her imagination. "What are you doing here?"

"Had to make a trip into town for supplies." He surveyed the wagon. "Seems you're doing the same thing," he added innocently. "Maybe we can travel together."

"Well, uh. . . ." She glanced nervously toward Mr. Bennett. "I, uh. . . ."

Tanner's gaze followed hers. "Hello." He nodded politely to the man beside her before turning back to Elise.

"I thought you'd be with your fiancé. Isn't he here?"

Elise blushed. "This is my fiancé. This is Mr. Percival Bennett."

Tanner was stunned. He hoped the shock he felt didn't register on his face. This was the competition? He turned toward the man again. "Well, hello there!" His warm greeting dripped with hospitality. "We've heard so much about you; it's a pleasure finally to meet you." He silently congratulated himself on his quick recovery.

This was Elise's fiancé? Somehow he'd pictured him differently. Someone tall and sophisticated, someone whose good looks would complement hers. Not a man old enough to be her father, who was balding and overweight to boot.

It's not what you think. Isn't that what she said? What an understatement. Tanner shoved his dark hat down on his head. It was time to find out what was going on. He urged Gypsy around to the other side of the wagon to get some answers. "So," he said, striking up a conversation, "the name's Bennett?"

Bennett nodded regally from his perch on the bench. "That's right. Percival Bennett here, of the Boston Bennetts." He looked down the end of his nose to inquire, "And you are?"

"Tanner Dalton, one of Seth Garver's hands." He deftly turned the attention back to the other man. "Boston Bennetts, huh? Seems I've heard of the family. . . ," he said.

"I should say you have, sir." He puffed out his chest with pride. "The Bennett family has been a bastion of social refinement and propriety for generations. We trace our lineage all the way back to the royal families of Europe," he boasted. "We have wealth, prestige, and what's more, the rare distinction of an untainted name. Never once in our proud history has even a breath of scandal touched the Bennett name."

Tanner gave a low whistle of appreciation. "That's mighty impressive." Inwardly, he cringed. Had Bennett just given him the evidence to convict Elise as a gold digger? What else besides money could she possibly see in the aged, overbearing windbag?

No. This time he would not jump to conclusions. Elise deserved better than that.

He inclined his head in her direction and lowered his voice. "No slight intended against Miss Garver there, but how is it a child like that ended up with a powerful man of the world like yourself? She must be one lucky woman."

Tanner could tell by the pleased look on the man's face that his strategy had worked. The size of the man's ego was exceeded only by the size of his waistline.

"You're very perceptive for a cowboy, Mr. Dalton. Actually, Miss Garver had nothing to do with it. She's too young and inexperienced to understand these things. The fact is, Claudia Stephens was instrumental in our alliance."

"That must be Miss Garver's Aunt Claudia?"

Bennett nodded. "Shrewd woman. I've handled a few investments for her over the years, always mutually profitable, so when she came to me with a proposition about her niece, I was all ears."

Bennett leaned out from the wagon toward Tanner to confide, "Claudia was concerned about the girl's prospects for marriage. One can never be too careful about that sort of thing. I was willing to overlook her obviously inferior bloodlines," he cast a glance toward Elise, whose attention was directed straight ahead, "because she's a lovely thing, and quite innocent. With the proper training at the hand of my mother, she'll make a fine Bennett."

The party rounded the corner into the town proper just then, and Tanner decided not to press the conversation further. They rode up to the general store in silence.

After helping Elise and Bennett alight from the wagon, he lingered outside for a moment to tend the horses and sort things out.

Bennett spoke of his engagement to Elise as unemotionally as one would describe any business venture. He never once mentioned love or mutual respect or any of the ingredients Tanner would have assumed would go into a marriage proposal. Tanner felt sick. Poor Elise. How could he have ever have been so wrong? And what could he do now to make it right?

As he stood by the team in front of the store window, he prayed. "God, show me what You want me to do. Amen."

Tanner stepped inside the store and paused to locate Elise. He started toward the back of the room where she was standing with Bennett, when he heard muttering coming from behind the counter. He leaned over to see Nathan, down on all fours. "Problem?"

"Huh?" Nathan glanced up in surprise. "Oh, howdy, Tanner. Didn't hear you come in. I spilled these nails and just wasted a good half hour picking 'em up. Don't know why they can't build a better box to keep them in." He dusted off his pants as he got to his feet. "Kinda surprised to see you in here again so soon." Nathan leaned across the counter with a twinkle in his eye. "How's the pretty little woman?"

Tanner failed to make the connection. "Little woman?"

"You know," Nathan winked knowingly, "the one you were kissing in my store."

Tanner glanced toward Bennett and Elise. Luckily, they did not seem to hear. "She's fine, thanks." He hoped his unenthusiastic response would quell Nathan's curiosity.

"Oh, I get it," Nathan persisted. "Don't want to talk about her, being she's the boss's daughter and all." He winked again. "Funny, I never figured you for the shy type."

From the corner of his eye, Tanner could see Bennett and Elise making their way toward the counter, and he knew the time for subtlety had passed. If Bennett heard Nathan's prattle, Elise's engagement would be ruined. Kissing one of the ranch hands would be just the sort of situation the Bennett clan liked to avoid.

Suddenly, Tanner smiled.

"Well, Miss Garver!" Nathan exclaimed, glancing nervously between her and Tanner. "Didn't know you were here." He shrugged apologetically at Tanner, before turning back to her. "What can I do for you, ma'am?"

"Nothing for me, thanks, but Mr. Bennett here needs your assistance with some hair preparations."

Nathan stepped out from behind the counter. "Yes, sir. I'll be glad to show you what I've got. Right this way."

Tanner caught Elise's arm before she could follow them. "Wait. I need to ask you something." He felt his heart melt as she raised emerald eyes to meet his. "Is this what you want? Marriage to Bennett?"

She didn't answer immediately. Instead, she dropped her gaze to her hands. A long moment passed before she looked at him again. This time, tears glittered in her eyes. "No," she said simply.

Tanner breathed a loud sigh of relief. He reached out to stroke her silken cheek. "I know I've been a fool. I don't deserve anything from you, but do you think you could find it in your heart to forgive me?"

A large tear slid from her eye as she nodded.

He took her chin and gently tipped her face up to his.

"I love you, Elise. I won't lose you."

She smiled tremulously in response as more tears fell.

"Why the tears?" he asked softly.

"I'm trapped in an engagement to a man I do not love and will love forever a man I cannot have."

Tanner resisted the urge to sweep her into his arms. She loved him. God was so good. He gently brushed the tears away with his finger. "Things could change."

She shook her head sadly. "Not this time. Aunt Claudia and Mr. Bennett have finalized all the arrangements. I have nothing to say about it." Her tone was hopeless. "You don't know them, Tanner. Once they've made a decision, it would take nothing short of a miracle to stop them."

fifteen

"You comfortable enough back there, Bennett?" Tanner called over his shoulder.

"I most certainly am not," Bennett snapped from his seat on the floor of the wagon, directly behind Elise, where he sat with his back against the side plank. "A sack of flour provides pitiful little insulation against the pits in this rotten road. And your dog stinks."

"You have my apologies, sir. A fine gentleman like yourself shouldn't have to accept such crude accommodations. You know you're welcome to ride my horse."

Bennett glanced fearfully at the enormous black beast tied to the back of the wagon. "No, no indeed." His voice became hopeful, "Perhaps I could join you two on the bench?"

Tanner shook his dark head. "Sorry, Bennett, it's strictly a two-seater. If you could handle a team, you and I could trade places. But seeing as how you can't, I'll have to drive. Wouldn't do to have Miss Garver at the reins, not when there are two healthy men around. Just isn't done in these parts. A man like yourself understands the importance of propriety."

"Indeed I do. It's just. . ." He cast a longing look at the bench. "How much longer to the ranch?"

"Not more than twenty minutes." Tanner smiled reassuringly. "Sit back and enjoy the view."

Bennett's silence lasted only briefly. "Is it always so hot here?" he complained.

Tanner nodded again. "Aw, this is nothing. Come August, it's so hot, it's hard to draw a breath." Bennett could not see the wicked smile hovering around Tanner's mouth as he continued, " 'Course, folks around here got a solution. Why, Miss Garver is already a big proponent of it."

"And what would that be?" Bennett sounded bored.

"Skinny dipping," Tanner pronounced casually, carefully ignoring Elise's gasp of horror and Mr. Bennett's sharp intake of breath. "Isn't that right, Miss Garver? Tell him how nice and cool the pond is."

Elise's flushed expression was pained. "Tanner, I don't think Mr. Bennett is interested. . . ."

"No need to be shy, Miss Garver. Mr. Bennett's a practical man; he under- stands the need for comfort. Besides, he's your intended." Tanner swung around on the bench to face Bennett. "And let me put any worries you might have to rest. The pond we're talking about is real private. Only me and Rosa were there with your fiancée." He turned back to the team before Bennett could see his smile.

"You were there?" Bennett choked. "With Miss Garver?"

Tanner's head bobbed up and down enthusiastically. "Well sure. Sounds a bit crowded I suppose, but actually, it's a real big pond."

"You and Miss Garver. . .?" Bennett couldn't seem to make himself finish.

"Isn't it nice to know we've become such close friends?" He flashed a cheerful smile over his shoulder. " 'Course," he added thoughtfully, "I guess we were obliged to get to know each other pretty quick, what with her sleeping in my arms and all."

Elise gasped and gripped the bench to keep from falling from the wagon.

"Guess that sounds pretty compromising, but you'd have to understand the circumstances."

Elise turned hope-filled eyes to Tanner and nodded for him to continue.

"Yes, yes, tell me," Bennett's words came out in a rush. "What were the circumstances?"

Tanner shrugged. "Simple, really. You see, we were so warm and comfortable on that mattress, one of us was bound to fall asleep."

"Mattress?" Bennett's voice was a loud, high-pitched squeak.

Tanner ignored the man's distress. "Look here." He pointed up ahead. "We're back already. Wasn't that a quick trip." He turned to smile into Bennett's beet red face. "Bennett, I wouldn't be surprised if all this riding has made you a bit stiff. You know, Miss Garver here had the same trouble." He patted Elise's shoulder companionably. "We found a bath to be the most soothing. Seemed to melt the aches away."

"We found?" Bennett's voice sounded weaker.

Tanner stopped the wagon in front of the house. "That's right. Now, of course, you won't be wanting one of them flowery smelling ones like Miss Garver," he added helpfully. "Though I've got to say, it smelled real fine to me."

"Tanner! I don't think Mr. Bennett wants to hear any more—"

"You're right!" Bennett shouted as he scrambled from the back of the wagon and marched stiff-legged up the stairs of the house. "I've heard all I want to hear."

The sound of the door slamming loosened Elise's tongue. "Tanner Dalton! What would make you tell him all those things?" she demanded incredulously. "He's likely to take them all the wrong way." Her eyes flew open with her next fearful thought and she gasped, "He'll probably even tell Aunt Claudia." Elise wrung her hands. "What do you think will happen now?"

Tanner shoved his black hat back from his forehead and grinned down at her, his dark eyes twinkling. "Nothing short of a miracle."

sixteen

"Claudia?" Bennett shouted as he swept into the house. "Claudia?"

Rosa stepped out from the kitchen. "No need to holler, Señor. She is upstairs with Señor Garver."

Bennett was too overwrought to consider the impropriety of his actions as he took the stairs two at a time, raced down the hall, and exploded into Seth's room unannounced. "The deal's off!" he pronounced with his last burst of energy before collapsing into a chair, gasping for breath.

"What's the matter with you, Percival?" Claudia demanded from her place at the window. "What are you talking about?"

"I've just ridden halfway across Texas on a plank is what's the matter with me," he answered irritably. "And I'm talking about your niece. She doesn't suit. The deal's off."

Seth's interest was piqued. He sat up in bed, shoving his pillows behind him for support. "What deal?"

"Shut up, Seth!" Claudia snapped at her brother-in-law before whipping her head around to glare at Bennett. "Now look here, Bennett," she snarled, "the deal's been made. There's no backing out."

Bennett shook his balding head with defiance. "The deal was that I marry your niece, a sweet, innocent girl with a malleable disposition. Someone deserving of the Bennett name." He wagged an accusing finger at Claudia. "Your niece is neither malleable nor innocent. And this entire ranch wouldn't be worth the blemish she'd bring to my name."

"What ranch?" Seth became more agitated. "And what deal?"

"Shut up, Seth!" Claudia reddened.

Elise and Tanner arrived outside Seth's door in time to hear Claudia's rebuke. Elise gasped her outrage. How dare Aunt Claudia address her father that way. Tanner pressed a finger to his lips and shook his head, imploring her to be silent. He moved back slightly from the door frame, pulling her with him, so as not to be seen.

Bennett shrugged. "What difference does it make if he knows? He hasn't got long to live." He ignored Claudia's threatening scowl and turned to Seth. "Claudia and I have been business associates for some time. I make investments for her," he said by way of explanation.

"Several months ago," he continued, "Claudia came to me with a proposition. She needed someone to marry her niece. Elise is getting to a marriageable age, and it wouldn't be long before some fella would marry her and carry her off. Without the support you send for Elise, Claudia would be a penniless spinster."

Claudia obviously took offense at his remark and fixed him with a frosty glare.

"That's why she needed me. I could marry Elise and guarantee a comfortable income to Claudia."

"All out of the goodness of your heart, I suppose?" Seth mocked.

Bennett laughed. "Don't be a fool, Garver. I'm a businessman first. This ranch will one day be Elise's, pretty soon from what I can surmise, and if she were married to me, the ranch would be mine. Whether I sold the place or hired someone to run it, there'd be big money involved." He nodded toward Claudia. "I guaranteed Claudia a percentage. It's unlikely any other suitor would be so generous to Claudia."

Seth suppressed his anger long enough to satisfy his curiosity. "But now you've decided the ranch isn't enough?"

Bennett raised his double chin a notch. "Garver, I'm a man of principle. Your daughter may be wealthy and beautiful, but I've got my good name to consider and hundreds of years of impeccable lineage to protect." He shook his head vehemently. "Elise and her exploits would bring our proud heritage crashing down around us."

"You're a fool, Bennett," Claudia hissed venomously.

"Shut up, Claudia!"

Her mouth fell open in surprise. "How dare you—?"

"How dare *you*?" Seth's eyes flashed with fury. "Try and sell my daughter off for a percentage? To a man old enough to be her father."

Claudia stomped over to Seth's bedside. "She owes it to me," she screeched. "I've raised her, I have put up with her all these years. She owes me."

"Claudia," Seth's voice was suddenly calm, "you've told the lie so long, you've convinced yourself." He shook his head sadly. "You didn't have to put up with her. I wanted her back. I begged you to give my daughter back to me. But you had already turned her against me. She hates me."

Elise wrenched free from Tanner's restraining grip and burst into the room. "Oh, no, Father," she cried as she fell to her knees before him. "I don't hate you. I love you." Tears streamed from her eyes as she confessed, "I've always loved you."

Seth was struck silent. Time stood still as he stared at Elise, trying to find the truth. She said she loved him. Could it be? He found his answer in her eyes. He extended his arms to her and, as she came to him, he pulled her to his chest and held her tightly. "All these years," he whispered into her hair.

"She told me you hated me, that the thought of me gave you nightmares. All these years I thought. . ."

Elise pulled back slightly so she could see his face. Her slender finger traced a tear streak across his whiskered cheek. She shook her head in denial. "I've always loved you. Every day, every hour, every minute. . . always."

Seth looked from his daughter to the woman standing over him. "You. . . you conniving scoundrel. How could you do this?"

"Simple," she said haughtily, without a trace of remorse. "Elise is my meal ticket." She sneered into his astonished face. "It didn't take me long to realize that with her in my possession, my future was guaranteed. You'd do anything for her. No amount of money was too much to send for her. I'd have been a fool to send her back to you."

Bennett spoke up. "Claudia, I'm shocked. Your behavior has been most improper. To provide for oneself is important, but to deprive a father of his daughter?" Bennett shook his head in disapproval. "Shocking."

Claudia turned on him. "Shut up, Percival! How could you possibly understand? You've never been poor. You've never been hungry or cold. Well, I have. My parents had nothing. They died with nothing. I vowed I would never suffer that way again."

"And you shall not," Seth pronounced. "This very day I will establish a trust for you. An income for you for the rest of your life. . .on one condition."

"And that is?"

"That I never see your face again."

"Well!" Claudia huffed.

"I mean it, Claudia. You carry yourself back up to Boston and never come back. Or I promise I'll cut you off without a dime."

"Very decent of you, Garver." Bennett nodded his approval.

Seth turned to him. "And Bennett, I trust I don't have to worry about ever seeing you again?"

"Most assuredly. Texas is no place for a gentleman. I'll be leaving first thing in the morning."

"No, sir." Seth shook his head. "You leave today. Both of you. I'll have James take you back to town as soon as you can get your things packed."

"But—"

"Move!"

෨

Father and daughter clung to one another long after Bennett and Claudia left the room. Finally, Seth drew back to look at her. "You have to believe me, Elise. I wanted you back. I always wanted you back. I tried everything I knew to do."

"I do believe you," Elise assured him. "Even when you didn't answer my letters, I knew it would happen."

Seth was incredulous. "Letters? You wrote me letters?"

"Every week."

"I never got one." Seth's voice broke. "I thought you hated me."

"Oh, no," Elise smiled into his troubled eyes, "I love you. I told you so in each letter. I gave them to Aunt Claudia to mail." She shook her head ruefully. "I never dreamed she wasn't sending them to you."

Seth rubbed his chin. "I knew the old girl was evil, but I didn't realize she was capable of anything so low. She must really hate me."

"And yet you agreed to support her?" Elise asked in wide-eyed amazement.

Seth chuckled. "Beats all, doesn't it? I don't know where the idea came from, but you can bet it wasn't mine." He raked a hand through his silver-streaked hair. "The only thing I can figure is that Rosa was praying again. She and God get to running things and I never know what's gonna happen next."

"Oh, I think I do," Elise said with a satisfied smile. "God'll be busy answering the prayers of His children."

seventeen

"I believe I'll have another one of them fine biscuits, Rosa," said Seth, smacking his lips in anticipation.

"That's your fourth one this morning," Rosa scolded. "Your recovery has been quite remarkable, Señor."

Seth scowled good-naturedly. "Guess I deserved that. You gonna tease me about it forever?"

"Tease you, nothing." Tanner wagged his fork at Seth. "I am far more tempted to skin you alive for scaring me so bad. Here I thought you were dying."

Seth's response was genuinely remorseful. "Tanner, son, I hope you can find it in your heart to forgive me. I know what I did was wrong, but I was desperate."

Elise reached over to pat her father's hand. "Don't fuss at him, Tanner. Under the circumstances, I think he was ingenious." She favored him with a bright smile. "I, for one, am grateful, and I forgive you."

"Don't encourage him, *querido*." Rosa laughed. "I'd hate to think where he'll go from here."

Seth shook his head. "No worries, Rosa. My days of deceit are over." He beamed at Elise. "I've got my little girl home now."

"Speaking of your little girl," Tanner chimed in. "Mind if I borrow her for a while? Thought maybe she and I might go for a ride."

"That's a fine idea." Seth crammed the biscuit into his mouth and started to stand. "Fine weather for it. Think I'll come, too."

Rosa grabbed his arm and pulled him back into his chair. "No, Señor. You can stay here and help me with the dishes."

"But I. . ."

Rosa cut her eyes meaningfully at him. "I think the young people would like to be alone."

Seth's face fell as he grumbled. "Fine. 'Course, I'll get as fat as ol' Bennett if I don't get some exercise."

Elise and Tanner rose from the table. "Thanks for breakfast, Rosa." Elise slipped her arm through Tanner's, and they started for the door.

"Speaking of Bennett," Seth said, stroking his chin thoughtfully, "there's something I never have understood."

Elise cast a worried look at Tanner before turning to ask, "What is that, Father?"

"Why the man would set up the whole plan with Claudia, even go so far as to travel to Texas to see the ranch, and then back out at the last minute." Seth settled back into his chair and stared up at his daughter. "He said you wouldn't suit." He was truly perplexed as he looked back over the table at Rosa to ask, "What could he possibly find about my little girl that was anything less than perfect. I've never met a more proper lady anywhere."

Tanner winked at Elise whose face was flushed a bright red. "Maybe someday you'll find out, sir."

The two of them ducked into the hall to avoid any more questions and disappeared out the back door in a peal of laughter.

❧

The riders raced into the wind, across the sun-kissed range. Even the horses seemed to sense the joyous spirit of the morning, and Becky cavorted gaily at their sides.

They slowed at the crest of a hill, under a small stand of trees to gaze out across the land. Tanner dismounted, then helped Elise to the ground.

Elise released a deeply contented sigh. "I'll never tire of Texas. There's no more beautiful place on earth."

Tanner wrapped an arm behind her waist and smiled down at her. "Beautiful."

Elise turned her face into the breeze to breathe deeply of the fresh air. "I feel so blessed. God has truly answered my prayers."

"Uh," Tannner began sheepishly, "about prayers. Remember what I said about me handling things pretty well without God?"

Elise nodded. "I remember."

He kicked at the dirt with the toe of his boot. "Well, that was the dumbest thing I've ever said." He focused his dark eyes to meet hers. "I've been thinking about the things you said, you know, about being in God's family and Him caring about us an' all, and I've committed to becoming a man of Bible study and prayer." He took her hand in his. " 'Course, I'll be needing your help."

She squeezed his hand and smiled warmly into his face. "It will be my pleasure."

Becky, who'd disappeared into the underbrush, suddenly appeared at their sides and began to yap excitedly at the twosome.

"What is it, girl?" Elise asked. "Did you find something?"

"Shucks, no." Tanner shook his head in dismay. "She's just a mite impatient. Never could keep a secret." He turned to admonish the dog. "Now, if you'll just mosey on out of here, I'll get on with what I was doing before you interrupted me."

Becky withdrew a respectful distance and sat down with her back to them.

"That's better." Tanner turned back to Elise who was clearly bewildered. "There's something else." He cleared his throat several times and pushed his hat back on his head. "Your father made me a partner—"

"Oh, Tanner," Elise squealed, "I'm so happy for you. It's just as it should be. Father and son running things together."

"Whoa, now. I don't want to be your brother."

She raised startled eyes to his.

"I want to be your husband." He took his hat in his hands. "Will you marry me?"

"Yes!" Elise threw her arms around his neck. "Yes, I'll marry you!"

❧

"Fine ceremony, Reverend Douglas." Seth slapped the younger man on the back. "Appreciate you coming out to officiate."

"Glad to do it, Seth." Reverend Douglas sipped his cup of coffee. "Your little girl's a beauty. I know you're proud to have her back."

Seth beamed. "You bet I am. Have I told you she's here to stay? She and Tanner are gonna settle in the house I built for her mother. 'Course, it's not a very big place. Once there's a couple of young un's around, I figure I'll give them this old barn," he gestured around the room, "and I'll move into their place. I always feel closer to Elizabeth there, anyway."

Rosa appeared at his side. "James says the buggy's ready, Señor Garver. Any sign of the newlyweds?"

Seth shook his head. "Not yet. Hope she's not fretting over what colors to wear again."

Rosa nodded. "I'm gonna have to work on her. I'm afraid Claudia's cruel comments about Elise's taste in colors have hurt her. I don't know what it will take to help build her confidence back."

"Rosa! I am disappointed in you," Seth said with a teasing glint in his eyes. "I figured a praying woman like you would have already taken that to God."

"You're right, Seth." Rosa was completely serious. "I'll do it right now." She bowed her head for a brief moment. There was a broad smile on her face when she raised it again. "All done."

The noise in the hall indicated the newlyweds had appeared. Seth and Rosa pressed their way through to the front of the crowd just as Tanner and Elise stepped from the stairs.

Rosa gathered Elise into her arms. "I love you, *querido*."

"I love you, too." Elise kissed her cheek before turning to her father.

"I love you, Father." She hugged him tightly. "And thank you. Thank you for everything."

A heavyset woman pushed her way through the crowd to Elise's side. "Thank heavens I caught you before you left," she puffed, her round face red from exertion.

"Mrs. Teekle!" Elise exclaimed with delight as she took the older woman's hand. "How good to see you. I didn't realize you had made it to the wedding."

"Well sure I did. I was plenty tickled to get your letter invitin' me. Wouldn't have missed it." She rolled her eyes in exasperation. " 'Course, I'd have been here on time, if ol' Wilbur wasn't such a slowpoke."

"Wilbur?" Elise inquired politely.

Mavis pointed to a reed-thin man at the edge of the crowd. "My man. Slower than molasses."

Elise smiled. "I'm so glad you were able to come. May I present my husband, Tanner Dalton. And this is my father, Seth Garver, and my dear friend, Rosa Viegas."

Mavis inclined her head. "Nice to meet all of ya." She wrung her chubby hands. "Actually, honey, there's something I'd like to ask of you, before you go."

"Yes, Mrs. Teekle?"

Mavis seemed hesitant to speak. "It's like this. After I met you on the train, I went home and bragged to a couple of my friends about you. You know, what a fine city lady you were and how you dressed so purty with all them fine colors."

"That's lovely of you to say."

Mavis put up her hand to silence her. "That ain't all. When I told them I was coming to your wedding, and that you were gonna be in Fort Worth, they pestered me half to death asking if you'd come and speak to our women's club."

Mavis's voice was pleading, "Honey, I know you're gonna be busy on your wedding trip, but do you think you could take a little time out to speak to us?"

"I'm not sure I understand. What is it you want me to speak about?"

Mavis clucked admiringly. "You city girls are so humble. Now what else would I be wanting you to teach us? About colors, of course. Ain't nobody got a fashion sense for color like you."

Rosa couldn't resist nudging Seth, whose jaw fell slack upon hearing Mavis's request. "Mercy, He was quick to answer that one," she whispered with a smug grin.

A delighted giggle erupted from Elise. "I. . .I'd be happy to, Mavis."

Mavis sighed her relief. "Oh, thank you, honey." She placed a piece of paper in Elise's hand. "This here's my address. Give me a holler when you can." She hugged Elise quickly before disappearing into the guests.

Tanner smiled tenderly at his bride and planted a quick kiss on her forehead before grasping her hand and starting through the throng of well-wishers toward the front door. The crowd moved outside to the porch and continued to cheer as the newlyweds loaded into the buggy and headed toward Fort Worth.

Rosa stood at the porch railing and watched as the buggy disappeared down the road. She wiped a tear from her cheek. "God bless them," she whispered.

Becky wagged her tail and barked.

Seth smiled. "I believe He already has."

Threads
of Love

Judith McCoy Miller

JUDITH McCOY MILLER
Judy makes her home in Kansas with her family. Intrigued by the law, Judy is a certified legal assistant currently employed as a public service administrator in the legal section of the Department of Administration for the State of Kansas. After ignoring an "urge" to write for approximately two years, Judy quit thinking about what she had to say and began writing it, and then was and has been extremely blessed! Her first two books earned her the honor of being selected **Heartsong Presents'** favorite new author in 1997.

Dedicated to

Tracie J. Peterson,
with love and heartfelt thanks for your
friendship, encouragement, and prayers.

one

The sounds in the kitchen caused Delphinia to startle awake and she immediately felt the dreadful taste of bile rise in her throat. Jumping from her bed, she ran to the washstand, removed the pitcher, and expelled the few remains of last night's supper into the chipped bowl. Looking into the small mirror that hung over the washstand, she was met by a ghostly likeness of herself. *I can't bear this, I just can't,* she thought as she rinsed her mouth and reached for a small linen towel to wipe her perspiring forehead. Making her way back to bed, she wrapped herself in a quilt and prayed that this was a bad dream.

"Oh please, dear Lord, let me go to sleep and wake up to my mama's laughter in the kitchen. Let this all be a horrible nightmare."

Instead, she heard her father's harsh command, "I hear ya awake in there, Delphinia. This ain't no day to be lazin' around. You get yourself dressed and do it now. You still got things to pack and time's gettin' short."

"I know, Pa, but I'm feeling poorly. Maybe you'd better tell that man I won't be able to go with him. I'm sure he won't want some sickly girl," she replied in a feeble attempt to dissuade him.

She heard her father's heavy footsteps come across the kitchen floor toward her room, knowing that she had tested his patience too far. The bedroom door swung open and he said in a strained voice, "Either you get yourself dressed or you'll travel as you are."

"Yes, Pa," she answered, knowing her efforts to deter him had failed and that she would soon be leaving home.

Trying to keep her stomach in check, she donned a green gingham dress and quickly pinned her hair in place. Not giving much care to her appearance, she sat down on the bed and placed her remaining belongings into the old trunk. Her hands trembled as she picked up a frayed shawl, threw it around her shoulders, and lay back on the bed, willing herself to think of happier days.

The noise outside the house brought her back to the present. How long had she been lying there? The streaming rays of sunlight that patterned the room told her that it must be close to noon. Her heart began to pound and immediately she began pressing down the gathers of her skirt in a slow, methodical motion. There was a loud knock at the heavy wooden door, followed by footsteps and the sound of voices. Minutes passed and then she heard her father calling out her name. She picked up her bonnet and sat staring at it, unwilling to accept that the time of departure had arrived. Her father called out again and she could hear the impatience in his voice. Knowing she dared not provoke him further, she compelled herself to rise from the bed and walk to the kitchen.

There, standing before her, was Jonathan Wilshire, the man who had bargained with Pa to take her away from the only home she had ever known. It was a certainty that she would dislike him. She had prayed and prayed about her predicament, but somehow God had not seen fit to eliminate this man from her life. She had begun praying that his horse would break a leg and he would not arrive. But soon she was asking forgiveness for thinking in such an unkind manner. She briefly considered a plea to God that Mr. Wilshire get lost on the journey, but she knew that would not be a Christian prayer, for he had children at home that required his safe return. So, in desperation, she did as her mama had told her many times: "When you don't know for sure what to pray for, just turn it over to the Lord for He knows your heart and will provide the best way." Fervent prayers had been uttered each night outlining the folly of the decision to send her west and requesting the Lord's assistance in finding a remedy. Although she was not sure what was best for her, she knew that leaving for Kansas with Mr. Wilshire would be a mistake. Given the amount of time she had spent in dissertation, she had been positive the Lord would agree and save her from this pending disaster.

Just look at what results that had produced! Here was Jonathan Wilshire, standing in her kitchen and looking fit as a fiddle, ready to take her to some farm in Kansas and turn her into a mama for his children. Where had her mother ever gotten the notion that praying like that would work?

Her heart had slowed down somewhat and she began to feel outrage and frustration begin to take over. She stepped toward her father and had just begun to open her mouth and voice that anger when, sensing her wrath, he said, "Delphinia, this is Jonathan Wilshire, the gentlemen we have discussed."

Once again, her palms began pressing down the gathers in her skirt and, looking directly at her father, she blurted out, "We never *discussed* Mr. Wilshire, Papa. You merely announced you were sending me away with him."

Delphinia could sense the discomfort she was causing for both men. Feeling she must press any advantage that could be gained, she continued with her tirade. "Papa, I've told you over and over that I don't want to leave you. It's been only a few months since Mama died and I don't want to lose you, too. . .and my home, Papa. Must I leave my home?" Tears had begun to roll down her cheeks and onto the pale green bodice of her frock. Her father stared at her in disbelief. She had never, in all of her seventeen years, questioned his decisions. Now, here she was, humiliating him in front of a total stranger. Not knowing if it was caused by anger or embarrassment, she watched as his short, thick neck and unshaven face quickly began to turn from deep tan to purplish red, clear to his receding hairline. Given the choices, she was hoping for embarrassment because her papa was not easy to contend with when angry. But as soon as their eyes met, she knew he was not only angry, but that he had reached the "boilin' stage" as Mama used to call it. Well, so be it. He was sending her away and she was going to tell him how she felt. After all, she had given God a chance to get things in order and He had certainly missed the mark!

"Delphinia," her father roared, "you will fetch the rest of your possessions immediately and place them in Mr. Wilshire's wagon. We've already loaded the other trunks. I'll hear no more of this nonsense. You know you're goin' along with Mr. Wilshire to look after his children. He's ready to pull out. Now mind your tongue, girl, and do as you're told."

Eyes downcast and knowing that her fate was sealed, she quietly murmured, "Of course, Papa. I'll only be a minute."

Walking back to her room, Delphinia allowed herself one last look at the small dwelling that she had called home for all of her seventeen years. She entered her sparsely furnished bedroom for the last time, grabbed the handle on the side of her trunk, and pulled it into the kitchen.

Making her way toward the center of the kitchen, her father once again began with his issuance of instructions. "Now mind your manners. I've told Mr. Wilshire that you know your reading and writing and can teach his youngsters what schooling they need to know."

Turning to the stranger, he continued his diatribe. "She even knows how to work with her numbers and so if there isn't a school nearby, she'll make a fine teacher for you."

He sounds like he's selling a bill of goods, Delphinia thought. Besides, all of her studies had been through her mama's efforts. Pa had always said it was a waste of time and had chided Ma for spending time on Delphinia's lessons. But her mother had stood firm and said it was important for both girls and boys to know how to read, write, and do their figures. When Pa would become too obstinate about the subject, Ma would smile sweetly and tell him that no child of hers would be raised not knowing how to read God's Word. Then Pa would back down and Delphinia's lessons would continue. Now here he was, using that bit of education to get rid of her.

Her thoughts ran rampant, wondering what kind of bargain had been struck between her pa and this man. Delphinia was not told the particulars and she knew her pa would never divulge all of the information to her. She knew he just wanted to be free of any responsibility. Ever since Mama had died, all he could talk about was his going to search for gold and how he would be rich and free of his worries. He had talked about it for years, but Mama had always managed to keep him level-headed and made him realize that going in search of gold was not the way of life for a married man with a family.

Well, he was "free" now. Mama had died and Delphinia was being shipped off with this stranger to some unknown place out west. Once again, she began to feel the tears well up in her eyes, but she made up her mind that she would not cry in front of her pa again. If he wanted to be rid of her, so be it. She had no choice in the matter.

Suddenly, she felt a hand reach across hers and heard Mr. Wilshire saying, "Here, I'll take that out to the wagon for you. You tell your pa good-bye and we'll be on our way. I'll be waiting outside."

Delphinia glanced up. Her father's anger had diminished and he looked as though he might feel a bit of remorse. "I'm sorry, Pa, I know I shouldn't have talked to you with such disrespect. Mama would be very unhappy with my behavior. But I don't think she'd be very happy with yours, either," she added.

When he gave no response, she continued, "Don't you think she'd want us to be together, now that she's gone?"

"I suppose, Delphinia, your mama would think that. You gotta remember, though, your mama knew I was never one to stay in one place too long. I've been living in the same place for nigh onto twenty years now. I kept my bargain with your ma and we never took off for the unknown lands farther west. But now I just have to go. There's nothing left here for me."

His words were like a knife in her heart. Was she really nothing to him? Could he think so little of her that it was more important to go searching for something he would probably never find?

"I've made proper arrangements for you, girl, and I know you'll be well cared for. Mr. Wilshire has a nice homestead in Kansas and needs help. It's a good arrangement for all of us and once I get settled, I'll let you know my whereabouts. It'll all work out for the best." He bent down, put an arm around her, and started leading her toward the door.

"What's to become of our home? Will I never see it again? You can't just go off and leave it." She pulled back and looked up at him. Her large, brown eyes were once again wet with tears.

"Now never you mind; I've taken care of all of that. Mama and I had to borrow against this place when times was bad and I'm just turning it back over to the bank. I got a little cash to get me going and what with. . . Well, I've got enough to get set up when I hit the gold fields." Once again, he was moving her toward the door.

"Oh, Pa, I just don't think I can bear it," she murmured, reaching up and throwing her arms about his neck.

"Now, now, girl, come along. It's all gonna be just fine. . .you'll see," he said, drawing her toward the wagon.

With Mr. Wilshire's help, Delphinia made her way up onto the seat of the buckboard and, without looking back, she raised her hand in a small, waving gesture to her pa.

Mr. Wilshire slapped the reins and the horses moved out.

two

A wave of panic began to take over Delphinia. Here she was, on her way to who knew where, with a man she did not even know and her pa thought it was just fine. And to think she had prayed so fervently about this! God must have been extremely busy when she issued her petitions, because she was absolutely sure that this could not be His plan for her life. Anyone could see this was a mistake. After all, she was only seventeen and she could see the folly of this situation. And God was. . . Well, nobody knew how old God was but He was certainly well over seventeen. Surely He would get her out of this mess. There must be some rescue in store for her. That was it! God had already planned her deliverance from Jonathan Wilshire!

Feeling somewhat comforted by that thought, Delphinia realized she hadn't even gotten a good look at Mr. Wilshire since his arrival. She didn't want to talk to him just now, but she was curious. Cautiously she glanced over his way, only to be met by two of the bluest eyes she had ever seen, and they were staring directly into hers.

She was so startled that she blurted out the first thing that came to mind. "Why would you need to come all the way to Illinois to find someone to care for your children?"

He did not answer but let out the deepest laugh she had ever heard.

"Just why is that such a funny question?" she countered.

"Well," he slowly answered, "I've not had a line of ladies waiting at my front door whom I'd consider suitable to meet the needs of my homestead."

Delphinia was not quite sure what that meant but she knew she did not want to pursue the matter further, at least for now. "Why are we traveling to Kansas with a wagon train? Wouldn't it be quicker and easier to travel by train?" she queried, not sure which would be worse: an arduous trip by wagon train or arriving in Kansas quickly.

"You're right. It would be faster by train, and that had been my intention. I arrived in Illinois a couple days before I was to fetch you and I was staying in town, planning to secure you shortly before our train would depart for Kansas. But, the day I arrived in Cherryvale, a group of folks from the wagon train were also in town. Their wagon master had become ill and wasn't able to continue his duties. Of course, they need to keep moving or the snows will stop them in the mountains," he explained.

"What does that have to do with us returning by train?" she interrupted, having expected a simple answer.

"They weren't able to find anyone to help them. The hotel owner heard of their plight and related it to me. I believe God puts us in certain places at certain times for a purpose," he continued. "The folks on this wagon train are good people with a need. I can fulfill that need by leading them as far as Kansas. I've talked with the wagon master and he thinks he'll be able to take over by then. . .probably before."

"But what if the wagon master isn't well by the time we reach Kansas? What if he dies?" she asked. "Then what?"

"Well, I don't believe either of those things will happen. But, if they should, I've talked with the folks on the wagon train and explained I can go no farther. They'll either have to winter in Kansas or find someone else to lead them the rest of the way. They're willing to put their trust in God that this will work, and so am I," he responded.

She was trusting in God, also, but not for the same things as Jonathan Wilshire.

"I'll be needing to pick up our supplies," he stated, pulling the horses to a halt in front of the general store, "so if there's anything you think you might be wanting for the journey, better get on down and come in with me."

"Oh, I'll just trust your judgment, Mr. Wilshire, as I've certainly never purchased supplies for a long journey and wouldn't have any idea what you might be needing," she stated rather smugly. He needn't think he was getting someone here in Illinois who was all that suitable, either! Besides, she hadn't fibbed for she didn't have the faintest idea what might be needed on such a journey.

Delphinia watched him jump down from the wagon and she could not help but admire his strength and size. Her pa was not a small man but Mr. Wilshire was quite tall and his shoulders were remarkably broad. She had never seen a man quite so large. Now that she thought about it, he was somewhat intimidating in his size. *Why hadn't I noticed that before?* she wondered. She was surprised she hadn't been frightened by him but then he had been sitting down in the wagon before she had actually taken notice of him. *Well,* she determined, *I'll not be afraid of anyone and that includes this giant of a man.*

A loud voice roused her from her thoughts. "Phiney, Phiney, are you sleeping up there?" Delphinia looked down in horror at Mr. Wilshire standing beside the wagon.

"You weren't speaking to me, were you, Mr. Wilshire?" she inquired.

"Of course I was," he stated, wondering who else she thought he might be talking to. "I was asking if you'd be wanting to choose some cloth to make a few dresses and britches for the children. They have a good selection here. . .better than the general store back home. Besides, we'll probably not go into Council Grove going back."

She stared at him, dumbfounded. "No, wait. What was it you were calling me?"

"Well, your name of course. I was trying to get your attention. Seemed like you were off daydreaming."

"I mean, what name did you call me?" she persisted.

"Phiney. I called you Phiney. Why?" he questioned.

"Mr. Wilshire," she said with as much decorum as she could muster, "my name is *Delphinia*. Delphinia Elizabeth Hughes—not Phiney, not Delphie, and not Della. Why would you ever call me such a name?" she asked in disgust.

He looked up at her and grinned. "Seems a mite formal to me. And you just feel free to call me Jonathan if you like. I been meaning to tell you that anyhow. Mister Wilshire. . .well, that's kind of formal, too. Besides, I always think people are addressing my pa when they call me that."

A frown was etched on Delphinia's face as she looked down at him, her brown eyes flashing fire. "Mr. Wilshire, I do not think my name is too formal. My mother took great care in choosing my name and I am very proud of it."

Jonathan's eyes sparkled with humor as he watched her trying to restrain her temper. If he was any judge, she would soon be stomping her foot to make a point of this whole issue. He knew he should let it drop, but for some reason he was enjoying the display of emotion she was exhibiting for him.

"I'm mighty pleased you're proud of your name, Phiney. I've always thought it was nice if folks liked their names," he said with a benevolent grin. With that, he moved on toward the general store, while calling over his shoulder, "Better hop on down if we're gonna get some yard goods picked out."

It took all her forbearance not to scream after him, "Don't call me Phiney," but before she could give it further thought, he had disappeared into the store.

She was fairly bristling as she climbed down from the wagon, her bonnet askew and tendrils of blond hair poking out in every direction. Jonathan stood behind some shelves of dry goods and, with wry amusement, watched her dramatic entry. He did not wish to continue upsetting her, but she really was quite a picture to behold, her cheeks turned rosy and skirt gathered up in her fists. Realizing she was looking for him, he stepped out from behind the shelves.

"Glad you decided to come in and have a look around," he grinned. Ignoring his barb, she made her way to the table of yard goods.

"You realize, of course, Mr. Wilshire, that I have no idea what anyone in your home may need. I don't even know who lives there," she proclaimed, wanting to be sure he realized she was not a willing participant in the future that her father had planned.

"Guess you've got a point," he commented, leaning against the table and causing it to almost topple with his weight. "There's surely no time for going into that now, so just pick some material you like for boys and girls and maybe some for new curtains. Oh, and Granny might like something for a new dress, too."

Her mouth had formed a large oval by the time he had finished his remarks, but before she could even exclaim, he added, "And don't forget to get something for yourself, too."

Not waiting for a reply, he immediately moved on to look at tools and Delphinia found herself staring back at the clerk, an older woman she had never seen before, who was impatiently waiting to take Delphinia's order and get to other customers. Having never before had such a task placed before her, Delphinia smiled pleasantly and approached the expectant clerk. "I'll take some of each of these," she said, pointing to six different fabrics.

Delphinia straightened her shoulders, her arms crossed in front of her and stood there, waiting. When the clerk made no move to cut the yard goods, Delphinia, looking perplexed, urged her on, stating, "That's all I'll be needing. You can cut it now."

"Would you care to give me some idea just how much you'd like of each fabric?" the clerk questioned in a hushed voice and added a smile.

Sensing that she had the sympathy of this woman, Delphinia answered, "Just whatever you think I should have."

"I'll cut enough for curtains to cover four windows out of this cream color, and you'll be able to get a dress for your little girl and a skirt for you out of this blue calico. Let's see, we'll cut a measure of this heavy fabric for some britches for your little boys and this brown print might make up into a nice dress for your grandmother."

Delphinia watched in absolute astonishment. Did this woman actually think she looked old enough to have a husband and houseful of children? Well, she was not about to explain her circumstances to a total stranger. She would just smile and take whatever help the Lord provided and He certainly knew she needed all the help she could get. Of course, Mr. Wilshire was also going to need all the help he could get for she was going to educate him to the fact that he had chosen the wrong person for his Kansas family.

"Will you be wanting any thread or lace to go along with this?"

Delphinia was so deep in thought that the question caused her to startle to attention. "Whatever you think. I'll just trust your judgment," she smiled.

The clerk finished quickly, wrapped the goods in brown paper, and tied it with heavy twine. Jonathan moved forward and requested the clerk to add the cost to his other purchases, which were being totaled, and he began to usher Delphinia out of the store.

Turning back, Delphinia walked to the clerk and whispered, "Thank you for your help. I'll be praying for you this evening and thanking the Lord for your help."

"Oh, my dear, thank you," the clerk replied. "It was a pleasure to assist you. It's a long trip you're making, but you're young and strong. With that able-bodied husband of yours, you'll do just fine."

"He's not my husband," Delphinia retorted before thinking.

"Oh. Well, I'll certainly be praying for you, too, my dear," the clerk replied.

Delphinia felt her cheeks turn a crimson red and she began to stutter a reply but the clerk had already turned and was helping another customer. Feeling totally humiliated, she briskly made her way out of the store and back to the wagon where Jonathan was waiting.

Without a glance in his direction, she made her way around the wagon and quickly climbed up onto the seat. Not knowing how many people had overheard their conversation, Delphinia was anxious to join the wagon train as soon as possible.

"I thought maybe you'd like to have dinner in town. There's a good restaurant down the street," Jonathan offered.

"I'm not hungry. Let's get going," she answered, her voice sounding somewhat shrill.

"What's wrong?" he questioned.

"Nothing. Let's just go," she replied.

"I'm not going anywhere until you tell me what's wrong," Jonathan said.

Delphinia knew from the set of his jaw that she was not going to have her way. Grudgingly she recounted the conversation, trying to keep as much composure as possible.

"Is that all?" he questioned. "I'll be right back after I explain our situation to the woman," and he started to make his way into the store.

"No, please," she countered. "I'd rather go no further with this. Let's just go. I'm honestly not hungry."

Sensing her discomfort and not wishing to cause her further embarrassment, Jonathan jumped up onto the seat, flicked the reins, and yelled, "Giddyup," to the team of brown mares.

Neither of them said anything, but as they grew closer to the wagon train camp, Jonathan sensed an uneasiness come over Delphinia. She was moving restlessly on the wooden seat and her hands began pressing the gathers in her skirt, as he had seen her do on several earlier occasions.

In an attempt to make her feel more comfortable, he said, "You'll not be staying in my wagon at night. Mrs. Clauson has agreed you can stay with her." Delphinia did not respond, but he noticed she was not fidgeting quite so much. This pleased him, though he was not sure why.

Slowing the team, he maneuvered the buckboard beside one of the covered wagons that had formed a circle for the night.

"Thought maybe you wasn't gonna make it back afore supper," a voice called out.

"I'd have gotten word to you if we weren't coming back this evening," Jonathan replied as he jumped down from the wagon and held his arms up to assist Delphinia.

As she was making her descent from the wagon, Jonathan matter-of-factly said, "Mr. and Mrs. Clauson, I'd like you to meet Phiney. . .Phiney Hughes. It was *Hughes*, wasn't it?"

He watched her eyes once again take on that fiery look as she very formally stated, "Mr. and Mrs. Clauson, my name is Delphinia Elizabeth Hughes. Mr. Wilshire seems to find it a difficult name. I, however, prefer to be called *Delphinia*. . .not Phiney." Smiling sweetly at the Clausons, she added, "Pleased to meet you both."

Turning, she gave Jonathan a look meant to put him in his place. He grinned back at her, but soon found himself trying to control a fit of laughter when Mr. Clauson replied, "We're real pleased to meet you, too, Phiney."

Not wanting to give him further cause for laughter and certain that a woman would better understand the proper use of her name, Delphinia decided she would discuss the matter of her name privately with Mrs. Clauson.

Jonathan and Mr. Clauson began unloading the wagon and the older woman, while placing her arm around Delphinia's shoulder, said, "Come on over here with me, Phiney. I'm just finishing up supper and we can visit while the menfolk finish unloading."

So much for another woman's understanding, Delphinia decided, moving over toward the fire. Perhaps she should just let the issue of her name drop with the Clausons. After all, once they arrived in Kansas, she would probably never see them again. Mr. Wilshire, though, was another matter!

"Is there anything I can do to help?" Delphinia inquired.

"No, no. Just set a spell and tell me about yourself. You sure are a pretty thing, with all that blond hair and those big brown eyes. Jonathan figured you probably weren't a looker since your pa was willin' to let you go west with a stranger. Thought maybe you couldn't get a husband."

Noting the look of dismay that came over Delphinia's face and the effect her words had on the young woman, Mrs. Clauson hurried to add, "He didn't mean nothin' bad by that. It's just that most folks wouldn't let their daughter take off with a complete stranger, let alone be advertisin' in a paper to. . . Oh, I'm just jumblin' this all up and hurtin' you more. Mr. Clauson says I need to think 'fore I open my mouth. I'm real sorry if I upset you, Phiney."

Lifting her rounded chin a little higher, Delphinia straightened her back and said, "There's no need for you to feel concern over what you've said. After all, I'm sure you've spoken the truth of the matter."

three

Neither Delphinia nor Mrs. Clauson spoke for a time, each lost in her own thoughts. Delphinia was not sure how long she had been reflecting on the older woman's words when she noticed that Mrs. Clauson was about to serve the evening meal.

"It looks like you've about got dinner ready. Shall I ladle up the stew?"

Mrs. Clauson turned toward the large pot hanging over a slow-burning fire and shook her head. "No, no. I'll do it. You just tell the menfolk we're ready. They should be about done unloading the buckboard and can finish up after supper."

Delphinia rose and, after locating the men and announcing dinner, slowly continued walking toward Jonathan's wagon. Jonathan pulled off his wide-brim hat, wiped his brow with a large, dark blue kerchief, and watched Delphinia as she continued toward his wagon. Her head lowered, her shoulders slumped, she was a picture of total dejection.

"Where are you going? You just told us dinner was ready."

Acting as though she did not hear, Delphinia continued along the outer edge of the circled wagons.

"Hey, wait a minute," Jonathan called as he quickened his step to catch up. When he came even with her, she glanced over and said, "I'm not hungry. You go on and eat. Mrs. Clauson's waiting on you."

Realizing something was amiss, Jonathan gently took hold of her shoulders and turned her to face him. "Phiney, you've got to eat. I know it's hard for you to leave your home, but please come have some dinner."

When there was no reaction to his use of "Phiney," he knew she was upset, but she turned and walked back to the campfire with him. She took the steaming plate of food offered by Mrs. Clauson who, Jonathan noted, seemed somewhat downcast.

Giving him a tentative smile, Mrs. Clauson asked, "Would you be so good as to lead us in prayer before we begin our meal, Jonathan?"

Bowing their heads, Jonathan gave thanks for the food provided and asked God's protection over all the folks in the wagon train as they began their journey. Delphinia was surprised, however, when Jonathan proceeded to ask the Lord to give her strength as she left her father and all those she knew to make a new home in Kansas. She was pleased that he cared enough about her feelings to ask God to give her strength. As she looked up at

Jonathan after he had pronounced "Amen," he was smiling at her and remarked, "Well, eat up, Phiney." At that moment, she was not sure if she needed more strength to endure leaving home or to put up with his determination to call her Phiney!

As soon as the meal was over, Delphinia and Mrs. Clauson proceeded to wash the dishes while the men finished loading the covered wagon and Jonathan returned the buckboard to town. By the time he got back to the campsite, folks were beginning to bed down for the night.

"Why don't you get the things you'll be needin' for tonight and bring them over to our wagon. We best turn in soon," Mrs. Clauson advised.

Nodding in agreement, Delphinia made her way to the wagon. Climbing in, she spotted the old brown trunk and slowly lifted the heavy lid. Pulling out her nightgown, she caught sight of her beloved quilt. Reaching in, she pulled it out of the trunk and hugged it close.

She was so caught up in her thoughts that Mrs. Clauson's, "Do you need help, Phiney?" caused her to almost jump out of her skin.

"No, I'm coming," she replied, wrapping the quilt around her and closing the trunk. She made her way down, careful not to trip over the covering that surrounded her.

After preparing for the night, Delphinia and Mrs. Clauson made themselves as comfortable as possible on pallets in the wagon. "Jonathan's been having some Bible readin' for us since he came to our rescue, but since he was gone so late tonight, he said we'll double up on our readin' tomorrow night. The mister and me, well, we don't know how to read much, so it surely has been a pleasure to have Jonathan read the Scriptures for us," she whispered almost ashamedly.

"Oh, Mrs. Clauson, I would have read for you tonight, if I had known," Delphinia replied.

"Why aren't you just the one. Such a pretty girl and bright, too. That Jonathan surely did luck out," she exclaimed.

Delphinia could feel her cheeks grow hot at the remark and knew it was meant as a compliment. All the same, she wished Mrs. Clauson would quit making it sound like Jonathan had just secured himself a wife.

Bidding the older woman good night, Delphinia spent a great deal of her prayer time petitioning the Lord to execute His rescue plan for her as soon as possible. She did give thanks for the fact that Jonathan seemed a decent sort and that she would have Mrs. Clauson with her for the journey. Once she had finished her prayers, she reached down and pulled the quilt around her, not that she needed the warmth for, in fact, it was nearly summer. Instead, it was the security that the wonderful quilt gave her, almost like a cocoon surrounding her with her mama's presence and love.

Many hours of love and laughter had been shared in completing what had seemed to Delphinia an immense project. Now, she was somewhat in awe that her mother had given so much time and effort to teaching her how to sew those many blocks and make the tiny, intricate stitches required for the beautiful pattern she had chosen.

When Delphinia had announced she wanted to make a quilt, her mother had explained it would take many hours of tedious work. She was doggedly determined about the idea, however, and her mother had patiently shown her each step of the way, allowing Delphinia to make and repair her own mistakes on the beloved project. How they had laughed over some of those mistakes and oh, the hours spent ripping out and restitching until it was just right. Mama had always said that anything worth doing was worth doing right. And when that last stitch had been sewn and the quilt was finally completed, Mama had abundantly praised her hard work and perseverance. She had even called for a celebration and, using the good teapot and china plates, served Delphinia some of her special mint tea and thick slices of homemade bread, smeared with strawberry preserves.

Tears began to slide down Delphinia's cheeks as she thought of those wonderful memories. Had it been only three years since she had enjoyed that special celebration? It seemed an eternity. In fact, it seemed like Mama had been gone forever, yet she knew it wasn't even six months since she had died. Sometimes she had trouble remembering just what her mother looked like and yet other times it seemed that Mama would walk in the door any minute and call her for supper or ask for help hanging a curtain. How she missed her and the stability she had brought to their home! It seemed to Delphinia that her life had been in constant change and turmoil since the day Mama died.

Delphinia closed her eyes, hoping that sleep would soon overtake her. Her mind wandered back to stories her mother had related of how she had come west to Illinois after she and Pa had married. Mama had tried to convince him it would be a better life for them back east but he was bound and determined to see new lands. It had been a difficult trip for Mama. She had lived a life of relative ease. Having been born the only daughter in a family of six boys had been cause for much jubilation and, when she later contracted rheumatic fever as a child, it had made her family all the more determined to protect her. Delphinia remembered Mama talking about all those uncles and the grandparents she had never known. Mama had made certain that Delphinia knew that her grandfather had been a preacher and that he had held great stock in everyone's learning how to read—not just the boys. He had made sure that Delphinia's mama was taught the same lessons as the boys. In fact, she had gone to school longer than any of the boys so that she could receive a teaching certificate, just in case she did not get married. Her pa wanted to be sure she would have a respectable profession. But she did get married. She told Delphinia about meeting Papa at a tent revival meeting the family had attended in a nearby town. They started to keep company shortly after that and were married six months later. Less than two months after the ceremony, they made their trip west to Illinois.

They had settled in a small house a few miles from Cherryvale. Pa had gone to work for the blacksmith who owned the livery stable. Delphinia knew her mama had been lonely. They did not get to town often and she had longed for the company of other people. Papa would give in and take them to church about once a month to keep Mama in better spirits, but he was usually anxious to get home afterward. Mama always loved it when there would be a picnic dinner after services in the summer and everyone would gather under the big elms, spread out their lunch and visit, or when the preacher would hold Bible study in the afternoon. Papa had always seemed uncomfortable and would stay to himself while Mama fluttered from person to person, savoring each moment. Papa was not much of a churchgoer and had never studied the Bible. His folks had not see any reason for his learning to read or write. They felt children were needed to help with the chores and plow the fields. Delphinia remembered Mama telling her how much she had wanted to teach Papa to read but he had put her off saying he was too old to learn. Sometimes, when Mama would be teaching Delphinia, Papa would become almost angry and storm out of the house. Mama always said it was nothing to worry about, that Papa just needed a breath of fresh air. *Maybe,* Delphinia thought, *Papa was angry at himself because he hadn't let Mama teach him and now his little girl knew how to read and he didn't.* Strange she hadn't thought of that before tonight.

She reflected on the time shortly before Mama's death, when she had overheard their hushed talk about not having money. That must have been when Papa borrowed against the house and how they had managed to make ends meet until Mama died. When she once questioned about money, her mother had told her there was time enough for that worry when you became an adult and that she should not concern herself. Her parents had never included her in any family business or, for that matter, anything of an unpleasant nature. She had always been protected. . .until now.

Burrowing farther under the quilt, Mrs. Clauson's remark about Pa advertising to send her west was the last thought that lingered in her mind as she drifted into a restless sleep.

four

Delphinia bounced along on the hard wooden seat, the blistering sun causing rivulets of perspiration to trickle down the sides of her face. She could feel her hair turning damp under the bonnet she was forced to wear in order to keep the sun from scorching her face. It seemed she had been traveling forever and yet, in spite of the heat and dust, she found joy in the beauty of the wildflowers and rolling plains.

Except for the short period of training that Jonathan had given her on how to handle the wagon and team, or those times when it was necessary to cross high waters and climb steep terrain, Jonathan rode his chestnut mare and few words passed between them. She was somewhat surprised when today he had tied his horse to the back of the wagon and climbed up beside her. Taking the reins from her hands, he urged the team into motion and, with a slight jolt, they moved forward in the slow procession taking them farther west.

"Sorry we haven't had more opportunity to talk," Jonathan commented, "but it seems I'm needed more to help keep the train moving. Besides, you've been doing just fine on your own with the wagon."

Delphinia did not respond but smiled inwardly at his compliment. When Jonathan had told her she would be driving the team, she had nearly fainted dead away. She, who had never handled so much as her pa's mules, was now expected to maneuver a team of horses and a lumbering wagon. With Jonathan's patience and her determination, she had finally mastered it, at least well enough not to run into the wagon in front of her.

"We're getting close to home and I thought we should talk a little beforehand about what you can expect," Jonathan stated.

Delphinia expelled a sigh of relief. Finally, he was going to acquaint her with what lay ahead. Nodding her encouragement that he continue, she gave a slight smile, folded her hands and placed them on her lap.

"My brother, Jacob, and his wife, Sarah, died some four months ago. Since that time Granny, that would be Sarah's mother, has been staying in the big cabin with the children. She's become quite frail and isn't able to handle five children and do chores any longer. Tessie, she's the oldest, doesn't think she needs anyone else to help out. At twelve, she's sure she can raise the others and take care of everything on her own."

Delphinia's face registered confusion and alarm. "Are you telling me the children I'm to take care of aren't yours? They are your brother's children?

That there are five of them under age twelve? And I will be caring for all of them as well as doing chores and nursing their ill grandmother?" she questioned in rapid succession.

"Whoa, wait a minute," he laughed. "How can I answer your questions if you throw so many my way I can't even keep them straight?"

"I'm glad you find this a matter to laugh about," she exclaimed, feeling tears close at hand and not wanting to cry, "but I'm not at all amused."

"I'm really sorry, Phiney. I guess because I know the situation, it doesn't seem all that bleak to me. You'll get used to it, too. It's just a matter of adjustment and leaning on the Lord. The children are fine youngsters and although the older ones are having a little trouble dealing with the deaths of their folks, they're a big help."

"Just what ages are the children?" she asked, almost afraid to hear the answer.

"Well, there's Tessie, she's twelve and the oldest. She has the prettiest mop of red ringlets hanging down her back, which, I might add, match her temper. She also has a bunch of freckles, which she detests, right across the bridge of her nose. She's not very happy that I'm bringing you home to help out. She thinks she's able to cope with the situation on her own even though she knows her ma and pa wouldn't want it that way. They'd want her to have time to be a little girl and get more schooling before she starts raising a family and taking care of a household. She's had the most trouble dealing with the deaths of her parents. Then there's Joshua; we call him Josh. He's seven and all boy. A good helper, though, and minds real well. He misses his ma's cooking and cheerfulness. I've tried to fill some of the gaps left by his pa. Then there's Joseph. We call him Joey, and he just turned four. He follows Josh around and mimics everything his big brother does, or at least gives it a good try. He doesn't understand death, but we've told him his folks are with Jesus and he'll see them again when he gets to heaven. I think he misses his ma most at bedtime. Then there are the twins, Nathan and Nettie. They're eight months old now and quite a handful. I guess that just about sums up the situation," he said, giving the horses a slap of the reins to move them up closer in line.

"*Sums it up?*" Delphinia retorted. "That doesn't even begin to *sum it up.*"

"Well," he drawled, "why don't you just ask me questions and I'll try to answer them. . .but one at a time, please."

"All right, number one," she began, with teeth clenched and eyes fixed straight ahead, "why did you tell my pa you needed someone to help with your children if they're your brother's children?"

"From the way you asked that question, Phiney, I'm sure you think I concocted a whole string of untruths, presented them to your pa, and he just swallowed it like a fish swallowing bait. Believe me, that's not the way it was. He knew the truth. He knew the children weren't mine. I wrote him a letter telling him of my need and explaining the urgency for a young woman to help out."

"My pa can't read," she interrupted, sure she had caught him in a lie.

Leaning forward and resting his arms across his thighs in order to gain a look at her, he answered, "I know, Phiney. He had a friend of his, a Mr. Potter, read the letter to him and write to me. Mr. Potter started out the letter by telling me your pa could neither read nor write but Pa was corresponding on his behalf."

Delphinia knew what Jonathan said was probably the truth. After Ma had died when there was anything he did not want her to know about, Pa would get Mr. Potter at the bank to help him.

Jonathan watched as Delphinia seemed to sift through what he had said. It was obvious her father had told her very little about the plan he had devised, or the correspondence and agreement that had followed. Not one to keep secrets, Jonathan asked, "Is there anything else you want to know?"

"Yes," she responded quietly. "Did you pay my pa for me?"

"No. That wasn't the way of it. You're not a slave or some kind of bonded person. I don't own you."

"But you did give him money, didn't you?" she questioned.

"Well—"

"Did you or didn't you give my pa money, Mr. Wilshire?" she determinedly inquired.

"There was money that exchanged hands, but not like I was buying you. He needed some financial help to get started with his prospecting and said he'd pay it back when he had a strike. I told him it wasn't necessary. I guess if you had to liken it to something, it was more like a dowry. . .only in reverse." Noting the shock that registered on her face at that remark, he continued, " 'Course we're not gettin' married so maybe that's not a good way to explain."

Delphinia could feel herself shrinking down, total humiliation taking over her whole being. How could her pa have done this to her? How could he think so little of her he would sell her to a total stranger? She was his flesh and blood. . .his only child. She had never felt so unloved and unwanted in her life.

She did not know how far they had come when she finally said, "Mr. Wilshire, please, would you explain how all of this happened to me?"

The question confirmed his earlier belief that her father had intentionally kept her uninformed. Her voice was so soft and sad he couldn't possibly deny the request.

"I'll tell you what I know. Please understand, I won't be speaking for your pa or why he made his decisions. Only the choices I made. . .and the reasons."

When she did not respond but merely nodded her head, he continued. "Well, now, I've told you about the deaths of my brother and his wife. I had come out to Kansas a year or so after them because Jake thought if I homesteaded the acreage next to his, we could work the land together. You know, help each other. I wanted to move west and he thought it would give us an advantage. Sarah and Jake built their house near the western boundary of their land so when I arrived, we constructed a cabin on the eastern boundary of my tract, allowing me to be nearby. We'd always been close and we decided it would be good for both of us. And we were right. It has been good for all of us. . .or at least it was until now. Jake and Sarah brought Granny Dowd with them when they came west. Sarah's pa was dead and she didn't want to leave her mother alone. Granny's been a real wonder to all of us. What a worker! She was just like a little whirlwind, even when I came out here. Then about a year ago, she took ill and just hasn't snapped back to her old self. She seems to rally for a while, but then she has to take to her bed again. She was always a big help to Sarah. I'm sure you'll like her, Phiney. She loves the Lord, her grandchildren, and the West, in that order." He smiled and glanced over at the dejected-looking figure jostling along beside him, hoping for some sort of response.

Finally, realizing he was not going to continue further, Delphinia looked over and was greeted by a slight smile and his blue eyes, full of sympathy. "You needn't look at me like you're full of pity for me or my situation, Mr. Wilshire. After all, you're the cause of this," she criticized.

"I didn't cause this, Miss Hughes," he replied. "I merely responded to your pa's ad in the newspaper." Why couldn't this woman understand it was her father who was at fault?

"Ah, yes, the newspaper advertisement. I'd like to hear about that," she retorted, her face flushed not only from the rising sun, but the subject under discussion.

"Well," he fairly drawled, "it appears we're getting ready to stop for the noon meal. I think we better finish this discussion after dinner when you're not quite so hot under the collar. Besides, I don't plan on discussin' this in front of the Clausons," he said as he pulled the team to a stop and jumped down.

He watched in absolute astonishment as she pushed away the arms he extended to assist her, lost her footing, and almost turned a complete somersault at his feet.

Looking up at him, her bonnet all cockeyed and her skirt clear to her knees, she defiantly stated, "I meant to do that."

"I'm sure you did, Phiney. I'm sure you did," he laughed as he began to walk toward the rear of the wagon to untie his mare.

"You could at least help me up," she hollered after him.

Glancing over his shoulder, he grinned and remarked, "Why would you need my help? I thought you planned that whole performance!" She could hear him chuckling as he led his horse down to the small creek.

"Oooh, that man," she mused, as she gathered herself up and proceeded to brush the dust from her dress and straighten her bonnet. "The Lord has a lot of work to do with him yet!"

ঽ৯

Delphinia and Mrs. Clauson had just finished preparing the noon meal when Jonathan strode up to the older woman. "Phiney's wanting to be alone and talk to me, Mrs. Clauson, so I thought we'd take our plates down by the creek and eat, if you don't mind. I understand we're going to be makin' camp here since the Johnsons have a wagon wheel that needs repairing before we continue. It's been agreed that this is a fine spot to spend the night. Besides, we've traveled a considerable ways and the rest will do us all good."

"I don't mind at all. You two go on and have a chat. I can sure understand you wanting some time alone," she said with a knowing grin.

Delphinia was positively glaring at him as he said, "Come along, Phiney. Let's go down by the water." He smiled, noting her feet appeared to have become rooted to the spot where she was standing. "I thought you wanted some answers, Phiney. Better come along. I may not have time later."

She did not want to give in and let him have his way. It was childish of her to act peevish over such a little thing. Her mother had always told her to save her arguments for the important issues. Perhaps this was one of those times she should heed that advice. Besides, if she did not go, he might hold true to his word and not discuss the matter later. Picking up her plate and cup, she followed along, calling over her shoulder, "We'll not be long, Mrs. Clauson," only to hear Jonathan respond, "Yes, we will." Mrs. Clauson merely smiled and nodded.

Hurrying to catch up, Delphinia watched as her coffee sloshed out of the metal cup, dribbling onto her apron. "Don't walk so fast. Your legs are longer than mine and I can't keep up," she chided, angry that he once again had the last word.

"I'm sure that haughty little temper of yours gives you enough strength to keep up with anyone," he retorted.

"You needn't make unkind remarks, Mr. Wilshire," she exclaimed.

"I needn't make unkind remarks?" he exploded. "I've been listening to your thoughtless insinuations and comments all morning, but when I point

out that you've got quite a little temper, you call that an unkind remark. I'd find that funny if I weren't so aggravated with you right now." He plopped himself down in the shade of a large tree that overhung the stream of water, and shoved a large forkful of beans into his mouth.

"You have control over my life, but don't expect me to be happy about it. I'm not one to apologize unless I feel it's in order, Mr. Wilshire. However, since I don't know all that occurred between you and my pa, I will, just this once, offer my apology. Of course, I may withdraw it after I've heard all you have to say about this odious matter," she informed him authoritatively.

"Odious? Well, that's extremely considerate of you, *Miss Hughes,*" he responded, trying to keep the sarcasm from his voice but missing the mark.

Settling on the grass not far from him, she arranged her skirt and commanded, "You may now continue with your account of what occurred between you and my father, Jonathan."

He was so startled she had called him Jonathan, that he didn't even mind the fact that he had been given a direct order to speak. "I believe we left off when you asked about the newspaper advertisement," he began.

She nodded in agreement and he noticed she was again pressing the pleats in her skirt with the palm of her hand as he had observed on several other occasions. *Must be a nervous habit,* he decided to himself.

"I've been trying to find help ever since Sarah and Jake died, but the few unmarried young women around our area were either, shall we say, unwholesome or looking for a husband in the bargain. Granny Dowd wouldn't accept unwholesome and I wouldn't accept a wife. . .not that I plan to stay a bachelor forever. I want to, you know, marry. . . ," he stammered. "It's just that I plan on being in love with the woman I marry, and sharing the same beliefs and goals. I don't want it to be some sort of bargain—"

"Mr. Wilshire, I really am not interested in your marriage plans. I'm just trying to find out why I'm here," Delphinia interrupted.

"That's what I'm trying to explain, if you'll just quit breaking in! Now, like I said, we didn't seem to find anyone that was suitable. Granny and I kept praying we would find an answer. A few weeks later, I was in town to pick up supplies. While I was waiting for my order to be filled, I picked up an old St. Louis newspaper that someone had left in the store. I looked through the advertisements and noticed one that stated, 'Looking for good home and possible teaching position immediately for my daughter.' There were instructions to write a Mr. Potter at the Union National Bank in Cherryvale, Illinois. I was sure it was an answer to prayer and so was Granny.

"That night, we composed a letter to your pa telling him about Jake and Sarah, the children, and Granny's failing health. We told him we were Christians who tried to live by God's Word and would do everything possible to give you a good home in return for your help with the children and the house. We also told him we would pay you a small stipend each month so you'd have some independence."

Jonathan got up and moved toward the creek. Rinsing off his plate, he continued, "We sent that letter off the very next day and waited anxiously for a reply. When it finally came, we were almost afraid to open it for fear it would be a rejection of our offer. Instead, it started out with Mr. Potter telling us your pa could neither read nor write, and that he was acting as his intermediary. Mr. Potter said your pa was pleased with the idea of your coming out to Kansas, and that I should make arrangements to come to Illinois because he wanted to meet with me personally."

"If that's supposed to impress me as loving, fatherly concern for my well-being, I'm afraid it doesn't persuade me," Delphinia remarked.

"I'm not trying to justify anything. I'm just telling you how it all happened."

"I know. I'm sorry. Please continue and I'll try to keep quiet," she murmured.

"I left Kansas the next morning. When I arrived in town, I went straight to the bank and met with Mr. Potter. He sent for your pa and we met the afternoon I arrived in Cherryvale. I presented him with letters I had secured from our minister and some folks in the community during the time we waited for your father's response. Granny said she was sure you were the Lord's answer, and we were going to be prepared."

Delphinia couldn't help but smile at that remark. It sounded just like something her ma would have said.

"Mr. Potter looked over the letters I had with me, read them to your pa, and he seemed satisfied that we were upstanding folks who would do right by you. He said he was wanting to go farther west in hopes of striking gold and that it would be no life for a young woman. I agreed with him. . .not just because we needed you, but because I felt what he said was true."

Jonathan paused, took a deep breath, and continued, "He told me he had fallen on hard times and mortgaged his house for just about all it was worth. Mr. Potter confirmed the bank held notes on the property and that your pa was going to deed it back over to the bank for a very small sum of money. Your father said he needed extra funds to get supplies and have enough to keep him going until he hit gold. I gave him some money to cover those expenses, but nobody considered it to be like I was buying you, Phiney. I was just so thankful we had found you, I didn't want anything like your pa needin' a little money to stand in the way. Then when the wagon train needed help, I was sure God's hand was at work in all that was happening."

"Did you ever stop to think that if you hadn't given him the money, I could still be at home, where I belong?" she countered.

"Phiney, your pa had made up his mind he was going to go west and search for gold. Nothing was going to stop him. He'd have taken you with him if he had to, I suppose, but he was right. . .it would have been a terrible life for you. But if you're determined this is not what you want, I'll not fight you. The next town we get close to, I'll put you on a train and send you back to Cherryvale."

"To what?" she asked. "My father's gone and if he isn't, he won't want to see me back. The bank owns our land. I have no one to go to," she said dejectedly.

"Your pa loves you, Phiney. He just has a restlessness that needs to be filled. He was careful about the arrangements he made for you. Your father was very concerned about your safety and well-being"

"He cared as long as I was out of his way," she retorted.

"You know, we all get selfish at times and your pa was looking out for what he wanted first. That doesn't mean he loves you any the less. I guess we just have to learn to believe what the Bible tells us about all things working for good to those that love the Lord."

Delphinia picked up her cup and plate, slowly walked to the water's edge, and rinsed them off as Jonathan issued a silent prayer that God would help Delphinia forgive her father and find peace and happiness in her new home with them.

"We better get back. Mrs. Clauson said we should wash some clothes since we don't get many opportunities like this one," she remarked, walking past him.

Jonathan was still sitting and watching her as she moved toward the wagons when she turned and said, "I guess you weren't at fault, so my apology stands."

five

For the remainder of the day Delphinia was completely absorbed in her own thoughts. She wandered from one chore to another without realizing when she had begun one thing and ended another. After the evening meal, Jonathan led them in devotions and the moment the final "Amen" had been uttered, Delphinia excused herself, anxious for the solitude the wagon would provide, even if only for an hour or two.

As Delphinia lay there, she began to pray. This prayer was different, however. It was not a request that God rescue her or that anything terrible happen to Mr. Wilshire. Rather, this prayer was that God give her the ability to forgive her father for deserting her and to grant her peace. Almost as an afterthought, she added that she could also use a bit of joy in her life. She fell asleep with that prayer on her lips.

Their few remaining days with the wagon train had passed in rapid succession when Jonathan advised her that the next day they would break away on their own. "I think the wagon master will be happy to see me leave. I've noticed it seems to upset him when folks look to me for leadership now that he's well again," he said with a grin.

"I think you may be right about that. I don't think some of the folks will look to him unless you're gone. They take to you more. Maybe it's because they view you as an answer to prayer," she responded.

"I hope I have been. Maybe someday I can be an answer to your prayers, too," he stated and then, noting her uneasiness, quickly changed the subject. "It's faster if we break off and head north on our own. We can make it home by evening without pushing too hard and it's safe, since the Indians around our area are pretty friendly. Besides, I've been gone quite a spell and I'm anxious to get home, if that's all right with you."

"Whatever you think is best," she replied, but suddenly a multitude of emotions began to envelope her. She was going to miss the Clausons and the other folks she had gotten to know on the train. She was frightened that Granny and the children would not accept her. And how, oh how, was she going to be able to take care of a houseful of children? The thought of such responsibility almost overwhelmed her. "Lord, please give me peace and joy and lots and lots of help," she quietly prayed.

The next morning they joined the Clausons for breakfast and Jonathan led them in a final prayer, while Delphinia attempted to remain calm. Mrs.

Clauson hugged her close and whispered in her ear to be brave, which only served to heighten her level of anxiety. She forced a feeble smile, took up the reins, and bid the horses move out.

Delphinia found herself deep in thought as they made their way to the Wilshire homestead. Jonathan rode the mare, scouting ahead and then riding back to assure her all was well, not allowing much time for conversation. With each mile they traversed, she felt fear beginning to well up inside. As Jonathan came abreast of the wagon to tell her they would be home in about three hours, he noticed she was holding the reins with one hand and pressing down the pleats of her skirt in that slow, methodical motion he had come to recognize as a sign of uneasiness.

"This looks like it might be a good spot for us to stop for a short spell. I'm sure you could use a little rest and the horses won't mind, either," he remarked, hoping to give them a little time to talk and perhaps find out what was bothering her.

"I thought you wanted to keep moving. . .get home as early as possible. Isn't that what you've told me every time you rode back from scouting?" she asked, her voice sounding strained.

"You're right, I did say that," he commented as he reached across his mare and took hold of the reins, bringing the team and wagon to a halt. "But I think a short rest will do us both some good."

Climbing down from his horse, he tied it to the back of the wagon and then, walking to the side of the wagon, stretched his arms up to assist her down. As her feet touched the ground, Delphinia looked up and Jonathan was met by two of the saddest brown eyes he had ever seen. Instead of releasing her, he gathered her into his arms and held her, trying his best to give her comfort. Standing there with her in his arms, he realized he truly cared for this young woman.

Pushing away from him, Delphinia retorted, "I'm not a child anymore, Mr. Wilshire, so you needn't feel you have to stop and coddle me. I'll be fine, just fine," she said. Not wanting to ever again experience the pain of losing someone she cared about, Delphinia knew she would have to hold herself aloof.

"Is that what you think? That I feel you're a child who needs to be coddled? Well, believe me, Phiney, I know you're not a child, but I also know there isn't a soul who doesn't need comforting from time to time. . .even you."

Immediately, she regretted her abruptness but was not about to let down her defenses. Turning, she saw Jonathan walking down toward the dry creek bed below. Not sure what else to do, she followed along behind, trying to keep herself upright by grabbing at tree branches as the rocks underfoot began to slide.

"You sure wouldn't do well sneaking up on a person," he remarked without looking back.

"I wasn't trying to *sneak up* on you. I wanted to apologize for acting so precipitous. You've probably noticed that I sometimes lack the art of tactfulness. At least that's what Ma used to tell me on occasion."

When he did not respond, she looked at their surroundings and asked, "Is there some reason why you've come down here?"

"I guess I just wanted to look around. About two miles up this creek bed is where Sarah and Jake died. It's hard to believe, looking at it now."

"What do you mean by that? You never mentioned how they died. I thought they probably contracted some type of illness. Was it Indians?" she asked with a tremor in her voice.

Sitting down on a small boulder, he pulled a long piece of grass and tucked it between his teeth. "No, it wasn't illness or Indians that caused their death. It was a much-needed rain."

"I don't understand," she commented, coming up behind where he sat and making her way around the rock to sit next to him.

"I wasn't with them. Granny and I had stayed back at the farm. She hadn't been feeling herself and we needed supplies from town. Sarah hadn't been in town since the twins' birth and she was wanting to get a change of scenery and see folks. The children wanted to go along, too. Going to town is just about the next best thing to Christmas for the youngsters.

"So they got all loaded up, Sarah and Tessie each holding one of the twins and the boys all excited about showing off the babies and maybe getting a piece or two of candy. They packed a lunch thinking they'd stop on the way home and eat so Granny wouldn't have to prepare for them. We watched them pull out and Granny said she was going to have a cup of tea and rest a while so I went out to the barn to do some chores. The morning passed by uneventfully. I noticed some clouds gathering but didn't think much of it. We needed rain badly but every time storm clouds would appear, it seemed they'd pass us by and we'd be lucky to get a drop or two out of all the thunder and darkness.

"Granny and I just had some biscuits and cold meat for lunch and I told her I was going to move the livestock into the barn and pen up the chickens and hogs since it looked like a storm was headed our way. We always took precautions, figuring rain had to come behind some of those clouds one day.

"As it turned out, that was the day. It started with big, fat raindrops and I thought it was going to be another false alarm. But shortly, the animals started getting real skittish and it began to rain at a nice steady pace. I just stood there letting it wash over me it felt so good. I ran back to the cabin and Granny was standing on the porch, laughing and holding her hands out to feel that wonderful, much-needed rain. It must have been a full ten minutes we stood there in delight when all of a sudden, there was the loudest clap of thunder and a huge bolt of lightning. The skies appeared to just open up and pour water down so fast and hard I couldn't believe it.

"Granny and I got into the cabin as quick as we could when the downpour began and as soon as we got our senses about us thought of Jake, Sarah, and the children, praying they hadn't begun the trip home before the rain started. I think it was probably the longest time of my life, just waiting there. I couldn't leave to go search for them, knowing I could never make it through that downpour. It seemed it would never stop.

"It was the next day before it let up enough so I could travel at all. I started out with a few supplies and had to go slowly with the horse, the ground was so soaked. I wasn't sure which way Jake would be coming back from town, so I told Granny to pray that if they'd left town I'd choose the right direction. There are two ways for us to make it to town, and we usually didn't come by way of this creek bed. I was hoping that Jake hadn't chosen this, of all days, to come the creek bed route, but I felt led to start my search in this direction.

"The going was slow and rough and I became more and more frightened as I continued my search. I stopped at the Aplington's homestead but they hadn't seen anything of Jake and Sarah. After having a quick cup of coffee, I continued on toward the creek bed. . .or at least what had been a creek bed. It had turned into a virtual torrent of rushing water, limbs, and debris. As I looked down into that flood of water, I saw what I thought was one of the baskets Sarah used to carry the twins. I just stood there staring at the rushing water, completely out of its banks and roaring like a train engine, whipping that tiny basket back and forth.

"When I finally got my wits about me," he continued, "I knew I had to go farther upstream in hopes of finding the family. I tried to holler for them but the roar of the water drowned out my voice. I stayed as close to the creek as I could, hoping I'd see something to give me a clue about where they might be. I wasn't giving in to the fact that anything could have happened to any of them. Finally, after hours of searching, I stopped to pray and, as I finished my prayer, I looked up and spotted Tessie, waving a piece of Josh's shirt high in the air to get my attention. They were inside a small natural cave that had formed above the creek bed. I had no doubt the Lord had placed me in that spot so that when I looked up the first thing I would see was those children.

"I made my way up to them. They were in sad condition, all of them. Not just being without food and water, but sick with worry and fear knowing their ma and pa were gone. That was a rough time I'd not like to go through again."

Delphinia stared fixedly at Jonathan as he related the story. It seemed he was almost in a trance as he recited the events. She reached over and placed her hand on his, but he didn't even seem to realize she was there. "What happened after you found them?"

"Even in the midst of all the sadness, the Lord provided. I had just managed to get two of the children down when Mr. Aplington and his older son arrived with a spring wagon. They worked with me until we had everyone down and loaded into the wagon.

"Tessie managed to tell us that Jake and Sarah were dead but it was much later before she was able to tell us what had happened. It seems that when the thunder and lightning started, the horses began to get excited. Jake decided to locate shelter and couldn't find any place to put them, except in that small cave. He went back down to try and get the horses and wagon to higher ground when a bolt of lightning hit, causing the horses to rear up and go out of control. They knocked him over and the wagon turned, landing on top of him. Sarah climbed back down, determined to get that wagon off of him, even though I'm sure he was already dead. Tessie said she screamed and screamed for her ma to come back up to them but she stayed there pushing and pushing, trying to get the wagon off Jake. When the water started rising, she tried to hold his head up, determined he was going to live.

"I imagine by the time she realized the futility of her efforts, the current was so strong there was no way she could make her way back. We found both of their bodies a few days later." His shoulders sagged as he finished relating the event.

"Oh, how awful for all of you. How those poor children ever managed to make it is truly a miracle," she said, having difficulty holding back the hot tears that threatened to spill over at any minute.

"You're right. It was God guiding my steps that caused me to find the children. I must admit, though, that the whole incident left some pretty deep scars on Tessie. The younger ones seem to have done better. Those poor little twins were so bedraggled and hungry by the time we got them back to the Aplingtons, I didn't ever expect them to pull through. The Lord provided for them, too, though. Mrs. Aplington had a goat she sent home with us and those twins took to that goat milk just like it was their mama's. Granny had me take the goat back just before I left to come for you. The twins seem to get along pretty well now with milk from old Josie, one of our cows, and food from the table, even if they are awful messy," he chuckled.

"I guess it's about time we get back to the wagon if we're going to get home before dark. Give me your hand and I'll help you back up the hill."

Several hours later, Delphinia spotted two cabins and looked questioningly at Jonathan who merely nodded his affirmance that they were home.

Growing closer, Delphinia could make out several children standing on the porch, waving. Jonathan grinned widely at the sight of those familiar faces, and Delphinia felt a knot rise up in her stomach.

six

Jonathan reached up in his familiar stance to help Delphinia down from the wagon, and as she lowered herself into his arms, three sets of eyes peered at her from the porch. They were such handsome children!

Tessie was all Jonathan had described, and more. She had beautiful red hair and eyes of pale blue that seemed to flash with anger and then go dull. Josh and Joey were towheads with big blue eyes, like Jonathan. "Uncle Jon, Uncle Jon," called Joey. "Is this our new mama?"

"She's not our ma, Joey. Our ma is dead. No one can take Ma's place and don't you ever forget that," Tessie seethed back at the child.

"Mind your manners, young lady," Jonathan said, reaching down to lift Joey and swing him high in the air. "Joey, this is Phiney and she's come to help Granny and Tessie take care of you," he said, trying to soothe Tessie's outburst.

"And this is Joshua, the man of the house when I'm not around. You've already figured out who Tessie is," he said, giving an admonishing look to the redhead.

"Where are Granny and the twins?" he questioned the pouting girl.

"In the house. The twins are having supper early so we can enjoy the meal," Tessie remarked.

Jonathan laughed and grabbed Phiney's hand, pulling her through the doorway. "Granny, we've finally made it, let me introduce you to—"

"Delphinia Elizabeth Hughes," she interrupted.

Delphinia was met by a radiant smile, wisps of gray-white hair, and a sparkling set of eyes amid creases and lines on a well-weathered face. "Delphinia, my dear, I am so pleased to have you with us. I have prayed daily for you and Jonathan, that your journey would be safe. You can't imagine how pleased I am that the Lord has sent you to be a part of our family," she beamed.

"Jonathan, we'll get dinner on the table soon. Hopefully the twins will have finished their mess before we're ready. Delphinia, let me show you where your room will be and Jon, bring her trunk in so she can get comfortable. Better get the horses put up, too, and might as well have Josh help you unload the wagon before we sit down to eat," she continued.

"Granny, I don't know how we made it back home without you telling us what to do and when to do it," Jonathan laughingly chided.

"Oh posh, just get going and do as I say. By tomorrow I'll probably be bedfast again and you can enjoy the peace and quiet."

Granny led Delphinia into a bedroom off the kitchen and she immediately knew it had belonged to Sarah and Jake. Judging from Tessie's critical looks, she surmised the room was regarded as sacred ground by the eldest child. Hoping to diffuse the situation, Delphinia requested a bed in the loft with the smaller children.

"The room is to be yours and I'll hear no more about it," the older woman insisted.

Delphinia placed her clothes in the drawers of the ornately carved chest and hung her dresses in the matching wardrobe, which had been brought from Ohio when Sarah and Jake had moved west. The room had been cleaned until it nearly shone; there was nothing left as a reminder that it had ever belonged to anyone else. Delphinia spread her quilt on the bed in coverlet fashion and placed her brush, mirror, and a picture of her parents on the chest in an attempt to make the room feel more like home.

She had just about completed her unpacking, when she saw Tessie standing in the doorway, peering into the room.

"Why don't you come in and join me while I finish?" Delphinia offered.

"I like your quilt," Tessie ventured, slowly entering the room.

"Why, thank you. It's a precious treasure to me. My mama and I made this quilt before she died. I don't think my mother ever thought I'd get it finished. She spent lots of hours teaching me how to make the different stitches until they met her inspection. I wasn't much older than you when I started making the quilt. Mama told me quilts were sewn with threads of love. I thought it must have been threads of patience because they took so long to make. Especially the ones Mama supervised! She was a real stickler for perfect stitches," she laughed.

"I've found great comfort having it since my mother died and through the journey here, it was like I was bringing a part of her with me, more than a picture or piece of jewelry, because her hands helped sew those threads that run through the quilt. I'm not near as good as she was, but if you'd like to make a quilt, perhaps we could find some old pieces of cloth and I could help you," she offered.

Overhearing their conversation, Granny commented, "Why, Sarah had started a quilt top last winter and I'll bet it's around here somewhere, Tessie. We'll see if we can find it and you and Delphinia can finish it. Once winter sets in, it'll be a good project for the two of you."

"No, I'm not making any quilt, not this winter, not ever, and I don't want her touching Mama's quilt, either," Tessie hastened to add, her voice full of anger.

Not wanting to upset the girl, Delphinia smiled and moved into the kitchen to assist with dinner. Shortly, they were all around a table laden with wonderful food and conversation. Granny told them she had been sure they would arrive home that very day, which was why she and Tessie had prepared a special dinner of chicken and dumplings. Delphinia was quick to tell both women the meal was as good as anything she had ever tasted. The children tried to talk all at once, telling Jonathan of the happenings since his departure. All but Tessie. She remained sullen and aloof, speaking only when necessary.

After dinner while they sat visiting, Delphinia watched as Nettie crawled toward her with a big grin. Attempting to pull herself up, she looked at Delphinia and babbled, "Mama." No sooner had she uttered the word than Tessie became hysterical, screaming to the infant that her mama was dead. Startled, Nettie lost her balance and toppled backward, her head hitting the chair as she fell. Reaching down, Delphinia lifted the crying child into her arms, cooing and rocking in an attempt to soothe her.

"Give her to me! She's my sister," Tessie fumed.

"Leave her be. You march yourself outside right now," Jonathan instructed, his voice cold and hard.

Delphinia did not miss the expressions of hatred and enmity that crossed Tessie's face as she walked toward the door. They were embedded in her memory. When Jonathan and Tessie returned a short time later, she apologized, but Delphinia and Tessie both knew it came only from her lips, not her heart. The child's pain was obvious to everyone, including Delphinia, for she, too, knew the pain of losing parents.

Lying in bed that night and comparing her loss to Tessie's, she realized the Lord had answered her prayers. She no longer was harboring the resentment for her pa and feeling sorry for herself. It had happened so subtly she hadn't even discerned it, and the realization amazed her. She slipped out of bed and knelt down beside her bed, thanking God for an answer to her prayers and then petitioning Him to help Tessie as He had helped her.

"Please, Lord," she prayed, "give me the knowledge to help this girl find some peace." She crawled back into bed and the next thing she heard were noises in the kitchen and the sound of the twins' babbling voices.

Jumping out of bed she quickly dressed, pulled her hair back, and tied it with a ribbon at the nape of her neck. *I'll put it up later when there's more time,* she decided. Rushing to the kitchen, she was met by Granny's smiling face and the twins' almost toothless grins.

"I'm so sorry. I must have overslept. I'm usually up quite early. You can ask Mr. Wilshire. Even on the wagon train, I was almost always up before the others," she blurted without pausing for breath.

"You needn't get so excited, child. Jonathan said to let you sleep late. He knew you were tired, as did I. There's no need to be upset. When I'm feeling well enough I always get up with the twins and fix Jonathan's breakfast. I usually let the others sleep until after he's gone to do his chores. That way we get to visit with a little peace and quiet. Jonathan and I both enjoy having a short devotion time in the morning before we start the day and I hope you'll join us for that," she continued. "One other thing, Delphinia, *please* quit calling Jonathan *Mr. Wilshire*. Either call him Jonathan or Jon, I don't care which, but not Mr. Wilshire. We don't stand on formality around here, and you're a part of this family now. I want you to call me Granny just like every other member of this family and I'll call you Delphinia. Jonathan tells me your name is very important to you. Now then, let's wake up the rest of the family and get this day going," she said. "I'll let you have the honor of climbing to the loft and rousing the children," she said, moving to set the table.

&

Delphinia could not believe the way the day was flying by. Granny seemed to have enough energy for two people. Leaning over a tub of hot water, scrubbing a pair of work pants, Delphinia commented that she did not understand why anyone felt that the older woman needed help.

"Well, child," Granny answered, "right now I'm doing just fine, and I have been this past week or so. But shortly after Jon left for Illinois, I had a real setback. Course this has been happening more and more lately. Jonathan made arrangements for Katy McVay to come stay if I had trouble. I sent Josh down to Aplington's place and Ned Aplington went to town and fetched Katy for me. She's a nice girl. Not a whole lot of sense and doesn't know how to do as much as some around the house, but she's good with the young children. Course, Tessie helped a lot, too. Once I got to feeling better, I sent Katy back home. Her folks run the general store in town and they need her there to help out, so I didn't want to keep her longer than necessary."

Tessie was hanging the clothes on a rope tied between two small trees, intently listening to the conversation of the older women as they performed their chores.

"Katy's got her cap set for Uncle Jon. That's why she wanted to come over to help out," Tessie injected into the conversation, with a smirk on her face. "I think he's sweet on her, too, 'cause Katy told me they were going to the basket dinner after church next week. He's probably going to ask her to marry him," she said, watching Delphinia for a reaction.

Delphinia wasn't sure why, but she felt a dull ache in the pit of her stomach.

"Tessie, I don't know where you get such notions," Granny scolded. "I sometimes think you must lie awake at night, dreamin' up some of these stories. If Jonathan was of a mind to marry Katy, I think someone besides you and Katy would know about it."

"Did I hear my name?" Jonathan asked as he came striding up from the barn, a bucket of milk in each large hand.

"Oh, Tessie's just going on about Katy having her cap set for you and telling us you two have plans to get married. How come you're carrying that milk up here? I thought Josh would have brought it up hours ago," Granny replied.

"Think he must have his mind on something besides his chores today. I told him he could go do some fishing at the pond when he finished milking since he worked so hard while I was gone. Seems he forgot that bringing the buckets up to the house is part of milking. Besides, I don't mind doing it, but I'm sure you women can find something better to talk about than my love life," he chuckled.

Not wanting to miss an opportunity to put Delphinia in her place, Tessie said in an almost syrupy voice, "But Uncle Jon, Katy said you had asked her to the church picnic. Everyone knows you're sweet on each other."

"Well, Tessie, I don't think you've got the story quite right, which is what usually comes of idle gossip. In any event, Katy asked me if I'd escort her to the church dinner and I told her I didn't know if I would be back in time. I feel sure she's made other arrangements by now, and I'm planning on all of us attending as a family. Why don't you get out to the chicken coop and see about collecting eggs instead of spreading gossip?" he ordered as he continued toward the house.

seven

The following days were filled with endless chores and wonderful conversations with Granny. Her love of the Lord caused her to nearly glow all the time. She could quote Scriptures for almost any situation, and then she would smile and say, "Praise God, I may not be as strong as when I was young, but I've still got my memory." That statement never ceased to make Delphinia grin.

Delphinia felt as if she had known Granny all her life and a closeness emerged that she had not felt since her mama died. Kneeling at her bed each night, Delphinia thanked God for the older woman and all she was teaching her about life and survival in the West, but most of all, how to love God and find joy in any circumstance.

Sunday morning found Delphinia musing about mornings long ago when she would rise and have only herself to clothe and care for. How things had changed! Granny advised her to dress the twins last, since they always managed to get themselves dirty if given an opportunity. Jonathan had already loaded the baskets of food and everyone was waiting in the wagon. With great care, she placed a tiny ribbon around Nettie's head, lifted her off the bed, and walked out to join them.

Jonathan jumped down to help her, a wide grin on his face. "I think Nettie's more prone to eating hair ribbons than wearing them," he laughed, pulling the ribbon out of the baby's chubby fist and handing it to Delphinia. Smiling, she gave a sigh and placed the ribbon in her pocket.

The twins slept through most of the church service with Jonathan holding Nathan, and Nettie snuggled in Delphinia's arms. Tessie made sure she was seated between the two of them. Josh and Joey were on either side of Granny, who managed to keep their fidgeting to a minimum by simply patting a hand on occasion.

After services, Granny tugged Delphinia along, telling her she wanted to introduce the pastor before they unloaded the wagon. Granny presented her to Pastor Martin and continued with a recitation about all of her fine qualities until Delphinia was embarrassed to even look at him. She merely extended her hand and mumbled, "Pleased to meet you. I think I better change Nettie's diaper."

Turning to make her getaway, she nearly collided with Jonathan, who was visiting with a beautiful young woman.

"Delphinia, I'd like you to meet Katy McVay," he said as they walked along beside her to the wagon.

Just as they rounded the corner of the church, Tessie appeared. "Oh, Katy, please join us for lunch. It won't be any fun without you," she pleaded.

"Well, if you all want me to, I couldn't refuse," Katy responded, smiling demurely as she looped her arm through Jonathan's.

Jonathan wasn't quite sure how to handle the turn of events and looked from Katy to Delphinia. His eyes finally settled on Tessie who was beaming with her accomplishment but quickly looked away when she noted her uncle's glare.

Watching the unfolding events from her position just outside the church, Granny decided to invite the young pastor to join them and share their meal. Realizing Tessie was enjoying the uncomfortable situation she had created, Granny assigned her the task of caring for the twins and Joey after dinner. Josh was off playing games with the other young boys, while the adults visited with several other families. Delphinia was introduced to everyone as the newest member of the Wilshire household and the afternoon passed all too quickly when Jonathan announced it was time to load up and head for home.

Delphinia took note that Katy was still following after Jonathan like a lost puppy. Smiling inwardly, she wondered if Katy would climb in the wagon with the rest of the family—not that she cared, of course. *Jonathan could spend his time with whomever he chose,* she thought to herself.

Granny organized the children in the back of the wagon, firmly plopped Nettie and Nate in Tessie's lap, and waited until Delphinia was seated. She then ordered Jonathan to help her to the front, telling him she wished to visit with Delphinia on the return trip. Delphinia slid to the middle of the seat and once Jonathan had hoisted himself into place, the three of them were sandwiched together in much closer proximity than Katy McVay would have preferred. With mounting displeasure the young woman stood watching the group but tried to keep her composure by saying, "Be sure and put that shawl around your shoulders, Granny. It's getting chilly."

"Not to worry, Katy," smiled the older woman, a twinkle in her eye. "We'll keep each other warm. You better run along before your folks miss you." The dismissal was apparent as Granny turned to Delphinia and began to chat.

"It sure was a fine day. I don't think I've gotten to visit with so many folks since Zeb and Ellie got married last year. I'm glad you got to meet everyone so soon after your arrival, Delphinia. You probably won't remember all their names, but the faces will be familiar and it makes you feel more at home when you see a friendly face," Granny commented. "Pastor Martin seemed mighty impressed with you, I might add."

Jonathan let out a grunt to her last remark and although Delphinia did not comment, Jonathan saw a slight blush rise in her cheeks and a smile form on her lips.

"It seemed to me you were pretty impressed with Pastor Martin yourself, Phiney," Jonathan bantered. "Every time I saw you, you were at his side."

Delphinia felt herself bristle at his remark. Why, he made it sound like she had been throwing herself at the pastor. She, with two tiny babies to diaper and feed, while he was off squiring Miss Katy McVay, fixing her a plate of food, carrying her parasol like it belonged to him, and making a total fool of himself. She all but bit her tongue off trying to remain in control.

"You might as well say what's on your mind 'fore you bust a button, Phiney. I can see you've got a whole lot of things you're just itching to say," he goaded.

Glancing over her shoulder, she observed the children were asleep. Looking at him with those same fiery eyes he had seen at the general store before he brought her west, he felt a strong urge to gather her into his arms and hold her close. Instead, he listened as she went into a tirade about how Katy McVay had been attached to him like another appendage and how foolish he had looked carrying her parasol.

"Well, I thank you for your insights, *Miss Hughes*," he responded as he lifted her down from the wagon and firmly placed her on the ground, "but I doubt I looked any more foolish than you did prancing behind Pastor Martin. I'm surprised you didn't ask to carry his Bible."

"How could I?" she retorted. "I was too busy carrying your nephew most of the time." With that said, she turned and carried Nathan into the cabin without so much as a good night. *I'm not going to let myself care for any man,* she thought to herself. *I've forgiven Pa for sending me away, but I've not forgotten. I don't need that kind of pain ever again.*

"My, my," smiled Granny as she gathered the other children and walked toward the cabin. "You two certainly have hit it off well. I'm so pleased."

Jonathan stood staring after her, wondering if she had lost her senses.

❧

Life began to fit into a routine for the family and although Delphinia still relied on Granny for many things, Granny had fewer and fewer days when she was up and about for any period of time. Jonathan made a bed for her to lie on in the living area so she could be in the midst of things. Granny still led them in devotions each morning and continued to be a stabilizing factor for Tessie, whose resentment of Delphinia seemed immeasurable. Everyone else was accepting Delphinia's presence and enjoying her company, particularly Pastor Martin.

It was a warm day and Delphinia had risen early, hoping to get the bread baking done before the heat of the day made the cabin unbearable. Her back was to the door as she stood kneading the coarse dough, methodically punching and turning the mixture, her thoughts occasionally drifting to Pastor Martin's good looks and kind manner. This was the last batch of dough and she was glad it would soon be done. She could feel droplets of perspiration forming across her forehead when she heard Granny say from the narrow cot, "Delphinia, don't be alarmed and don't scream. Just slowly turn around and smile like this is the happiest moment of your life."

Not knowing what to expect, the younger woman whirled around to be greeted by three Indians who were solemnly staring at her as her mouth fell open and she began moving backward.

"Smile, Delphinia, smile," Granny commanded.

"I'm trying, Granny, I'm honestly trying, but I can't seem to get my lips to turn upward right now. What do they want? Is Jonathan anywhere nearby?"

"Oh, they're friendly enough and they belong to the Kansa tribe. Just don't act like you're afraid. It offends them since they've come here from time to time and have never hurt anyone. They seem to know the days when I bake bread and that's what they want. I thought they had moved to the reservation, it's been so long since they've been here. They used to come every week or two and expect a loaf of bread and maybe some cheese or a chicken. Then they just quit coming. They never knock, just walk in and stand there until they're noticed. Gives you quite a start the first time, though.

"You want bread?" Granny asked, pointing at the freshly baked loaves resting on the wooden table.

Nodding in the affirmative, they each reached out and grabbed a loaf of bread.

"Now just a minute," Delphinia chastened. "You can't each have a loaf. You'll have to settle for one loaf. I have children here to feed."

"Well you lost your fear mighty fast, child," Granny commented as she looked over to see both twins toddling into the kitchen.

"You papoose?" one of the Indians asked, pointing first at Delphinia and then the twins, seeming amazed at the sight of them.

"They haven't been here since the twins were born," Granny commented. "I don't know if they realize you're not Sarah, but just nod yes."

"Yes, my papoose," Delphinia said, pointing to herself and to each of the twins while the Indians walked toward the babies, looking at them curiously. Then, reaching down, the spokesman picked up Nettie in one arm and Nathan in the other. He began bouncing the babies as he talked and laughed with his companions. Both infants were enthralled with the attention and were busy stuffing the Indian's necklaces into their mouths.

Delphinia glanced at the older woman and knew she was becoming alarmed by the Indian's interest in the babies. Forgetting her fear, she walked to the Indian and said, "My papoose," and extended her arms. Grunting in agreement, the Indian passed the children to her, picked up a loaf of bread, held it in the air, and the three of them left the cabin without saying another word.

"Wow," said Josh, coming from behind the bedroom door. "You sure were brave."

"Yeah, brave," mimicked Joey.

"I don't know about brave," Delphinia answered, "but they were making me terribly nervous and I was afraid they'd walk out with more than a loaf of bread."

Jonathan was just coming over from his cabin when he was met by Joey and Josh, both trying to give an account of everything that had happened, even though they had witnessed very little of the actual events.

"Slow down, you guys, or I'll never be able to understand. Better yet, why don't you let Granny or Phiney tell me what happened."

Joint "ahs" emitted from both boys at that suggestion and they plopped down on the bed with Granny as she began to tell Jonathan what had occurred.

"Seems you finally put that temper of yours to good use, Phiney," Jonathan responded after hearing Granny's account of what had happened.

"I what? Well, of all the—"

"Now, now child," Granny interrupted, "he's just trying to get you riled up, and doing a mighty fine job of it, too, I might add. Pay him no mind. He's as proud of you as the rest of us."

"She's right, Phiney. I should be thanking you instead of teasing. That was mighty brave of you and we're grateful although I can't say as I blame those Indians for wanting some of Granny's bread. Those are some fine looking loaves."

"They're not mine, Jonathan. I couldn't begin to knead that bread the way I've been feeling. Delphinia's baked all the bread around here for weeks now."

"Well, I think Granny's bread is much better, and so was Mama's," came Tessie's response from the other side of the room. "I don't know why you're making such a big fuss. Those Indians weren't going to hurt anyone. They were just curious about the twins and wanted a handout. She's no big deal. We've had Indians in and out of this cabin before she ever came here."

"You're right, Tessie. I'm sure the Indians meant no harm and I did nothing the rest of you wouldn't have done. So let's just forget it and get breakfast going. Tessie, if you'll start more coffee, I believe I'll go to my room for a few minutes and freshen up."

Once inside her room, Delphinia willed herself to stop shaking. Leaning against the closed door, her ghostlike reflection greeted her in the bureau mirror. Aware the family was waiting breakfast and not wanting to appear fainthearted, she pinched her cheeks, forced a smile on her face, and walked back to the kitchen realizing she had been thanking God from the instant the Indians left the cabin until this moment. Immediately, she felt herself quit shivering and a peaceful calm took the place of her fear.

Granny's supplication at the morning meal was more eloquent than usual and Jonathan was quick to add a hearty "amen" on several occasions throughout the prayer. Delphinia silently thanked God for the peace He had granted her. She was not aware until this day that some time ago she had quit praying for God to rescue her and had allowed laughter and joy to return to her life. It was not the same as when she had been at home with her parents, but a warmth and love of a new and special kind had slowly begun to grow in her heart.

eight

Autumn arrived and the trees burst forth in glorious yellows, reds, and oranges. The rolling hills took on a new beauty and Delphinia delighted in the changing season. The warm air belied the fact that winter would soon follow.

For several days Josh and Joey had been hard at work, gathering apples from the surrounding trees, stripping them of the tart, crisp fruit. An ample supply had been placed in the root cellar and she and Granny had spent days drying the rest. Hoping she might find enough to make pies for dessert that evening, Delphinia had gone to the trees in the orchard behind the house. Once the basket was full, she started back toward the cabin and, when coming around the house, she noticed Pastor Martin riding toward her on his sorrel. Waving in recognition, he came directly to where she stood, dismounted, and joined her.

"I was hoping to catch you alone for a minute," he commented as he walked beside her, leading the horse. "I've come to ask if you'd accompany me to the social next Friday evening," he blurted, "unless you're going with Jonathan. . .or has someone else already asked you?"

Before she could answer, Tessie came around the side of the house, a twin at each hand. "You'd better take him up on the offer, Phiney. Jonathan will be taking Katy McVay, and I doubt *you'll* be getting any other invitations," she prompted, a malicious smile crossing her face.

"I don't know if I'll be attending at all, Pastor Martin. I had quite forgotten about the party and I'm not sure I can leave the family. Granny hasn't been quite as good the last few days."

"Really, Phiney. We're not totally helpless, you know. We managed before you got here and I'm sure we could manage for a few hours on Friday night," came Tessie's rebuttal.

Not sure whether she should thank Tessie for the offer to assist with the family or upbraid her for her rude intrusion, Delphinia invited the pastor to join her in the cabin where they could discuss the matter further and gain Granny's opinion.

Granny was always pleased to see Pastor Martin and her face shone immediate pleasure as he walked in the room. "I didn't know you made calls this early in the day," she called out in greeting.

Smiling, he sat in the chair beside the bed where she rested and he took her hand. "Normally I don't and only for very special occasions. I've come to ask Delphinia if she'd allow me to escort her to the social Friday night," he answered, accepting the cup of coffee Delphinia offered.

"Well, I'd say that's a pretty special event. What kind of answer did you give this young man, Delphinia?" she asked the embarrassed young woman.

"I haven't answered him just yet, Granny. I didn't think I should leave the children with you for that long. Tessie overheard the conversation and said she could help but I wanted to talk it over with you first."

"Why, we can manage long enough for you to have a little fun, Delphinia. Wouldn't want you away too long, though. I'd miss your company and sweet face."

Delphinia leaned down to place a light kiss on the older woman's wrinkled cheek. "I love you, Granny," she whispered.

"Does that mean you've accepted?" asked Tessie, coming from the doorway where she had been standing out of sight and listening.

"Well. . .yes. . .I suppose it does," she replied. "Pastor Martin, I'd be pleased to accompany you. What time should I be ready?"

"I'll be here about seven, if that's agreeable."

Glancing over at Granny for affirmation and seeing her nod, Delphinia voiced her agreement.

Downing the remains of coffee in the stoneware cup, the young parson bid them farewell, explaining he needed to stop by the Aplingtons' for a visit and get back to town before noon. Walking outside, Delphinia strolled along beside him until he had come even with his mare. "If you're going to attend the social with me, Delphinia, I think it would be appropriate for you to call me George," he stated and swung atop the animal, which was prancing, anxious to be allowed its rein.

"Fine, George," she answered modestly, stepping back from the horse.

Smiling, he lightly kicked the mare in the sides and took off, reaching full gallop before he hit the main road, his arm waving in farewell.

Delphinia was standing in the same spot when Jonathan came up behind her and eyed the cloud of billowing dust down the road. Unable to identify the rider, he asked, "Who was that just leaving?"

"Jonathan, you frightened me. I didn't hear you come up behind me," she said, not answering his question.

"I'm sorry if I startled you. Who did you say that was, or is it a secret?"

"I didn't say, but it's not a secret. It was George. . .I mean, Pastor Martin."

"Oh, *George,* is it? Since when are you and the parson on a first name basis, Phiney?"

"Pastor Martin. . .George. . .has asked me to attend the social with him on Friday night," she responded.

"You didn't agree, did you?" he demanded, his anger evident. The look on his face almost defied her to admit her acceptance.

"I checked with Granny. She found no fault in my going. I'll make sure the twins and Joey are ready for bed before leaving, if that's your concern." Irritated by the tone he was taking, Delphinia turned and headed back toward the house, leaving him to stare after her.

"Just you wait a minute. I'm not through discussin' this," he called after her.

"You needn't bellow. I didn't realize we were having a discussion. I thought it was an inquisition," she stated, continuing toward the house. *Why is he acting so hateful?* she wondered. *Jonathan knows George Martin is a good man. He should be pleased that such a nice man wants to keep company with me.*

"The problem is that I planned on taking you to the social and here you've gone and promised to go with George," he retorted.

Stopping short, she whirled around almost colliding with him. "You planned on taking me? Well, just when were you going to tell me about it? This is the first time you've said one word about the social. Besides, Tessie said you were taking Katy McVay."

"Tessie said what?" he nearly yelled at her. "Since when do you listen to what Tessie has to say?"

"Why wouldn't I believe her? I've heard enough rumors that you and Katy are a match. She's got her cap set for you and from what I've been told, the feeling is mutual," she retorted.

"Oh, really? Well, I don't pay much heed to the gossip that's floating around. For your information, we are not a match. I've escorted Katy to a few functions but that doesn't make us betrothed or anything near it. If Tessie told you I invited Katy, she spoke out of turn. I've not asked anyone to the social because I planned on taking you."

"I can't read your mind, Jonathan. If you want me to know what you're planning, next time you need to tell me," she answered, his comments making her more certain that men were not to be trusted.

The kitchen was filled with an air of tension throughout the noon meal until Granny finally questioned Jonathan. Hearing his explanation, she let out a whoop and sided with Delphinia. "Just because she lives here doesn't mean you can take her for granted," she chided.

Feeling frustration with Granny's lack of allegiance, Jonathan turned on Tessie, scolding her mightily for interfering.

"That's enough, Jon. I know you're upset, and the girl was wrong in telling an outright lie, but all your ranting and raving isn't going to change the fact that the preacher is calling on Delphinia Friday night,"

Granny resolutely stated.

Not willing to let the matter rest and hoping to aid Katy in her conquest, Tessie suggested Jonathan ride into town and invite her. "I'm sure she'll not accept an invitation from anyone else," she added as her final comment.

"Tessie, I would appreciate it if you would spend as much time performing chores as you do meddling in other people's affairs. If you'd do that, the rest of us wouldn't have to do a thing around here!" His face was reddened with anger as he pushed away from the table and left the house.

✶

When Friday evening finally arrived, Granny made sure that Josh fetched water and it was kept warm on the stove for Delphinia's bath. After dinner, she ordered Jonathan to carry the metal tub into Delphinia's room, then smiled to herself as Jonathan made a dash for his own cabin to prepare for the evening.

Scooting down in the tub, Delphinia let her head go completely underwater and, sliding back up, began to lather her hair. She rubbed in a small amount of the lavender oil that had belonged to her mother and finished washing herself. Never had she taken such care in preparing herself. She towel dried her hair and pinned it on top of her head. An ivory ribbon surrounded the mass of curls except for a few short tendrils that escaped, framing her oval face. Her mother's small, golden locket was at her neck and she placed a tiny gold earring in each lobe.

She had decided upon wearing a deep blue dress that had belonged to her mother. Granny helped with the few necessary alterations and it now fit beautifully. She slipped it over her head and fastened the tiny covered buttons that began at the scooped neckline and trailed to the waist. Slipping on her good shoes, she took one final look in the mirror and exited the bedroom.

Her entry into the living area was met with lusty approval from the boys. Granny beamed at the sight of her and Tessie glared in distaste. Jonathan had gone to sit on the porch when he heard the raves from inside. Rising, he entered the house and was overcome by the sight he beheld. She was, without a doubt, the most glorious looking creature he had ever seen. Noting the look on his face, Tessie stepped toward him. "Aren't you leaving to pick up Katy, Uncle Jon?"

Gaining his attention with her question, he looked her straight in the eyes. "I told you earlier this week I was not escorting Katy. Have you forgotten, Tessie?"

"Oh, I thought maybe you'd asked her since then," she murmured. Gathering her wits about her, she quizzed, "Well, who are you taking?"

"No one," he responded, unable to take his eyes off the beautiful young woman in the blue dress. "I'm just going to ride along with George and Phiney."

"You're going to *what*?" stammered Delphinia.

"No need in getting my horse all lathered up riding into town when there's a buggy going anyway. Doesn't make good sense, Phiney. Besides, I'm sure the parson won't mind if I ride along."

No sooner had he uttered those words, when the sound of a buggy could be heard coming up the roadway. Jonathan stepped to the porch and called out, "Evenin', George. Good to see you. I was just telling Phiney I didn't think you'd have any objection to my riding into town with the two of you. Didn't see any need to saddle up my horse when I could ride along with you."

The pastor's face registered a look of surprise and then disappointment. "No, no, that's fine, Jon. Might be a little crowded—"

"Don't mind a bit," interrupted Jonathan. "You just stay put and I'll fetch Phiney."

"I think perhaps I should fetch her myself, Jon," he said, his voice hinting of irritation.

Both men arrived at the door simultaneously and for a moment Delphinia thought they were going to be permanently wedged in the doorway until the pastor turned slightly, allowing himself to advance into the room. "You look absolutely stunning, Delphinia," he complimented, watching her cheeks flush from the remark.

"She's a real sight to behold, that's for sure," responded Jonathan as every eye in the room turned to stare at him.

Nate and Nettie toddled to where she stood, their hands extended to grab at the flowing gown. "No you don't, you two. Tessie, grab the twins or they'll be drooling all over her before she can get out the door," ordered Jonathan.

"Seems to me you're already drooling all over her," Tessie muttered under her breath.

❧

The evening passed in a succession of dances with Jonathan and George vying for each one, occasionally being bested by some other young man who would manage to whisk her off in the midst of their sparring over who should have the next dance. By the end of the social, Delphinia's feet ached but the gaiety of the event far outweighed any complaint she might have. The only blemish of the evening had been overhearing some unkind remarks from Katy McVay at the refreshment table. When she noticed Delphinia standing close by, she had given her a syrupy smile and excused herself to "find more appealing company."

Although they were cramped close together on the seat of the buggy, the autumn air had cooled and Delphinia felt herself shiver. "You're cold. Why didn't you say something? Let me help you with your shawl," Jonathan offered as the pastor kept his hands on the reins. Unfolding the wrap, he slipped it around her shoulders and allowed his arm to rest across her shoulders in a possessive manner. Much to George's irritation, he remained thus until the horses came to a halt in front of the house. Jumping down, George hurried to secure the horses in hopes of helping Delphinia from the buggy, but to no avail. Jonathan had already assisted her and was standing with his arm draped across her small shoulders. Delphinia attempted to shrug him off but he only tightened his grip.

"It's getting late, Parson, and you've still got to make the trip back to town. Thanks for the ride and good night," Jonathan stated, attempting to dismiss the preacher before he could usher Delphinia to the house.

"Now just a minute, Jonathan. I'm capable of saying thank you and good night for myself. You go on to your place. George and I will be just fine," Delphinia answered.

"Nah, that's okay. Want to make sure everything's okay here before I go over to my place so I'll just wait here on the porch till George is on his way."

Knowing that Jonathan was not about to leave and not wanting to create a scene, the pastor thanked Delphinia for a lovely evening and bid them both good night.

"Of all the nerve," she shouted at the relaxed figure on the porch. "You are the most vexing man I have ever met. George Martin made a trip here especially to invite me to the social, made another trip to escort me and return me safely home, and you have the nerve to not only invite yourself along, but won't even give him the opportunity to spend a moment alone with me!" The full moon shone on her face and he could see her eyes flashing with anger.

"I'll not apologize for that, Phiney. After all, I have a responsibility to keep you safe. You're a part of this family," he said with a boyish grin.

Hands on her hips and chin jutted forward, she made her way to the porch where he stood and she said, "I'll have you know, *Mr. Wilshire,* that I do not need your protection from George Martin, nor do I want it."

But, before she could move, he leaned down and kissed her full on the mouth. When he released her she was so stunned that she stared at him in utter disbelief, unable to say a word, her heart pounding rapidly. A slow smile came across his lips as he once again gathered her into his arms and his mouth slowly descended and captured her lips in a breathtaking kiss. She felt her legs grow limp and, as he leaned back, she lost her balance causing her to reach out and grab Jonathan's arm for support.

"Now, now, Phiney, don't go begging me to stay any longer. I've got to get over to my place and get some sleep," he said with an ornery glint in his eye.

That remark caused Delphinia to immediately regain her composure. "Beg you to stay? Is that what you think I want? Why, you are the most conceited, arrogant, irritating, interfering—"

"You just keep on with your chattering, Phiney. Think I'll get some sleep," he interrupted, stepping off the porch and walking toward his cabin.

"Oooh, that man! I don't think the Lord is ever going to get around to straightening him out," she muttered under her breath as she turned and opened the cabin door.

nine

The beginning of the school year brought excitement to the household and the children were anxious for the change in routine. Delphinia made sure that each of the youngsters looked their very best for the first day, especially Joey, since this marked the beginning of his career as a student. Although he was not yet five, the new schoolteacher had come to visit and, much to his delight, declared him bright enough to begin his formal education with the other children. Delphinia and Granny packed their tin pails with thick slices of bread and cheese, an apple, and a piece of dried peach pie. The two women stood at the cabin door watching as the young Wilshires made their way toward the dusty road, their happy chatter floating through the morning air.

With the older children gone to school each day, Delphinia and Granny were left at home with only the twins to care for. Although she loved all the children, even Tessie with her malicious ways, Delphinia cherished the additional time it allowed her to be alone with the older woman.

Granny took advantage of the new-found freedom and devoted most of the extra hours to teaching Delphinia all the things that would assist the young woman in running the household once she had only herself to rely upon. Shortly after her arrival, Delphinia confided that her mother had given her a wonderful education, insisting she spend her time studying, reading, and doing fancy stitching rather than household tasks. It was soon evident that she had much to learn. During the months since her arrival, she had proven herself a capable student of the older woman's tutelage. But there remained much to learn and Granny spent hours carefully explaining how to use the children's clothing to make patterns for new garments; how to plant and tend a garden; how to preserve the meats, vegetables, and fruits that would provide for them throughout the winter and early spring; how to make tallow candles and lye soap, being sure to wrap each candle and bar in straw for storage; how to make big wheels of cheese, being sure to allow time for aging; and how to prepare meals for the large threshing crews that would hopefully be needed in early summer. Listening intently, she absorbed everything Granny taught her.

Delphinia's true pleasure came, however, when Granny would call for a quiet time during the twins' nap and the two of them would read from the Bible and discuss the passages. Their sharing of God's Word caused a bond of love to flourish between the two women, just as the one that had grown between Delphinia and her mother when they stitched her cherished quilt. Both women were especially pleased when Pastor Martin would stop by, which was happening more frequently. He never failed to raise their spirits. Delphinia enjoyed his attentiveness and insights, while Granny hoped the visits would light a fire under Jonathan.

As winter began to settle on the prairie, Delphinia thought she would never see a blade of grass or a flower bloom again. The snows came in blizzard proportions, keeping the children, as well as the adults, inside most of the time. Although everyone made great effort to create harmony, boredom overcame the children and tempers grew short.

After several days, Delphinia was sure something would have to be done to keep the children diverted. That evening as Jonathan prepared to go to the barn and milk Josie, their old brown and white cow, Delphinia began putting on her coat and hat. "Where do you think you're going?" he asked. "I want to go to the barn and unpack some things from one of my trunks stored out there," she answered, falling in step behind him.

Barely able to see, the snow blowing in giant swirls with each new gust of wind, they made their way to the barn and, while Jonathan milked, Delphinia began going through the items in one of her trunks. She found her old slate and schoolbooks, an old cloth ball, a rag doll from when she was a small child, and some marbles her father had bought for her one Christmas, much to her mother's chagrin. She bundled the items in a heavy shawl and sat down on top of the trunk to await Jonathan.

"Come sit over here and visit with me while I finish," he requested.

Picking up the parcel, she walked over and sat on one of the milking stools, watching intently as the milk pinged into the battered pail at a steady rhythm.

"Granny tells me George has been coming out to see you some."

"He's been here occasionally."

"I take it that makes you happy?" Jonathan questioned, noting the blush that had risen in her cheeks.

"George is a fine man. I enjoy his company. And what of Katy McVay? Do your visits with her make you happy?" she questioned.

"I haven't been visiting with Katy. I don't know how I've missed George when he's come calling," he replied, rising from the stool. "Guess I need to be a little more observant," he grumbled as the two of them headed back toward the house.

"From the looks of that bundle, it appears your trip was successful," Granny said, watching the children assemble around Delphinia who was struggling to remove her wet outer garments.

"Perhaps more successful than the children will care for in a few days," she answered with a slight smile, pointing at the teaching materials she was removing from the shawl. Handing the rag doll to Nettie, she smiled as the baby hugged it close and toddled away, with Nate in close pursuit.

"Here Nathan, catch the ball," she called, just as he was reaching to pull the doll away from Nettie. Chortling in delight, he grabbed the ball with his chubby hands as it rolled across the floor in front of him.

"Where are our toys?" asked Josh, a frown crossing his face.

"I don't have a lot of toys, Josh," she replied. "I do have some marbles my pa gave me one Christmas that I'd be willing to let you boys earn by doing well with your lessons."

"Ah, that's not fair," they replied in unison. "The twins don't have to do no lessons."

"Any lessons," Delphinia corrected. "The twins are still babies. You boys are old enough to know you must work for rewards. . .in this case, marbles. Tessie already understands that the true reward of a student is the knowledge you receive," she explained, although Tessie's look of boredom belied a real zeal for knowledge, or anything else at the moment.

"I did, however, find this tortoise-shell comb and, if you'd like, Tessie, I would be willing to consider it a little something extra, over and above the reward of knowledge."

Tessie eyed the comb trying to hide her excitement. It was the most beautiful hair piece she had ever seen and she desperately wanted it. As much as she wanted it, however, she would never concede that fact to Delphinia.

"I suppose it would make the boys try harder if they knew we were all working toward a reward," she responded.

Granny and Delphinia exchanged knowing smiles and the lessons began. The children worked hard on their studies and the days passed, some with more success than others. The boys finally were rewarded with all the marbles and Tessie had become the proud owner of the tortoise-shell comb.

When at last the snows abated and the roads were clear enough for school to resume the first week in December, both women heaved a sigh of relief, along with a prayer of thanksgiving. They waved from the doorway as the three older children climbed up on the buckboard and Jonathan drove off toward school, all of them agreeing the weather was still not fit to walk such a distance.

The children returned home that first day, each clutching a paper with their part for the Christmas pageant. Delphinia quickly realized the evenings would be spent with the children practicing elocution and memorization. Tessie was to portray Mary, but had detailed instructions that her red hair was to be completely tucked under a scarf.

"Why'd they pick her if they didn't want a redhead? It's not like she's the prettiest girl in class," Josh commented, tiring of the discussion of how to best cover Tessie's hair.

"They picked me because I'm the best actress in the school," Tessie retorted.

"I must be one of the smartest since the teacher picked me to be one of the Wise Men," Josh bantered back.

By this time, Joey was totally confused. "How come they picked me to be a shepherd, Granny?" he inquired. "Does that mean I have to take sheep with me to the school?"

Everyone broke into gales of laughter at his remark, as he stood there with a look of bewilderment on his face.

"No, sweet thing, you don't need any sheep," Granny replied. "But I think you all better get busy learning your lines instead of telling us how wise and talented you are."

After school the next day, Miss Sanders arrived to request that Nate or Nettie portray the Baby Jesus in the pageant. Just as Delphinia was beginning to explain that neither of them would hold still long enough for a stage production, both twins came toddling into the room. Squealing in delight and their hands smeared with jelly, they headed directly for the visitor. Delphinia was unable to head off the attack and Miss Sanders left soon after with jelly stains on the front of her dress and a withdrawal of her request for a Baby Jesus from the Wilshire home.

Granny, Jonathan, and Delphinia had been making plans for months, hoping the upcoming holiday would be a special time since this was the first Christmas the children, as well as Delphinia, would be without their parents.

"I want it to be a good Christmas, one we'll all remember fondly," Granny kept reminding them.

Jonathan made several trips to town for special purchases and while the children were at school, gifts were ordered through the mail or made by the women. Oranges, a rare treat for all of them, were poked full of cloves, and tins of dried apricots and candied fruits arrived. Gingerbread men were baked with the distinctive spice Granny ordered from back east and the children delighted in helping cut and bake them the Saturday before Christmas. Even Tessie seemed to enjoy the preparations, helping the younger children make decorations.

The day before Christmas Jonathan and the two older boys went in search of a tree with instructions from Granny that it not be too large. They came back with a somewhat scraggly cedar and placed it in the corner. The homemade garland and strings of popcorn were placed on the branches and Delphinia hung ornaments and a star that she had brought from home. The tin candle holders were clipped onto the tree, with a promise that the candles would be lit Christmas morning.

The day went by in a stir of confusion and soon everyone scurried to get ready for the Christmas pageant being held at the church. Jonathan worried the weather would be too hard on Granny, but she insisted on going. Dressed in her heaviest woolen dress and winter coat, Jonathan wrapped her frail figure in blankets, carried her to the wagon, and, placing her on a mattress stuffed with corn husks, tucked a twin on either side. Finally, he covered all of them with a feather comforter. The rest of the children piled in the back, all snuggling together to gain warmth from each other. Jonathan helped Delphinia to the seat beside him. Starting down the road, he pulled her closer with the admonition she would certainly be too cold sitting so far away. She did not resist, nor did she respond, but his touch caused her cheeks to feel fiery in the frosty night air.

The program was enchanting with each of the children performing admirably. The audience gave its enthusiastic approval and the evening ended with the group of delighted parents and relatives sharing cocoa and cookies. Miss Sanders proudly presented each of the children with a stick of peppermint candy as a gift for their hard work.

"I'm sorry I haven't been out to see you," George told Delphinia, offering her a cup of cocoa. "The weather has made it impossible, but I hope to come by again soon."

"We always look forward to your visits, George. I'm sorry I've missed you the last few times you've come to call," came Jonathan's reply from behind Delphinia. "You just come on out anytime. I'll make a point to be watching for you," he continued. "We're getting ready to leave, Phiney," he stated, holding out her coat and giving her a wink, sure that George would notice.

"Pastor Martin plans on coming out to visit soon," Delphinia informed Granny on the trip home.

"I think he's more interested in visiting Phiney than the rest of us, but I told him we'd be happy to have him anytime," Jonathan stated. "You two be sure and let me know when he comes calling so I don't miss another visit," he instructed and was disappointed when Delphinia did not give one of her quick retorts.

Once home, the children were soon tucked into bed, anxious for morning to arrive. Granny was quick to admit that she, too, needed her rest and apologetically requested that Delphinia complete the Christmas preparations. Before retiring, the older woman instructed Delphinia where everything had been hidden, fearful that a gift or two might be forgotten. Smiling and placing a kiss on her cheek, Delphinia reassured her that all would be ready by morning.

Christmas Day was a joyous event of sparkling eyes and joyous laughter. The children were in good spirits, the tree was beautiful, and the gifts well received. Jonathan had gone hunting the morning before and returned with a wild turkey, which was the main attraction of the festive holiday meal. After dinner, Granny read the Christmas story from the Bible while the family sat in a circle around her listening intently, even the young twins. When she had finished, Jonathan began to sing "Silent Night" and the others joined in. One by one, they sang all the Christmas carols they could remember until Jonathan declared it was bedtime for the children. Not long after, Granny bid them good night, thanking them both for all they had done to make it such a wonderful day. "Don't stay up too long," she admonished, always in charge.

"We won't, Granny," answered Jonathan, smiling back at her.

As the burning candles flickered, Jonathan reached in his pocket, pulled out a small package, and handed it to Delphinia. Her face registered surprise.

"What's this for?" she inquired.

"It's a Christmas gift, from me to you. I didn't want to give it to you in front of the others."

"You shouldn't have, Jonathan," she chided as she slowly untied the ribbon and removed the wrapping to reveal a beautiful gold thimble on which the initials DEH had been engraved. Her face radiated as she examined it and placed it on her finger. "It's beautiful, Jonathan. I love it. How did you ever happen to choose a thimble?" she inquired.

"Granny told me about the quilt you and your mother stitched and how special it was to you. I figured sewing was important to you and I'd never seen you using a thimble when you were sewing. Granny said she didn't think you had one. The initials were Granny's idea."

"I'm surprised you didn't have it engraved P-E-H instead of D-E-H."

"To tell you the truth, I wanted to have in engraved with P-H-I-N-E-Y but Granny wouldn't hear of it and the engraver said it was too many letters for such a small piece," he laughed.

"I'd better be getting over to my place. It's getting late and Granny will have my hide if I'm not out of here soon," he said, rising from the his chair.

At the door he reached down and placed his hand alongside her face and lightly kissed her on the lips. "Merry Christmas, Phiney. I'll see you tomorrow," he said and headed toward his cabin.

Delphinia sat on the edge of her bed staring at the golden thimble and remembering Jonathan's kiss, still unsure she should trust any man again. *If I were to trust someone, George would probably be the safest choice.*

ten

Delphinia sat in the rocker, Nettie on one arm, Nathan on the other, watching their eyes slowly close in readiness for a nap. They had developed a real sense of independence, seldom wanting to be rocked anymore, except at bedtime. It was hard to believe that almost a year had passed since she left home. The birds were once again singing and the aroma of blooming honeysuckle gave notice of spring's arrival. New life had begun to appear in everything, except Granny. Her health fell in rapid decline throughout the winter and she lost the will to battle her debilitating illness any longer. It had been only a few weeks since her death, but life had taken a turn for the worse since her departure. Delphinia's sense of loss was extraordinary. Tessie had grown more sullen and less helpful, the boys seemed rowdier, the twins fussier, and Jonathan tried to cheer all of them, with sadness showing in his own eyes.

Delphinia thought of Granny's final words the morning she lay dying. "Remember I love you like a daughter, and the Lord loves you even more. Never turn from Him, Delphinia. I can see the peace you've gained since coming here and I don't want you to lose it. Nothing would make me sadder than to think my death would cause you to stumble in your faith.

"One more thing, my dear. Jonathan loves you and you love him. I'm not sure either of you realize it yet, but I'm sure God has wonderful plans for the two of you. You've learned well and there's nothing to fear. Jonathan will be close at hand whenever you need him," the dying woman had said as she reached up and wiped the tears from Delphinia's cheeks.

Shortly thereafter, she summoned Jonathan and, in hushed murmurs, they said their final good-byes.

The services were held at the church and everyone in the surrounding area came to pay their tribute. Granny would have been pleased, not because they came to honor her, but because some of them hadn't been inside the church since it had been built!

Several days after the funeral, Pastor Martin came to visit and confided that the services had been planned by Granny. She had known it might be the only opportunity the minister would have to preach the plan of salvation to some of the homesteaders. Determined her death might provide eternal life for one of those settlers if they heard the message of God's love, she had ordered, "Don't talk about me, tell them about the precious Savior I've gone to join."

There had been no flowery eulogies, no words of praise about her many acts of charity, or sentimental stories about her life. Pastor Martin had given an eloquent sermon based on Romans 10:9–13 telling all those assembled that Granny's deepest desire had been consistent with that of her Lord. She wanted them to have the opportunity to receive Jesus Christ as their Savior. She wanted them to experience the joy of serving a Lord Who would be with them in the times of happiness as well as sorrow. She wanted them to know the pure joy and peace that could be attained in service to the living God. Yes, he pointed out, there would still be sorrow, even while faithfully serving the Lord. He told them there was no promise made that our lives would be free of unhappiness and grief but, he added, the Word of God does tell us we will not be alone at those times. We have comfort through our Lord, Jesus Christ.

"That is what Jesus wanted you to know, and that is what Granny wanted you to know," he had said as he finished the message.

The service ended more like a revival meeting than a funeral. The pastor explained to those attending that if they had not received Jesus as their Savior, nothing would make Granny happier than to use this opportunity to take that step of commitment at her funeral. When two men and one young girl stepped forward, Delphinia was sure the angels in heaven were singing and that Granny was probably leading the chorus!

It had been a unique experience for all of them. The burial had taken place, followed by a baptism at the river and everyone had then returned to the church for dinner and visiting afterward.

Granny would have loved it!

The twins stirred in Delphinia's arms and carefully she placed them in bed, hoping they would not awaken. Hearing the sound of a horse coming toward the house, she walked to the porch and watched as George Martin approached, quickly returning his smile and wave. "It's good to see you, George," she welcomed as he climbed down from the horse. "Come in and I'll pour you some coffee."

"It's good to see you, too. Coffee sounds good. I hope you have some time so we can visit privately," he stated as they walked into the house.

"It appears you're in luck. The twins are napping, Tessie's gone to pick berries, and the older boys are with Jonathan," she answered.

"I really don't know how to begin," he stammered, taking a sip of coffee, "so I guess I'll just get to the heart of the matter."

"That's usually best," she encouraged, leaning forward.

"Delphinia, I don't know if you realize that I've come to care for you a great deal. We don't know each other well. . .I don't really think we could ever get to know each other very well as long as Jonathan's around. Anyway, I've been called to another church and must leave here by the end of the month. I'd like you to come with me. . .as my wife, of course," he stated.

"George. . .I don't know what to say. You've taken me by surprise," she said, her voice faltering. "You're a wonderful man but I don't think I could marry unless I was sure I loved you. I don't think a few weeks would assure us of that. Furthermore, I couldn't just leave the children. That's why I'm here, to care for them. I have an obligation to the bargain that was made, even if I wasn't a part of it," she stated, sadness evident in her voice.

"I'm not worried about the fact that you're not in love with me. I think our love for each other will grow once we're married. Your feeling of obligation to the Wilshires is admirable, and I certainly don't want to see the children left without someone to help, but I'm sure we can overcome that problem. That is, if you really want to," he said in a questioning manner.

"I'm not sure, George. I don't think I can give you an answer so quickly," she responded. *I'm just not ready to trust a man again,* she thought, *especially one I don't love.*

"Please don't think I'm placing pressure upon you, Delphinia, but I want to be absolutely honest. I've been calling on Katy McVay from time to time, also. I would prefer to marry you, but if you're going to turn me down, I need to know now," he replied.

"You mean if I reject you, you're going to ask Katy to marry you?"

"I am. I think highly of Katy, also. Unlike you, I believe love truly blossoms after marriage. You are my first choice, but I want to be married when I start my new assignment," he responded.

"Under the circumstances I hope she will accept your offer and the two of you will be very happy," Delphinia answered. Rising from her chair, she held out her hand to him. "I have truly enjoyed our friendship, George. I wish you much happiness and thank you for all the kindness you've extended. I am honored you would ask me to marry you but I think we both now realize our thoughts on love and marriage differ enough that your choice should be someone else."

"I'm sorry we can't make this work," he replied as they walked outside and he got on his horse.

"Good luck with Katy," she called out, watching him ride down the path. Slowly she walked into the house and sat down in the rocker, contemplating the consequences of her decision, wondering if she should change her mind and go after him.

Voices from outside brought her back to the present and the twins began to stir in the bedroom. Jonathan, Josh, and Joey came rushing into the room, concern and excitement evident as they all tried to talk at once.

"I need your help, Phiney. The boys can watch the twins," Jonathan shouted above the boys' chatter.

"Let's find Tessie. I'd rather have her stay with them. What's going on?" she asked, not yet convinced it was necessary to leave the twins in the care of their over-anxious brothers.

"She's gone to pick berries. I need you now. The cow's giving birth and she's having a hard time. Come on," he shouted, rushing to the barn to grab some rope and then running for the pasture.

Soon after Delphinia left the cabin, she could hear the cow's deep bellowing and she wondered what Jonathan could possibly expect her to do. She did not know anything about birthing children, let alone animals, and besides, *Couldn't a cow do that without help?* she wondered.

Nellie, the small black heifer was lying down as Josie, the older brown and white cow, appeared to stand guard a short distance away. Jonathan was already at Nellie's side, motioning Delphinia to hurry. Not sure what to expect, her gait had grown slower and slower as she approached the laboring animal. Nothing could have prepared her for the experience. The cow's eyes were open wide, registering fear and pain. A low, bellowing moan came from deep in the animal's throat just as Delphinia walked up beside Jonathan.

"I don't know what to do. I think we should have Josh ride for Mr. Aplington. He'll be able to help," she offered, near panic.

"There's no time for that. If we don't get this calf out, we'll lose both of them. I don't want to lose the calf, but it's probably already dead. I'll hold onto Nellie while you reach up inside her and see if you can grab hold of the calf's legs. If you can, pull with all your might."

"I can't do that! You want me to reach up inside the cow? That is the most absurd thing I've ever heard. . .not to mention how offensive. If it's so important, do it yourself," she retorted, her face registering disgust.

"*Delphinia,* this cow is going to die! I don't have time to listen to your nonsense. You can't hold onto Nellie. Now reach in there and pull!" he commanded as froth oozed from Nellie's mouth and her tongue lolled to the side.

Going down on her knees, Delphinia closed her eyes and felt her hands begin to shake. *All right, I can do this,* she told herself, peeking out of one eye. Taking in a gulp of air, she thrust her arm high inside the cow. The assault was met by Nellie's bellow and a flailing leg. "I thought you were going to hold her!" Delphinia screamed.

"I'm trying. Can you feel anything?"

"I think so. . .yes. Jonathan, hold her still! How do you expect me to take care of this when you're not doing your part?"

He looked at her in astonishment. *"You're taking care of it?"*

"I don't see you doing much of anything," she grunted, leaning back and pulling with all her might. "This isn't working. I think it moved a little but I can't get a good hold."

Jonathan grabbed the piece of rope he had brought from the barn and tossed it to her. "Reach in and tie that around its legs. Be sure you get both legs."

"This isn't a quilting party, Jonathan," she rebutted. "Next you'll be telling me to embroider a lazy-daisy stitch on its rump."

Her remark brought the hint of a smile to his face. "Make a loop in the rope, slide it around the legs, and tighten it. When you're sure the rope is tight, try pulling again. Once you feel it coming, don't let up. If you slack off, it might get hip-locked and we'll lose both of them," he instructed.

All of a sudden, the heat was stifling and Delphinia felt herself begin to retch. "Not now, Phiney. There isn't time for you to be sick," he commanded.

"I'll try to keep that in mind," she replied curtly, tying a slipknot into the rope.

"You need to hurry!" he yelled.

"Jonathan, you are not helping this predicament with your obtrusive behavior! How do you expect the cow to remain calm if you keep hollering all the time," she preached at him. "I have the rope ready, and if you will kindly hold Nellie still this time, I will begin. Everything is going to be fine."

His jaw went slack as she finished her short speech. Where had that come from? She seemed totally in command and a calmness had taken the place of the near hysteria she had exhibited only minutes before. He kept his eyes on her and tightly gripped the heifer when she nodded she was ready to begin.

With almost expert ease, and over the vigorous protests of Nellie, she managed to secure both of the calf's front legs. Being careful not to let up, she worked arduously, pulling and tugging, her arms aching as the calf was finally pulled into the world. The calf's feeble bawl affirmed its birth. "It's alive," she said, tears streaming down her face.

"Let's hope it stays that way, and let's hope Nellie does the same," Jonathan answered.

"They're both going to be fine," she replied confidently.

"Take your apron and clean out it's nose, while I check Nellie," he ordered.

"Yes, sir! Any other commands?" she inquired, watching the new mother turn and begin lapping her tongue over the calf in a slow, deliberate manner.

"Not right now. It looks like Nellie's going to be a good mama. She's got her a nice lookin' little calf," he said, ignoring the barb she had given.

Delphinia sat back on her heels watching the two animals in wonderment. "There surely was a transformation in your attitude when you were helping me," Jonathan commented. "At first I thought you were going to be less help than Josh. One minute you were retching and the next you were ordering me around and taking charge," he laughed.

Turning to look at him, she quietly replied, "It was God Who took charge,

Jonathan. I merely prayed. But I knew that as soon as I finished that prayer for help, everything was going to be all right."

"You're quite a mystery, Phiney," he said, slowly shaking his head. "First, you're giving me the devil and next, you're praising God."

"I'm not sure I'm such a mystery. I criticize you only when it's needed," she laughed. "I do know I fail to praise God enough for all He does. I sometimes forget we serve a mighty God and that much can be wrought through prayer. My mother taught me that when I was very young, and I watched Granny live it daily." She reached up from where she sat and grasped his extended hand.

"Thanks for your help, Phiney. I couldn't have done it without you. I'm sure if Nellie and her baby could thank you, they would." Almost as if on cue, the tiny calf let out a warbling cry, causing both of them to smile.

"By the way, was that George Martin I saw leaving a while ago?" he questioned later, as they walked toward the house.

"Yes. He's been called to another church and will be leaving the end of the month," she answered.

"George is a fine preacher, but I can't say I'm sorry to see him leave," he responded.

"You may be. He's gone to ask for Katy McVay's hand in marriage," she told him, sure that that would take the smug grin from his face.

"Katy? Why would he be asking for Katy's hand? I know he's fond of you."

"He asked for my hand," she answered, saying nothing further.

"He what?" Jonathan pulled her to an abrupt stop. "What did you tell him?"

"I told him, no."

"So now he's gone to ask Katy?"

"It appears so," she answered and then related enough of their conversation to hopefully stop his questions, while watching his face for reaction.

"I didn't know she had taken a shine to the preacher. They might make a good match," he replied. "The less competition the better, as far as I'm concerned," he mumbled under his breath.

"What did you say?" she asked, turning toward him.

"Nothing to concern yourself with," he replied and began whistling as they walked to the house.

eleven

With the coming of early summer, the days grew longer and the beauty of nature began to unfold. The twins were able to play outside as Delphinia, aided by Jonathan, prepared the ground for her garden. Surprisingly, she found herself anxious to begin the arduous task, wondering if she would remember all that Granny had taught her. She felt challenged to prove she had been a capable student, worthy of the older woman's confidence.

Jonathan assured her she would be an adept gardener, pointing to the fact that she had nagged him almost continuously until he had given in and tilled enough ground for an early planting of potatoes in late March. Besides, the strawberries were already beginning to blossom, thanks to her attentive care and the cooperative weather.

Nate and Nettie found enjoyment following behind and playing in the turned soil, occasionally spotting a worm or some other crawling creature that they would attempt to capture. In late afternoon, the older children would return from school and go about their chores, enjoying the freedom that the change of season allowed. All but Tessie. If she found enjoyment in anything, she hid it from Delphinia.

It seemed that no matter how earnestly Delphinia prayed, she had not been able to make an inroad with Tessie. She tried everything from cajoling to ignoring her but nothing seemed to work. The young girl was determined to do all in her power to make those around her miserable, particularly Delphinia. She was not unkind to the other children, yet she did not go out of her way to help them. She performed her chores but if Delphinia requested additional help, she would become angry or sulk. When Jonathan was about, she was on her best behavior although it was obvious that even at those times, she was unhappy.

Saturday arrived bright and sunny and Jonathan declared it would be a wonderful day for fishing down at the creek. In return for preparation of a picnic lunch, he offered to take all of the children on the excursion and give Delphinia some much-needed time alone. She was overwhelmed by the offer and questioned whether he thought the twins would allow him to do any fishing. When he assured her he would be able to handle the twins, she began packing a lunch for their outing.

"I'm not going," Tessie announced in a voice that almost defied either of them to oppose her decision.

"I'd like you to come with us, Tessie," her uncle answered, sitting down at the kitchen table with a cup of coffee. "Delphinia has little time to herself. She's had to care for all of us without much opportunity for leisure. I hope you'll reconsider your decision."

"If she doesn't want me around, I'll stay out on the porch or in the orchard," she petulantly answered.

"No, I'd like to have you stay with me, Tessie. If you don't want to go fishing, we can enjoy the day together," Delphinia replied sweetly, looking over at Jonathan to let him know she would not mind.

The children were so excited that Delphinia finally sent them outdoors until she completed packing the lunch and Jonathan was prepared to leave. Following him to the porch, Delphinia noticed the questioning look in his eyes as he turned to bid her farewell.

"We'll be just fine," she assured him. "It's you who will be in for a day of it, believe me! I'm sure there will be no fish returning with you, so I'll have some beans and corn bread ready," she bantered.

"We'll see about that!" Jonathan responded, accepting her challenge. Lifting Nettie upon his shoulders, he grabbed Nate's chubby hand and cautioned Josh not to forget their lunch. Joey ran along carrying the fishing poles Jonathan had crafted, all of them full of eagerness to catch a fish for supper. Waving after the departing group, Delphinia wished them good luck and stood watching until they were out of sight.

Slowly returning to the kitchen, she began clearing the breakfast dishes from the table. "I think I'll make gooseberry pies for dessert tonight, Tessie. If you'll wash off the berries while I finish up the dishes, we can be done in no time. I thought I'd go out to the barn and go through my trunks. I have some things stored out there I'd like to use."

Although there was no response, Tessie picked up the pail of berries and headed toward the well to fetch water. Delphinia noticed that instead of returning to the kitchen to visit, she sat isolated on the porch until her task was completed, and then reappeared.

As Delphinia mixed the pie dough and began to roll it, she asked if Tessie would like to accompany her to the barn.

"I suppose. There's nothing else to do," came the girl's curt reply. Nothing further passed between them and once the gooseberries had been sweetened and poured into the pie shells, Delphinia placed them in the oven.

"I think these will be fine while we're down at the barn. You remind me they're in the oven, if I get forgetful. Once I get going through those trunks, I may get absent-minded." She smiled, removing her apron and throwing it over the back of a wooden chair.

Tessie followed her, giving no acknowledgment that any words had been spoken.

The barn was warm and the smell of hay wafted through the air as Delphinia proceeded to the far stall to see the calf she had pulled into the world only a few weeks ago. How he was growing! Josh had named him "Lucky" and they had agreed it was a good choice.

Tessie stood by waiting, a look of boredom evident on her face, but Delphinia pretended not to notice. They made their way toward the rear of the barn and, after brushing off the dirt, unlatched the hasp and opened the trunk. Lifting the items out one by one, Delphinia began sorting into piles those belongings she wished to take into the house and the ones she would leave packed. From time to time, Tessie would show a spark of interest in an item, but would not allow herself to inquire. Near the bottom of the trunk, wrapped in a woolen blanket, Delphinia found her mother's china teapot. She carefully unwrapped it and stared at it as if she expected it to come to life.

"We've already got a teapot," Tessie exclaimed, wanting her to hurry up.

"Yes, I know. But this was my mother's teapot and her mother's before her. It is very special to me. In fact, I remember the last time it was used," she continued, not particularly caring if the girl listened. She needed to recall the memory, just to validate who she had been, even if no one else cared.

"You may remember I told you about the quilt that's on my bed. My mother and I spent many hours making that quilt. It's probably my most precious possession. When I had finally completed the final stitches and it had passed Mama's inspection, we had a celebration. My mother seldom used this china teapot. It sat on a shelf in the cabinet because she feared it might get broken. It was one of the few possessions her mother had passed on to her when she married and moved to Illinois," Delphinia related as Tessie stared toward the barn door.

"Anyway, that day my mother had baked bread and she said we were going to have a tea party to commemorate the completion of my first quilt. She brewed a special mint tea in this teapot and cut slices of warm bread for us. She even opened one of her jars of preserves and we had such a gay time," she reminisced.

"Do you think the pies are done yet?" was Tessie's only remark to the account Delphinia had just given.

"What? Oh, yes, I suppose they'll soon be ready," answered Delphinia, coming back to the present. Lovingly she wrapped the teapot back in the woolen blanket and placed it in the trunk, knowing this was not the time to move it into the cabin. *Perhaps, one day it will sit on a shelf in my home,* she hoped.

Swiftly, she placed one pile of her belongings back in the trunk and bundled the rest in a tablecloth. Walking back to the house with her collection, she could smell the pies and quickened her step.

"Tessie, check those pies while I put this in my room, please," she requested as she stepped into her bedroom, coming face to face with a large Indian bouncing on the edge of her bed.

Stifling the scream that was caught in her throat, she attempted to smile and remain calm. "Tessie, there's an Indian sitting on my bed," she said, staring directly at the warrior. "Try and quietly leave the cabin. I'm hopeful he thinks I'm talking to him, so don't say anything, just leave. He doesn't look like the other Indians that have been to the house. Go to the Aplingtons' for help."

The Indian continued to bounce on the mattress until she quit speaking and then, with alarming speed, he jumped up, pushed his way by her, and ran into the kitchen. Delphinia turned to see him holding Tessie by the arm, pulling her back inside the house. He slammed the door shut and, standing in front of the barrier, motioned they should not attempt to leave.

Slowly he walked toward Tessie and began circling her, occasionally stopping and staring. Tears began to trickle down the girl's face and Delphinia moved closer to place an arm around her, only to have it slapped away by the intruder.

"Stay," he commanded Delphinia, pointing to the spot where she was standing. He moved closer to Tessie and grabbed a handful of her hair and grunted. He stood transfixed, rubbing the locks of red hair back and forth between his fingers, occasionally making some sound.

Tessie, overcome by fear and sure he was planning to scalp her, could stand it no longer and lunged toward Delphinia for protection.

"You—sit," he commanded, pushing the young girl into a chair.

"Obviously, he understands some English, Tessie. Just try to remain calm and I'll see if we can communicate," Delphinia said as soothingly as possible.

Issuing a prayer for help, Delphinia smiled at the uninvited visitor and, while making hand motions, asked, "You hungry? Want to eat?"

She walked toward one of the pies cooling on the table and lifted it toward him as an offering. Lowering and raising his head in affirmation, he reached across the table and, forming his hand into a scoop, dug into the pie and brought out a handful of steaming gooseberries. Letting out a howl, he flung his arm, causing the berries to fly in all directions about the room. Tessie was close to hysteria, unable to control her high-pitch laughter, which further angered the injured warrior.

Dear God, Delphinia prayed silently, *I'm relying on Mark 11:24. You promise that if we believe we've already received what we're praying for, it will be ours. Well, Lord, I believe this Indian is going to leave our house and not harm either of us. The problem is, I'm afraid things have gotten out of control, what with his burned hand and Tessie's continual outbursts. So I'd be real thankful if I could claim that promise right now.*

Assured the matter was safely in God's hands and would be favorably resolved, Delphinia confidently offered the glowering trespasser a wet towel for his hand. He grunted and wrapped the moist cloth around the burn. Tessie became silent until the Indian once again walked to where she sat and began caressing her hair.

"Please, Tessie, try to remain composed. The Lord is going to see us through this, but you must act rationally. I'm going to try and find out what he wants," Delphinia quietly advised. The blue eyes that looked back at her were apprehensive, but Tessie did not cry.

Considering the pie disaster, Delphinia thought it best she try to distract the Indian with something other than food. Eyeing a small mirror, she tentatively offered it. Although somewhat suspicious, curiosity won out and he took the object from her hand. At first, his reflection startled him but then, as he made faces at himself in the glass, he seemed pleased. Soon, he was walking around the room holding it up to objects and peeking to see what had been reproduced for him. Standing behind Tessie, he held the mirror in front of her, producing an image of both their faces that, from the sounds he was making, he found highly amusing.

While the Indian continued his antics with the mirror, Delphinia tried to assemble her thoughts. It was obvious he was quite fascinated with Tessie's red hair. If only she knew what he was planning. No sooner had that thought rushed through her head than the Indian grabbed Tessie's arm and started toward the door.

"We go," he pronounced in a commanding voice.

Once again Tessie broke into wails and Delphinia's heart began pounding as she screamed, "No, stop!" and motioned him into her bedroom. Dragging Tessie along, he followed and was met by Delphinia's display of belongings she had just carried from the barn.

"Take these things," she said, pointing to the array on her bed. "She stays here," she continued, trying to pull Tessie beside her.

A deep grunt emitted while he sorted through the items. He was smiling, which pleased Delphinia, and she whispered to Tessie she should move behind her. He did not seem to notice the movement, or so they thought, as he pulled the tablecloth around the items and tied a large knot.

"I take," he said, placing the bundle on the floor and pointing to himself. "Her, too," he said, indicating Tessie.

Well, this is really beginning to try my patience, Delphinia thought. *Not only is he going to take all my treasures, but he wants Tessie, to boot. I just won't tolerate that kind of behavior. After all, fair is fair!*

Moving a step toward him and placing both hands on her hips, Delphinia looked him full in the eyes and vehemently retorted, "No. Not her." She shook her head negatively and pointed to Tessie. "She's mine," and placed an arm around the girl to indicate possession.

Somewhat taken aback by Delphinia's aggressive behavior, the Indian stood observing the two young women. Raising an arm to his head and lifting a bit of hair, he pointed toward Tessie.

"Oh, no! He wants to scalp me!" the child screamed.

"I don't think he's ever seen red hair before, Tessie. Perhaps if we would just cut a lock or two and give it to him. . . What do you think?" asked Delphinia, not sure of what the Indian wanted.

Tessie merely nodded her head and Delphinia walked to her bureau, removed her sewing scissors, and walked toward Tessie, all under the close observation of the man. Reaching toward the mass of red ringlets, Delphinia snipped a thick lock of hair and handed it to the warrior. He smiled and seemed in agreement.

"You—go now," Delphinia ordered.

Stooping to pick up the bundle, he reached across the bed and in one sweeping motion pulled the quilt from Delphinia's bed and wrapped it around himself.

"Oh, no you don't," yelled Delphinia. "Not my quilt. That's mine and you can't have it," she screamed, attempting to pull it from his shoulders.

Angered by her actions, the Indian threw down the quilt and reached to grab Tessie.

Realizing she had provoked him and was about to lose her advantage, she tried to calm herself. "No, not her. Take me," she said, throwing herself in front of the girl.

The intruder backed up slightly and Delphinia, with tears in her eyes, pleaded, "You can have my quilt, you can have me and all of my belongings. Just don't take this child. She needs to be here with her family. I'll go with you willingly, and I'll give you anything from this house you want. . .just not the girl. Please, not her," she begged.

She did not know how much he understood, or what he would do, but she lifted the quilt back around his shoulders and then held out the bundle that had been resting on the floor.

Looking directly in her eyes, he took the bundle and, wearing her quilt across his shoulders, slowly walked from the room and out of the house.

twelve

Hearing the door close, Delphinia rushed into the kitchen and lowered the wooden bar they used as a lock. Returning to the bedroom, she found Tessie huddled in the far corner of the bedroom, legs drawn to her chest and with her head buried low, resting on her knees. Going to her, Delphinia enveloped the child with both her arms and began talking to her in a soothing, melodic voice. Tessie did not respond and Delphinia began to worry that she had slipped away into the recesses of her own mind, like those people she had heard about, who were sent off to insane asylums.

"Tessie," she said quietly, "this isn't going to do at all. The Lord has kept His promise and we're safe from harm. Now you're going to have to do your part." Moving back slightly and cupping her hands under the girl's chin, she lifted the beautiful crown of red hair until Tessie was eye to eye with her.

Her eyes are vacant and she's not going to respond, Delphinia thought.

"Tessie, I know you may not hear me, but in case you do, I apologize," and then Delphinia landed a resounding slap across the girl's cheek.

"What are you doing?" Tessie asked, dismayed by the act.

Overjoyed with the results, Delphinia hugged her close, laughing and crying simultaneously. "Oh, Tessie, I was so worried you weren't going to respond. I tried to arouse you, but to no avail. I'm so sorry, but I didn't know what else to do but give you a good whack."

"Are you sure he's gone?" the girl sobbed, tightly embracing Delphinia.

"Yes, he's gone, and everything is fine," she reassured, returning the embrace.

Tessie's body trembled and once again she broke into racking sobs. "Why did he try to take me? What if he comes back? What are we going to do?" she wailed between sobs and gulps of breath, her body heaving in distress.

"Tessie, calm yourself. Everything is fine. He won't come back. He's probably miles away by now," she crooned, wiping the girl's tears.

"But what if he isn't? What if he's outside lurking about, just waiting for one of us?" she questioned, faltering in her attempt to gain composure.

"If he wanted one of us, he wouldn't have left the cabin," Delphinia answered, holding the girl and stroking her hair. "We're fine, Tessie, just fine," she assured for what seemed like the hundredth time.

Slowly Tessie's body began to relax and finally she gave Delphinia a half-hearted smile. "Perhaps we should go sit in the kitchen where it's a bit more comfortable," she suggested.

"That's a wonderful idea," Delphinia responded, her cramped body needing to stretch. "I'll put the kettle on for tea."

"We need to talk," Tessie whispered.

"I'd like that very much," came Delphinia's response.

Making their way into the kitchen, Tessie wearily dropped onto one of the wooden chairs. "I know I've been spiteful to you for no apparent reason. You didn't do anything but try to be nice to me. I've treated you horribly and in return you offered yourself to that savage. You allowed him to take your beautiful quilt and other belongings. I know that quilt was very special and yet you gave it willingly for me. Why did you do it?" she coaxed, tears slipping down her face.

Delphinia poured two cups of steaming tea and sat down beside her. "When I first came here I anticipated you would resent me. Your Uncle Jonathan had forewarned me you had not accepted the deaths of your parents. I must add, however, that I didn't expect your bitterness to last this long! Granny and I prayed for you every day, Tessie, and I have continued since her death. We both realized you were in torment and, although it has been difficult at times, I have tried to remember your pain when you've treated me impertinently." She smiled, pausing to take a sip of tea.

"Yes, but *why* did you do it?" she implored.

"This is going to take a few minutes of explanation, Tessie. Please try to be patient. I've been waiting for a very long time for this moment to arrive."

Tessie smiled and Delphinia continued. "You're right about the quilt. It was my pride and joy. But it is merely an object, not a living, breathing child of God, like you. In my prayers, I have consistently asked God to show me a way to give you peace from your anger and turmoil. That Indian's appearance while we were here alone was God's answer to my prayers. Had I not offered myself and those possessions that were important to me, you might never have believed that anybody loved you. I'm sure you know the verse in the Bible that says, 'Greater love hath no man than this—' "

" 'That a man lay down his life for his friends.' John 15:13," interrupted Tessie. "Granny taught me that verse long ago."

"I love you that much, Tessie, and Jesus loves you that much, too. He sacrificed His life for you, so that you could live. . .not be consumed by hate and anger," she said, watching the play of emotions that crossed the girl's face.

"I'm not just angry because Ma and Pa died, Phiney," she began. "Nobody knows everything that happened that day, except me."

"Perhaps you'd feel better if you confided in someone. I know Jonathan would sympathize with anything you told him," Delphinia encouraged.

"No, I think perhaps I should tell you. Uncle Jonathan might not be so understanding. You see, it's my fault. I killed my parents. *Do you still love me now?"* she asked, her voice trembling.

"Yes, Tessie, I still love you. But since you've taken me into your confidence, would you consider telling me what part you played in their deaths?" she asked in a kindly manner.

Her eyes seemed to glaze over as she recounted the events of that day. Delphinia noted the story was almost identical to what Jonathan had previously related to her on the wagon train.

"So now you can see how I am the cause of their deaths," she said, ending the narrative.

Delphinia stared at her, dumbfounded. "No, Tessie, I don't. Jonathan related that exact account to me before my arrival. Please explain what was your fault," she queried.

"Don't you see? I was the one who wanted to go the creek bed route. If we had gone the other way, we would have been safe," she wailed.

"Oh, Tessie," Delphinia whispered, embracing the child, "there is no way we can possibly guess what would have happened if you'd taken the other route. Perhaps the wagon would have been struck by lightning, causing it to go up in flames. Perhaps one of the horses would have broken a leg in a chuckhole causing the wagon to overturn and crush all of you. Any number of things could have happened. We'll never know. What we do know is that the lives of you children were saved. You're not guilty of anything. You asked your father to travel a different road. He knew the dangers that route held and he made a decision to go that direction. His choice was based on knowledge he had available to him. It didn't appear it was going to rain and there were no more hazards than the other road might have had in store for his family. You have no fault in their deaths and no reason to condemn yourself. Somehow, you must accept that fact. Don't die with your parents, Tessie. Let them live through you. If you'll only allow it, others will see the love and gentleness of Sarah and Jake Wilshire shining in your eyes. That's what they would have wanted and I think if you'll search your heart, you know that already."

"I know you're right, but it hurts so much and I don't want them to be forgotten," she confided.

Clasping her hands around Tessie's, Delphinia looked at her with a sense of understanding and said, "How could they ever be forgotten with five such wonderful children? You're a testimony to their lives. It's not easy to lose your parents, but God will help fill that emptiness, if you'll allow it. It's up to you, but I don't think you want a life full of unhappiness and brooding any more than I do. Pray for peace and joy, Tessie, and it will come to you when you least expect it."

The girl gave a half-hearted smile through her tears and whispered, "I'll try."

"I know you will and I'll be praying right along with you."

❧

Jonathan had never been so exhausted. *I don't know how Phiney keeps up with these children all day long, day after day.*

He lost count of the times he had chased after the twins, both of them determined to wander off and pick a flower or run after a squirrel. When they weren't trying to explore, they were playing at the edge of the water, caking mud in their hair and all over their clothes. With no soap or washcloth available, he decided the only way to get them presentable was to dunk them in the creek before starting home. Josh and Joey thought it was hilarious watching their Uncle Jonathan put a twin under each arm and wade into the cool water. Their squeals of protest only added to the boys' enjoyment of the event.

"You guys quit your laughin' and get our gear picked up. It's time we headed back to the house. They'll be expecting some fish for supper, so get a move on."

The air was warm as they made their way through the orchard and, as they approached the cabin, the boys were still chattering about who caught the biggest fish and who tangled the fishing lines. On and on it went, Jonathan ignoring them for the most part and hoping the twins were "dried out" before Phiney got hold of them.

"Wonder why they got the door closed, Uncle Jonathan. You suppose they went visiting somewhere and you'll have to cook the fish?" Josh questioned.

"I don't know, Josh. But if they're gone, you can forget the fish. I'm not cooking. I've about had all the women's work I can stand for one day."

"Ahhh, Uncle Jon, please," came from both boys in unison.

"Let's just wait and see if they are home. Run ahead and check the door, Josh."

"I can't get in, Uncle Jon. It's locked," he yelled back to them.

Terror ran through Jonathan. Why would Phiney have the door barred? There had been no rumors of problems with the Indians and it did not appear that anyone else was at the cabin. Placing the twins on the ground, he took off at full speed toward the cabin, calling back to Joey to remain with the smaller children until he was sure all was safe.

"Phiney, Phiney!" he yelled as he reached the entry and began pounding on the door.

"I'm coming, Jonathan. You needn't yell," she answered, allowing him entry.

His eyes immediately fixed on Tessie. Bedraggled, a red hand print across her cheek, her face wet from tears, and her eyes puffy from crying, he went racing to her, swooping her into his arms.

"What's happened here?" he asked in an accusatory tone, looking directly at Delphinia.

She could feel the hair on the back of her neck begin to bristle at his tone. "Why I've just finished beating her, Jonathan. Why do you ask?" she quietly responded with an angelic smile.

Both women began to laugh, causing Tessie to erupt into loud hiccups. Jonathan stared at the two of them as if they had gone mad. "If you'll quit acting so preposterous, we'll explain what happened. Where are the twins?" Delphinia inquired. "I hope you haven't forgotten them," she smirked.

"That's enough," he answered, calming somewhat. "Joey, you can bring the twins up now," he called out the door.

"Josh, go help him and bring the fish. I'm sure Phiney is ready to eat crow while we eat fish," he said, tilting his head to one side and giving her a crooked grin.

As Josh came in, carrying a string of fish and pulling Nettie along under protest, Jonathan said, "I'd be happy to sit here and listen to the events of the afternoon, ladies, while you fry that fish." But he was not prepared for the story he heard and continually interrupted them, pacing back and forth while they related the tale. Tessie completed the narrative by telling how the Indian finally left the cabin with Delphinia's possessions and her quilt wrapped around him.

"There's an even more important part, but I'll tell you that when we're alone, Uncle Jon," Tessie remarked.

Delphinia smiled and nodded toward the door. "Why don't the two of you take a short walk while I finish supper. We'll be fine in here."

When they returned, Jonathan immediately went to Delphinia and, placing his arms around her, whispered, "How can I ever thank you? She's finally come back to us."

"It wasn't me that did it, Jonathan. It was answered prayer," she responded. "However, if you're determined to find a way to thank me, you can fry this fish for supper," she said, laughing at the look of disdain he displayed with that request.

Grinning, he released her and said, "I should have known you'd be quick with an answer."

thirteen

The morning dawned glorious with puffy white clouds that appeared to almost touch the earth. A pale orange sun shone through, causing a profusion of magnificent colors and the promise of a gorgeous day. Looking out the front door of the place she now called home, Delphinia wondered how anything could be more beautiful. The view nearly took her breath away.

She waved her arm in welcome to Jonathan who was coming from the barn, apparently already through with some of his morning chores. "Breakfast is just about ready. Isn't it a splendid morning?" she called out.

"That it is. We couldn't have planned a better day for going to town," he responded.

Delphinia watched as he continued toward her, knowing Granny had been right. She did love this giant of a man who had turned her world upside down. Her day became joyful just watching him walk into a room. Her feelings were undeniably true and they had been for quite some time, although she did not want to admit it. She had given this thing called "love" a considerable amount of thought. Late at night lying in bed, she had gone through the diverse emotions she had felt for Jonathan since that first day when they had met back in Illinois. They seemed to range from dread and dislike to admiration and caring. For some time she had had difficulty keeping herself from staring at him all the time. Even Tessie had mentioned it and knowingly grinned.

When she considered how Jonathan might feel toward her, she was not so sure her feelings were fully returned. He treated her well, was kind and considerate, and listened to her before making decisions. But that was not love. He treated everyone that way. He had kissed her on a few occasions but it seemed that each of those times had either ended in a quarrel or could be interpreted as pity. She realized he had tried to make the preacher jealous with his attention but she was sure that was so he would not have to go looking for someone else to care for the children. On several occasions, he had mentioned he could not get along without her, but she reasoned that that was because he needed help with the children, not because of love.

"Are those the biscuits I smell burning?" Jonathan asked, bringing her back to the present. "That's just about once a day now you're scorching something, isn't it?" He sat down at the table with a cup of freshly poured coffee. "Is there something wrong with the stove or have you just forgotten how to cook these days?" he joked.

"I think she's in love," Tessie teased.

"That will be enough out of you, Tessie. Get busy and dress the twins so we can get started for town," Delphinia responded angrily, knowing the girl had spoken the truth.

"She's only having fun, Phiney. You don't need to bite her head off," Jonathan responded, giving Tessie a quick hug and nodding for her to get the twins ready.

Irritated with herself for scolding the girl, Delphinia walked into the other room and sat down on the bed. "I'm sorry, Tessie. My remark was uncalled for. Perhaps it made me uncomfortable."

"Why, because it's the truth? Anyone can see you're in love with Uncle Jon. You look like a lovesick calf when he comes into a room, so it's hard not to notice." They both burst out laughing at her remark and Jonathan, hearing the giggles from the bedroom, smiled in relief, pleased that this had not caused discord between the two now that they had become friends.

"How 'bout we get this burned breakfast eaten and get started toward town before nightfall, unless you two would rather stay here and do chores all day," Jonathan called from the kitchen.

That statement brought everyone clamoring for the table and they all agreed the biscuits weren't too bad if you put lots of gravy on them. Delphinia good-naturedly took their bantering and soon they were loaded into the wagon and on their way. Tessie offered to sit in back with both of the twins, allowing Jonathan and Delphinia a small amount of privacy.

"How many supplies do you plan on buying today?" Jonathan queried.

"Just the usual, except Tessie and I want to spend a little time looking about for some thread and fabric. In fact, if you could keep an eye on the younger ones while we do that, I'd be thankful," she responded.

"What are the two of you planning now?" he asked with a grin.

"Tessie's asked me to help her finish the quilt that Sarah started before her death. She wants to use it for her bed. We decided to purchase the items needed to finish it today and, as soon as harvest is over, we'll get started with our sewing."

"You hadn't told me about that. I can't tell you how pleased it makes me that Tessie has finally accepted your friendship. I know Sarah and Granny would be mighty happy," he smiled.

"I think they would be, too, Jonathan. She's a sweet girl and I hope completing the quilt with her will be good for both of us. Somehow, quilting with my mother gave me a feeling of closeness. We would visit and laugh together as we sewed the stitches, knowing each one helped hold the quilt together and made it more beautiful. It's much like the threads of love that tie folks' hearts together. There are the small, tightly sewn stitches, close together, like a family. Then there are the larger, scattered stitches, like the friends we make in our lifetime. I believe God weaves all those threads together in a beautiful pattern to join our hearts and make us who we are, don't you think?"

He looked down at her and a slow smile crossed his face. "You know, you never cease to amaze me with your ideas. That's a beautiful thought, and I agree," he answered, placing his hand on top of Delphinia's.

She glanced toward him and he was staring down at their two hands. She watched as he enveloped hers and gave a gentle squeeze. Slowly, he looked up and met her watchful eyes as Delphinia felt her cheeks flush and a quiver of emotions run through her entire being. The question in her eyes was evident.

"Yes," he said, looking deep into the two, dark brown liquid pools.

"Yes, what?" she inquired. "I didn't ask you anything."

"Yes, you did, Phiney, and the answer is, yes, I love you very much."

Leaning over toward him, she said, "I can't hear you above the children's singing."

"I said I love you, Delphinia Elizabeth Hughes," he said and leaned down to gently place a kiss on her lips.

The children burst forth with hoots of laughter and loud clapping at the scene unfolding in front of them. Jonathan joined in their laughter and then lifted Delphinia's hand to his lips for a kiss, just as they arrived at the general store.

"Jonathan, there's some mail over here for ya'," called Mr. McVay from the rear of the store. "Think there's one in there for Phiney, too."

"For me?" she questioned, looking at Jonathan. "Who would be writing me?"

"Only one way to find out. Let's take a look," he answered as they headed toward the voice.

Jonathan quickly perused the mail and handed over the envelope bearing Delphinia's name. He could see from the return address that it was from her father.

"It's from my pa," she commented. "From the looks of the envelope, he's in Colorado. I think I'll wait until I get home to read it," she said, folding the letter in half and placing it in her skirt pocket.

"I'll go give my order to Mrs. McVay and as soon as she's finished, Tessie and I can look at fabric. I better get back to the children. It looks like the twins are going to try and get into the cracker barrel head first," she exclaimed, moving toward the front of the store at a quick pace.

Jonathan smiled after her but could not shake the feeling of foreboding that had come over him ever since he had seen the letter.

Why now? he thought. *What does he want after all this time?* He did not know how long he had been wandering through the store, aimlessly looking at a variety of tools and dry goods when Tessie's voice brought him to attention.

"Uncle Jon, come on, we've got the order filled except for the thread and fabric. It's your turn to look after the twins."

"Sure, be right there. You women go pick out your sewing things," he smiled back at her.

He could hear them murmuring about the different thread and what color would look good with the quilt top while he helped the younger children pick out their candy.

"Oh, Jonathan, not so much," he heard Delphinia exclaim. She was looking over her shoulder at the twins who had their hands stuffed full of candy.

His attempts to extract the candy from their clenched fists resulted in wails that could be heard throughout the store. Grabbing one under each arm, Jonathan looked over at Delphinia and with a weak smile replied, "Guess I'm not doing my job very well. Think we better get out of here."

"We'll be along in just a few minutes," she called after him.

"Tessie, I think we'd better make our choices soon. Otherwise, your Uncle Jon may be forced to leave without us. I don't think he's feeling particularly patient today," she said as the two women gave each other a knowing smile.

Shortly out of town Jonathan spotted a small grove of trees and pulled over so they could have their picnic. Dinner finished, the twins romped with Joey and Josh while the women discussed getting started on the quilt and the preparations they would need to do for the harvest crew. Jonathan seemed distracted and paid little attention to any of the activity surrounding him, appearing lost in his own thoughts until quite suddenly he said, "Tessie, I'd like to visit with Phiney for a few minutes. Would you mind looking after the children?"

"No, of course not, Uncle Jon," she answered, rising from the blanket where she had been sitting.

As soon as Tessie was out of earshot, Jonathan took Delphinia's hands in his, looked directly in her eyes, and asked, "Have you read your pa's letter yet?"

"No, I'd almost forgotten about it. I planned to read it when we get back home. I thought I had mentioned I was going to wait," she answered with a questioning look as she patted the pocket where she had placed the letter.

"You did. I just thought perhaps you had glanced through it and had an idea of what he wanted. I'm concerned why he's writing after all this time," Jonathan remarked.

"Do you want me to read it now? In case it's bad news, I didn't want to spoil our trip, but I'll open it if you prefer," she responded.

"No, you wait like you planned. I suppose we really ought to be getting packed up before it gets much later," he answered, starting to gather their belongings and placing them in the wagon.

"You're right," she said, forcing a smile. "Tessie, would you get the children together while I finish packing the food and dishes. We need to be getting started," Delphinia called to the younger woman.

Noting Jonathan's solemn disposition, Delphinia made every attempt to pull him out of his mood. She sang, made jokes with the children, and even tried to get him to join in their word games but her attempts were fruitless and finally, she ceased trying.

Nearing home a light breeze began to blow across the fields of wheat, causing the grain to bend and rise in gentle waves. "Isn't it beautiful, Jonathan? I've never seen the ocean, but my guess would be it looks a lot like that field of wheat, moving in a contented motion to greet the shore," she smiled.

A smile crossed his face as he looked at her. "I never heard anybody get quite so poetic about it, but you're right. It's downright pretty. Almost as pretty as you!"

"Why, Jonathan Wilshire! You keep up that kind of talk and you'll have me blushing."

"Looks to me like you already are," laughed Tessie from the wagon bed as they pulled up in front of the house.

"Tessie, Josh, let's get this wagon unloaded while Phiney gets Joey and the twins ready for bed," Jonathan instructed as he lifted Delphinia down.

With one of the twins on either side and Joey in the lead, they made their way into the house and, without any difficulty, the younger children were in bed and fast asleep.

"I've got to get a few chores done, so I'll be back in shortly," Jonathan advised Delphinia from the doorway.

"Fine," she smiled. "I'll just put a pot of coffee on and it should be ready by the time you're finished."

After Tessie and Josh had gone to bed, Delphinia sat down in the kitchen. She slid her hand into the pocket of her skirt, pulled out the letter, and slowly opened the envelope.

fourteen

Dearest daughter,

I have asked an acquaintance to pen my letter. I hope this finds you well and happy in Kansas. First, I must say I am sorry for not writing you sooner. I know it was thoughtless of me, and in these almost two years, I should have acted more fatherly. However, I can't change what's in the past, and I'm hopeful you don't hold my unkind actions against me.

I wanted you to know I am in Denver City, Colorado, which is not so very far by train. As you know, I had planned on going to California in search of gold, but I stopped in Colorado and never got farther. I don't expect I will, either.

Delphinia, I am dying. The doctor tells me there is no cure for this disease of consumption but. . . .

Reading that dreaded word caused Delphinia's hand to begin shaking, and the sound of Jonathan coming through the door captured her attention.

"What is it?" he asked, seeing the look of horror written on her face.

"It's Pa. He's got consumption," she quietly answered.

"How bad is he?"

"I'm not sure. I haven't finished the letter yet. Here, let me get you some coffee," she said, starting to rise from her chair.

Gently placing his hand on her shoulder, he said, "No, you finish the letter. I'll get us coffee."

Nodding her assent, she lifted the letter back into sight and read aloud.

"I have implored him to keep me alive so that I may see the face of my darling daughter before I die. He is doing all in his power, practicing his painful bleeding and purging remedies upon me. I am a cooperative patient although at times I feel it would be easier to tell him, 'No more. I shall die now.' If it were not for the fact that I must see you and know you've forgiven me, I would give it up.

"My dearest, darling daughter, I implore you to come to Denver City with all haste so that I may see you before the end comes to me. I have taken the liberty of having a ticket purchased for your departure on the eight o'clock morning train out of Council Grove. You will go

*north to Junction City and board the Kansas Pacific, which will
depart at four-twenty in the evening and arrive in Sheridan at ten the
next morning. It will then be necessary for you to embark by stage
into Denver City on the United States Express Company Overland
Mail and Express Coach. My acquaintance has made all arrangements for your departure on the tenth of July. Your boarding passes
will await you at each stop.*

"I beg you, please do not disappoint me.

"Your loving father."

They stared silently at each other, the lack of noise deafening in their ears.
Finally, Delphinia gave a forced smile and commented, "I wonder who
penned that letter for Pa. It certainly was eloquent."

"Somebody else may have thought up the proper words for him, but it's
his command. He wants you there. What are you going to do?"

"I don't know. It's just so. . .so sudden. I don't know what to think or
what to do. How could I leave now? We've got the harvest crew due here
in a week and if I went I don't know how long I'd need to be gone. Who
would do all the cooking during harvest? Who would take care of the children? Who would look after everything? It's too much of a burden for
Tessie, and yet. . ."

"And yet you're going, isn't that right?" Jonathan queried, knowing his
voice sounded harsh.

"He's my father, Jonathan. My only living relative."

"Right. So where was your only living relative when you wanted to stay
in Illinois? He was selling you off so he could go live his own dreams. He
didn't care about you," he rebutted.

But as soon as the words had been spoken, Jonathan wished he could pull
them back into his mouth for he saw the pain they had caused her.

"Oh, Phiney, I'm so very sorry," he said, pulling her into his arms as she
burst forth into sobs that racked her body. "I'm criticizing your pa for being
selfish and unfeeling and here I am doing the same thing to you."

She buried her head in his shoulder, his shirt turning damp from the deluge of tears. "Please don't cry anymore. You must go to your father. I know
that as well as you. I'm just full of regret for waiting so long to declare my
love and afraid of losing you just when I felt our lives were beginning."

"You're not losing me. I would be gone for only a short time and then I'd
return," she replied.

"I know that's what you think now, but once you get to Colorado, who
knows what will happen. I realize your intentions are to return, but if your
father's health is restored and he wants you to stay, or if you meet someone

else. . . It's better you leave and make no promises to return."

"That's unfair, Jonathan. You make it sound as though I have no allegiance to my word and that I could not honor an engagement—if you ever asked me to marry," she haughtily answered.

He looked down into her face, feeling such a deep love rise up in him he thought he would die from the thought of losing her. "Phiney, I would be honored to have you as my wife but I'll not ask you for your hand in marriage until you return to Kansas. You're an honest, courageous woman and I know you would make every effort to honor your word, but I'll not try to hamper you in that way. It would be unfair. We'll talk marriage if you return. Right now, we need to talk about getting you ready to leave."

"If that's what you truly want, Jonathan. But we will talk marriage when I return," she answered adamantly.

They talked until late deciding how to accomplish all that needed to be done before Jonathan could take her to Council Grove to meet the train. By the time they had completed their plans, both of them were exhausted. Delphinia bid Jonathan good night from the front porch and, as she watched him walk toward his cabin, her heart was heavy with the thought of leaving this family she had grown to love. Yet deep inside, she ached to once again see her father and knew she must go.

❧

Morning arrived all too soon and both Delphinia and Jonathan were weary, not only from their lack of sleep but from the tasks that lay ahead. The older children uttered their disbelief that Delphinia would even consider leaving, sure they could not exist without her. Amidst flaring tempers and flowing tears, preparations for her departure continued.

Mrs. Aplington agreed to make arrangements with the neighboring farm women to feed the harvest crew and she talked to Jennie O'Laughlin who knew a widow who agreed to come and help care for the children. Delphinia packed her smallest trunk in an effort to assure Jonathan she would not be gone long, and the next morning, after many tears and promises to write, they were on their way to meet the train.

It was a trip filled with a profusion of emotions. Fear of riding the train and meeting a stage by herself, traveling such a great distance, leaving the farm, the children, and man she now loved so dearly, all mixed with the anticipation of seeing her father.

"We've got time to spare. Let's go over to the hotel restaurant and get a hot meal," Jonathan suggested, trying to keep things seeming normal.

The meal smelled delicious but somehow the food would not pass over the lump in her throat and she finally ceased trying. The two of them made small talk, neither saying the things that were uppermost in their minds.

"Better finish up. The train is about ready to pull out. They're loading the baggage," Jonathan remarked.

"I guess I wasn't as hungry as I thought. Let's go ahead and leave," she answered, pushing back the wooden chair, causing it to scrape across the floor.

She waited as Jonathan paid for their meal and slowly they trod toward the waiting train.

"Looks like there's not many passengers so you should be able to stretch out and relax a little," Jonathan stated, trying to keep from pulling her into his arms and carrying her back to his wagon.

She smiled and nodded, knowing that if she spoke at this moment, her voice would give way to tears and she did not want to cry in front of these strangers.

"Them that's goin', let's get on board," the conductor yelled out.

Jonathan pulled her close and Delphinia felt as though his embrace would crush the life out of her. She tilted her head back and was met by his beautiful blue eyes as he lowered his head and covered her mouth with a tender kiss.

"I love you, Delphinia Elizabeth Hughes, and the day you return, I'll ask you to be my wife," he said as he lifted his head.

"I love you also, Jonathan, and I shall answer 'yes' when you ask for my hand in marriage," she responded, smiling up at him.

He leaned down, kissed her soundly, and then turned her toward the train. "You need to board now. You'll be in our thoughts and prayers," he said as he took hold of her elbow and assisted her up the step and onto the train.

Standing on the platform, he watched as she made her way to one of the wooden seats, trying to memorize every detail of her face for fear he would never see her again.

Peering out the small window, trying to smile as a tear overflowed each eye, she waved her farewell while the train slowly clanked and chugged out of the station, leaving nothing but a billow of dark smoke hanging in the air.

Exhausted from the days of preparation for her trip, Delphinia leaned her head against the window frame and was quickly lulled to sleep by the clacking sounds of the train. She startled awake as the train jerked to a stop and the conductor announced their arrival in Junction City. Gingerly stepping onto the platform, she made her way into the neat, limestone train depot and inquired about her ticket to Sheridan, half expecting to be told they had never heard of her. Instead, the gentlemen handed her a ticket, instructed her as to the whereabouts of a nearby restaurant, and advised her that the train would leave promptly at 4:20 P.M. and that she best not be late.

The information she received was correct. As they pulled out of the station,

Delphinia noted it was exactly 4:20 P.M. She found pleasure in the sights as they made their way farther west but as nightfall arrived, she longed to be back at the cabin, getting the children ready for bed and listening to their prayers. They were due to arrive in Sheridan the next morning at 10:00 but the train was running late, causing Delphinia concern she might miss her stage although the conductor assured her they would arrive in ample time.

Once again, she found her ticket as promised when she arrived at the stage line, although the conductor had been wrong. She had missed the last stage and would have to wait until the next morning. That proved to be a blessing. She was able to make accommodations at the small hotel and even arranged to have a bath in her room. It was heavenly! In fact, later she tried to remember just how heavenly that bath had been, sitting cramped on the stage between two men who smelled as though they hadn't been near water in months. The dust and dirt billowed in the windows of the stage, making her even more uncomfortable, but at least she hadn't been forced to eat at the filthy way stations along the route. The hotel owner's wife had warned her of the squalid conditions she would encounter on the trip, counseling Delphinia to take along her own food and water, which had proved to be sound advice.

The trip was long and arduous and when the man beside her said they would soon be arriving in Denver City, she heaved a sigh of relief. The stage rolled into town with the horses at full gallop and then snapped to a stop. Delphinia's head bobbed forward and then lurched back, causing her to feel as though her stomach had risen to her throat and then quickly plummeted to her feet. Not to be denied refreshment at the first saloon, her traveling companions disembarked while the coach was still moving down the dusty street. She almost laughed when the stage driver looked in the door and said, "You plannin' on jest sittin' in there or you gonna get out, ma'am?"

"I thought I'd wait until we came to a full stop," she answered with a slight smile.

"Well, this is about as stopped as we'll be gettin, so better let me give ya a hand," he replied as he reached to assist her down.

"Thank you," she answered, just in time to see the other driver throw her trunk to the ground with a resounding thud.

"You got someone meetin' ya?" he inquired.

"I'm not sure. Perhaps it would be best if you'd move my trunk from the middle of the street into the stage office. I would be most appreciative," she said.

Delphinia was on her way to the office to inquire if her father had left a message when she heard a voice calling her name. Turning, she came face to face with the man who had called out to her.

"Miss Hughes, I'm sorry I'm late. We expected you on the last stage. Your father was so upset when you didn't arrive, that I've had to stay with him constantly. He went to sleep just a little while ago and I didn't notice the time. Please forgive me. The time got away before I realized. I hope you've not been waiting long."

"No. I just arrived," she responded. "But how did you know who I was?"

"Your father told me to look for a beautiful blond with big brown eyes. You fit his description," he answered with a grin.

"I find it hard to believe my father would say I'm beautiful, Mister. . . I'm sorry but I don't know your name."

"It's Doctor. . .Doctor Samuel Finley, at your service, ma'am. And your father did say you are beautiful, you may ask him," he replied.

"You're the doctor my father wrote about? The one that diagnosed and has been treating him for consumption?" she questioned.

"One and the same. I'm also the acquaintance that penned the letter to you and made arrangements for your trip," he advised.

"Well, I suppose my thanks are in order, Dr. Finley. I'm sure my father appreciates your assistance as much as I do. Will you be taking me to my father now?"

"Since he's resting, perhaps you'd like to get settled and refresh yourself."

"If you're sure there's time before he awakens, that would be wonderful," she answered.

Having loaded her trunk, he assisted her into his buggy and after traveling a short distance, they stopped in front of a white frame house with an iron fence surrounding the neatly trimmed yard. Small pink roses were climbing through latticework on each end of the front porch, and neatly trimmed shrubs lined both sides of the brick sidewalk.

"Is this my father's house?" she asked with an astonished look on her face.

"No," he replied. "This is my house. Your father needs almost constant care and since he had no one here to stay with and I'm alone, we agreed this arrangement would be best."

When she did not respond but gave him a questioning look, he continued by adding, "It's really easier for me. I don't have to get out to make house calls since he's right here with me."

"I understand," she answered as he led her into the fashionably appointed parlor, although she was not quite sure she understood anything.

"You just sit down and make yourself at home while I fetch your trunk and then you can get settled," he advised, exiting the front door.

Delphinia watched out the front window as Dr. Finley walked toward the buggy. He was tall, although not as tall as Jonathan, perhaps an inch or two shorter. He had hair that was almost coal black with just a touch of gray at the temples and a slight wave on either side, gray eyes, and the complexion of a man who worked outdoors rather than practiced medicine. His broad shoulders allowed him to carry her trunk with apparent ease and he carried himself with an air of assurance, perhaps bordering on arrogance, Delphinia thought.

She moved away from the window as he entered the house and when he beckoned for her to follow him, she did so without question.

"This is to be your room; I hope you will find it adequate. But if there is anything you need, please let me know. You go ahead and freshen up and I'll check on your father. I promise to let you know as soon as he's awake," he said as he left the room, pulling the door closed behind him.

After washing herself, she unpinned her hair and began to methodically pull the short-bristled brush through the long blond tresses. Leaning back on the tapestry-covered chair, she took note of her surroundings. The walnut dressing table at which she sat was ornately carved with a large oval mirror attached. The bed and bureau were both made of matching walnut and boasted the same ornate carving. All of the windows were adorned with a frilly blue-and-white sheer fabric, the coverlet on the bed matching the blue in the curtains. A beautiful carpet in shades of blue and ivory covered the floor, complementing the other furnishings. It looked opulent and was a startling contrast to the rudimentary conveniences on her journey. She found herself wondering why a doctor would have such a feminine room in his house. Everything, she noted, including the blue-and-white embroidered scarves on the dressing table, emphasized a woman's touch. A knock on the door and Dr. Finley's announcement that her father was awake brought Delphinia's wandering thoughts to an abrupt halt.

fifteen

When Delphinia finally opened the door, Samuel Finely came eye to eye with a beautiful young woman. Her hair, golden and wavy, hung loose to her shoulders, making a wreath around her oval face. The paleness of her skin was accentuated by her deep brown eyes that held just a glint of copper and her lips seemed to have a tiny upward curve with a very slight dimple just above each end of her mouth.

He stood staring at her until Delphinia, not sure what he was thinking, reached toward her hair and remarked, "I guess I was daydreaming. I didn't get my hair pinned up just yet."

"You look absolutely radiant," he replied and smiled as a deep blush colored her cheeks.

"I'll take you to your father now," he said, breaking the silence that followed his compliment.

"Does my father know I've arrived?" she asked, following him down the hallway.

"He does, but try not to look surprised by his appearance when you see him. He's lost weight and his general health is very poor," he responded.

Opening the door for her, he stood back as she brushed by him to enter the room, a distinct scent of lilac filling his nostrils.

"Papa," she almost cried as she made her way to the emaciated figure that lay on the bed, his thin arms outstretched to embrace her.

"Ah, Delphinia, you've let your hair down the way I like it. Come give your papa a hug," he responded in a weakened voice she almost did not recognize. Dr. Finley momentarily watched the unfolding reunion and then quietly backed out the doorway, pulling the door closed behind him.

Her heart ached as she held him, but she forced a bright smile and then said, "I'm not a child anymore, Pa."

"You'll always be my child," he said, reaching up to lay his hand alongside her face. "I know I've done wrong by you and before I die I need your forgiveness for sending you off the way I did. I know now it was selfish and wrong. Say you'll forgive me, Delphinia," he requested in a pleading voice.

"I forgave you long ago, Pa. I was angry when you sent me away and then when I found out you'd gone so far as to advertise in a newspaper to find someplace to send me, I was horrified—"

"I just wasn't—" he interrupted.

"No, Pa. Let me finish. I was shocked and devastated you would do that. Later, though, after some time had passed and I had prayed steadfastly for understanding, I no longer resented your actions. It caused me a lot of pain, but that's behind me now. I've missed you but my life with the Wilshires has been good. You must now concentrate on making yourself well and quit worrying about my forgiveness," she finished.

Tears brimmed his sunken eyes as her father gave a feeble smile. "I don't deserve your forgiveness or love, but I am thankful for both. As for concentrating on getting well, I'm afraid that's not possible. This illness seldom allows its victims to regain their health. Besides, your forgiveness is all I want. Now I don't care when I die," he said, caressing her hand.

"Papa, my forgiveness is not most important," she said. "It's God's forgiveness we must always seek. It is important to ask those we offend to forgive us, but most importantly we must repent and ask God's forgiveness for our sins. I know you used to go to church, but did you accept Jesus as your Savior and invite Him into your heart? Did you repent and ask God's forgiveness of your sins? Have you tried to live a life that would be pleasing to God? If not, Papa, you're not ready to die and I won't get to see you in heaven. I want us to be together again one day. Just think, you and Mama and me, together in heaven," she said, not sure how he would react to her intonation.

"You're a lot like your mama, young lady," he said. "Maybe you're right and I have been looking in the wrong direction for my forgiveness. You continue to pray for me and I'll ask for some forgiveness. It probably wouldn't hurt for me to have a talk with the preacher," he said and then broke into a spasm of racking coughs.

Hearing the sound, Dr. Finley entered the room just as Delphinia rose from her chair to fetch him.

"Don't worry. This is common with his illness. Why don't you let him rest a while. Sometimes talking causes these bouts to come on, but it will cease shortly," he reassured her. "Why don't you take a few minutes and relax outside. We'll be having dinner soon."

Sitting on one of the two rockers that faced each other on the front porch, Delphinia uttered a prayer of thankfulness for her father's receptive attitude to their conversation about God. As she finished her prayer, Dr. Finley walked out the door and sat down in the chair opposite her.

"He's doing fine," he said in answer to the questioning look she gave him.

"Is there anything I can do to assist? I'm a decent cook and would be happy to help," she offered.

"Well, I thank you kindly but I'm afraid my neighbor, Mrs. O'Mallie, might take offense. She's been cooking for me ever since my wife passed away. She likes making the extra money and I like having a warm meal. She looks after your pa when I have to be gone on calls, and she even does my laundry. Her husband passed away a week after my wife, Lydia, so we've been a help to each other," he responded.

"I'm sorry about your wife," she said, not sure how to react to his casual declaration of her death.

"Don't be. She suffered from severe mental depression after the death of our baby and never got over it. Several months after the baby died, she contracted typhoid and was actually happy about it. She wanted to die. It's been eight years now and I've made my peace with the situation," he responded, giving her a slight smile.

"And you never remarried?" Delphinia asked, realizing too late that her question was intrusive and wishing she could take it back.

Dr. Finley burst into laughter as he watched how uncomfortable the young woman had become once she issued her question.

"No," he replied. "I've never met the right woman, although I believe that may have changed several hours ago. Your father told me what a beautiful, high-spirited daughter he had, but I thought it was the usual boasting of a proud parent. I find he spoke the truth and I couldn't be more delighted."

Disconcerted by the doctor's remarks, Delphinia began pressing down the pleats in her skirt with the palm of her hand in a slow, methodical motion. "I'm sure my pa told you of my temper and feisty behavior, also," she replied, trying to make light of the compliments.

"I believe he did, at that," he answered and gave a chuckle. "Looks like Mrs. O'Mallie is on her way to the back door with dinner. I better go meet her," he said as he bounded out of the chair and into the house.

Later, lying in bed, Delphinia reflected upon the events of the day. Exhausted, she had unpacked only what was necessary for the night and then had fallen into bed, sure she would be asleep before finishing her prayers. But instead of sleep, her mind kept wandering back to the conversation on the front porch with Dr. Finley. During dinner he had insisted that she call him Sam and he had certainly made her feel at home. Yet she was not sure how to take some of the remarks he made, nor how much her pa had told him about why she lived in Kansas.

❧

The next week passed quickly. Sam was always there, willing to help in any way she asked. He arranged for the preacher to visit with her father, posted her letters, insisted on showing her around town, and still maintained a thriving medical practice. Most of the time she spent with her father and when she would mention returning to Kansas, he would beg her to remain until his death.

Toward the beginning of the second week she confided in Sam that she planned to leave within the next few days.

"I'd rethink that decision. If you leave, I'm sure it will break your father's heart," he said, knowing he was arguing as much for himself as he was for her father.

"But you've told me he may live for a month or longer. I couldn't possibly wait that long," she argued, feeling selfish. "Besides, I told the Wilshires I would be gone for only a few weeks at the most," she continued, trying to defend her position, his statements adding to her guilt.

She was torn by uncertainty, feeling that she would fail someone, no matter what. Her prayers had been fervent about where she belonged, but no answer had been forthcoming, at least none that she could discern. She hadn't even unpacked all her clothing, fearing she would begin to feel settled.

As the days passed and her indecision continued, Sam and her father felt assured that she would remain in Denver City. She accompanied Sam to several socials at the church and he proved to be an enjoyable companion, making her realize that city life held a certain appeal. But she found herself missing Jonathan and the children. The letters she received from them were cheerful and told of missing her, but not to worry about them. They did not ask when she would return, and she did not mention it in her letters to them.

Delphinia's father watched out the window by his bed as she and Sam came up the sidewalk returning from an evening stroll, her arm laced through his. Her father gave a slight smile as they stepped out of his sight and onto the porch.

"Let's sit here on the porch and visit a while, if you're not too tired," Sam invited.

"How could I be tired?" she bantered. "I do nothing but sit all day."

"You are growing restless, aren't you? I could sense it all day," he responded.

"Sam, I'm used to hard work and keeping busy. I've been caring for five children and a homestead out on the Kansas prairie. I miss the children and I guess I miss the work, too," she admitted.

"You're far too beautiful to work on a farm. There's no need for you to return to that kind of life. You should be living in a city, married, and having children of your own. Don't you want to have your own children?" he asked.

"Of course I want to have my own children, but that doesn't cause me to love or miss the Wilshires any the less. You say there's no need to return to that kind of life. My father doesn't have much longer to live by your calculations and once he's gone, I'll have no one but my substitute family in Kansas. I think that is where I belong," she stated.

Reaching toward her he took hold of her hand and lifted it to his lips, gently placing a kiss in the center of her palm. "No, Delphinia, you belong here with me. I care for you more than you can imagine. I have from the first day you arrived."

"Oh, Jonathan. . .I. . .I mean, Samuel," she stammered. "I think I had better retire," she said, rising from the chair and moving toward the front door.

"So I do have competition. It's not just the children you miss. Are you in love with this Kansas farmer?" he asked, blocking her entry to the house.

"I. . .well, I think so," she finally answered.

The last word had barely passed her lips when he drew her into his arms and kissed her with an impatient fervor that almost frightened her.

"Please, don't. I must check on my father," she said, entering the house and leaving him on the front porch.

୬

"I wasn't sure if you'd still be awake, Pa," Delphinia said, approaching his bedside.

"You two have a nice walk?"

"Why, uh, I guess so. Yes, it's a pleasant evening. I wish you could be outdoors a while and enjoy it with me," she answered, trying to hide her emotions over the recent incident with Sam.

"I get a nice breeze through the window. Sometimes I even hear people talkin' on the porch," he said with a grin.

She did not respond but began to tidy the room and straighten his sheets.

"He's a good man, Delphinia. You couldn't ask for a better catch to marry up with. I know he's thinkin' hard on the prospect of asking you 'cause he asked if I'd have any objection," her father continued.

Her head jerked to attention at his remark. "What did you tell him?" she asked, her voice sounding harsh to her ears.

"I didn't mean to upset you. I thought you'd be happy to know he was interested in you. I told him I didn't know anyone I'd be more pleased to have marry my daughter, but he'd have to take it up with you," he answered, seeing that she was disturbed by the conversation.

"Pa, I'm not looking for a prize catch. I'm not even looking for a husband. The only reason I came to Denver City was to see you and then I'll be returning to Kansas. In fact, I should have returned a week ago," she responded.

"Now, I've gone and made you unhappy and you're gonna run off and leave me here to die alone, aren't ya?" he asked, hoping her tender heart would not allow her to rush off in anger.

"You've not made me unhappy, Pa. I know you're thinking about my future, but I've been on my own for some time now and I don't need anyone making marriage plans for me. Besides, Jonathan Wilshire has pledged his love and intent to marry me once I return to Kansas," she told him as she rearranged the small bottles on a nearby table for the third time.

"Those bottles look fine; you've straightened them enough. Now come and sit down here," he said, indicating the chair beside him.

"Delphinia, I'll not try and push you into any marriage. Folks need to marry those they love. I know that. I loved your ma like I could never love anyone else. But there's a lot to be said for finding the person you're suited to. It makes things run smoother."

"I know that. But I think Jonathan and I are suited," she answered.

"Maybe so. I thought your ma and I were, too. I tried to make her happy but she longed for city life and even though I helped her as much as I could, it was a hard life. She always wanted the kind of life she'd had as a child, but she gave in to my dreams and left it behind. I'm not sure she ever got over leaving her family," he continued.

"She wasn't unhappy and you know it, Pa. We both know she would have preferred living in the East, close to her family, but she understood."

"I was married to her, child. You saw what she wanted you to see. But many's the night I listened to her cry about life out in the middle of nowhere and longin' to see her family and lead a city life. I'm real sorry I did that to her," he said, a distant look in his eyes.

"You did the best you could," Delphinia answered, not knowing what to say that would relieve some of his pain.

"That's true. I did. The only thing I could have done different would have been to stay in the city. You got that chance to stay now. It's what your ma would have wanted for you and here you are with this wonderful opportunity. Denver's not like those big eastern cities, but it's an up-and-coming kind of town. One day it's gonna be grand, for sure," he boasted.

"That was Ma who wanted the big city. I've never said that."

"Perhaps, but you could have a good life here. You're too young to be tied down to somebody else's children. Doc Finley's a fine man and he could take care of you. You'd never want for anything and you could eventually have children of your own. You'd be able to give them what they needed without worrying about money," he said, beginning to cough from the exertion of talking so much.

"That's enough for tonight, Pa. You're getting excited and you're going to make yourself worse. I'm going to get your medicine ready and then I want you to get some rest," she said as she moved toward the bottles and poured out a spoonful of the yellow liquid.

"I'll take the medicine and go to sleep if you promise to think on what we've talked about," he responded and then clenched his mouth together like a small child.

Looking at his face she was unable to hold back her laughter. "It's a deal. Now open up," she said as she cradled his head and lifted him to take the spoon.

She leaned down and placed a kiss on his cheek. "Good night, Papa. I love you."

Smiling, he bid her good night with the admonition she think hard on his words. She smiled and nodded her assent as she left the room and pulled the door closed behind her.

"How is he?" Sam asked.

Delphinia jumped at the sound of his voice. "You startled me. I thought you'd gone to bed," she said, turning to find him sitting on the stairway outside her father's bedroom. "He's doing pretty well. He got a bit excited and talked too much, which caused his cough to start up. I just gave him his medicine and hopefully he'll get a good night's rest," she answered.

"I want to apologize for my behavior this evening. I didn't mean to offend you. I care for you very much and it's been difficult for me not to kiss you before now," he stated.

"Perhaps this is something we should talk about another time. I'm really very tired," she answered and moved toward her bedroom.

"Whenever you're ready, my love," he said, going up the stairway.

Quickly, she made her way down the hallway to her bedroom, but could not deny the small flutter she felt when he used the term of endearment.

She lay in bed thinking of the things both her pa and Sam had said. *I do want children of my own and I wonder if I'll grow weary of raising my Kansas family and never really have time for my own.*

Tossing restlessly, she questioned the excitement she felt when Dr. Finley had called her by a term of endearment.

"Can I be in love with Jonathan and still feel something for another man?" she whispered to herself.

That night her prayers were fervent for God's direction.

sixteen

Delphinia awakened to a day that had dawned bright and sunny with a crispness to the air, giving notice that summer was over. Just as she finished making her bed, she heard the back door slam and Mrs. O'Mallie enter the kitchen.

"I'll be right there to help you, Mrs. O'Mallie," she called out.

"Take your time. I'm in no hurry," the older woman answered.

"Here, let me take that tray," Delphinia offered as she entered the room, reaching toward the huge silver platter and placing it on the kitchen table.

"It's a beauty of a day out there and I've been thankin' the Lord for that. Don't want anything to spoil our meeting tonight," Mrs, O'Mallie said.

"You have special plans for today?" Delphinia inquired hospitably.

"Why, sure. It's the autumn revival. Thought maybe Doc Finley might have mentioned it. All the churches get together and have one big revival each fall. It's going be wonderful. There's a service every night this week so if your pa is doing all right, I hope you'll come," Delphinia invited.

"I'd love to, but I'll have to see how he's feeling later this afternoon. Thank you for telling me about it," Delphinia answered.

"Well, guess I better be gettin' back home. You give thought to coming tonight," Mrs. O'Mallie said, leaving out the back door.

"Looks like Mrs. O'Mallie's already been here and gone," Sam said as he entered the kitchen.

"She just left. I'll take Pa's tray to him. You go ahead and eat," she responded.

"I'll wait for you," he answered as she left the room.

"There's no need to do that," she said, walking out of the kitchen before he could respond.

"Good morning, Pa. How are you feeling today?" she inquired, thinking he looked thinner each day.

"Not too bad, but I'm not hungry. You go eat. I'll try and eat later." But seeing the look of determination on his daughter's face, he shook his head and said, "I'm not going to eat now, so you needn't argue with me. Go!"

"All right, all right," she answered with a smile. "I'm going."

"He's not hungry," she announced, walking into the kitchen and sitting down opposite Sam at the wooden table.

"Don't look so downcast. That doesn't necessarily mean anything bad. We all have times when we're not hungry. Looks to me like you'd better quit worrying about your pa's eating and take a nap this afternoon. Those dark circles under your eyes tell me you didn't get much sleep last night."

"You're right, I didn't. I'll think about the nap if you'll tell me about the revival," she said.

"Revival? How'd you hear about that?" he questioned.

"Mrs. O'Mallie told me. I'd love to go if Pa is all right. Do you think that would be possible?" she asked.

He smiled as he watched her face become animated and bright, like a child seeing a jar of peppermint sticks.

"There's really nothing to tell. Several years ago the churches here in Denver City decided to have one big revival each autumn. They all get together and select a preacher to come and they hold services outdoors every night. If the weather doesn't cooperate, they go over to the Methodist church, since it's the biggest. I don't see any reason why you couldn't go, but not unescorted since it's held during the evening," he responded.

"Perhaps I could go with Mrs. O'Mallie," she suggested.

"If your pa's doing all right, I'll escort you," he said, "at least this one evening, but you must promise to rest this afternoon."

"I will," she answered delightedly. "Our breakfast is probably cold. Do you want to give thanks?" she asked.

"You go ahead and do it for us," he answered.

"Mrs. O'Mallie certainly knows how to start off the day with a hearty breakfast," he said, having devoured all that was on his plate and wiping his hands with the large cloth napkin. "I'd better get busy on my house calls. Don't forget your pa's medicine this morning and I expect you to be taking a nap when I return," he admonished.

"Oh, I will be," she answered, excited by the prospect of the evening.

"Guess what, Papa," she exclaimed, almost skipping into his room.

"I don't know what to guess except that something has made you happy," he ventured.

"There's a revival beginning tonight and Sam said that if you're doing all right this evening and if I take a nap this afternoon, he'll escort me. Isn't that wonderful?"

"Well, it certainly is wonderful and I'll be doing just fine. You just be sure and get that nap and find yourself something to wear," he said, pleased to see her so happy about going out with Sam.

"Something to wear. Oh, yes. I'd not even thought of that. I'll need to look in my trunk and see if I can find something extra special. Oh, and then I'll need to get it pressed. I'd better get that done or I'll not have my nap taken before Sam returns," she said.

"You get a move on then. I'm feeling fine and I'll ring the bell if I need anything," he promised.

He waved her out of the room as she blew him a kiss and headed toward the doorway. *Perhaps she's decided that Sam would be the right man for her, after all,* he thought, pleased by the prospect.

Delphinia lifted the lid on the partially empty trunk. She still hadn't completely unpacked the contents. *I hope I packed something warmer in the bottom of this trunk,* she thought, methodically removing each item. Lifting a dark gold dress, her eyes flew open at the fabric tucked within the folds of the dress. It was Sarah's quilt top! And there, underneath the dress was a neatly folded piece of paper. She sat down on the edge of the bed and slowly opened the page.

Dear Phiney,
    While you were busy with the twins, I packed Mama's quilt top in with your dress. I want you to come back to Kansas. I didn't know how else to be sure of your return. I'm hoping the threads of love in this quilt are strong enough to bring you home to us.

                                                            Love,
                                                            Tessie

Tears rolled down her cheeks as she read the letter a second time. The words tugged at her heart and made her even more lonely for Kansas and the family she had left behind. *I've got to make a decision soon,* she thought, folding the letter and placing it with the quilt top in her trunk. *Surely God will give me an answer soon.*

She carried her dress into the kitchen, searching until she found a pressing board and then heated the iron. Carefully she pressed the gown, watchful not to burn the silk fabric. Certain all the wrinkles had been removed, she draped it over a chair in her bedroom and took the promised nap.

Later, she could hardly wait for dinner to be over in order to clear off the dishes and get ready. Sam had declared her father was doing fine and they would leave in an hour. She took her time getting ready, pinning her hair up on top of her head, and then securing it with a thin, black and gold ribbon. A white lace collar surrounded the neckline of her dress and she placed a gold earring in each lobe. Looking at her reflection in the mirror above the walnut bureau, she remembered that the last time she had worn the earrings had been when Pastor Martin escorted her to the dance. She smiled, thinking about that night when Jonathan had become their uninvited guest. *It seemed so long ago, almost a different world,* she mused.

"You about ready? Your pa wants to see you before we leave. I'll wait in his room," Sam said, knocking on the door.

"Be right there," she answered. Taking one last look in the mirror, she pinned a wisp of hair and then went to her father's room.

Her entry brought raves from her father who insisted that she twirl around several times so he could see her from all angles. Sam was silent, although she could feel his eyes on her from the moment she entered the room.

"We'd better leave or we'll be late," he said, rising from the chair.

"Are you sure you'll be okay, Pa?"

"I'm sure. Now you two go on and have a nice time," he instructed.

Sam had drawn his carriage to the front of the house and carefully assisted her into the buggy, his two black horses appearing sleek in the semidarkness.

"You look quite beautiful. I didn't want to tell you in front of your father for fear of causing you embarrassment. Besides, it would have been difficult to get a word in," he said, smiling down at her.

"Fathers tend to think their daughters are beautiful, no matter what," she responded.

"Perhaps. But in your case it's true," he answered as he pulled himself into the buggy and flicked the reins.

"How far is it to the meeting place?" she asked, wanting to change the subject.

"Not far, just south of town. There's a large grove and they set up benches and chairs, whatever they can move from the churches. There's been ample seating when I've been there," he commented.

The crowd had already begun to gather by the time they arrived. Mrs. O'Mallie had saved seats, hopeful they would attend. She was in the third row, waving them forward with unbridled enthusiasm.

"Oh, there's Mrs. O'Mallie. Come on, Sam, we can sit up front. She's saved seats," Delphinia pointed out, tugging his arm.

"I'd rather sit farther back, if it's all the same to you," he answered, holding back.

"Oh," she said, somewhat surprised, "that's fine. I'll just go tell Mrs. O'Mallie. Why don't you see if you can find a spot for us."

The older woman was disappointed and Delphinia would have much preferred to sit up front, but deferred to Sam's choice since he had been kind enough to escort her.

The services were all that Delphinia had hoped for. The preacher was dynamic and the crowd was receptive to his message. They sang songs, read Scripture, and heard the Word preached, and when the service was over, Delphinia could hardly wait to return for the next evening.

"Wasn't it wonderful?" she asked Sam as they made their way to the buggy.

"It was interesting," he responded, saying nothing further.

Delphinia was so excited about the meeting, she did not note how quiet Sam had been, nor the fact that he had little to say the whole way home.

When they finally reached the porch, she said, "Do you think we could go tomorrow?" She sounded so full of anticipation. He thought once again of a child being offered candy.

"I don't think so," he answered, watching as her face became void of the animation it had held just minutes before.

"Why? Do you think it unwise to leave Pa again?" she asked.

"No, that's not why. I think one night of observation is sufficient," he answered.

"Observation? What an odd thing to say. Attending church or revival is not something one observes. It's something you do. It's worshiping God," she said, looking at him through a haze of confusion.

"Not for me," he responded.

"Whatever do you mean, Sam? You believe in God. You've accepted Jesus as your Savior. . .haven't you?" she asked, doubt beginning to creep into her thoughts.

"I attend church because it's the respectable thing to do and people expect it of a doctor. As for your question, however, the answer is no, I don't believe in God."

With that pronouncement, Delphinia almost fell onto the chair just behind her and stared at him in open-mouthed disbelief.

"I'm sure that comes as a shock to you, but I consider myself an educated man. I believe in science and have studied in some of the best schools in this country and Europe. There is absolutely nothing to support the theory of your God, Delphinia. I realize most people have a need to believe in some higher being and so they cling to this God and Jesus ideology. I don't need it. I believe in myself and when life is over, it's over," he said, sitting down opposite her.

"But. . .but. . .you've acted as though you believe. You went and got the pastor for my father and you attend church and you talk to Mrs. O'Mallie about God and you pray—"

"No," he interrupted, "I do not pray. I allow others to pray over their food and I discuss God with Mrs. O'Mallie because she enjoys talking about such things. You have never heard me pray, and you won't. When a dying patient wants a preacher, I see to it. That doesn't mean I think it's needed," he answered.

"I don't know what to say. I just can't believe you're saying this," she said, rising from the chair and pacing back and forth. "I know you place great value in your education, but I hope you'll heed the words of 1 Corinthians 3:18 where it tell us that if any man seems to be wise in this world, let him become a fool so he may become wise," she said, hoping he would listen, but realizing from his vacant stare that he did not care to hear.

"I've heard that rhetoric preached all my life. My parents took me to church every Sunday. My mother was devout, although my father confided in later years that he never believed, but for my mother's sake, he acted like he believed," he said.

When she did not respond, he continued, "I wanted you to know how I felt before we marry. I'll not stop you from attending church, and on occasion I'll escort you. But I'll not want you there all the time, nor would I want our children indoctrinated with such nonsense," he added.

"Before we marry? I never said I would marry you. I never even gave you cause to think that," she fired back at him.

"I never doubted you would accept. I realize how much I have to offer a woman. A nice home, security, I'm kind, and, I've been told, good-looking," he said with a smile.

"I'm sure to many women those would be the most important qualities, but your confidence in my acceptance is unfounded. I would never marry a man who didn't believe in Jesus Christ as his Savior. I feel sorry for you, Sam, if you've hardened your heart against the Lord, but I want you to know I'll be praying for you," she said, walking toward her father's room. "I think I'd better check on my father and get ready for bed. Good night, Sam."

"Good night, Delphinia. I've not accepted what you said as your final word, however. We'll discuss this further tomorrow," he answered, not moving from the chair.

Her father was fast asleep when she stepped into his room. She backed out quietly and made her way down the hall to prepare for bed.

Sitting at the dressing table, she gazed at the reflection of herself. *How could I have been so blind?* She forced herself to think back over the weeks she had lived in this house. It was true, she had never seen Sam pray. At meals he always deferred to someone else and now that she thought about it, whenever she would pray with her father, he would leave the room. When she had tried to discuss the sermons they had heard on Sundays or ask his opinion about a verse of Scripture, he would always change the subject.

She slipped into her nightgown and dropped to her knees beside the bed and earnestly thanked God for answered prayer, certain His intent was for her to return to Kansas and be joined with a godly man. She prayed regularly for those she loved and tonight she added a prayer for the salvation of Dr. Samuel Finley, an educated man, walking in darkness.

Arising the next morning, Delphinia hastened to get herself dressed, wanting to talk with her father. Sam was waiting in the kitchen when she entered and requested she join him for breakfast.

"I'd rather not this morning. I'm not very hungry and I'd like to visit with my father. I didn't spend much time with him yesterday and we need to talk," she said, lifting the tray of food and moving toward the door.

"We will talk later," he said tersely.

"There is no doubt about that," she answered emphatically, without looking back.

Who does he think he is? she thought, marching down the hallway to her father's room. She stopped before entering, knowing she must change her attitude before seeing him and taking a moment to issue a short prayer that God assist her in this discussion.

"Good morning, Papa," she greeted, smiling brightly.

"Good morning to you," he said, indicating the chair by his bed. "Sit and tell me all about your evening."

"I plan to do just that, but first you must eat," she told him, lifting a napkin off the tray and placing an extra pillow behind him.

"I'll eat while you talk. Have we got a deal?" he asked.

"As long as you eat, I'll talk," she said, glad to see a little more color in his cheeks.

He lifted a small forkful of food to his mouth and nodded at her to begin.

"Papa, I know you have a desire for me to marry Sam and he has asked for my hand."

"I'm glad to hear that, Delphinia. When's the weddin' to be? Maybe I'll be well enough to attend," he said excitedly.

"There won't be a wedding. At least not a wedding between Sam and me," she answered.

"What do you mean? You're confusing me," he said, slapping the fork on his tray.

"There's no need to get upset. I'm going to explain, if you'll just eat and let me talk," she admonished. "Sam has asked for my hand but I could never marry a man unless he's a Christian. Sam doesn't believe in God. Besides, Papa, I don't love Sam. I love Jonathan Wilshire. I have to admit that I was swayed by Sam's good looks and kind ways and that it was nice to be escorted about the city and have his attention. But that's not love. A marriage between us would be doomed for failure."

"You can't be sure of that. You just said he's good and kind and you enjoy his company. I don't want you livin' out your days workin' like your mama, always unhappy and wishin' for more," he said.

"Just because Mama was unhappy some of the time doesn't mean she would have changed things. She loved you, Pa, and that's where a woman belongs. With the man she loves. You've got to understand that I could never love Sam. Not unless he turned to the Lord, and then I'm not sure. He's hardened his heart against God. Why, he told me he wouldn't even allow his children to be brought up as Christians. You know I couldn't turn my back on God like that," she responded adamantly.

"I understand what you're saying and I know you're right. I guess I'm just being selfish again. I want you to have all the things I could never give your mother, even if you don't want them."

"Don't you see, she had the most important things: a family that loved her and the love of our Savior. That's all any of us really need to be happy," she said, leaning down and placing a kiss on his cheek.

seventeen

When Sam returned later in the afternoon, Delphinia was sitting on the front porch, enjoying the cool breeze and silently thanking God for the afternoon discussion with her father and his agreement that she return to Kansas.

"I thought you'd be in tending to your father," Sam said with no other greeting.

"I just came out. He's asleep and I wanted some fresh air," she answered defensively.

"Good, then we can have our talk," he rebutted, sitting down and moving the chair closer.

"There's really nothing further to say, Sam. I can't marry you. I've explained that I could never marry a non-Christian and besides, I'm in love with Jonathan Wilshire," she said, leaning back in her chair in an effort to place a little more distance between them.

"As I recall, you weren't quite so sure of your love for that Wilshire fellow when I kissed you on this very porch."

"I'm not going to defend myself or my actions to you, but I hope you'll believe and accept my decision in this matter. It will make life easier for all three of us," she responded, hoping to ease the tension between them.

"I think your pa will have something to say about this. I've already asked for your hand and he as much as promised it. So you see, the decision really hasn't been made yet," he answered with a smug look on his face.

"I've discussed the matter fully with my father, Sam. He is in agreement that I should follow my heart and return to Kansas. He was unaware of your disbelief in God, as much as I was. There is no doubt in his mind that I could not be happily married to a non-Christian. The Bible warns Christians about being unequally yoked."

"Don't start quoting Scripture to me. That's the last thing I want to hear. What I want to know is how you talked your father into allowing you to return to Kansas?" he interrupted.

"I've already explained and he realizes the folly of my marrying someone like you. He may have discussed the fact that he thought a marriage between us would be good, but you deceived him, too. I'm not sure it was intentional, since you find faith in God so unimportant. I would rather believe you didn't set out to mislead either of us. I'd prefer you didn't upset my father by discussing this further, but you're the doctor. Do as you see fit," she said, hearing the small bell at her father's bedside and rising to go to his room.

"Stay here. I'll see to him," Sam said, standing and picking up his bag.

She did not move from the chair, but it was not long before Sam returned. Leaning against the thick rail that surrounded the porch, he looked down at her, his eyes filled with sadness.

"We could be happy, you know. If I'm willing to overlook your foolish beliefs and allow you to practice your Christian rituals, why is it so difficult for you to think our marriage wouldn't work?" he asked.

"That's exactly why—because you don't believe. It would always be a struggle between us. I want to be able to share my love of the Lord with my husband and raise my children to know God. I want God to be the head of our house and that could never happen if I were married to you," she answered.

"You've done a good job of convincing your father. I found no allegiance from him when we talked. I guess there's nothing more to say, except that I love you and if you change your mind, we can forget this conversation ever took place," he said and walked in the house.

Delphinia remained, not wanting to discuss the matter further. When she was sure Sam had gone upstairs, she went to her father's room.

"I wondered if you'd gone to bed without a good night kiss for me," he said, watching her enter the room.

"No, I'd not do that," she replied, straightening the sheet and pulling the woolen blanket up around his chest. "How are you feeling this evening?"

"Not too bad," he answered. "I talked with Sam."

"I know. He told me," she said, sitting down beside him.

"He's not happy with either of us. Maybe one day he'll open his heart to the Lord. If not, I suppose someday he may find a woman who thinks as he does. I have something I'd like for you to do tomorrow," he said, taking her hand.

"I'll try," she answered.

"I want you to go to town," he instructed, pulling a small leather pouch from beneath his pillow. "I'd like for you to purchase your wedding gown here in Denver City. I know I can't attend the ceremony, but it would give me great pleasure to see you in your wedding dress. Would you consider doing that?"

"You don't need to spend your money on a wedding gown, Pa. I have a dress that will do," she answered.

"Always trying to look out for everyone else, aren't ya? I can afford to buy you a dress and it would give me great pleasure. Now, will you do that for me? Mrs. O'Mallie has agreed to go with you. Quite enthusiastically, I might add," he said with a smile.

"If it would please you, I'll go shopping with Mrs. O'Mallie. Did you and Mrs. O'Mallie decide when this shopping trip is to take place?" she inquired, plumping his pillow.

"Tomorrow morning, just as soon as the shops are open. She said she'd come over for you and I told her you'd be ready," he answered.

"Pretty sure of yourself, were you?" she asked, letting out a chuckle.

"I know you pretty well, girl. You wouldn't deny an old man his dying wish."

"Don't talk like that, please," she said, shaking her head.

"It's better to face up to the facts. We both know I've not long for this world. You mustn't get sad on me. After all, it's you who gave me hope, knowing I'd be seeing you and your mother again one day. You just keep thinking on that and forget this dying business," he said and then waved his hand, gesturing her to leave the room. "You get off to bed now. You need your rest for all that shopping you're going to do tomorrow, and I need my sleep."

She leaned down and placed a kiss on his cheek. "I'll stop in before I go tomorrow. You sleep well," she said, departing for her own room.

❧

Delphinia took care in dressing, wanting to look her best when she visited the shops in Denver City. Just as she was tying on her bonnet, Frances O'Mallie arrived. The older woman was so excited at the prospect of purchasing a wedding dress, she talked nonstop from the time she entered the house until they reached the door of the first small shop.

The store owner was a lovely woman, delighted to see her first customers of the day. It was immediately obvious to her that these women were going to make purchases, and she needed the business. Mrs. O'Mallie instantly took charge, asking to see what fabrics and laces the woman had in stock, fingering each item with a knowledge that surprised Delphinia. Taking her assignment seriously, the older woman inquired about how long it would take to make the dress, how many yards of fabric for each of the patterns they had viewed, and the exact cost for everything from the tiny buttons to the lace trimming. Just when the clerk was sure the women were ready to make their decision, Mrs. O'Mallie took Delphinia by the elbow and said, "Come, my dear, we must check the other stores."

Opening the door to exit, she informed the store owner, "We'll be back, unless we find something more to our liking."

Delphinia, somewhat stunned by Mrs. O'Mallie's actions, was quick to tell her she particularly liked one of the patterns and wanted to discuss it further.

"Tut, tut, don't you worry. These merchants always need business, and it's good to know what the competition has to offer," she said, ushering Delphinia into a shop with beautiful gold lettering on the windows proclaiming the finest needlework west of the Mississippi.

"Lucy Blodgett owns this place," Mrs. O'Mallie whispered. "She can be real hard to deal with, but her sign on the window is true. She does the finest needlework I've ever seen. Just let me do the talking," she instructed.

The brass bell over the front door announced their entry and the women observed Lucy Blodgett making her way from the back room of the shop.

"Mornin', Lucy. This is Delphinia Hughes. She's out here from Kansas looking for a wedding dress and I told her you do the handsomest needlework in these parts," Mrs. O'Mallie praised.

"Good morning to you, Frances. Nice to make your acquaintance, Miss Hughes. Why don't you ladies come back and have a seat. I find it much more expeditious to discuss just what my customer is here for, and then proceed to show you my line of goods," she smiled, leading them toward four elegant walnut chairs that encircled a matching table.

Flitting through patterns that were neatly stacked on a shelf, she produced five different styles. "Why don't you look at these while I get us some tea," she offered.

"She knows how to run a business, wouldn't you say?" Mrs. O'Mallie asked, thoroughly enjoying the opulent surroundings.

"It would appear that way, but are you sure this shop isn't too expensive?" Delphinia questioned.

"We'll see, we'll see," the older woman replied, pushing the patterns toward the younger woman. "I rather like this one."

"Here we are, tea and some biscuits," Miss Blodgett said, placing a tray in the middle of the table. "Why don't you pour for us, Frances, and I'll visit with Miss Hughes."

Mrs. O'Mallie was glad to oblige. The silver tea service and china cups seemed exactly what should be used while discussing wedding gowns with Miss Lucy Blodgett. Delphinia's escort sat back and had her tea and biscuits, not missing a word that passed between the other women.

"How long would it take for you to complete the gown?" Delphinia asked, having finally settled on one of the patterns.

"At a minimum, three weeks. I have many orders to fill and once I give my word that a purchase will be ready, I am never late. Isn't that right, Frances?"

"Absolutely," said Mrs. O'Mallie, wiping the crumbs from her mouth and taking a swallow of tea.

"Well, I'm sorry to have taken your time, Miss Blodgett, but I must leave for Kansas within the week. My father wanted me to purchase a gown here in Denver City so he might see it before I depart. It appears that isn't going to be possible," Delphinia said, rising from the chair.

"I'm sorry, too, Miss Hughes. You're a lovely young woman and I could make you into a beautiful bride," Miss Blodgett replied.

"You'll not find a seamstress in this city who can make you a wedding gown within the week, I'm sorry to say," she continued as Mrs. O'Mallie and Delphinia tied their bonnets, preparing to leave.

"We appreciate your time, Lucy," Mrs. O'Mallie said as they walked out the store and walked toward another shop down the street.

The two women had walked as far as the livery stable when they heard Lucy Blodgett calling, and observed her motioning them to return.

"Lucy Blodgett, I've never seen you make such a spectacle of yourself," Mrs. O'Mallie said, feigning surprise.

"I've been making a fool of myself for years, Frances. At least whenever I felt there was cause to do so," she answered with a smile.

"Come back in the shop. I just may be able to solve your problem, Miss Hughes," she said, leading Delphinia to the rear of the store and into her workroom.

"Stand right here," she said, placing Delphinia along the wall opposite her cutting table. Moving across the room, Miss Blodgett walked to a closet and removed a hanger that was draped with a sheet. In one dramatic swoop, she pulled off the sheet revealing a beautiful white gown that absolutely took Delphinia's breath away.

"Oh, Miss Blodgett, it's beautiful. . .truly beautiful," Delphinia said, staring at the creation. Walking toward the dress, she reached out and touched the tiny beads that had been sewn in an intricate pattern on the bodice. The long sleeves were made of a delicate lace that matched the overlay of the floor-length skirt, flowing into a short train.

"It appears to be just about your size, I would guess," Miss Blodgett replied, ignoring the compliment.

"Perhaps a mite big," Mrs. O'Mallie responded.

"Well, certainly nothing a good seamstress couldn't remedy in short order," the shop owner replied rather curtly.

"What difference does it make?" Delphinia interrupted, exasperated that the two women were arguing over alterations on a wedding dress that had been made for another bride.

"That's why I called you back to the shop," Miss Blodgett responded, looking at Delphinia as if she were dimwitted. "This dress is available."

"Available? How could it be available?" she asked, stunned by the remark.

"I hesitate to tell you why for fear you'll not want the dress, but with all the folks Mrs. O'Mallie knows, I'm sure she'd find out soon enough anyway. This is the dress I made for Mary Sullivan's daughter, Estelle," Miss Blodgett began.

"Ah, yes," Mrs. O'Mallie said, nodding her head in recognition.

"Estelle Sullivan was to be married last Sunday afternoon. Her intended made a little money mining for gold, but his claim went dry. They decided to settle in California so he went out in June to look at some possible investments. Two weeks before the wedding, she got a letter saying that he had married a California woman and wouldn't be returning. Her dress had been ready for two months. Her future husband even picked the pattern," she commented in disgust.

"Would it bother you to wear a dress that had been made for another who met with misfortune?" Mrs. O'Mallie asked.

"I don't think so," Delphinia answered. "It's so pretty and it's never been worn. Would they be willing to sell it, do you think?"

"It's mine." Miss Blodgett said. "Estelle was so devastated and Mary doesn't have the money to pay for a dress her daughter will never wear. I told them I'd take it apart and use the pieces for another gown. Would you like to try it on, Miss Hughes?"

"Oh, yes, I'd love to," she said, the excitement evident in her voice. "Uunless you think it would make Estelle and her mother unhappy."

"I don't think they would mind a bit under the circumstances. Besides, your marriage won't even take place in Denver City," she responded.

"Then I'd like very much to see how it fits."

By the time they left the shop, Delphinia had purchased a properly fitted wedding dress, a matching veil, and a pair of shoes. Miss Blodgett was good to her word. She was able to stitch a few well-hidden tucks and the dress fit like it had been made for Delphinia. Mrs. O'Mallie was pleased because she had been able to convince Lucy to lower the price on the premise she was selling "previously purchased goods." That statement had caused a bit of a riff between the two older women, but eventually they came to terms. Delphinia, however, thought the dress was worth every cent of the original asking price.

The older women agreed that Delphinia made quite a spectacle in her finery, both feeling like they had championed a special cause.

Mrs. O'Mallie helped carry the purchases into the house and then bid Delphinia a quick farewell, knowing she would need to hurry with dinner preparations.

"Thank you again for all your assistance," Delphinia called after her as the older woman bustled out the back door.

Delphinia heard the jingle of her father's bedside bell and quickly hastened to his bedroom. "I thought I heard voices," he said, holding out his hand to beckon her forward. "Did you and Mrs. O'Mallie have success with your shopping?"

"Oh, Pa, we did! I purchased the most beautiful gown you could ever imagine. I know that God led me to it," she said smiling, as she proceeded to give him a detailed report of their shopping excursion.

"I'm looking forward to having you model it for me after dinner this evening," he said. "I wonder if Mrs. O'Mallie thinks she or God should have credit for leading you to that gown," he said with a small chuckle.

"I don't think she'd mind giving God some praise as long as she gets credit for Miss Blodgett's lowering the price," she answered, which caused them both to smile in appreciation of their neighbor's love of a bargain.

"I think I'll take a nap. I've been tired today," her father said, shifting in the bed to try and become more comfortable.

"How thoughtless of me. Here I've been rambling on while you need your rest. How's that?" she asked, adjusting his sheets.

"Fine, and you've not been rambling. It's given me more pleasure than you can imagine to hear you relate the events of today and I'm looking forward to seeing that dress on you a little later," he said, closing his eyes.

❧

Sam arrived home for dinner and although somewhat subdued, he remained cordial during their meal. The minute they finished, he rose from the table, informing Delphinia that he would be making house calls for the next several hours. As soon as he had departed, she ran next door to Mrs. O'Mallie's, requesting assistance buttoning her gown.

"I'll be over shortly," the older woman told her. "You get your hair fixed and by then I should be done in the kitchen."

Thirty minutes later, Mrs. O'Mallie came scurrying in the back doorway, proceeded to Delphinia's room, and her nimble fingers went to work closing the tiny pearl buttons that trailed down the back of the dress. "Now, let's put your veil on," she said after Delphinia had slipped her feet into the new white slippers. Carefully, Mrs. O'Mallie pulled curly tendrils of hair from behind the veil to frame either side of Delphinia's face.

"There! God never made a more beautiful bride," she said, stepping back and taking full view of the young woman. "Let's get you down the hall to your pa. You wait here in the hallway and I'll see if he's awake," Mrs. O'Mallie instructed.

Delphinia could hear Mrs. O'Mallie talking with her father, propping him up to permit a good view as she entered the room.

"All right. You can come in now," Mrs. O'Mallie called out.

Delphinia watched her father as she walked into the room. He appeared awe-struck after she pivoted in a full circle allowing him to see the entire dress. Turning back to face him, she watched a small tear slide down each of his sunken cheeks.

"I wish your mama could see you," he said, his voice cracking with emotion. "I know I've never seen such a pretty picture as you in that dress. Hasn't God been good to allow me such joy?"

"I'm glad you're pleased with my choice," Delphinia said, walking to the bed and placing a kiss on his damp cheek. "Thank you for accepting my decision to marry Jonathan, Papa, and thank you for this lovely wedding gift. I just wish you could be there for the wedding," she said.

"Your mama and I may not be with you in person, but we'll be there. You just remember that," he answered, trying to force his quivering lips into a smile.

"I know you will. I know," she answered.

"I think we better get this young lady out of her gown before she has it worn out," Mrs. O'Mallie said, trying to brighten the spirits of both father and daughter.

"We wouldn't want that," her father answered, "at least not until she's said her vows. You go ahead and change. We can visit again before you go to bed."

Delphinia returned once Mrs. O'Mallie had gone home. She sat by her father's bedside, visiting when he was awake and holding his hand as he slept, aware he was now in constant pain.

Later that night, a knock on her bedroom door awakened Delphinia from a sound sleep. Thinking she had overslept, her feet hit the floor before she realized it was still dark outside. Quickly, she pulled on her robe and rushed to open the door. Sam's eyes told it all.

"He's gone, isn't he?" she asked.

He nodded his head in affirmation. "I got home a few minutes ago and went in to check on him. He was dead. I'm sure he slipped away in his sleep," he said, watching her reaction, not sure how she would handle the news.

"He was ready," she said. "I know the pain had worn him down. What time is it?" she asked.

"Around five-thirty," he answered sheepishly. "I was gone longer than expected."

She did not respond to his comment, but knew from the odor of his breath that he had been drinking.

"I think I'll put on a pot of coffee. Mrs. O'Mallie will be up and about soon. She'll want to know. Why don't you get some sleep? There's nothing that needs to be done right now," she said, hoping he would take her suggestion.

"If you're all right, I'll do that. I have several calls to make later this morning and I'm going to need some rest," he responded.

"I'm fine. You go ahead," she answered, already lost in her own thoughts.

When Mrs. O'Mallie arrived, Delphinia was dressed and sitting at the kitchen table, sipping her third cup of coffee.

"Aren't you the early bird? Coffee made and gone already," she said brightly.

Taking a closer look at the young woman, she saw her eyes were red and puffy. "Come here, child," she said, her arms outstretched to enfold and give comfort, her instincts telling her that death had come.

"Does Sam know?" Mrs. O'Mallie inquired.

"Yes, he went up to get some rest a little while ago. He didn't get much sleep last night," she answered without further explanation.

"I was hoping you would help me with the arrangements," Delphinia said, a sense of foreboding in her voice.

"Of course, I will. In fact, I'll take care of as much or as little as you'd like. You just tell me how much help you want," Mrs. O'Mallie answered, patting the younger woman's hand.

"Perhaps if you would go with me?" Delphinia asked. "Oh, and Mrs. O'Mallie, I was wondering. . ." She paused, not sure how to proceed.

"Yes? Come now, Delphinia, you can ask me anything," the older woman urged.

"I don't think it would be proper for me to remain in Dr. Finley's house. Would you mind very much if I stayed with you until after the funeral? I'll leave just as soon as I can make travel arrangements," she said apologetically.

"I would love to have you come stay with me. If I would have been thinking straight I would have already offered. Why don't you pack your things while I get myself ready," she replied, already heading for the door.

Two days later, Mrs. O'Mallie and Sam Finley took Delphinia to meet the stage heading east out of Denver City.

eighteen

The journey by stage was tiring but the air was cool and Delphinia felt exhilarated to be on her way home. The stage was on schedule, allowing her to make the train connections and the trip home, although long, went smoothly. Her body ached for rest, however, and she wished she had been able to notify Jonathan of her arrival.

The train lurched to a stop and the conductor walked the aisle of the coach calling out, "Council Grove." Wearily, Delphinia made her way to the end of the coach where the conductor assisted her to the platform. "We'll have your trunk unloaded in just a few minutes, ma'am. You can wait in the station," he said politely.

She nodded and thanked him, too tired to be concerned about her trunk. The station was empty of customers and Delphinia sat on one of the two long wooden benches, waiting as instructed.

Her eyes fluttered open when she heard a voice asking, "Do you often sleep in train stations, Phiney?"

Looking down at her were those two beautiful blue eyes that belonged to the man she loved. "Jonathan, how did you. . .? Why are you. . .? What. . . ?" she stammered.

"I don't believe you're quite awake. Seems like you can't get your words out," he said with a smile, lifting her into his arms and lightly kissing her lips.

"I don't. . . We ought not. . ."

"Seems my kiss wasn't quite enough to waken you. You're still stammering. I must be out of practice," he said and once again covered her mouth, enjoying the sweetness of her.

"Oh, Jonathan, I've missed you so. It's even good to be called Phiney," she said when he finally released her. "It seems I've been gone forever and so much has happened. How did you know I would be here?"

"I didn't know for sure, but I got a letter from your pa yesterday saying if things went as planned, he expected you'd be back today. I decided I wasn't going to miss the opportunity to meet your train. I checked the schedules and knew you couldn't make connections for another three days if you didn't get here today," he answered.

"You got a letter from Pa? Isn't that amazing," she said, wonderment on her face.

"Well, Mrs. O'Mallie had written it for him."

"Oh, I realize he didn't write it," she said. "I'm amazed because he wrote a letter telling you when I'd be home before he took a turn for the worse and died. It's almost as if he planned just what he wanted to accomplish and then died," she responded.

"I didn't know. . . I'm so sorry," he began.

"I know. It's all right," she answered. "Papa was ready to meet the Lord and I know he and Mama are enjoying their reunion," she said with a smile.

"Where are the children?" she asked, finally looking around to see if they were outside the station.

"Guess I was selfish. I left them at home with Maggie," he answered.

"Maggie?" she questioned.

"Maggie Landry, the widow who's been helping while you were gone," he responded.

"I guess I left in such a rush, I never knew her name. I only remembered that Jennie O'Laughlin knew of a widow. How has she worked out? Do the children like her? Is she a good cook? You and Tessie never mentioned her when you wrote and I guess I didn't think to ask," she said, her voice suddenly full of concern.

"I didn't worry too much about her cooking and cleaning or whether the children liked her," he answered, his voice serious. "She's such a beauty, I didn't care about her homemaking abilities," he said and then seeing the look on her face, broke into gales of laughter.

"She's probably close to sixty years old, Phiney!" His laughter continued until Delphinia stomped her foot in agitation and insisted he quiet down.

"Jonathan Wilshire, I was merely inquiring about the woman's expertise. You make it sound as though I were jealous," she said with an air of indignation.

"Weren't you? Now don't answer too quickly, Phiney. I don't want you to have to ask forgiveness for telling a lie," he said with a grin.

He watched her face as she tried to think of just the right answer. "Perhaps, just a little, but then my jealousy was quickly replaced by pity for the poor woman, since she'd have to put up with you and your antics if you took a fancy to her," she answered smugly.

"Is that so?" he asked, once again kissing her soundly as he lifted her onto the seat of the wagon. "You stay put until I get your trunk loaded. If I don't get you home soon, I know five little Wilshires that are going to have my hide."

"I'm not planning on going anywhere without you again," she said, smiling down at him.

The reunion with the children was full of chaos. The twins greeted her with sounds of "Mama" and clung to her skirt while the boys tried to shout over each other to be heard. In the midst of the confusion, Tessie and Mrs. Landry tried to get dinner on the table.

The meal reminded Delphinia of the day she and Jonathan had first come to Kansas. It seemed like yesterday and yet, in other ways, it was a lifetime ago. This was her home now. This was where she belonged.

After dinner, Jonathan hitched the horses to the buggy and delivered Mrs. Landry back home for a much-needed rest, leaving Tessie and Delphinia to visit while cleaning the kitchen. They had talked of the children's antics while she had been gone and news of neighbors, school, and church, when Delphinia mentioned her surprise at finding the quilt top in her trunk.

"I was pleased you sent your quilt top with me," Delphinia said. "I didn't find it until I had been in Denver City for over a week. I didn't unpack my trunk right away, thinking I'd be able to return sooner," she confided.

"I was afraid you wouldn't come back to us. I'm sure Denver City is wonderful and full of excitement. I guess I thought if I sent the quilt along, you'd be sure and return," Tessie said sheepishly.

"It was more special for me to find that quilt top than almost anything you can imagine, Tessie, and we're going to begin work on it right away," she said just as Jonathan came into the room.

"I don't think so," he said, interrupting their conversation.

"Why not?" they asked in unison.

"Because I plan on keeping you occupied for the next week or so," he said sternly.

"Is that so?" she responded, rising to the challenge in his voice.

"I've sure missed being able to spar with you, gal," he said with a laugh. "But the fact is, I intend to have a wedding right away and spend a few days with you all to myself. What have you got to say to that?" he asked.

"I'd say it sounds wonderful," she answered. "I'm sure Tessie would allow us a little time before we start our project. Especially if she knows I've found something special for the binding on her quilt," she remarked, watching Tessie's eyes light up with anticipation.

"What did you get? Please show me and then I promise I'll be off to bed," she begged.

"I think she's convinced me," said Jonathan.

Delphinia opened the trunk that Jonathan had placed just inside the door and, reaching down along one side with her hand, she pulled out a roll of soft fabric. With a smile that showed her pleasure, she placed the coil of lustrous ivory fabric in Tessie's hands.

"Oh, it's so elegant. Where did you ever find it?" Tessie asked.

"It's the same material that my wedding dress is made from. When I was being fitted for my gown, I told the shopkeeper about the quilt we were going to finish when I returned to Kansas. She suggested we might like to use the leftover fabric from my gown. I hoped you would like the idea," she answered.

"How could I not like it?" she asked, giving Delphinia a hug.

"And now, young lady, off to bed," Jonathan said. "I'd like to visit with Phiney a little while before I go over to my cabin. It's not too cool outside. Why don't we sit on the porch?" Jonathan said, moving toward the door.

Once they were seated, he continued, "I know you're tired and I don't plan to keep you up long, but I hope you'll consent to our being married a week from Saturday. Mrs. Aplington and the other women at church have already begun planning the festivities for afterward, and I announced in church we'd be getting married on your return. The preacher says he'll keep the date open and I've got some ideas about a wedding trip. You've got your wedding dress, so there's nothing to hold us back," he said convincingly.

"I think that sounds fine, except I don't want to go on a wedding trip. I've just gotten home," she answered.

"Don't you think we need a little time alone, without the children around?" he asked, not wanting to sound selfish but sure he did not want to marry and return home to the five children on their wedding day.

"What would you think about our staying at your cabin for a week or so after we're married? Just the two of us. We could see if Maggie would stay with the children, but we'd still be close by."

"I think that would be just fine," he answered, giving her a hug. "It's so good to have you home. You can't imagine how must I've missed you. Now I think I'd better let you get some rest. I'll see you in the morning," he said and gave her a kiss.

She stood on the porch watching as he made his way toward the smaller cabin. He was almost to his cabin when he turned and shouted loudly, "I love you, Phiney."

Smiling, she turned and walked into the house, savoring the pure joy of being back home with her Kansas family.

❧

A light tap on the door awakened Delphinia from a sound sleep and she was surprised to see the sun already beginning its ascent. A cool autumn breeze drifted through the small bedroom window as she called out, "Who is it?"

"Just me," came Tessie's voice. "May I come in?" she asked.

"Of course, you can," Delphinia answered and watched as the young red-head walked into the room and plopped herself at the foot of the bed.

"How can you be sleeping like this? You're always first up and here it is your wedding day when you should be all fluttery or something, and you're sleeping like a baby," Tessie exclaimed, full of frustration that she was the only one awake on a day she considered should be full of excitement from dawn until dark.

"I'm not sure why I'm still asleep," Delphinia answered. "Perhaps because I wasn't able to doze off until a short time ago," she admitted.

"Well, now that you're awake, what do we do first?" Tessie questioned, beginning to bounce on the side of the bed, unable to control her anticipation.

"For starters, you can quit jostling the bed," Delphinia answered with a smile. "If you really want to help, you can get breakfast started. Jonathan will be through with chores before I get out of bed, at this rate," she said, throwing back the covers and swinging her feet over the side of the bed.

"Aw, that's not what I meant. I want to really do something. You know, for the wedding," Tessie replied.

"Wedding or not, we still have to eat breakfast, Tessie. The wedding isn't until this afternoon and we've got to finish our regular work before we can get ready," Delphinia prodded.

"Okay, I'll get breakfast started," she answered, somewhat disheartened.

Delphinia smiled inwardly at the girl's excitement over the wedding. *Seems like only yesterday she didn't even want me on this homestead, and now you'd think this wedding was the greatest event of her life,* Delphinia mused, thankful that God had been so good to all of them.

By three o'clock, the appointed time to leave the cabin, Delphinia wasn't sure anything was ready. If Maggie Landry hadn't shown up early to help, they wouldn't have been to the church until dusk. Insistent that Jonathan not see her before the wedding, the Aplingtons agreed Delphinia would go to the church with them and Jonathan could bring the rest of the family in the buckboard. The twins protested vehemently when Delphinia began to leave. Ned tugged on her gown, while Nettie kept calling after her in a tearful voice, trying to suck her thumb and cry at the same time.

Mrs. Aplington and some of the other women had been to the church earlier that day, carrying in food and bringing fall flowers from their gardens to decorate the church. Their handiwork was beautiful and Delphinia was touched by all they had done, but even more by their love and acceptance.

As she began her slow walk down the aisle to meet her future husband, Jonathan smiled broadly, noting she was pressing down the gathers in the skirt of her wedding dress as she walked to meet him. When she reached his side, Jonathan leaned down and whispered, "There's nothing to be nervous about, Phiney."

"I'm not nervous. I'm very calm," she replied, her quivering voice belying that statement.

"Now, Phiney, we're in the house of God and there you go, trying to fib to me," he muttered back.

"Why are you trying to upset me, Jonathan?" she questioned, her voice louder than she intended, causing the guests to wonder just what was taking place.

The pastor loudly cleared his throat and whispered to both of them, "May we begin?"

"Well, I wish you would. We're in our places," came Delphinia's feisty response.

"She's something, isn't she?" Jonathan remarked to the preacher with a broad smile. "Sorry for the delay, but I wanted her to relax and enjoy the wedding. She needs to get a little fired up before she can calm down," he said to the pastor who merely shook his head, not sure he even wanted to try and understand that explanation.

As they exchanged their vows and pledged their love, Delphinia knew her parents and Granny were with them. In fact, if the truth were known, Granny was probably up in heaven impatiently tapping her foot and saying, "It's about time!"

The festivities were still in full swing at the church when the young couple made their way back to his house.

"Tessie said she put something in the back of the buggy for us," Delphinia advised Jonathan when they arrived at his cabin.

Reaching behind him, he pulled out a wicker basket. The handle was wrapped with white ribbon and topped with two large bows. Entering the house, he placed it on a small wooden table and then returned to the buggy, lifted Delphinia into his arms, and carried her into the cabin.

Placing her on the floor in front of him, he gathered her into his arms and kissed her with such passion, she felt her body go limp as she leaned against him. "That, Mrs. Wilshire, is how I intend to be kissed every morning, noon, and evening from now on," he announced, being careful to hold her upright.

"I'm not sure how much work I'll get done if you kiss me like that all day long," she answered with a smile.

"Let's see what Tessie sent along for us," he said, keeping her by his side as he lifted the covering from the basket.

"Looks like she didn't want you to spend your first day of married life having to cook for me," he told her. She peeked around him and saw fried chicken, a jar of homemade preserves, two loaves of bread, pickles, and sandwiches that had been cut into heart shapes, causing both of them to smile.

"There's a note in here, too. I'll let you open it," he said.

The note was written on a heart-shaped piece of paper and on the outside it said, *Before you open this, walk into the bedroom.*

Jonathan took her hand, guiding her into the small bedroom, and watched as Delphinia's face shone with absolute joy. "Oh, Jonathan, it's my quilt. How did you ever get my quilt back?"

"I didn't," he said. "The last time we were in town Tessie saw the Indian who had been to the cabin. He was carrying your quilt over his arm. There was no holding her back. She went straight to him and the next thing I knew, she had his knife and was cutting off some more of her hair. I sat watching to make sure nothing would happen. A short time later she returned to the wagon with your quilt," he answered.

"What does her note say?" he asked.

She opened it and read out loud.

"Dearest Delphinia and Jonathan,

   "May the threads of love that hold this quilt, tie your hearts with love and joy forever.

"Love,
"Tessie."